Rainey saw her dau[...] dow in the classroom door. Sasha w[...] on top of a five-foot-tall filing cabinet next to the teacher's desk. Her legs crossed Indian-style and her hands clasped tightly in her lap, she sat with her back perfectly straight and gazed at the far wall with an air of regal calm.

The walk to the front of the classroom was a long one. Rainey sat down quietly on the blue rug where students normally gathered for reading groups. She smiled up at Sasha, and Sasha looked down at her slowly, the beginnings of a warm smile in her extraordinary blue eyes. Maybe this time it would be easy. But then a barrage of thunder hammered outside and Sasha's smile dissolved. She returned her line of sight to the far wall and sat as still as stone.

"We're going home, Sash," Rainey said patiently. There was no response. "Emma's making dinner tonight, and I thought maybe we could all watch *Pinocchio* together. How about it, sweetheart? Will you come out front and help me get the Ford started?"

Sasha didn't move.

"They said on the news there's going to be a meteor shower tonight—lots and lots of shooting stars," Rainey said. Stars always struck a chord with Sasha, even when all else failed.

Without a word, she climbed down off the filing cabinet and took her mother's hand and they walked out of the school with quiet dignity.

THE STARRY CHILD

Lynn Hanna

AN ONYX BOOK

ONYX
Published by the Penguin Group
Penguin Putnam Inc., 375 Hudson Street,
New York, New York 10014, U.S.A.
Penguin Books Ltd, 27 Wrights Lane,
London W8 5TZ, England
Penguin Books Australia Ltd, Ringwood,
Victoria, Australia
Penguin Books Canada Ltd, 10 Alcorn Avenue,
Toronto, Ontario, Canada M4V 3B2
Penguin Books (N.Z.) Ltd, 182–190 Wairau Road,
Auckland 10, New Zealand

Penguin Books Ltd, Registered Offices:
Harmondsworth, Middlesex, England

First published by Onyx, an imprint of Dutton NAL,
a member of Penguin Putnam Inc.

First Printing, October, 1998
10 9 8 7 6 5 4 3 2 1

Copyright © Lynn Hanna, 1998
All rights reserved

 REGISTERED TRADEMARK—MARCA REGISTRADA

Printed in the United States of America

Without limiting the rights under copyright reserved above, no part of this
publication may be reproduced, stored in or introduced into a retrieval
system, or transmitted, in any form, or by any means (electronic, mechanical,
photocopying, recording, or otherwise), without the prior written permission of both the copyright owner and the above publisher of this book.

PUBLISHER'S NOTE
This is a work of fiction. Names, characters, places, and incidents either are
the product of the author's imagination or are used fictitiously, and any
resemblance to actual persons, living or dead, events, or locales is entirely
coincidental.

BOOKS ARE AVAILABLE AT QUANTITY DISCOUNTS WHEN USED TO PROMOTE PROD-
UCTS OR SERVICES. FOR INFORMATION PLEASE WRITE TO PREMIUM MARKETING DIVI-
SION, PENGUIN PUTNAM INC., 375 HUDSON STREET, NEW YORK, NEW YORK 10014.

If you purchased this book without a cover you should be aware that this
book is stolen property. It was reported as "unsold and destroyed" to the
publisher and neither the author nor the publisher has received any payment for this "stripped book."

For Jack, my loyal knight; for family and friends who never lost faith; and for those who treasure all things Gaelic—*Bruidhinn Rium!* With special added thanks to my two guardian angels, Susan Ginsburg and Audrey LaFehr, the true miracle workers.

Chapter 1

"I'm afraid little Sasha is on top of the filing cabinet again, Mrs. Nielson. We can't seem to reason with her this time. I believe the thunder we experienced this morning may have triggered her actions. Certainly, we are all working toward getting her to tell us why these things affect her so. But that goes to the heart of the problem, doesn't it?"

"Yes, it does, Mrs. Pitney." Rainey Nielson glanced at her daughter's portrait on the mantel. Sasha's dark curls and brilliantly blue eyes were the image of her own. But even in the photo, the distance was there, an ethereal quality that far transcended eight short years of life and somehow set her apart from the rest of the world.

Sasha, the Queen of the Woodland Fairies, Alan had always called her.

Alan . . . God, how she missed him. And Sasha had thrived on his every word. He had been more than a husband, more than Sasha's father. He had been a lifeline, a rock of optimism and stability, two of the qualities Rainey had always felt she lacked. He had probably been the only man in America with a master's degree in business administration who carried around a sketch pad and a full set of charcoal pencils in his briefcase so he could draw on his lunch breaks.

There were a dozen boxes of his drawings, all neatly stacked under the bed. She couldn't bring herself to sort through them. The time wasn't right. There was some question in her mind whether the time would ever be right. The pain of loss still ached inside her, and each time she looked into Sasha's troubled eyes, she knew all the unspoken sorrow a little girl could possibly hold in her heart was welled up there with nowhere to go. Was there anger there, too, a feeling of abandonment or misplaced responsibility for the death of her father? A word, one simple phrase from her, would be a miracle in their lives. But it had been three long years of silence from Sasha, three years since she had been told her father was never coming back.

Mrs. Pitney broke into her thoughts. "Let me assure you, Sasha isn't expressing fear, Mrs. Nielson, so much as determination, shall we say? I'm sorry, but she is altering the focus of the rest of the class, and we feel a time-out at home might be the best answer for now. Communication is, as always, our primary goal with Sasha, but it appears that today may not be a day for a breakthrough."

"I'm on my way, Mrs. Pitney. I know things have been difficult, and I'm sure you and Mrs. Johnson are doing your best."

"Let me remind you that we don't categorize incidents like this as negative, Mrs. Nielson," Mrs. Pitney was careful to assure her. "Sasha is simply giving us notice that we are failing to reach her for the moment, and we have a great deal of work to do if we are to reintroduce her into the mainstream. This is her statement of impatience with the teaching process. In its own way, her resistance, shall we say, to conventional methods demonstrates again the extraordinary intelligence we saw in her visual testing.

I'm sure tomorrow will be a more learning-positive day for all of us."

"Thank you for your patience, Mrs. Pitney. I'll be there in ten minutes."

"Very good. Oh, on a related subject, Mrs. Nielson, I had a rather unsettling phone call from a Dr. Evanston today regarding Sasha's classes. He said he was Sasha's personal physician, although I noticed he was not mentioned on her file card."

"Evanston is in no way Sasha's doctor, Mrs. Pitney," Rainey said firmly. It felt like a straight pin was being drawn up her spine, and she shuddered. "Under no circumstances are you to discuss her status or her progress with him. I must insist on your cooperation in this."

"Certainly, that is your prerogative. But I feel compelled to mention that this Dr. Evanston is not the most diplomatic individual. It seems he has very set ideas about the direction Sasha's therapy should be taking. There was a particular drug he mentioned, I believe—something new and highly recommended in cases such as Sasha's where there has been a long period of no verbal communication. Have you spoken with him about this?"

"He wants to institutionalize Sasha, Mrs. Pitney. He wants to take that beautiful little girl and lock her away in a medical facility so he can test his drug discoveries on her. There was even some mention of a new form of shock therapy. I cannot and will not cooperate with him in any way."

"Believe me, Mrs. Nielson, I had no idea of the nature of his interest in Sasha."

"I'm aware of how persuasive he can be. One of Sasha's previous schools recommended him. But I found out later he was paying them substantial kickbacks for referrals. It's no exaggeration to call him a monster, Mrs. Pitney. He has been hounding us for months, and I'm looking into the possibility of getting a restraining order against him."

"The very idea of institutionalizing Sasha for such illicit purposes is quite beyond my comprehension. Is there no way to remove him from practice?"

"Unfortunately, no one has had the courage to stop him yet, Mrs. Pitney. If I had the resources, I'd go after him myself. But as you know, my hands are full. The bottom line is, he doesn't want to help Sasha. He wants to further his own career at any cost, and once I found out his intentions, I made it very plain to him that we wanted nothing to do with him or his so-called cutting edge research. Sasha is not a lab specimen, Mrs. Pitney. She simply has certain issues to work through. And Evanston is part of the problem, not part of the solution."

"Understood. But please be warned, he has made it patently clear he is planning to bring legal charges, not only against you, Mrs. Nielson, but against the school as well for continuing Sasha's enrollment. We must consider the well-being of all our students. To be sure, we all want what's best for Sasha. By the same token, I'm sure you can understand why it would be wisest for everyone involved if this matter has treated with the utmost discretion. Please call on me if there is any way I can be of assistance."

"Thank you, Mrs. Pitney. I'll handle it." Rainey hung up the phone and tossed a message pad halfway across the room. What Mrs. Pitney was really saying was that she'd like Rainey to place Sasha elsewhere.

"Damn it, why can't Evanston leave us alone?"

She looked to the family portrait that sat next to Sasha's picture. Alan's handsome face smiled back at her, so full of life, confidence, and a gentle sense of humor. Where was that glorious sense of humor now? They could have handled this situation together. The truth was, there wouldn't have even been a situation if Alan hadn't been lost to them. Now all the decisions, for better or worse, were hers alone to make.

"It was the thunder again, wasn't it, Sash?" she said to herself. "From the beginning, it was always the thunder." Images of the hellish night when Sasha had first reacted to a storm flashed through her mind, the night when Alan's commercial flight had gone down in what they had termed "the storm of the decade." It had been a night of unspeakable sadness. Unspeakable.

The past was a demon she couldn't wrestle with at the moment. The present was challenge enough. She threw on her jacket and grabbed her purse.

They were running out of schools. This one had been promising. The faculty was progressive and tolerant, the classes small and custom-tailored to children with extraordinary needs. Of course, it was impossibly expensive. The latest Winston Academy invoice had been sitting unopened on the kitchen table for three weeks, and she had to question her own wisdom at cutting her hours at the ad agency to part-time so she could spend more time with Sasha.

And now Evanston had found them again. That sick old vampire just wouldn't give up. He was determined to take over Sasha's life to further his own ends. But Rainey was equally determined that he would never get the chance.

If there was just one hint from Sasha, one sign that anything had changed for the better . . .

The marine air hung heavy with electricity and moisture as she walked out to her old Ford. Thick clouds the color of smoke and charcoal rolled overhead, stalled against the densely forested Santa Cruz Mountains. The garden soil she had turned the day before smelled rich and dark, and the branches of the big redwood in the front yard groaned like aching bones. There was going to be more thunder.

She had hoped to get away from lightning storms by moving from Connecticut to northern California. But the elements followed Sasha. Sometimes she wondered if Sasha somehow called to the thunder when she took the notion. It was always hard to remember which had come first, the crashing of a storm or Sasha's need to be sitting higher than everyone else in the room.

The car was badly in need of tires and a tune-up, and Rainey concentrated her energy on convincing it to start one more time as she put the key into the ignition. Alan had thrived on toying with the mechanics of the old junker she had bought for herself her first year out of college. A total classic, he had called it. Car trouble was just one more ugly feature of widowhood.

A tap on the glass startled her, and she turned to find her next-door neighbor, Emma Ferguson, smiling at her warmly. Dressed in a huge Mackintosh raincoat and sloppy, old-fashioned galoshes, Emma motioned for her to roll down the window.

Rainey had always felt a sense of kinship with Emma. Emma had raised her only son, Robbie, alone, after the loss of her husband in World War II. And when Robbie had had the good fortune to get a high-tech job in the Silicon Valley, for the first time in her seventy-five years Emma had left her native Glasgow. She had accompanied Robbie to California with the clear understanding that she would maintain a household of her own. The friendship between Rainey and Emma had only been reinforced by Sasha's steadfast affection for Emma. Sasha didn't warm to many.

"I've made a simply brilliant barley soup for supper, love," Emma said with a merry gleam in her light brown eyes. Her lilting Scottish burr was infectious. "Now, if only I knew of two wee lassies with appetites like teamsters who might be willin' to take a bit of it off my hands."

Rainey did her best to smile. "It sounds great, Emma. Really." She said it without enthusiasm and looked away as she rolled her hands on the steering wheel.

Emma frowned with concern. "What is it, dear, problems with the wee bairn?" She touched Rainey's shoulder kindly and saw a single tear slide down her friend's cheek.

Thunder rumbled overhead, and a shiver slid down Rainey's back. "She's having a rough day because of the storm. Evanston is hounding us again."

"Och, *dearg nàmhaid*, he's a hateful enemy, Rainey. Can I be of any help to ye?" She offered her a plain linen hankie, but Rainey shook her head, defying her tears. "Ye made mention of callin' yer mother in Connecticut to see about gettin' a wee loan."

"I can't ask her, Emma. Ever since my dad died of a heart attack, Mom's just been so emotionally fragile. Even if I told her I needed the money to get Sasha braces, she'd go into a full-blown depression. No, I have to take care of this on my own. I'm going to bring Sasha home, now." Her voice caught. "Tomorrow we'll start fresh. Tomorrow we'll . . ." She was at a loss, but recovered long enough to add, "Come by about five-thirty, Emma. Please. I'll make a salad and bake some biscuits. The TV cable is out because of the storm, so I thought we could all watch *Pinocchio* together for the hundredth time. The little wooden boy who couldn't talk . . ."

Emma plucked a fallen oak leaf from the roof of the car. "Sasha'll talk again when the time is right, Rainey. She spoke before the accident, did she no? A language of her own much of time, ye said." Rainey nodded. "Then she has the capacity. It's a burden to her, losing her father at so tender an age. Just ask my own dear Robbie." She wrapped her coat tighter around herself to fight off a chill far greater than the weather. "She's waitin', love, pure and simple. Soon enough she'll be jabberin' a streak, till ye canna finish a sentence of yer own."

Rainey turned to Emma with a look of hope in her eyes. "I want that more than anything else in the world. I've had to come to grips with losing Alan. Sasha and I have to get on with our lives. But it's like she refuses to make any progress. Therapists, counselors, teachers—they all have their own so-called solutions. But the only one who really has any answers is Sasha, and she's not saying a word."

Emma twirled the weathered leaf between her fingers thoughtfully. "Ye must give it a wee bit more time, love. At this age, the harder ye push, the more she's likely to dig in her heels. She's independent-minded, our little Sasha. Ye got to have faith in her."

"Faith," Rainey said softly.

"Aye, lass, a pinch of faith and a healthy dose of homemade barley soup now and again," Emma said with a spirited wink.

Rainey gave her a world-weary smile. "Got it, Emma. By the time the soup's ready, I'll arrange to have the faith."

"There's the sturdy soldier." Emma disciplined a loose strand of her rosy-gray hair back inside her hood and gave Rainey a solid thumbs-up. Then she turned on her sensible heel and started up the worn path to her house. "Five-thirty sharp, ducks," she called over her shoulder. "Not a tick later, mind, or Angus'll be havin' himself quite the merry feast for his supper."

"You spoil that mutt rotten, lady," Rainey teased. "He already weighs a ton."

"Posh! 'Tis the breed. They're all big-boned. Besides, it's the neighbor girl tossin' him all those sausages, that's what's given the poor wee tyke all that baggage. It's completely beyond my control, ye ken."

"Right, Emma. See you soon." She switched on the ignition. The car coughed in protest, then died. This was going to take a while.

Mrs. Pitney met her at the door to Sasha's classroom, and Rainey experienced an all-too-familiar sinking feeling in her chest. Sasha's special schools had become synonymous with setbacks.

The color of the principal's neatly tailored gray suit matched the color of her hair beautifully. She gave Rainey a carefully controlled smile and took her hand kindly. In spite of the gesture, Rainey felt very much on her own.

"We arranged to move the rest of the class to the Making Friends with Science Room," Mrs. Pitney told her evenly. "We were careful to protect Sasha from any demonstrations of resentment by the other members of the class. In cases like this, it's important for the child to comprehend that while we cannot condone disruptive behavior, we do realize these unusual manifestations of personality always have a root cause, an incident or encounter we hope to identify and understand."

"Of course," Rainey said. She saw Sasha through the window in the classroom door. As was often the case, Sasha was sitting on top of a five-foot-tall filing cabinet next to the teacher's desk. Her legs crossed Indian-style and her hands clasped lightly in her lap, she sat with her back perfectly straight and gazed at the far wall with an air of regal calm. Apparently, it was of no consequence to her that she was the only person in the room. Other children seemed to have little meaning to her.

Some little girls her age might have used this time to converse with imaginary friends or test their art skills on the chalkboard. Sasha appeared only to be waiting for something that was owed to her. From her formal composure, one might surmise that a large crowd was scrutinizing her every breath.

Rainey squared her shoulders and turned to Mrs. Pitney with a professional smile she had perfected in her years in the advertising industry. "We'll be going home now, Mrs. Pitney," she said with renewed strength. "I'll give you a call in the morning, and we'll discuss Sasha's plans for the day."

Mrs. Pitney inclined her head in reserved agreement. "Certainly, Mrs. Nielson. These things can be quite a challenge for everyone. They take time and a great deal of patience."

"And faith," Rainey said as she pulled the heavy classroom door open.

"Faith. Certainly," Mrs. Pitney said, although the word seemed to strike her as archaic. "I'll leave the two of you alone now. By all means, if I may be of assistance in any way, don't hesitate to let me know. I'll be in my office."

"Thank you again, Mrs. Pitney. I'll be in touch."

"I'll look forward to hearing from you."

Mrs. Pitney started to walk toward her office, but she paused and turned back to Rainey. "Oh, by the way, Mrs. Nielson . . . this is always a bit awkward, but I received a memo from the accounting office this morning. Something really must be done about the atrociously bad service of the post office these days. It seems your monthly payment somehow got misplaced in the mails. They have postal tracers they can use, I'm told. Perhaps you should have a few words with the local postmaster."

Rainey never took her eyes off of Sasha. "It will be taken care of, Mrs. Pitney. I promise you."

"Excellent. I have every confidence . . . every faith in you and in Sasha, Mrs. Nielson." Rainey had already slipped into the classroom, and Mrs. Pitney frowned a bit. "An uncommon pair," she said under her breath.

The walk to the front of the classroom was a long one. Rainey sat down quietly on the blue rug where students normally gathered for reading groups. She smiled up at Sasha, and Sasha looked down at her slowly, the beginnings of a warm smile in her extraordinary blue eyes. Maybe this time it would be easy.

A barrage of thunder hammered overhead, and Sasha's smile dissolved. She returned the line of her sight to the far wall and sat as still as stone.

Rainey waited for the noise to die down. What had ever made her think this would be easy? "We're going home, Sash," she said patiently. There was no response. "Emma's making dinner tonight, and I thought maybe we could all watch *Pinocchio* together. Angus will be there. We can give him that big soup bone we've been saving for him. How about it, sweetheart? Will you come out front and help me get the Ford started?"

Sasha didn't move, and Rainey sensed Mrs. Pitney was observing them from the hall. She stood up and walked over to the filing cabinet to take Sasha's hand. "They said on the news there's going to be a meteor shower tonight—lots and lots of shooting stars."

Stars always struck a chord with Sasha, even when all else failed. She adored them. Her room was decorated with them, and her favorite clothing was covered with them. They seemed to give her comfort, and Rainey did what she could to keep them in her life.

"I set the lawn chairs out on the back porch so we

could all bundle up and watch the show. Stars, Sasha, hundreds and hundreds of them all sparkling across the sky like diamonds. What do you think? Shall we go look for the stars together? We can go get some yogurt first."

Sasha stared down at the bright red stars on her T-shirt. Then, without a word, she climbed down off the filing cabinet and took her mother's hand. They nodded to Mrs. Pitney in unison and walked out of the school with quiet dignity.

"What's the matter with you?" a little towheaded boy demanded of Sasha as she sat beside her mother on a park bench. Sasha continued to lick her strawberry yogurt cone, giving the boy no more attention than she would a troublesome fly.

"Has the cat got your tongue or something?" he persisted. "Are you a deaf person?" He frowned at her like she was a broken toy. "I asked you if you wanted to go on the teeter-totter with me," he shouted in her ear.

Rainey handed Sasha a paper napkin. "I don't think she's in the mood for the teeter-totter right now."

The storm had subsided long enough to allow a moment in the park. But the clouds still lingered, and this was no time for a mean-spirited inquisition.

When Sasha continued to ignore him, the boy turned to Rainey. "Eddie's deaf, you know," he informed her. "He's my cousin's friend. He talks with his hands. I think it looks kinda dumb, like he's trying to do magic or something. But Mommy says I should feel sorry for him 'cause he's not lucky like me. Can your girl talk with her hands? Make her talk with her hands. I wanna see it."

He gyrated his fingers wildly in Sasha's face. Sasha

held her head high against the boy's barrage of questions and demands. His attitude was hardly new.

"How come you let her be so rude, lady?" he insisted. "She'd go on the teeter-totter with me if you made her. It's not like her leg is broke." He considered Sasha's legs to confirm his own conclusion. "My mommy says there's no excuse for being rude."

As if on cue, a red-haired woman pushing a towheaded baby in a stroller came down the walkway. She was dressed in a magenta jogging outfit, and her attention was locked on the self-help magazine she had balanced on the stroller's handle. The boy ran up to her and yanked on her sleeve. He pointed to Sasha with a pout.

"She's being rude, Mommy. That girl right there. She won't talk to me. And she won't go on the teeter-totter. Tell her mommy to make her play with me."

The woman looked up from her reading material, sighing at Rainey and Sasha with a distracted frown. "What, Jared? Somebody said something mean to you?"

"That girl right over there," Jared reiterated with a stamp of his designer-label basketball shoe. He dragged his mother over to the bench.

The woman paid no attention to Rainey, but closed in on Sasha. "Wouldn't you like to go on the nice teeter-totter with Jared, little girl?" she wheedled with an artificial smile. "It's important to play with others. It helps you to grow and be a better person."

Sasha gave Jared an estimating look, her dark blue eyes clear and uncompromisingly honest. Jared jutted out his chin at her in defiance, very sure he had won this bit of mommy jousting. But Sasha merely shook her head and returned to her yogurt.

"She's rude, Mommy!" Jared wailed.

Now Jared's mother turned to Rainey. "I really think your daughter should apologize to my son," she said with an edge of anger. The baby in the stroller began to fuss. "If she's not going to be cooperative, the least she can do is say she's sorry." The baby's cries rose an octave.

"I'm afraid that won't be possible," Rainey replied. She wrapped her arm around Sasha's shoulder and drew her closer.

Jared's mother narrowed her eyes as she took in Sasha and Rainey from head to toe. She saw the book on the bench next to Rainey. It was a reference book on the symptoms and effects of childhood trauma.

"She's got a problem, I guess, like in *Rain Man,*" the woman said with a smug look. She glanced down at Jared. "The little girl is learning-impaired, sweetie. She's probably good with big numbers, but she doesn't know how to speak correctly, like you and I."

"That's you and me," Rainey said calmly. "And the fact is, she speaks very well. It's just that she hasn't felt like saying anything lately." Sasha smiled up at her mother serenely, and Rainey could see no reason to add that lately could be defined in years.

A distant crack of thunder reached them, and Sasha rose from Rainey's embrace. Her yogurt cone fell to the sidewalk, utterly forgotten, and Jared's face lit up as he watched her walk toward the park's playground equipment. Convinced he had triumphed after all, he started after her.

But Sasha walked past the teeter-totter and climbed to the top of the slide. She sat down there cross-legged and locked her arms through the curved handles, blocking the way of the would-be sliders stacked up behind her. No amount of pushing and yelling could get her to budge as she stared off into the distance. Rainey started toward the slide.

Jared turned to his mother and pointed at Sasha. "She's doing it again, Mommy, she's being really rude this time. That girl needs a spanking."

His mother called after Rainey, "You shouldn't expose other people's children to this kind of performance. I'm all for helping the handicapped. My husband's an attorney, and he gives a small fortune to charity. But my babies are going to have nightmares now. You've disrupted Jared's routine. You should get your daughter some professional care, for chrissakes. There are psychiatrists and special schools for people with mental illnesses." She wrestled the stroller over the grass to grab Jared by the arm as the baby screamed to high heaven.

"I wanna go on the slide, Mommy!" Jared howled.

"Mommy's talking, Jared!" his mother snapped as her two children warmed to their dueling tantrums. "You get her off that slide now, lady, or I'm going to report this to the authorities as child abuse. And for godsakes check her into some kind of mental hospital."

"I assure you, she's already receiving professional care," Rainey said calmly. She had been dealing with this kind of ignorance for a very long time. "The biggest disability we have to cope with is the distinct lack of education we have to put up with from people who should know better."

"You get her out of here, or I'll call the cops!" Jared's mother fumed.

Rainey walked over to the foot of the slide. She ignored Jared's rantings, but she was so angry her hands were shaking. It was anger over the world's cruelty and her own feeling of helplessness. They couldn't even sit in the park in peace. She extended her hands toward Sasha, focusing only on her and not the yelling mob behind her.

"Come on, sweetheart, it's time to go."

Mercifully, the skies were quiet, and Rainey was able to get through to her. Sasha looked down with the beginnings of recognition and reached out to her.

At that instant, two boys pushed her from behind, and she slid down into her mother's arms. A shout went up from those waiting on the ladder, and Jared's mother smirked in triumph.

Rainey paused in front of her, looking at the baby crying and kicking in the stroller. Jared squirmed under Sasha's unrelenting gaze and burst into fresh shouts of indignation.

"They're quite a handful," Rainey said, tsking loudly. "Perhaps you should get some professional help." She smiled down at Sasha, her eyes bright with unshed tears. "You know what, Sash, I think we're going to put in a whole year's supply of strawberry yogurt so we can have it any time we want. What do you say?"

Sasha smiled bravely. But Rainey noticed she was rubbing a wide scrape on her arm, one of the "benefits" of playing with other children. When they reached the Ford, she glanced back toward the park. Jared's mother was writing down their license plate number.

Rainey left Sasha's bedroom door open a crack and tiptoed back into the living room. The skies had cleared, and they had watched the shooting stars for hours, until Sasha had finally given in to sleep. Emma sat on the couch now, staring intently at the TV with Angus on her lap. The little Scottie dog's hair was nearly as gray as his mistress's, but he was as alert and devoted as ever. Emma still had on the coat and head scarf she'd worn while watching the dazzling light show in the night sky.

It had helped a little to recount the horrors of the day to Emma. They had all watched *Pinocchio* earlier in the evening. The cable service had never come back on, and Rainey had grabbed a video out of a cardboard box and stuck it into the player without even looking to see what it was so Emma would be entertained while she got Sasha settled into bed.

"Would you like a cup of tea, Emma?" she offered. It had been a long day, and she knew she could use a cup.

Emma's attention never left the screen. "Is there any decent Scotch whiskey in the house, by chance?" Emma asked.

Rainey had never seen Emma touch a drop, not even when she had mourned for a month over the loss of Angus's sister the year before.

"I'm sorry, Emma. I think there's a beer somewhere in the fridge. Is that okay?"

"Never mind, lass. Get over here." Emma sat forward on the edge of the couch and gestured for Rainey to come sit beside her quickly.

The video was of Sasha's fifth birthday party, and Rainey winced. She hadn't seen it for a very long time. It hurt to see Sasha dressed all in pink lace and bows, laughing and playing with other children her own age. At times on the video, Sasha said complete, understandable sentences in English, talking about her presents and the party. Then, she would lapse into her other language, the one only she understood. It had a beautiful, poetic quality to it, and it was complete gibberish.

But most painful was the footage of Alan. Seeing his clear brown eyes flirting with her through the lens of the video camera was an unexpected shock, and her sight blurred with tears before she had a chance to get control of her emotions. He cracked a silly joke, and it nearly destroyed her. The hard ache she carried in her heart like a stone doubled in size, and for a moment she forgot she wasn't alone. She jumped when Emma spoke.

"Rainey?"

She blinked back her tears and tried to overcome

the lump in her throat. "I-I'm not being a very good hostess. Did you want that beer?"

Emma grabbed her arm as she stood up to escape to the kitchen. "Rainey, did your Alan speak the language?"

"English? Of course he did, Emma. He was born and raised in Pennsylvania. His family came over on the Mayflower, or something. They've been all-Americans for as long as anybody could be such a thing." Was Emma losing her hearing? The video was filled with Alan's comments and endearments.

Emma scowled at her like her IQ had just dropped a hundred points. "Not English, lass. Gaelic. Did any of his kin or yours speak Scottish Gaelic around Sasha?"

"You mean one of the dead languages? No, I'm sure they didn't."

"For shame, lass. You're speakin' sacrilege. Gaelic is no more dead than you or me. You're goin' to think I'm daft for what I'm about to tell ye, Rainey, but I never heard Sasha utter a word till this night, ye understand. I'm tellin' ye true, what the lassie is usin' on the film is the old style, far older than what my brothers and I were taught. But I know Gaelic when I hear it. The wee kitten's overflowin' with it. Speakin' it like she was born to it, too."

"You're joking, right, Emma? I mean, I know for a fact that she's never been around anyone who speaks Gaelic. She might have picked up a few words of Spanish since we moved to California. But I've known all her friends and family from the start, and nobody taught her anything like Gaelic. What you're describing is out of *The Twilight Zone*."

"I wouldn't hurt ye for the world, Rainey. You know that. It's no a joke. I'm tellin' it to ye straight as I know how. I'm a bit rusty, ye ken, and there's parts of it slippin' by me, but it's mostly clear as a bell in my head. I canna wait to share this bit o' news with my Robbie. Your Sasha has a rare gift."

"A gift." It hardly seemed like a gift so far. It was more like a curse. Rainey stared at the TV screen as Sasha first pointed to her birthday cake, then looked directly into the camera and said a complex sentence in her own language with total authority. She crinkled her nose and shrugged when her mother didn't respond, then ran off to find her father.

"What did she say that time? Could you catch it?" Rainey's heart gave a tug as she watched Alan dance to a ridiculous Chipmunks song with Sasha balanced on his shoes.

Emma turned to her slowly and pressed her lips together in thought before she spoke. "You'll be thinkin' I'm daft and off the dock for sure."

"Daft is what we do best in this household, Emma, remember? I want to know."

"What she said, love, and you understand these are her words, not mine, is that a brown cake isna befittin'. It should have been white."

Rainey rewound the video and watched Sasha's expressions as she spoke the exotic words. They fit her body language. But how was any of this possible? How could she believe any of it?

Emma sighed. "There's more, lass," she said cautiously as she listened to the words of the video one more time.

"Tell me." Rainey laid her hand on Angus's head and took comfort from the feel of the sleeping dog's silky fur.

"Our little Sasha says it isna a proper cake for the company of royalty, and that because she's of royal blood, she should by rights have stars on her birthday cake."

Chapter 2

Rainey nursed her morning coffee as she watched the birthday video for the dozenth time. It still made no sense that Sasha could somehow know how to speak Gaelic. And yet, each time she replayed the part about the cake, she could see the conviction in Sasha's eyes. She could see that what Emma had told her about Sasha's words was true.

The last thing they needed in their lives was another mystery to be solved. The question was, would this new knowledge help to overcome Sasha's problems somehow, or merely make them far more complex?

It was nearly time to call Mrs. Pitney at the school to explain that Sasha wouldn't be returning to her classes. She wanted to get it out of the way before Sasha woke up because she knew any mention of Dr. Evanston's name in the conversation would upset Sasha terribly. The old man had frightened the wits out of Sasha with a single look. And now that he knew where to find her, the school was no longer a viable sanctuary. Where could they go from here?

As she turned off the VCR, she heard a loud crash from the direction of Sasha's bedroom. For a fleeting moment, she envisioned Evanston escaping through the bedroom window with Sasha a prisoner in his arms. It wasn't inconceivable. He had money, influence, and a malignant streak of madness. The old man had no conscience, and she had been putting obstacles between him and something he wanted very badly—Sasha. Her heart pounded as she raced down the hall. She would kill him with her bare hands if he so much as tried to touch a hair on Sasha's head!

"Sasha?" she called as she pushed the bedroom door open. The bed was empty. The room was empty. "Sasha, where are you, sweetheart?" But she knew there would be no answer. Cautiously, she came into the room. She glanced at the window. It was closed, thank God. But the sliding door to the closet was open. The closet was small, with a series of poorly built shelves. As Rainey drew near, she heard a muffled sob.

Sasha was there, lying on the closet floor. Her face was smudged with tears and filled with silent pleading as she reached toward her mother. Rainey fell to her knees and swept Sasha into her arms, rocking her gently.

"Are you hurt, Sash? Tell Mama, where does it hurt? Please say something just this once, Sasha. Just this once. I won't ask you to talk again." She wanted to scream from the frustration of Sasha's refusal to speak.

Sasha shrugged to let her mother know she was okay, but she did rub her backside a bit. Several of the shelves had broken free from the wall. She had been trying to climb again, this time without the sound of thunder. She might have broken her neck. Fortunately, all the folded clothes had come down first to cushion her fall. But the danger to Sasha's safety was reaching new and terrible proportions.

Sasha's predilection for climbing was still very hard for Rainey to understand. She, herself, had a fear of heights, a fear that had intensified in the past

few years. The fact that Sasha found comfort in being
higher than the rest of the world only added to
Rainey's anxiety. One day, she might have to climb
up after Sasha, and she wasn't sure she would have
the courage.

"Ah, Sash, what are we going to do with you?"
she said with a heart-wrenching sigh. Sasha hugged
herself, then wrapped her arms around Rainey's neck
and laid her head against her mother's shoulder.
They sat there, taking comfort from each other, until
Sasha pointed to her school backpack which lay on
the floor next to her bed.

"I think we're going to take the day off, sweetheart. What do you think of that?"

Sasha didn't smile much anymore, but Rainey
could see it in her eyes that she was relieved to be
staying home. They stood up slowly and headed for
the kitchen, hand in hand. Sasha had her usual corn-
flakes, and Rainey was about to sit down with her
toast and jam when the phone rang.

"Yes, Mrs. Pitney, I was just about to call you."
Rainey walked into the living room with the phone.
"Sasha won't be—I beg your pardon? You're telling
me Evanston's attorneys had the audacity to come to
school? No, Mrs. Pitney, I assure you I never signed
any papers. This is unbelievable! He has no right to
interfere in our lives this way. I'm sorry you were
subjected to that kind of harassment. I'll see what I
can do. Yes, yes, Sasha will be staying home for now.
No, let's not get the police involved just yet. I assure
you, I'll call them if we have any more problems. I'll
be in touch. Thank you. Good-bye."

Things were out of control. If Evanston's legal
sharks had tried to take Sasha on the spot, would
Mrs. Pitney have had the courage to refuse them?
This had been a very close call. She went back into
the kitchen and hung up the phone. Sasha gave her

an inquiring look but Rainey could only lean against the wall and shake her head. The phone rang again, and she was almost afraid to answer it. Thankfully, it was Emma.

"Emma, thank goodness it's you. I—You're kidding! Right now? But what does she want?"

"She's callin' herself Harriet Malinsky, or some such," Emma said barely above a whisper. "I'd say she's an old witch, if ye were to ask the likes of me, and I've got her waitin' in the livin' room with a cup o' cold tea. But she says she's from Child Protection Services, Rainey, and she's come to interview some of the neighbors about how Sasha's bein' tended."

"God, what's going on?"

"The woman says a series of formal complaints have been filed by somebody she's no at liberty to name. I gotta go, love, but rest assured, she'll hear nothin' but pearls rollin' off this old tongue. Guard yer back, Rainey, the infidels're closin' in on us."

Rainey let the phone fall from her hand. As she turned toward the kitchen, she found Sasha standing beside her with the pieces of toast in her hand. Sasha held them up for her, but Rainey's hands were shaking too badly to take them.

"I'm afraid I've lost my appetite, sweetheart."

Sasha set the toast down on the coffee table in disappointment, and Rainey did her best to smile through her worry. "I'll get to it later, Sash." She knelt down and took Sasha into her arms. "We have to be strong women, Sash. Nobody's going to bring us down. We're going to make it all right, no matter what it takes. We're going to win this war, I promise." She crossed her heart, and Sasha smiled.

"My name is Lorraine Nielson, and I'm here to see Dr. Macinnes, please."

Rainey gave the rather dowdy secretary her most

glowing smile. The nameplate on the woman's utterly organized desk read MS. PHOEBE GIVENS, and the disapproving way she peered over her bifocals definitely filled one with "misgivings." But according to Emma's son Robbie, Matthew Macinnes was a friend and a master of languages, past and present. She had to pursue this. Maybe Gaelic would prove to be a key to getting Sasha to communicate. The pressure was on. They had to try everything to get Sasha to talk.

An envelope with the California state seal had arrived in the mail. She hadn't opened it because she was determined to present a strong front for this interview with Macinnes. Looking at that letter might have set her courage back. This was a long shot, but for the moment, it was also her only shot.

"Are you enrolled?"

Ms. Givens's words might as well have been "Are you prepared to die?' as far as Rainey was concerned, and she said no to both questions. Ms. Givens threw open the large black ring binder next to her right hand.

"Have you an appointment?"

"In a manner of speaking."

Phoebe's rubber finger protector squeaked down a binder page that was thick with names and numbers. She shook her head ominously.

"That is to say . . ."

The secretary's head snapped up, and her small eyes narrowed.

"A friend of mine, Robbie Ferguson, knows Dr. Macinnes," Rainey said diplomatically. "They golf together, and Dr. Macinnes told Mr. Ferguson to have me stop by his office when it was convenient."

"When it was convenient?" Ms. Givens slid her spectacles a bit further down her long nose so that her glasses chain clattered.

"It's convenient for me today, Ms. Givens."

"I see."

Ms. Givens was going to be a pain in the lower lumbar. It didn't matter to Rainey why Phoebe's life had gone sour. She had very real problems of her own.

"If you would indulge me, Ms. Givens," she said. "I took time away from my work to come here today. You have things to do. I have things to do. So if you'd be so kind as to tell me if Dr. Macinnes is behind that door over there, we can all get back to business." She inclined her head toward Macinnes's office, and Phoebe stiffened.

"The doctor is in seminar. He won't be available for the remainder of the day," she said like a declaration of national policy. "If you would like to make an appointment . . ." She flipped forward a dozen full pages in her black book. "There's a fifteen-minute opening at three p.m. on the twelfth of next month. Will that also be convenient for you, Miss Nielson?"

"Mrs."

"As you say."

The twelfth was two days short of a month away. It might as well have been a decade. She was beginning to hate this Macinnes, and she had never even met him.

"Is the seminar being held here on campus?" Rainey asked.

"At Stanford?" Ms. Givens asked, somewhat in awe at Rainey's ignorance of the doctor's professional magnitude. "On Fridays, he spends the day at the University of California at Berkeley. He feels he has a duty to share his language expertise with carefully chosen students at the more prestigious institutions of higher learning."

What an incredibly pompous snob he must be, Rainey concluded. She had had enough.

"Have you ever heard of Harvard, Ms. Givens?" she asked politely as she wrote down her name, address, and phone number on one of the countless Post-it pads on the desk.

Phoebe slammed shut her appointment book, her nose decidedly out of joint. "Yes, of course I have. Why do you ask?"

"If the good doctor ever decides to 'share his expertise' east of the Mississippi, tell him to give me a call. I'll draw him a map to the real Ivy League."

Ms. Givens couldn't seem to come up with a snappy rejoinder, and Rainey closed the door politely behind herself.

"And the woman at the university was that rude?" Emma marveled as she helped clear away the dinner dishes. She had resisted the temptation to communicate with Sasha in Gaelic. A streak of home-grown intuition cautioned her she wasn't the one to make this breakthrough, that it might be somehow dangerous if it was done in the wrong way. "Hard to believe they'd let the help act such a way," she continued. "I'll be havin' a word or two with my Robbie about it, I promise ye. There's no excuse for such brackish behavior."

Sasha carried her dishes to the sink and gave her mother a questioning look to see if it was her turn to wash them.

"My turn tonight, honey," Rainey assured her. "Why don't you go in the living room and play with Angus?" Sasha smiled her distant smile and headed for the living room.

"Did ye open the envelope yet, love?" Emma asked softly.

"No. Maybe tomorrow."

Emma patted her shoulder. "Time enough. It'll wait."

"I hope so."

The skies had been mercifully storm-free. In fact, the moon had risen clear and bright through the trees. But the good weather was small help. Another neighbor had called to tell her that Harriet Malinsky from Child Welfare had paid a call. It was only a matter of time before the woman showed up on their doorstep as well. The way things were going, it might be wisest to disappear before that happened.

She hadn't been able to come up with another school for Sasha, much less the money to pay for it. Worse still, she would have to consider using an alias at the next school to dodge Evanston's pursuit. It infuriated her to think she would be reduced to acting like a criminal to ensure Sasha's safety.

"Don't bother Robbie any more about this Macinnes guy, Emma," she said. "It was kind of him to try to help. We took a shot, and it didn't work out. If I can't reach Macinnes by phone next week, I'll just have to come up with another plan. I'm sure there are other local authorities on language. Maybe someone at the community college will have an idea. It sounded like this high-and-mighty Macinnes was going to be a pompous royal pain, anyway. He's probably a hundred years old and incredibly senile." She gave a halfhearted laugh at the image she had created as she carried her dishes to the sink.

"Thirty-seven, in point of fact, and I'd like to think more lost in academic genius than senility," a deep male voice said from the doorway.

Rainey grabbed a carving knife from the dish drainer as she whirled. The intruder had come past Sasha to get where he was, and she edged her way forward, her maternal instincts bristling. Oddly enough, Angus hadn't made a sound, and the little Scottie usually barked at everything, real and imaginary.

The man was a head taller than she was and athletic-looking in his frayed jeans and worn blue sweater. He didn't appear hostile, but there was several days' worth of stubble along his jaw, and he was badly in need of a haircut. The cowlicks in his long, russet-colored hair were definitely having their own way. But most strikingly, he had a thin white scar running from the outside corner of this left eye across his cheekbone.

And something about the eyes behind his wire-rimmed glasses made Rainey extremely wary. She prided herself in being a pretty good judge of character. But she couldn't read him at all, and she wasn't sure she could take him if he made an aggressive move.

"Who the hell are you?" she demanded. "And how did you get in here? The doors were locked."

He kept an eye on the knife in her hand as he leaned his shoulder against the kitchen doorjamb and folded his arms across his chest. "The name is Pain, dear lady, Pompous Royal Pain." His speech had a strong Scottish burr, similar to Emma's. "And you must be Lorraine Nielson. You're a friend of Robbie Ferguson's mother, and you left your name and address at my office earlier today."

Rainey stared hard at him, the knife still held firmly in her hand. He certainly bore no resemblance to the tweedy university antique she had envisioned. "Macinnes?"

"Matt, if it please the court." The glasses gave him a serious look, but there was a genuine spark of humor in those blue-gray eyes. "The jewel in the livin' room opened the door for me before I reached the yard. And of course the dog came near to lickin' me to death. I drove up here in a Studebaker I've been restorin' in my off hours. You'll excuse my casual appearance, it's to be hoped, but Armani wool tends to cry at the sight of axle grease. It's still a bit temperamental, the Stude, so I parked it down the hill. You didn't hear me comin'." He looked at Rainey and the knife thoughtfully. "Robbie's goin' to owe me more than a couple of rounds of golf for this one," he muttered to himself. "Your daughter, Mrs. Nielson, she's psychic, then, amongst her other wondrous talents?"

"Sasha!" Rainey called. When Sasha strolled into the kitchen with Angus ambling happily at her heels, she gave the intruder a dazzling smile of familiarity, and Rainey relaxed a bit. Still, she kept her eye on Macinnes. "Emma, say something to him in Gaelic, just to be sure."

Emma thought for a moment, then rolled off a sentence that Rainey couldn't understand. The man and Sasha crossed to the kitchen sink as one and each picked up a fork. The two stared at each other, and the knife fell from Rainey's hand.

"Was the answer right, Emma?" she demanded.

Emma laid a hand on her shoulder. "Aye, that it was, Rainey. The pair of 'em. Right as ye please."

Matt Macinnes went down on his haunches beside Sasha and took her small hand between his own large, steady ones. "Your dear mother calls herself Rainey, does she? Like dark, misty nights among the heather, a name like that."

Sasha gave him a wistful look.

Matt's smile was warm and straight from the heart as he turned from English to slow, carefully spoken Scottish Gaelic.

"*A Sasha, ciamar a tha thu-fhèin?*"

"What did he say, Emma?" Rainey asked quickly.

"It's like, 'How are ye?' or 'How's yerself?' ye ken?"

Sasha made a circle of her thumb and forefinger, a clear response that she was fine. Matt looked to

Rainey in a silent request for permission to proceed. With a frown of skepticism, she gave it.

At first, Sasha nodded and shook her head to his questions tentatively. But gradually, her eyes began to glow with joy and recognition. She responded like a starving soul who had been granted a crust of bread at last. Still, she wouldn't say a word.

"What do you make of it, love?" Emma whispered into Rainey's ear.

"I'm not sure," Rainey said under her breath. "Can you tell if she actually understands his questions?"

Emma observed the pair closely. "I canna be certain what he's sayin' for her now. It's gone far beyond what I was taught, ye ken. But look at her face, Rainey. It's like she's . . . like she's found family."

Rainey felt the sting of tears behind her eyes. It was true.

With a friendly pat to Sasha's hand, Macinnes stood up and turned his attention to Rainey and Emma. To Emma he said, "You must be Mrs. Ferguson. *Tha mi toilichte d'fhaicinn.*" He extended his hand to her, and she took it demurely.

Out of the corner of her mouth, Emma said to Rainey, "He says he's pleased to see me."

"Robbie does little else but sing your praises, Mrs. Ferguson. And are you the caster of spells who taught the wee lassie this magic?"

"I never," Emma said with a silly giggle. She blushed like a schoolgirl under his praise.

He looked at Rainey and raised one russet brow in inquiry.

"I'm afraid I don't speak a word of Sasha's language," Rainey assured him. "But she's spoken it since she was a year old."

"And what of the father?"

Rainey glanced at Sasha. The smile melted from

Sasha's sensitive face, and she turned slowly to walk back into the living room. She was lost to them again.

Matt watched the change in Sasha's demeanor with interest. "I've said something inappropriate. I apologize. Perhaps if Robbie had given me a bit more background about your situation . . ."

Rainey set the knife back on the kitchen counter and faced Macinnes squarely. "Sasha's father, my husband Alan, was killed in a plane crash several years ago. Sasha hasn't spoken a word in any language since she was told of his death."

People reacted in predictable ways when she told them about losing Alan. Some expressed heartfelt sympathy. Some retreated emotionally. Some tried to hide their resentment toward her for darkening their day. Dr. Matt Macinnes did none of these.

"It's brilliant," he said, more to himself than to the others. He started to pace back and forth slowly, rubbing his brow in thought. "Her father fell from the sky, you say? She's guardin' somethin', that wee treasure. She understands the old dialects, to be sure. I asked her straight out if there was a time or a place where she would communicate to me verbally. And she nodded, cooperative as you please. But I'd bet a hefty grant she won't give us a thing till we're bright enough to pose the right questions—in the right order." His head snapped up as he remembered Rainey and Emma were still in the room. He gestured toward Rainey. "And you say she spoke before your husband's death?"

"Yes, English and her own language. I mean, what you and Emma say is Gaelic," Rainey provided.

Macinnes's eyes glowed with new challenge. "What about Irish? How is she with the Irish dialects and Latin? And the Nordic languages, of course. Has she been tested in Old English and Medieval French? We'll make her famous, that wee moonbeam. We'll take her on the lecture tour, of course, when her school schedule allows. Or better yet, we'll hire her a tutor. We'll make all the journals. They'll come from all over the world to see her in action."

Rainey bristled, her thoughts very much on Evanston's tactics. "Sasha is eight years old, Dr. Macinnes." She crossed her arms defensively and leaned back against the sink, not far from the knife. She didn't like the way this was going. If he hoped to make Sasha a laboratory specimen, she was going to throw him out right now. She would give him a one-way ticket to hell to match Evanston's. "Until two days ago, I had no idea she had any knowledge of Gaelic, much less all those other languages you mentioned."

She walked to the table where Sasha had left her slice of bread from dinner. Sasha had systematically torn it into the shape of a perfect five-pointed star, and Rainey held it lightly in her palm.

"What I do know," she said, "is that my daughter isn't finding happiness in her world the way it is now." She turned her hand so Macinnes could see the star. "Sasha has been stared at, psychoanalyzed, categorized, criticized, and generally excluded from life for a very long time." She raised her chin a notch and looked Macinnes in the eye. "It's going to stop. No more journal articles, no more clipboards, laboratories, and fancy experimental schools. No publicity, no media. If I have to move to a thousand different towns in a hundred different countries, I'm going to find a place where Sasha can be happy. Do you understand me?"

Macinnes frowned at her as if she had just snatched a box of his favorite candy from his hands. "I do, Mrs. Nielson," he said with some reluctance.

Sasha switched on the TV in the living room, and Macinnes lowered his voice. "Is there a place where we might talk and not be overheard?"

Rainey glanced at Emma, silently soliciting her opinion of their guest. It was plain that Emma Ferguson was smitten to the point of embarrassment, so Rainey made her own decision. She grabbed her jacket and held open the door that led out onto the back porch. The night air was heavy with the promise of fog, but the bright crescent moon still gilded the trees with silver as she and Macinnes looked over the deck's railing to the fragrant redwood groves beyond.

Matt eyed the moon with a hint of affection. "*Mar a' ghealach, mar a' reultan siùbhlach, dùisg às do shain.* Like the moon, like the wandering stars, awake from your profound sleep."

"One of yours?" Rainey asked.

He turned to her with a smile that held a touch of mystery. "In your honor, Mrs. Nielson."

She eyed him cautiously. "Is there more to it?"

"A great deal, I imagine. But these things take time. It's part of the creative genius, you understand." He frowned at her with mock seriousness.

"You aren't a California native, are you, Mrs. Nielson? Ye sing more of the north, Connecticut with a pinch of Harvard clip thrown in for good measure. It seems we've both run a long way from home." His attention returned to the moon.

Rainey gave him a wry smile. "I suspected Ms. Phoebe Givens was a Stanford landmark not to be missed. What else did she tell you about me?"

"Ah, Phoebe," he said wistfully. "She's that fierce, my Phoebe. I often picture her standin' like a figurehead at the prow of a Viking vessel of war, a great horned helmet on her head and a bronze breastplate on that monumental bosom."

There was little Rainey could do but smile at the picture he had created. Matt Macinnes definitely had a way with words. He smelled of fresh air, lamb's wool, and motor oil. It was a pleasing mixture, especially for a university professor. "That smacks of sexual harassment, Dr. Macinnes."

He drew back, feigning shock. "Harassment? Never. It's true love. Phoebe is ever my idol and my bodyguard. I only wish she were family so I could bring her to hearth and home at the holidays. As it happens, she had gone home for the day by the time I got back to the office. But she had left your note front and center, underlined in red. A sure sign that you'd given her a run for her money. I salute you for your courage, Mrs. Nielson." He favored her with a smart salute and a thick burr. "And as for that bit about Connecticut, lassie, it's somethin' of a parlor trick to me these days. But ye have to admit, do ye no, when first ye heard me speak, ye didn't for a minute suspect me to be Italian, now, did ye? It's the same when I do it. The only difference bein' that sortin' out language puzzles is my life's work."

Rainey's mood softened. "I apologize for threatening you in the kitchen. You took me by surprise."

He took off his glasses and fogged them with his breath to clean them. "I sincerely doubt I'll be given the advantage of surprise again, Mrs. Nielson. You don't strike me as a woman who gives a man more than he's earned."

"You may call me Rainey."

"A gift."

Shreds of ocean fog skidded over the moon, and macabre shadows danced in chaos across the yard. The air grew chill as the night lost its glow.

"I want Sasha to talk again." As she wrapped her jacket more securely around herself, Rainey was struck by the timeless quality of her own gesture. She felt a kinship to every living thing that had ever endured the need for more warmth.

Matt gave her a considering look. "When I asked

her there in the kitchen if she'd be willin' to eventually answer some of my questions in English, she was very direct with me that she would not. If we can get the lass to speak at all, it's most likely goin' to be in old Gaelic. She's quite the phenomenon, your daughter."

Rainey shook her head. "I don't understand how any of this is possible, Dr.—" He frowned at her. "Matt," she provided. "As far as I know, Sasha's had no exposure to contemporary Gaelic, never mind the ancient kind. I just don't see how she can have this knowledge. And how is she going to make it through life speaking nothing but a language no one else around her speaks?"

"That one?" he said with a tip of his head toward the living room. "She's cast of iron, that wee flower. Or more correctly, bronze, I have a feelin'. Runnin' circles around us all in that magic Celtic brain of hers." He settled his glasses back across the bridge of his nose in an elegant gesture. "The answers to why she possesses these gifts lie in gettin' her to talk things out with us. She may not be aware herself of why all of this is comin' to pass. The question is, how tightly locked is the door to her heart? If we could get her to share her secrets . . . give us the key that would let us know who she really is . . ."

Rainey flicked a twig over the edge of the railing. "Who she really is is Sasha Nielson, an eight-year-old American girl who's never left the States and who, as far as I know, never heard a word of Gaelic spoken by another person until today. You're the expert. I'm not a big believer in reincarnation and mystic mumbo-jumbo. How do you explain it?"

The moon cleared the blowing ridge of fog.

"Not a believer, is it? You see that wedge of shining rock up there?" he said, his focus on the moon once more. Rainey nodded. "What do you see when you look at it?"

"I see the moon."

"That's it, then? Nothin' more?" He rubbed the stubble on his chin thoughtfully. "No poetry, no silver, no faces beamin' back at you? Och, you were never so much for the liberal arts, I take it."

Rainey bristled. "I majored in business administration," she said defensively. "But I had to take some creative writing courses, too."

"All the better to put teeth into the ad copy, my dear," he replied with a comical twist to an imaginary handlebar mustache.

"I wanted a career. I didn't want to be a grade school teacher or a glorified secretary. I wanted something more, something with my own signature on it." She slammed her hand against the railing as the strain of the last few days caught up with her. Her nerves were in tatters, and she tucked her hair behind her ear as she had done since she was a child to calm her emotions. "I don't see what this has to do with Sasha's situation," she said briskly as she turned her back on him.

When he touched her sleeve to turn her around, he saw her eyes lock on the gold wedding band he wore. He took his hand away. "You don't see. That's just the point, dear lady. Livin' purely on facts is highly overrated. My thought is that Sasha's situation, as you call it, has more to do with silver and poetry than science. And if you're wantin' somethin' with your signature on it, love, that bonnie lassie wears your looks like a crown. She's that like her mother, though. Whatever gifts she's likely to bestow, she's goin' to make us work for them. She's a fair mystery to be solved. A queen of the fairies. Are you game for the job as I am, Harvard?"

"A queen of the fairies . . ." Rainey said softly.

Her heart caught in her chest, and the little hairs at the back of her neck stood on end. Alan's words had come back. It gave her a kind of comfort to be reminded of Alan. Macinnes was getting under her skin in more ways than one, and she needed to remember her true priorities. "I'm game for the job, Stanford. I promise you, I'm game."

Chapter 3

The moon had gone behind the hills for the night by the time Rainey was able to slip out onto the back porch again. She missed its glow.

Matt had been openly disappointed when they had gone back inside and found Sasha asleep on the couch with her arm around the snoozing Angus. He watched the birthday video with rapt interest, and left with a wink and a fervent promise to return the next day.

Rainey did what she could to rearrange her work schedule in anticipation of his visit. Gratefully, the ad copy she had to polish could be done on her home computer.

Her reactions to Matt Macinnes were definitely mixed. He was knowledgeable, as far as she could tell. But he also made her nervous with his poetry and his instant rapport with Sasha. He was a charmer, no question about it. She had even found herself falling under his spell a time or two. It was the hint of a dare in his eyes, she supposed, and the accent. She almost wished they had met under different circumstances. But it was unnerving to know he could reach Sasha in a way she couldn't, a way she couldn't supervise.

Her thoughts touched on his wedding ring. It made it easier to be assured that things would be strictly business. For so long, the entire focus of her life had been Sasha. She had forfeited a potential vice presidency at a prestigious Manhattan advertising agency to search for a better life for Sasha, and there was no such thing as a social life. She couldn't afford it, physically or emotionally. Was she going to be able to afford Matt Macinnes, she wondered?

The back door opened and closed softly behind her, and she knew it would be Emma, ready to scold her for being out in the night air.

"The weddin' ring belonged to his father," Emma said without preamble as she settled an overcoat across Rainey's shoulders. Rainey turned to her in surprise.

"His parents passed on some years ago," Emma continued, "and Robbie says the good doctor wears it for luck. A keepsake, ye might say. From the buccaneer cut of that scamp, it most likely helps to keep all those pantin' coeds at bay as well. There now, love, don't be givin' me that parson's wife look. I was 'round when Stonehenge was a Saturday night hot spot, and if that young dirk can put a blush in these old cheeks, I figure it's wise to set the record straight. It was best ye heard the information from me, understand, since it's doubtful ye'd believe it off the man himself. What with ye holdin' him at knifepoint and all."

Rainey flinched when her heart jumped over a beat at the news Macinnes wasn't married. She had to scramble to rebuild her defenses.

"Be fair, Emma," she insisted. "Macinnes walked in here like he owned the place." She threw a pinecone for distance. "For all I knew, from the shabby way he looked, he could have been some lunatic murderer up from the Boardwalk to get his jollies preying on defenseless women."

"Defenseless, ye say? Defenseless?" Emma gave

her a laughing snort. "Ye were fully prepared to skewer him, throat to throttle, lassie. Of the two of ye, I think we all know who was the more dangerous."

Rainey gave her a hard look. "I have to defend us all, Emma. It scares me to death when I think how big a job that is. Sasha is so vulnerable. You and I are her only protectors in the world, and we can't let her down. We can't let each other down. Macinnes is an outsider, a researcher. Don't you see, he may be thinking this is his big chance to make the cover of *Newsweek*. He talks in riddles half the time, and I won't have him manipulate Sasha."

"You've been a wonder in that wee lassie's life, Rainey. Never doubt it for a moment." Emma patted her hand in motherly fashion. "There's not a soul who could criticize ye for all ye've done. But if there's a chance this Macinnes fella can help get Sasha back in the swing of things, ye got to give it a go. It's owed to yerself as well as to her. And I don't have to remind ye, love, the wolves are closin' in."

Rainey gave Emma a grateful hug, her thoughts very much on the unopened envelope with the state seal she had taped to the refrigerator. "You're right. We have to try this. It's got to work, Emma. Sometimes I think it may be our last chance.

"But Macinnes rolls through here like a tidal wave. I don't feel like I'm in control of things when he's here. He throws me off balance. One minute I'm staring at him in awe, and the next minute I want to deck him. I never know what to expect from him."

Emma patted her back, then put her at arm's length. "All I know, lass, is my Robbie says Matt Macinnes is one feather shy of sainthood, despite the fact the man beats my boy soundly at golf on a regular basis. We'll keep a sharp eye on him to be sure, love. But my Robbie's never wrong—except in his choice of girlfriends, o' course. He needs a sound talkin' to in that regard now and again. But I can't help thinkin' the Macinnes is worthy of our trust. There's somethin' about him rings verra true to my mind."

There was still a strong element of doubt in Rainey's mind. She wasn't sure she could rely on her own instincts, so for now she had to trust Emma's.

"I don't know what I would have done without you the last couple of years, Emma," she said with all her heart.

"Ah, but it's you and Sasha who've been lifesavers for me, Rainey. What with my Robbie workin' the clock 'round, and him with a life of his own, I'd have been nothin' but a lonely old hermit without you and Sasha for company. Angus would have given me the toss for bein' a brooder long ago, and that's purely the fact of the matter."

The back door creaked, and they turned to find Sasha standing in the doorway. She had on a new pair of star-covered pajamas that were too big for her. After an enormous yawn, she made circles of her fingers and held them up to her eyes like glasses.

"Matt had to go home, sweetheart," Rainey explained as she took Sasha's hand. She was careful not to refer to him as "Doctor" for fear Sasha would retreat from the idea of him. The expression of complete sorrow on Sasha's face made her look far older than her years, and Rainey was quick to reassure her. "He said he'd come back to see us tomorrow, if we'd like. So we'll see what happens."

In reaction to the news that he would return, Sasha led her into the living room and started to rummage through the collection of oversized picture books on the coffee table. She pulled a crayon drawing from beneath the stack.

The picture was simply but elegantly done, and at first, Rainey thought it might be one of Alan's earlier works. But she had never seen Alan work in crayons, and the style was not quite his. It portrayed a tall young woman with Sasha's features—a self-portrait, perhaps. The woman in the drawing wore a long, flowing gown of dark green and a circlet of tiny stars around her head. And at her feet knelt a man dressed in the crude, ancient-looking armor of war. He held an impressive broadsword before him, the handle toward heaven, in a kind of tribute to the woman. His hair was a dark shade of red, and, quite out of character, he wore wire-rimmed glasses. There could be little doubt who he was.

The scene was electrifying, and Rainey's hand trembled as she held it. Sasha hadn't drawn people for years. Every time they had encouraged her to try, she had lost interest in her artwork. So they had settled for the steady stream of forests, birds, and endless stars she had provided in recent years.

Now, here were two very recognizable people. And the person other than herself Sasha had chosen to draw was hardly more than a stranger. Plainly, he was a very important stranger to her.

Rainey gave Emma a telling glance as she knelt beside Sasha. "Shall we show this to Matt tomorrow, honey? I bet he'll be pleased. You've done a fine job."

Sasha started to sort through the stack of books on the coffee table again, searching for something. Another drawing was stuck to the back of a glossy picture book, pressed away for safekeeping, and she peeled it off the cover impatiently. It showed a waterfall that plunged into a deep canyon. The falls were done in dark colors and the surrounding terrain was bare. On the rocky walls beside them perched a flock of black birds. The pool at the base of the cascading water was the stark color of blood.

Sasha pressed her circled fingers to her eyes again to indicate that she wanted this one shown to Matt as well. Rainey agreed numbly.

She had hoped for a breakthrough, a key, as Macinnes had called it. Now that she held the two disturbing pictures in her hand, she wondered if the solution to their problems was going to be more devastating than the problem itself. She handed the pages to Emma, who, to her credit, hid her true reactions behind a cough.

"How about a little TV, Sash?" Rainey asked as she settled Sasha beside her on the couch and clicked the remote. The cable was back, and after five minutes of *I Dream of Jeannie*, Sasha relaxed against her in sleep.

Emma sat down next to them on the couch, the drawings still in her hand. She gave Sasha a long look to be sure she had returned to her dreams before she spoke.

"She's haunted, love. I've never seen the like of it. But one thing's sure, we got to do somethin' about it quick because it's eatin' this poor wee thing up."

Rainey smoothed Sasha's dark hair. "I hope I'm doing the right thing by letting Macinnes work with her. The drawings . . . I don't know if we should help her to remember or forget." She frowned at the irritating situation comedy antics on the television. "It's not fair!" she said in a harsh whisper. "I shouldn't have to be making these decisions alone. Alan should be here to share the responsibility. Or maybe if he had stayed home just that one time, none of this would have happened to Sasha. When we lost him, it triggered all of this. Sometimes I wonder if I'll ever be able to forgive him for dying. I know how bitter and senseless that sounds. He can't be blamed for a plane crash, for godsakes. But I get so tired of having to carry the weight of it."

Emma patted her hand. "I know what ye're goin' through more than most, Rainey. We're sisters in tragedy, ye ken, what with me losin' Robbie's father all those years ago. It's an achin' in the heart that feeds on itself, if ye let it. But ye canna blame Alan for somethin' that started long before his passin'. Sasha was speakin' the Gaelic before the crash, remember? We have proof of it on your videola there. The loss of her dad just turned the page on another chapter of somethin' that was already in progress, ye see. I'm that convinced of it."

Rainey gave a heartfelt sigh. "You don't think the picture she drew of Macinnes tonight was just the product of too many fairy tales? I mean, she's at a very impressionable age, and the world has hardly been kind lately. It's probably just that she sees him as a hero figure, a knight in shining armor, so to speak, because of the language breakthrough."

"You're certain she drew this tonight, lassie?" Emma gave Sasha's drawing of Matt careful consideration.

"She must have." Rainey felt the little hairs on her arms prickle again.

"Well, she was watchin' the telly whilst ye were talkin' to the doctor in the kitchen, and she was playin' with Angus till she fell asleep when the two of ye were out on the porch. I was keepin' an eye on her, and ye know how she sinks herself into her art by the hour once she gets started. I got to tell ye, love, I never saw her take to the crayons once."

"The sword," Rainey said in a whisper as she studied the picture of the knight again. "She did it with the silver crayon. It got stepped on a week ago, and I watched her throw it into the trash." She traced the sword with her fingertip, and brought a bit of the shining color up for closer examination. "Macinnes talked about silver being part of the answer. Sasha knew he was coming."

"Aye, it seems so," Emma replied matter-of-factly. And then, in true Scottish fashion, she added, "It's good the lassie knows when he's bound to drop by, Rainey, so we'll have warnin' to set another place at the supper table."

Rainey closed her eyes and rested her head against the back of the couch as the last strains of the *I Dream of Jeannie* theme faded. "I have the feeling we'll all be wearing plaid before the week is out," she said as the TV announcer informed the world that tonight's late-night movie classic would be *Brigadoon*.

Her work wasn't going well. All morning Rainey had tried to polish up the ad copy she was supposed to turn in first thing Monday morning. But her fingers had a mind of their own, and last night's dreams kept creeping into her waking hours. She didn't want to dwell on the tangled forests and the dark, faceless pursuers that had twisted her sleep. She had had enough psychology to know that recent developments were hounding her subconscious.

Sasha strolled into the bedroom that doubled as Rainey's home office and set a warm mug of strong tea next to her mother's elbow. Rainey gave her a smile of thanks and looked around for Angus. Sasha made a walking motion with her fingers to indicate that Emma and Angus were off on their morning constitutional. With a nod of understanding, Rainey pulled up a chair and patted it so that Sasha could sit with her for a while.

It occurred to her every so often that even though Sasha could hear and understand perfectly well, they tended to communicate in silence the great majority of the time, through exchanged looks and gestures, even reading each other's thoughts. It was a language of its own, and she wondered if this kinship, this knowledge of each other, would remain as strong if Sasha's speech returned.

Sasha made circles of her fingers and held them up to her eyes in the now customary pantomime of Matt.

"He'll be by after lunch," Rainey provided.

Sasha held up her forefingers, then spread her hands far apart.

"Too long, huh? Well, if I don't get this mountain of work done this morning, things could get pretty complicated."

Sasha sprang out of her chair and raced for the door. She turned briefly and made a typing motion with her fingers, then closed the bedroom door softly behind herself.

"Right, Miss Slave Driver, I get the message."

Rainey returned to her work, but more often than not, she found herself off into a daydream as she watched the light winds tease the branches of the old redwoods outside her window. The faint scent of sweet pine smoke from a neighbor's chimney sent her off into thoughts of ancient fires and the people who tended them. By lunchtime, she had accomplished next to nothing, and with a sigh of defeat, she shut down the system.

Sasha was already seated at the kitchen table, her napkin in her lap and a soup spoon in her hand when Rainey walked in. Emma ladled a healthy portion of freshly made potato soup into three white porcelain bowls, and Rainey gave her a wave of greeting.

"She's been sittin' there at the table like that for an hour, waitin' for it to be lunchtime, haven't ye, darlin'?" Emma said with a wink and a grin. Sasha nodded dutifully. "I expect she thinks her new friend will get here sooner if we get the meal over."

Rainey carried two of the filled soup bowls to the table and took her place across from Sasha. "I told her Matt would be here after lunch." Sasha had already gulped down three spoonfuls of soup, and Rainey gave her a motherly look of warning. "Wait till Emma sits down with her soup, Sash. You know the rules. It was very nice of her to go to the trouble of bringing the lunch over for us, and wolfing down your food isn't going to make Matt get here any faster. He's a very busy man. Chances are, he won't be here for an hour or two."

Sasha looked at her mother thoughtfully for a moment, then politely wiped her mouth and left the table. She took the crayon drawings off the refrigerator and walked to the front door. And when she opened it, Matt walked up the steps as if she had conjured him up out of some mystical cloud. As before, there had been no sound of a car's arrival.

Before crossing the threshold, Matt went down on one knee and lightly took Sasha's hand in his own as she handed him her drawings. The scene's resemblance to the picture Sasha had done of the two of them was uncanny. He studied her artwork, then smiled warmly and said something only she could hear. In response, Sasha threw her arms around his neck and nearly knocked him over with the exuberance of her hug as they both dissolved in laughter.

Rainey cleared her throat as she approached the pair of them. Something caught in the pit of her stomach at the sight of Sasha's open joy at seeing Matt Macinnes. It was all happening too quickly. She was still unable to put the idea out of her mind that he would use Sasha to further his own career, that this was a masterfully orchestrated campaign he was carrying out to gain her trust.

Professors at the top universities were always under incredible pressure to publish new research material. Macinnes wasn't exempt. And as she watched him smoothly regain his feet, she put a leash on the surge of anger she felt at the idea that he might be manipulating them all for his personal gain. They needed him for now, she told herself firmly. And, in all fairness, she had sought him out. But if he betrayed their trust, she would bring him to his knees permanently.

"We're glad you could come, Matt," she said evenly as she extended her hand to him.

He shook her hand graciously, but she was careful not to let him hold it too long. She was forced to admit there was a certain electricity about the man. His teal blue sweater and casual slacks were newer and more tidy than what he'd worn the night before, and he carried a weathered, brown leather bomber jacket over one arm. But his hair was still too long and unruly for anyone to mistake him for a man who was thoroughly civilized. And this was the closest she had been to that enigmatic scar on his cheek. Put a sword in his hand and throw a couple of yards of plaid over those broad shoulders, and he might be a Highland warrior of old. She promised herself she would get it out of him how he had come by that scar. Soon.

Reluctantly, Matt handed Sasha's drawings to Rainey and gave a friendly nod of greeting to Emma. "A, Mrs. Ferguson, *dè do bheò?* How are you keepin'?"

Emma blushed behind a girlish smile. "*Tha gu doigheil, tapadh leat.* I'm doing nicely, thank you. Could ye do with a bowl of homemade potato soup, Matt?" Emma asked kindly.

He tested the air and picked up the delicious scent of Emma's soup. "Aye, dear lady, that would be grand if there's a spoonful to spare."

"Come and set yourself down, man," Emma insisted with a sweep of her hand.

Matt raised one eyebrow toward Rainey.

She realized she had been frowning at him, and quickly smoothed the look of doubt from her features. "Of course. Please join us. Emma always makes more than the three of us could ever eat."

"Thank you for your generosity."

His burr had doubled in strength. Had there been just a hint of tease in this thanks? The frown returned to her face.

Sasha took Matt by the hand and led him to the kitchen, where she placed him at the head of the table, a chair that had remained empty since they had moved into the house. He looked from the chair to Sasha's upturned face. There was no need to glance at Rainey's face to know what her reaction might be to this turn of events.

"Where do you usually sit, Sasha?" he asked.

She pointed to her chair at the right side of the table, and Matt pulled his chair around beside hers. "That's better, then, isn't it, love? All cozy, like." He caught Rainey's eye as he sat down. "Don't be hangin' me for treason just yet, Harvard. I've no desire to usurp the throne."

Rainey's knuckles were white around her spoon, but she spoke calmly, her eyes locked with his. "You're a welcome guest in our home."

"Never an ounce more than I've earned," he said to her with a sly wink.

Emma gave Sasha a curious look, and Sasha beamed in return.

"The soup is brilliant, Mrs. Ferguson," Matt said. "Are the mushrooms of a wild variety?"

"Wild? No. I collected 'em at the local supermarket. It's been years since I was able to gather fresh."

Matt gave a quick glance at Sasha's waterfall, which was now back on the refrigerator for safekeeping. He noticed, too, the ominous envelope posted there. Even at a distance he could see the return address said something about Child Welfare.

Rainey rose abruptly. "I'll get you some more milk, Sasha," she said quickly as she opened the refrigerator. Everyone could see that Sasha's glass was still full, so Rainey set the milk carton on the table next to Sasha's plate. She had managed to peel the envelope off the door and stuff it behind the orange juice container, but she had the sinking feeling she hadn't fooled Macinnes for an instant. He didn't miss a beat as she watched him out of the corner of her eye.

"Would you court the notion of huntin' the brown beauties in the woods, missus, if you were given the opportunity?" he asked Emma.

Emma's eyes shone with interest, and she leaned forward. "You know of a place, Macinnes?"

"I do." Matt set his spoon down with great dignity, then folded his arms across his chest as if he were guarding a state secret. "If you've a mind to, we can all go there this afternoon and be back in time for supper."

"So, you're after beggin' another home-cooked meal off us, ye young rascal," Emma said with a wag of her finger.

"That's a fact. Shall we make an afternoon of it, then?" He turned to Sasha, who nodded enthusiastically. Then he turned to Rainey with a look of pure challenge. "It's all in the line of duty, I promise you."

Rainey returned the challenge coolly. "I hope we won't have to go too far. My car isn't very reliable."

"Then we'll take mine," Matt offered.

"I thought you said you were having engine trouble or something." A bout of restlessness brought her to her feet, and she started to clear the table.

"Ah, that's because I had the Studebaker out for a romp last night. Today I brought the Land Rover.

It's a bit more conducive to family travel. Are you game for the hunt, Harvard?"

Family travel. Rainey felt a pang in her chest. She wished he had chosen different words. They didn't seem right somehow. And she wasn't certain she wanted to leave the relative safety of home ground.

"I'm not sure I understand why we're doing this," she said. But when she caught Sasha's imploring look, it was impossible for her to say no. "I guess it won't do any harm to go look for mushrooms." Sasha ran over and gave her a hug that demonstrated far greater thanks than a simple afternoon's walk warranted.

Chapter 4

The air was cool and rich with the scent of ancient redwoods and fallen leaves as they made their way along the forest path. They walked in no particular hurry as the trail took a gradual upward climb. The sun was warm, but the breezes teasing through the lower branches brought a touch of shiver with them. Below, hidden from sight by the dense curtain of fern, evergreen, and leafless maple, the song of water rushing over rock invited more daring exploration. But the steep journey down would be a hazardous one.

Rainey kept her eyes trained on the path. In itself, the trail wasn't too bad. But the downhill side made her vision swim, and the uphill side was just as steep in its own way. The important thing was to concentrate on the ground beneath her feet, or she might become claustrophobic as well. She was determined not to be the one to hold the expedition back.

Every so often, Emma paused to gather a mushroom or two of a favorite variety. She knew which ones were safe to eat, and she never put a strain on any one colony. She hummed to herself as she tucked her earthly treasures into an old linen bag with a faded painting of Edinburgh Castle on it. Now and again, she gave them all a wistful smile when she stopped to drink in the cleansing fragrance of moist evergreen. Angus tagged along at her heels, intent on his own diligent explorations. Every tiny bird or insect was worthy of his attention.

Sasha led the way with a limitless supply of energy. At each fork in the trail, she decided their direction without looking back for confirmation. No one questioned her judgment. Matt had shown her how to mark their progress with signs made of rocks and sticks so they could retrace their steps home, and Sasha marked each fork faithfully.

They lost sight of her, and Rainey started to race up the hill. But Matt caught her arm.

"She knows the way, Harvard. Let her go."

Their eyes held as Rainey wrestled with the idea that Sasha might know her own way. Macinnes was willing her to accept the notion, to believe. But reason wouldn't let her. "Sasha, wait for us!" she shouted. "Wait right there!"

Sasha appeared from around the next bend. She sat down in a disappointed huff and stripped the bark from the twig in her hand.

There was a note of indecision in Rainey's voice. "She doesn't 'know the way,' as you put it, Macinnes. She's never been here, remember? And this may look like the forest primeval, but we're only forty minutes from the city streets. A hiker was murdered on these trails a month ago, and there have been three mountain lion attacks since July. Maybe things like that don't click in your macho brain, but Sasha is all I've got, and I don't intend to jeopardize her safety for the sake of your fairy-tale notions about the world. Have you got that?"

Matt stood quietly through her speech, his eyes on Sasha. He was unscathed by Rainey's mood. "There's a waterfall about a quarter of a mile up the trail from here. I've hiked these woods, and I know them well. That lassie can smell the water, pure and simple. It's a place she's meant to go, and she's anxious to get there. Don't hold her back, Harvard. There's little enough time as it is. And, for the record, I have a feelin' if you gave that wee flower a dirk, she'd be happy to slay all the mountain lions you could throw at her." He glanced down the trail. "Come along, if you please, Mrs. Ferguson, Angus."

He started to walk toward Sasha at a brisk clip, and Rainey had to hustle to keep pace. She caught him by the sleeve and turned him around. "What did you mean when you said 'little enough time'?" she pressed. "Do you know something you're not telling me?"

Matt glanced at Sasha. Her eyes were intent on the path that led upward, and he laid his palm over Rainey's hand where she gripped the leather of his jacket. "It was her pictures spoke to me, the birds at the top of the canyon. And did you notice the bareness of the cliffs?"

"The what? I suppose . . ." Rainey felt the heat rise in her cheeks. She had missed that aspect of the picture. Macinnes was in motion again, and she and Emma raced after him.

The pale sunlight caught the burnt red shades of his hair, and as she watched his strong, uphill strides, she had the eerie feeling she was following him into an historic battle of old. A surge of adrenaline raced to her extremities. It felt right to be following him, even strangely familiar. And when he turned back toward her, there was an intensity to his blue-gray eyes, the beginnings of a new kind of communication of the soul that made her lose her concentration. She stumbled over a loose rock on the path, and he caught her firmly by the arm to prevent her fall. She regained her balance quickly and filed away his grin of amusement among the multitude of other sins he had committed against her.

"The Winter Solstice and the time of the fire rituals will be upon us soon, you know," he said.

"Fire rituals?" Rainey shook her head and took a step back. "No, I don't like the sound of that, Macinnes. Come up with another theory, or we're gone."

"Not to worry. These days most of the ancient ceremonies are little more than bluff and pyrotechnics for the benefit of the *sassenachs*, the tourists."

"And in the old days?" Rainey pursued.

Matt watched the swirling wisps of fog race over the treetops. "Ah, well, no religion worth its salt is without a great bit of showmanship and a wee touch of the occult. We'll educate you as we go along."

"What if it's something I don't want to learn? More importantly, what if it's something I don't want Sasha to be exposed to?"

He faced her squarely. "She's been 'exposed,' as you put it. In fact, I suspect there are things she could tell us about the old ways that would make us both cringe. But it's the timing more than the ceremonies themselves that are important to us."

"Riddles, Doctor. I came to you because of your knowledge of languages, not for a dose of old-time religion."

"You're missing the point, dear lady. The settin' in Sasha's artwork brought to mind an old tale I half-remembered from years ago. I know you're mad for facts, and there's not a one I can give you yet. But give her some space, Rainey. She's got a story to tell us, and we've got to have the brains and the patience to listen." He motioned to Sasha that she could go ahead. Sasha looked to her mother, and Rainey nodded.

"You're basing Sasha's future on some fairy tale you can't even remember?" she demanded.

"Not a fairy tale, a legend native to where I spent my summers as a boy. Legends are most often based

on fact if you search back far enough, you know."
He cocked a brow at her. "You've tried what modern
science has to offer, have you not? Why not grant
the metaphysical a bit of playing space?"

"I don't understand any of this," Rainey said with
a shake of her head. "And I already have more than
enough question marks in my life."

Matt adjusted his glasses a bit higher on his nose.
"You've a stiff backbone about you, Harvard. I can't
help wonderin' what it's goin' to take to get you to
bend to my way of thinkin'."

"An act of God, I imagine."

"Christian or pagan?"

Before Rainey could gather a reply, Emma huffed
up beside them. Her plastic rain bonnet was slightly
askew as she hefted her Edinburgh bag over her
shoulder. Matt extended his hand in an offer to carry
her burden for her, but she dismissed him with a
smile and a wave of her hand. She saw the look of
concern on Rainey's face as they all hurried to catch
up to Sasha.

"I heard ye speak of a legend, Matt," Emma said.
"To what legend of old might ye be referrin', if I
may be so bold as to inquire? I've learnt a wee fable
or two in my travels of the universe. Could develop
it's one familiar to me."

Matt plucked up a fallen redwood frond the size
of his hand and held it to the dappled sunlight as
they walked. The deep green width of it was covered
with a finely spun spider's web. It was coated with
tiny droplets of water, and the sun turned the silk
into a shimmering fan of exquisite color. But as they
passed into a patch of shade, the web dulled to the
gray of a shroud, and Matt set it reverently into
the branches of another tree.

"*Sgeula bheag àbhachdail,*" he said with half a grin.
Rainey and Emma exchanged looks.

"He said it was 'an amusin' little tale,' " Emma whispered. "I take it that's the only answer we'll be gettin' out of the man for now."

"That's not much of an answer," Rainey replied loudly enough for Matt to hear. "The man talks in riddles."

"Bi air t'fhaiceall, fuasgladh na ceiste!" Matt tossed over his shoulder with a dramatic wave of his fist.

"Now what?" Rainey asked.

"He says, 'Beware, the answerin' of the riddle.' "

"Fine, a comedian. Tell him he's hedging the issue."

Emma glanced at her. "Ye can tell him yerself, can ye not? Ye dunna need me for that."

Rainey blinked. "Right. I forgot for a minute." But she knew Matt had heard her. And what was more, it didn't seem to bother him in the least.

The sound of water plunging downhill grew stronger with each step they took, and as they rounded a bend in the trail, one end of a footbridge became visible through the trees. Sasha was nowhere to be seen, and Rainey cupped her hands around her mouth to call out to her. But Matt held a finger to his lips in warning.

As they drew near, a group of boulders came into sight, and then the falls themselves. More correctly, it was a series of falls that raced over rugged natural steps, careening and sending up spray between the piles of massive rock and fallen trees. The mists touched their skin with veils of cool moisture. These falls weren't the same as the single high cascade in Sasha's drawing, with its ominous pool below. But the similarity was there.

Emma touched Rainey's shoulder lightly and pointed to the top of the falls. Rainey trapped a gasp behind her hand and grabbed Emma's arm for support. Sasha was perched high on a boulder ledge fifty feet above where they stood. She sat cross-legged, her hands clasped serenely in her lap, her eyes focused straight ahead, just as she had been on the school filing cabinet. She seemed totally unaware of her companions or the dangerous drop beneath her.

"I'll never forgive you for this, Macinnes!" Rainey shouted as she started her climb. "If she so much as breaks a fingernail, I swear to you, I'll . . ."

"Wait, Rainey!" Matt and Emma called in unison.

The rocks were slick with moss as Rainey clambered over them, and the water was frigid. This was out of her league, and she knew it. She was no mountain climber. And if she didn't know better, she would swear all of nature was fighting against her. Her boots had been made for shopping malls, not rock climbing, and she shuddered from the sogginess of her socks after only a few steps. She glared down at Matt over her shoulder, and the world spun in chaos.

"Come down, Rainey," Matt instructed levelly.

"No, I have to get to her before she falls!" She glanced up and saw that Sasha had stood up, her eyes still fixed straight ahead. Rainey's heart stopped. Nausea gripped her stomach as she tried to steady her vision. "Sasha, sweetheart, sit down! I'm coming to get you. Sit down, Sash, please God, sit down."

Matt shouted something to Sasha in Gaelic, a short sentence followed by a long one. She nodded solemnly and sat down, resuming her original position. Then he turned his attention to Rainey.

"I know this is difficult, Rainey," he called to her, "but Sasha doesn't recognize you right now."

Emma tugged at his arm. "She'd boil me in oil for confidin' this to ye, Matt, but she's that petrified of heights. She can't even look at a tall set of stairs, ye ken?"

Matt's eyes flashed to where Rainey stood frozen

with fear. She lost her footing and slid down the rough surface of a boulder to land waist-deep in an icy pool. Before she could react, Matt was there to haul her out. She shivered, and as he draped his warm leather jacket around her shoulders, she darted a quick glance up at the ledge where Sasha sat like a regal statue.

"What do you mean she doesn't recognize me?" she ground out between chattering teeth.

"I mean, she's on duty, guardin' a trust of some kind, a promise, perhaps." He led her back onto the bridge where Emma waited with a look of sincere worry on her face.

"How do you know what's happening with her?" Rainey demanded. "And if you have the gall to tell me it's part of some crazy legend, I'll throttle you."

"Then, I'd have to say we have nothin' to discuss." Matt walked to the center of the bridge and shouted a string of sentences to Sasha in Gaelic.

Rainey threw off her wet boots in disgust. "What's he saying to her now, Emma?" she asked. "Figure out if he's telling her to jump, so I can pound a wooden stake through his heart." She got to her feet and wrapped Matt's jacket more securely around herself as she padded to the center of the bridge.

Emma concentrated on Matt's words as she tried to glean their meaning. She muttered the words she could understand as she struggled to unravel the ancient dialect.

"He's goin' up after her," she said under her breath.

To confirm Emma's words, Matt started to climb the rocks toward Sasha. He talked to her as he went, and the lilt of his Gaelic as it rose on the mist blended melodically with the rushing waters of the falls. From time to time, Sasha nodded or shook her head at something he said, reinforcing the impression that she understood.

"I can't watch, Emma," Rainey said in desperation. "Please. Tell me what's happening."

"Well, lass, he's plainly an experienced climber. We'll have to give him that much."

Rainey gripped the bridge railing with a vengeance. "I couldn't do it, Emma. I couldn't go up there to help her. What if this is the kind of thing she's going to do from now on? I can't handle these kinds of heights."

Emma patted her hand comfortingly. "Not to worry, love, the Macinnes will help us. He's sittin' on the ledge just below where Sasha is. The sun has broke through the trees and it's shinin' down on the two of them like a blessin' from above. It looks like somethin' the two of them do on a daily basis."

Rainey wanted to scream at the pair of them as she risked glancing up at the precarious set of ledges. "I wish to God I still had that kitchen knife in my hand," she declared. "He's crazy. This is at least five kinds of reckless endangerment. He doesn't give a damn about her safety. Or his own, for that matter. I don't want to have to rely on him." She tucked her hair behind her ears in agitation. "Once they get down here . . ." The word "if" came to mind, but she dismissed it. "I'm going to send him away. I can't take this." She paced the length of the bridge, not daring to look at the ledges above.

"Ye shouldna send him away, love," Emma said patiently.

Rainey whirled on her, glad for a nearby target for her frustrations. "Why not? She'd be safe at home right now if I hadn't been taken in by all of his blarney, or whatever you people call it."

Emma tore off her rain bonnet and planted her fists on her hips. " 'You people,' is it? 'You people'?

You're forgettin' yerself, Rainey. I'll be fergivin' ye this time because I know the kind of worry yer goin' through. But I'm tellin' it to ye straight, ye ken, Matt Macinnes does care for our Sasha. He talks to her like she's royalty. That's got to count for somethin'. And if ye ain't got the courage to take this route, then suit yerself, lassie. Take that wee angel home and never let her see the light o' day again. Keep her a prisoner in the dark just like she's been keepin' herself one. Or pack up and run till there's nowhere left to hide. Better still, open the front door and let Evanston or that harpie from Child Welfare steal her from ye. And I hope ye'll be verra happy in the lonely decades to come." She picked up her Edinburgh bag, and with a sharp salute, she trudged down the trail with Angus trotting at her heels.

"I'm sorry, Emma," Rainey called after. "Really, I'm sorry." Emma waved her off and continued her downward journey.

Emma's scolding cut deeply, and at the prospect of losing her friendship along with everything else, Rainey wanted to weep. As far as she was concerned, Matt Macinnes was destroying all their lives.

She glanced back toward the ledges at the top of the falls, only to find them empty. Matt and Sasha were nowhere to be seen, and a wave of panic rose in her heart.

"Dear God, he's stolen her!"

"Stolen who, our dear Emma?" Matt said behind her.

Rainey turned to find him and Sasha watching her with interest from the far side of the bridge. They both looked none the worse for wear, and Sasha seemed to be her old self as Rainey ran to her and hugged her for dear life.

"There's a wee path leads down on the other side," Matt said in reply to Rainey's accusing look. "It's perfectly safe and decidedly more comfortable than landin' on your, er, back, if you don't mind my sayin'." He answered her frown with one of his own. "What's become of Emma, then? She's not gone psychedelic because of a rogue mushroom, it's to be hoped."

Rainey kept a firm hold on Sasha's hand. "She started down ahead of us. It's time we all went home."

Matt gave her a considering look. "Whatever is your wish." He winked at Sasha, who beamed back at him. "Your dear mother's convinced we're both daft, lassie. Nuts, ye know." He crossed his eyes and wiggled his hands out of his ears until Sasha giggled with delight. "And yet, she's the one standin' about soaked to the bone in her stockin' feet, all of a brisk winter's day." He tsked loudly.

Rainey ignored their antics and shoved her feet back into her cold, waterlogged boots. She glared at Matt over her shoulder as she started cautiously down the path and mouthed the words "You are crazy" at him.

"Och, but you said you were game, Harvard, and I took you at your word."

"You ask too much. You can't expect me to go along with putting Sasha in this kind of danger."

Matt ran his hand along the fine moss that sloped up from the trail. "The only real danger came when you tried to interfere."

Rainey stopped in her tracks and whirled on him. "Interfere?' she demanded. "My daughter was hanging from the edge of a cliff!"

"Hardly. She knew precisely what she was about."

"Well, I don't know what she's about. And I don't see how all of this madness has gotten us any closer to solving our problems." She took a deep breath and looked him straight in the eye. "We won't ask you to sacrifice any more of your time, Dr. Macinnes. If you'll be so kind as to drive us home, we'll let you go on about your business."

Matt regarded her closely. "It's that easy to play the coward, is it, Harvard?"

"My name isn't Harvard, it's Lorraine," she shot at him. "Sasha and I don't need your so-called help anymore. We have some packing to do." She turned on her heel and started down the hill again with Sasha in tow. But Sasha broke away from her and stood poised halfway between her mother and Matt. She looked furtively from one to the other, then walked over to take Matt's hand.

Rainey watched in utter shock. Was his hold over Sasha already so strong she would choose this crazy Scottish poet over her own mother? "What are you doing, Sash?"

Sasha looked up at Matt imploringly, then led him forward. She took her mother's hand and became the living link between them.

Matt raised his eyes from Sasha to Rainey. "It seems the lassie won't settle for just one of us . . . Mrs. Nielson. I'm sorry. Never havin' had a wee one of my own, I can only guess how much this must offend you, given all the love and sacrifice you've invested in her upbringin'."

"That's right, you don't know," Rainey agreed. She pulled her hand away and wrapped her arms around herself defensively. "When you lose someone you love, you never want to have to live through it again. You'll do anything in your power to keep your family safe. Anything. Life is so very fragile." Rainey saw the tears of silent pleading in Sasha's eyes and felt her own emotions fill to the brim. "This is all happening too quickly. I need time to adjust."

Matt gave Sasha's hand a gentle squeeze. "I don't know how to emphasize this enough, Mrs. Nielson.

We have no time to give you. I swear to you I'll guard Sasha's safety as if she were my own daughter." He ran his hand through his hair in a restless gesture. "Would you like a promise in writin' that I will not use anythin' I discover about Sasha in print or to further my own career?"

"You would do that?" Rainey said in astonishment.

"I would. I don't know how I can possibly convey to you the importance of what's happenin' between us all. It goes far beyond grants and lecture circuits, to be sure. It's the opportunity of a lifetime, of a hundred lifetimes, perhaps." He looked down at Sasha. "You speak of investing the whole of your heart in a person, Mrs. Nielson. My heart was lost from the first moment I saw this wee lassie standin' in the doorway of your home. I cannot explain it. We're of the same mind much of the time, Sasha and I. There's an impatience between us, am I not right, Sasha?" He tousled Sasha's hair, but she frowned back at him.

"Mi-fhaighidinn, leannan," he provided, and she nodded her understanding.

Rainey pulled a sheet of drawing paper and a red crayon from her purse. A part of her said she was being foolish to go through with this kind of kindergarten contract. But another part of her insisted upon it. She presented the items to Matt, and he gave the scarlet color of the crayon a dubious look.

"It's to be drawn up in blood, I see," he said as he took the items from her. "So be it, ladies." He wrote out a declaration of his honest intent, first in English, then in Gaelic, and signed it with an elaborate scrawl.

When Rainey gave a questioning glance at the Gaelic portion, Matt handed it to Sasha, who studied the old words. She gave her mother an affirming nod.

"Call us in the morning," Rainey said as she

tucked the paper and crayon back into her purse and handed him his jacket. She felt drained of all warmth.

Sasha smiled at Matt and took her mother's hand.

"Would seven o'clock by satisfactory?" Matt asked as he threw on his jacket.

"Not a second before eight," Rainey said with a shiver as she concentrated on nothing but the path. "Emma's not speaking to me, so if you're hoping for another traditional Scottish meal, Macinnes, you'll have to ask her for it, or settle for tea and toast."

"Far be it from me to impose, Mrs. Nielson."

"Humph," Rainey scoffed, sounding for all the world like a native Scot.

Chapter 5

Sasha was up, dressed, and rummaging around for her crayon collection at the break of dawn. Rainey gave up trying to get any rest. She hadn't slept well, and she dreaded calling in to the agency tomorrow to try to buy more time to finish her work. The fact that she had always met her deadlines promptly probably wouldn't carry much weight, given the urgent nature of the ad copy she had been assigned. She hadn't been thinking straight when she told Macinnes he could come over first thing. Now she was going to have to find a way to juggle things for the rest of the day.

Most of all, she strained to hear the sound of Emma's familiar knock on the door. It was Sunday, and that traditionally meant Emma's homemade scones and jam. But this wasn't going to be like other Sundays in any respect. She was going to need all the support she could get in dealing with Macinnes. But this time, she was on her own.

He had wandered at will through her brief dreams, smiling a challenge at her one minute and dragging her by the hand through tangled forests the next. With a start, she remembered he had led her to the edge of a cliff, and he had kissed her as if they had been lovers a very long time. In the dream, she had responded to his kiss with all her heart. Her body responded to the memory even now.

The phone rang as she stepped out of the shower, and she threw a towel around herself, hoping the call was from Emma. If it wasn't, she promised herself she would go next door and beg for forgiveness before Matt had the chance to show up. She wasn't sure she could trust herself alone with him.

Thankfully, it was Emma on the phone.

"Emma, I'm sor—," Rainey began.

"Tosh, lassie, I'll not hear a word of it," Emma said briskly. "It's forgotten. But fair warnin', the Macinnes is on his way over. He was 'round to the house for scones and jam this mornin'. Sasha waved to him out the window 'bout an hour past, so it's to be hoped she gave ye notice of his comin'."

"No, nothing."

"Well, he'll be dashin' up the front steps by now. I'm off to church, love," Emma continued cheerily. "I'll pop 'round later."

"I—"

"Give the man a chance, Rainey."

Emma hung up without waiting for a reply, and at the same time, Rainey heard Sasha open the front door. Just as before, she found Matt Macinnes watching her from the doorway.

"Ah, Aphrodite on the Half Shell," he said with an appreciative smile at her bath towel. "I approve wholeheartedly of the new wardrobe."

"You're early," Rainey replied curtly. Her hair dripped down over her shoulders, and a sea of gooseflesh rose on her skin.

Matt neatly filled out his oatmeal-colored Aran sweater, and his jeans were clean, but well broken in. He seemed taller than she remembered. The dream was very much on her mind, and it wouldn't have surprised her to have him walk up to her and kiss her soundly in greeting. It took an instant for her to realize she was staring at him.

Matt glanced at his watch. "My watch says eight o'clock straight up, Harvard. I long since switched from Edinburgh time."

Out of reflex, Rainey glanced at her wrist where her watch would normally be, and her towel slipped precariously. She grabbed it and cinched it around herself so tightly she could hardly breathe.

"You were supposed to call first," she said through a blush that went from head to toe.

"Ah, well, I had Emma make the call for me to save time."

He ignored Rainey's glare and went down on his haunches next to Sasha.

"Emma sent over freshly baked scones for you and your mother, Sasha," he said with a smile. He produced a scone from his jacket pocket and handed it to her. The other he set on the letter table next to the door. There was a telltale stack of bills there, most with PAST DUE stamped on them. His eyes didn't linger there.

"Sasha, would you care to join me out on the front porch for a bit o' brekkie while your dear mother gathers herself? Emma said she'd leave that wee dragon Angus in our care."

Sasha gave Rainey a hopeful look.

"Five minutes," Rainey said with a firm grip on her towel. "And Sasha, you put on your heavy jacket, understood? And your ski hat. And your rain boots."

Matt gave Sasha a wink. "There's your five minutes' worth, right, love? By the time we've harvested that lot, your mum should have time to deck herself out sufficient for the coronation ball, should she not?"

Sasha nodded dutifully.

"Five minutes," Rainey reiterated. She made her

escape into the bedroom and slammed the door. The sound of Sasha's joyous laughter reached her ears, and she was torn between gladness and irritation at the ease with which Matt had once again lifted her daughter's mood. He was speaking to her in Gaelic again, she suspected, and for now, she didn't even have Emma's help in figuring out what he might be saying to her.

Once she had thrown on her slacks and sweater, she tore the brush through her dark curls and slapped on the only lipstick she could find. Her reaction to her own reflection was that she looked like she hadn't slept for a week, and it made her feel at a disadvantage. She had to be at a hundred and ten percent if she was going to spar with Macinnes. Was there ever a time when he wasn't absolutely in control of himself and his surroundings?

It had been a long time since she had felt the pressure to prove herself to anyone. A very long time. She still had it, the strength, the self-possession, the power to achieve whatever she chose to do. The drive to succeed had taken her to the top of her class and very near the top of her chosen profession. Qualities like that didn't just disappear. They were still there, and she was going to make sure Macinnes didn't get another opportunity to manipulate her. It was time for him to tell her what he had learned from all these Gaelic "conversations" with Sasha. She would insist upon it. She grabbed her jacket and marched out the front door, ready to take charge of the day.

But once she was out on the porch, she discovered she was alone, and she knew another moment of panic. He had stolen her again. No, he had never really stolen Sasha from her, she told herself. But he was impulsive and unreasonable with her safety, and he didn't give a damn about anybody's opinion but his own. That was very dangerous. And now, he and Sasha were gone.

She dashed down the steps toward Emma's house. The sound of Sasha's laughter reached her, and she gave a little groan of relief. Matt was on Emma's porch, fully engaged in a raucous game of sock tug-o'-war with Angus while Sasha tickled each of them in turn with a small pine branch she had found.

Matt handed the sock to Sasha and came over to Rainey with a warm smile of greeting. The smile persisted despite her look of open disapproval. That look definitely promised a sharp reprimand, and he didn't give her the chance to work up a head of steam. He took her by the arm and led her a short distance out of Sasha's earshot.

"It's time we had a talk, Mrs. Nielson," he said in more serious fashion.

Rainey turned so she could keep an eye on Sasha. "I couldn't agree more, Dr. Macinnes," she said, matching his tone. "I think it's time you—"

"Please, please, no need to apologize," he said quickly.

"Apologize?"

He leaned forward against Emma's fence rail, his eyes, too, on Sasha as she gave Angus a run for his money with the tattered sock. "I'm of the opinion that if you realize the scope of what we're dealin' with here, perhaps we could speed our progress."

The temptation to straighten him out about the notion of her apologizing to him for any reason was a strong one, but she recognized this window of opportunity.

"Enlighten me."

He turned to her and took a deep breath as if he were about to embark on a very long, steep journey.

"I am nothing if not a pragmatist, Mrs. Nielson," he began. "Perchance it stems from all those generations of Macinneses who slogged about knee-deep in the Highland bogs referrin' to each other by high-born titles while they picked the lice from their noble beards."

"You're losing me, Macinnes."

He removed his glasses and looked at her in all seriousness. "Sasha is living two lives, Mrs. Nielson. She's here with us. But she's also elsewhere from time to time."

"Elsewhere. Exactly what do you mean by elsewhere?" Every ounce of her common sense warned her she didn't want to hear what he had to say.

"A part of her dwells in another time and place. She's got obligations in the distant past."

As if she sensed they were talking about her, Sasha turned toward them with a cheery wave as Angus frolicked around her ankles. Matt and Rainey waved back simultaneously. Sasha looked angelic in the early morning sunlight, like a spirit being who had dropped her veils of invisibility only to them. And yet, she was still Sasha. Sasha who loved Emma's scones, computer games, and double scoops of strawberry frozen yogurt.

"So, you're saying she should be treated for classic schizophrenia, that she has two distinct personalities." Rainey felt her defenses rise. She had been told this one before by some of the biggest names in the psychiatric world. It was a simplistic diagnosis, as far as she was concerned, and she wasn't buying it.

Matt saw her stiffen, and gave her an enigmatic smile. "I'm not a shrink. I don't make lists of isolated symptoms and sum them up at the bottom of a page. Words are how I earn my supper, remember? Words and an abiding faith in human nature, past and present. She is one person, one person with two jobs to perform. She's here for you because you need her. But she's also there because someone else needs her. There's business of some kind she's sworn to finish. I'm convinced of it." He plucked a fallen maple leaf from the railing and spun it lightly between his fingers, much as Emma had done. "I don't want to tear that wee treasure apart just to count the pieces. I want to gather her together and give her freedom. And perhaps give her mother a bit of freedom into the bargain."

"I'll get by just fine," she assured him as she tucked her hair behind her ear. "I don't require anything more than Sasha's happiness."

"Is that a fact?" The leaf floated from his hand to the ground. "Martyrdom does not become you, Mrs. Nielson. You're no the type."

Rainey turned to him. "Oh, and since you've decided to be a shrink after all, just what type am I, Dr. Macinnes?" she insisted.

"You'll choose to misunderstand this, of course," he said with a sigh, "but I can find no other word sufficient in the English language to describe you. You are a passionate woman." She bristled instantly, and he was quick to explain. "By that I mean you are a person who grabs hold of something and won't let go, despite the odds."

She looked at him skeptically. "Stubborn, you mean."

He grinned at her. "Here, now, I'm supposed to be the wordsmith, and you've topped me, neat as you please. There was a better word."

She gave him a reluctant smile. "It's not a word I'm unfamiliar with."

"Interesting. We have somethin' else in common, it seems. They had it engraved on my nameplate at the university, along with pompous, arrogant . . . Ah, the glowing accolades could fill a wall."

Sasha started to walk toward them. She would soon be within hearing distance.

"I'll ask you to indulge me one more time, Mrs. Nielson," Matt said. "A campfire in the woods tonight. We'll tell some stories. I've given Emma somethin' of a script to follow, since much of what we'll be doin' will be in Gaelic. It'll be phonetic, much of it, but Emma has a feel for the inflections. And I'll be needin' your help, too. I know it's hard for you, not bein' able to understand, so I've written you up a translation." He tucked some folded sheets of paper into her hand. "The legend I spoke of before won't be included to-night because I don't want to set ideas into Sasha's mind. But the other stories will be taken from tradi-tional tales, and they may be familiar to her in some way if my theories are correct. We may be able to get her to respond verbally if the memories are strong enough. Do I have your permission?"

There was no time to think.

"No mountain climbing or waterfalls," Rainey said quickly. "And no rituals, understood? I don't want her frightened."

"She'll be fine. It's you we have to tend, isn't it?"

Sasha was nearly to them. She crooked her finger at Matt to get him to bend over the fence. It looked like she was going to give him a hug. Instead, she littered his hair with a handful of acorn shells and dashed back a few feet, laughing uproariously.

Matt straightened with great dignity as the acorns bounced off his broad shoulders in comical fashion. He looked at Sasha like a disgruntled general.

"You understand, lassie, this means war," he said with mock sternness.

Sasha froze at his words as if they had struck a chord in her memory. Her expression grew distant, and they were about to lose her to the past again.

Matt sprang into action. He leapt over the little fence and sprinkled a handful of grass over Sasha's head. It tickled her nose, and when she sneezed, it broke the spell. With a shriek of delight, she grabbed a double handful of grass and tore after him. But Matt was already in motion. They chased around the yard, laughing and sliding on the damp grass.

Rainey's heart constricted as she watched them play. This was right in so many ways. But Matt Macinnes was the wrong man. It should have been Alan out there with Sasha. This was a father's job, and Matt wasn't Sasha's father. Those wonderful times between Sasha and Alan would never happen again.

She wanted it all back, all that Alan had given her like so many brightly wrapped presents—the devotion, the support. And Sasha. But the past was dead, and she never wanted to risk that kind of commitment of the heart, that kind of pain, again.

The game of tag came back in Rainey's direction, and she locked her emotions back into storage. Matt and Sasha looked at her, then grinned. They had chunks of fresh grass ready in their hands, but Matt lowered his arm when he saw Rainey's expression.

"Oh, no, you don't," she said, forcing a smile as she eyed the chunks of grass. "I just had this sweater dry-cleaned." She held her hands up in defense as she backed away from the fence. But the enemy closed in.

"Do you wish to know the terms of your surrender, Mrs. Nielson?" Matt's words were mischievous, but he was watching her closely.

Rainey regarded the pair of them. The race had put color into their faces, and her eyes were drawn again to the long white scar on Matt's cheek. "Not surrender, Stanford, truce."

"A gift." He bowed to Rainey, and Sasha took the opportunity to toss all of her green ammunition on top of his head. When he rose slowly, the sly grin on his face set Sasha into immediate giggling flight. The two of them raced around the yard until they collapsed on Emma's porch in exhaustion.

Rainey walked up to them and folded her arms across her chest in maternal fashion. "Are the two of you quite finished?"

They both nodded contritely.

"Matt has invited us to a marshmallow roast around the campfire tonight, Sash," Rainey said. "What do you think?"

Matt tousled Sasha's hair affectionately. "I thought perhaps once Emma gets back from church, we could play a few rounds of miniature golf. And I do still owe us all dessert. Ice cream, maybe?" Rainey mouthed a hint to him, and he quickly corrected his offer. "Or frozen yogurt, perchance."

Sasha considered the idea for a moment. Then, with quiet grace, she rose from the step and headed toward home.

"We may have to postpone the campfire," Rainey said as she stood up to go.

Matt caught her sleeve. "Wait for it. She's up to somethin'."

Rainey's stomach tightened when she saw Sasha emerge from the house with two crayon drawings in her hand. Even at a distance, they didn't look like the ones from before. Sasha handed the pictures to them and waited calmly for their responses.

One drawing was of the waterfall at the height of a storm. The clouds were nightmarish, the waters lead-gray and in turmoil. The other picture portrayed a ring of white spirit figures above the waters, some large, some the size of a child. And at the center of the ring shone a broadsword with a crown of stars above it. It was a revelation and somehow a warning.

"Oh, Sash," Rainey sighed as she took Sasha's hand and brought her down to sit on the step.

Sasha produced a handful of crayons from her jacket pocket. She tucked her hair behind her ears, a copy of her mother's habit, and began to draw in one corner of the spirit picture. It was a perfect strawberry.

Rainey gave her a sad smile. "A double scoop, Sash, I promise."

Chapter 6

Darkness fell quickly. It didn't feel like they were inside the safe boundaries of the local state park. The camping facilities were closed to the public for the season, but through his ties to the university, Matt had pulled some strings to get them the use of the grounds. They parked the Land Rover in a lot at the end of a well-groomed dirt road and packed up their supplies for the bonfire.

In addition, Matt slung a brown leather backpack across his shoulder. He guided them by flashlight along the winding trail to their campsite. No one lagged behind as the woods closed around them like a living tunnel. Angus gave a soft whine of insecurity, and Emma lifted the little Scottie into her arms.

Rainey gave Sasha's hand a reassuring squeeze. "Are you okay, sweetheart?" she asked. "You aren't . . . cold, or tired, or anything, are you?" As far as she was concerned, if Sasha showed any sign she was afraid of all this, the expedition was going to come to a swift halt. Matt turned the light toward them so Rainey could see Sasha's reaction.

Sasha gave her mother a stalwart smile and shook her head. Then, with a regal wave of her hand, she gestured for Matt to lead them on.

Total blackness gave way to the dim, phosphorescent glow of the lush moss on the ancient trees, some of which dated back to the age of the Roman Empire. It gave their surroundings an ethereal atmosphere and melted away all sense of time.

They were so intent on following the trail, it was almost a surprise when they reached the clearing. The stone fire ring was a standard size and shape for government-maintained camp areas. But this wasn't a warm summer night filled with the echoing laughter of other campers and the songs of crickets. It was cold and quiet, and a bank of marine fog raced over the tops of the trees, bringing with it a blanket of damp chill that penetrated to the bone. The park was only half an hour from home, but it felt like they were a thousand miles from civilization.

The kindling they had brought was aged and dry, and within minutes Matt had a friendly fire started. To this he added a hefty log of native pine left for them by the ranger. The sound of the crackling wood bounced back to them off the ring of giant redwoods, and a burst of shimmering sparks floated heavenward like so many tiny spirits set free on a mission of great importance.

Sasha laughed with pure delight as she followed the sparks' upward journey, and Rainey caught Matt's smile. He had that Highlander look about him again in the fire's glow. And although he was wearing jeans, his teal sweater, and his leather jacket, it took very little imagination to picture him in weathered kilts with a sword slung behind his back. His hair was in wilder disarray than usual, and his eyes shone with the spirit of their surroundings. There was every possibility he had been born with that scar across his cheek, she decided. A memento from another, more dangerous time.

"Who's for hot dogs, then?" Emma proposed with enthusiasm as she unpacked the food. She took off her conservative head scarf and inhaled the cold, clean air with a look of contentment as Angus frolicked around her at the prospect of scraps. "Ah, now, this place'll give ye an appetite and put the color back in yer cheeks. What do ye say, Matthew, are ye willin' to supervise this bonnie wee barbecue?"

Matt bowed to her in courtly fashion. "*Le toileachas.* With pleasure, dear lady," he said humbly. "Dogs it is." He looked down at Angus with a mischievous gleam in his eye, and Emma wagged a scolding finger at him.

"Oh, no, ye don't, ye young heathen," she said with mock sternness. "This is no some godforsaken hut in the China Sea, nor is it the stones at Caisteal Grugaig. So I'll be askin' ye to mind your manners, if it's all the same." She winked at him through her supposed indignity and gave Angus a hearty hug.

Sasha had smothered a small gasp at the mention of Caisteal Grugaig, and Matt was quick to pursue the subject. "If I may ask, whatever brought you to think of Caisteal Grugaig, Emma?" he asked.

Emma stroked Angus's silky coat, a wistful smile on her face. "We used to summer on the Isle of Skye when I was a wee lass. Some of the tales my brothers spun about the rituals of Caisteal Grugaig positively drove a body to religion."

"Castle what?" Rainey asked as she slid a hot dog onto a stick. She started to hand it to Sasha to cook, but Sasha stood up slowly and turned away from the fire with a look of concern on her young face. There was a fallen tree just to one side of the fire circle, and she climbed it easily to take her place above them all.

Matt noted her actions, but continued as if nothing had happened. Her reaction to Grugaig hadn't been part of his original plan, but he was only too happy to capitalize on it.

"Caisteal Grugaig," he said lightly. "It's a *broch*, a fort that dates back to the Pictish Iron Age, back to the time of ceremonial sacrifice and the like. It's in the north country near Kyle of Lochalsh, where they have the bridge now to the Isle of Skye." He took a hot dog from Emma settled it onto a stick. It sizzled as it started to cook, and the air filled with the tantalizing aroma of food on the open fire. "Grugaig guards the juncture of two lakes, Loch Duich and Loch Lomond."

Sasha slid down from her seat and walked over to Matt with a look of censure. She gently took his face between her hands and shook her head at him.

"What is it, love?" he asked, his eyes locked with hers. "Have I misspoke myself, then?" Sasha nodded vehemently, and he frowned in thought. "Let's give it some work. Isle of Skye, that part was correct, was it not?" He was given the nod. "Caisteal Grugaig, is the error there?"

She inclined her head to indicate that he was getting closer to the source of the problem and stepped back to make a horizontal wave motion with her arm.

Matt rubbed his chin. "Oh, aye, the lochs, is that where the trouble lies?"

Sasha nodded solemnly.

"Ah, Loch Duich, perchance?"

Sasha stamped her foot in impatience as Matt took a leisurely bite of his hot dog. "Then it would have to be the other loch. Whatever did I say before? Give me a moment to recollect." He took another bite of hot dog, and Sasha looked close to violence. "I might have said most anythin', you know. It must be said we academic types are quite prone to early senility, you see." He winked at Rainey, and she pressed her lips together in disapproval. A smile broke across his face as he swallowed the last of his bite and put a second hot dog on his stick.

Emma tossed a pebble at him. "Ye said Loch Lomond, ye young clod," she scolded. "It's no been so long we wouldna remember Caisteal Grugaig bein' the meetin' place of Loch Druich and Loch Alsh, for pity's sakes! Even little Sasha here knew ye were sorely in the wrong."

The impact of what she had just said struck home, and Emma inadvertently dropped her hot dog into the flames as she shot a glance at Rainey. It was clear from the look on Rainey's face she wanted to ask a thousand pointed questions, of Macinnes and Sasha alike. But, for the moment, she held her peace.

Matt wiped the mustard from the corner of his mouth with great ceremony. "Loch Alsh, of course! Thank you, Sasha. Hang me for a thief if I didn't twist the topography 'round."

"A rather colorful and not altogether unappealing image," Rainey said sweetly under her breath as she took Sasha a hot dog.

Matt gave her a grin of challenge, and his Scottish burr grew a foot thick. "Th-e-e-re now, Harvard, I told ye, did I no, ye must but keep your vows of passion in the dark a wee bit longer, forebye. Did I no warn ye of the ter-r-rible consequences if the world were to discover the depth of yer heartfelt affection for me?"

Rainey's jaw dropped, and she felt color stain her cheeks as she watched Matt slip the second hot dog into a bun with tender care. Sasha smothered a giggle behind her hand, which only fueled Rainey's embarrassment.

"Insufferable," she shot at him.

"On a daily basis, *mo chridhe*." He handed the hot dog to Emma in chivalrous fashion.

"*Mo chridhe*, what does that mean, Emma?" Rainey asked.

Before Emma could answer, Sasha walked over to

Rainey and drew the outline of a heart over the breast pocket of her jacket. She looked into her mother's eyes and smiled.

"It means heart? Is that what it means, Sash?" Sasha nodded. Rainey looked to Matt, but he was making a great ceremony of putting more mustard on his hot dog. She didn't think for an instant he was complaining of a heart condition. The only assumption she could make was that it didn't mean the same thing in Gaelic as it might in English.

"Now, as I was sayin'," Matt continued, "the fort has quite a history. The walls are nine feet thick and thirteen feet high. Even today, wall chambers and parts of the staircase and the gallery still stand. There's a massive triangular block of stone above the doorway, you see. Weighs tons, I imagine. It was of great significance to those who understood its meanin'." His attention was focused on the tiny hisses of smoke sent up by the hot dog Emma had lost in the fire.

"And do you understand the stone's meaning, Matt?" Rainey asked. She watched Sasha climb on top of the fallen tree again. Sasha's eyes were trained on the fire, but she had not left them spiritually, nor had she taken her usual cross-legged pose. Still, her demeanor was guarded, and she seemed acutely aware of her surroundings.

Matt gave Sasha a smart salute, and she saluted him in return.

"The meanin' of the stone dwells in the hearts of those who lived then, Harvard," he said as he placed another hot dog in a bun. His eyes held Rainey's as he passed the food to her.

A wave of gooseflesh raced up the back of her neck as she took the food from him. She got the distinct impression he knew exactly what that triangular block of Scottish stone signified. The absurd question in her mind was in what century had he acquired the knowledge?

She tried to clear her head of such nonsense as the hot dog course led to the dessert course—toasted marshmallows. But Sasha's knowledge of the lakes of Scotland still mystified her. She decided it was something Matt had taught her. It was the only explanation that made any sense.

Once the tea and cocoa had been brewed and the picnic supplies had been neatly packed away, Matt stoked the fire and turned the pine log over in a spectacular explosion of embers. The fire gathered itself briefly before the flames embraced the new wood. It burned higher and brighter than before, and they were all silent as every tiny shift and burst hypnotically commanded their full attention.

Matt surveyed his audience, then reached into the leather backpack he had brought with him. He withdrew several items of interest: a very old looking dagger in a tattered leather sheath, a swatch of pale blue wool, and a silver button. The button's ornate decoration had been nearly worn away.

"Now, dear ladies," he said with theatrical panache, "the time has come for a wee bit of yarn spinnin', if you'll indulge me." He gave Sasha a sly wink, and she sat up with interest. Then he raised a brow in Emma's direction and received a smile of readiness.

When he made eye contact with Rainey, he took note of her tension. But she didn't mouth any protests, so he took it as temporary consent. He hoped she had read the outline he had given her. Once the story was in progress, it wouldn't do to have it interrupted. He took a deep breath and savored the prospect of letting the magic of old Gaelic roll from his tongue. Still, everything in its own sweet time. He

smiled at the thought and started the story in English
for Rainey's benefit.

"In the time of the old ways, there lived a beautiful
young woman who was called Derbhorgill," he
began. "Derbhorgill's father was a powerful king of
Lochlann, the land of many lakes where Norsemen
lived in those days." From the outset, it was poetic.
Without missing a beat, he switched to Gaelic.

Rainey lowered her gaze to the flames, disappointed at not being able to follow the flow of the
story anymore, even though she had read Matt's
notes. But Emma and Sasha didn't even blink at the
change. Rainey listened to the timeless, enchanting
rhythm of the words and tried to fit the pieces of the
story to the sound she heard. Names were the anchor
to which she clung.

The word *Fomorii* caught her attention. According
to the story, they were ugly, misshapen, violent crea-
tures who lived under the sea in ancient Celtic
mythology. Obnoxious little people, the *Fomorii* often
demanded tribute in exchange for keeping the peace.
And in this case, the king of Lochlann decided to
send them the lovely Derbhorgill in lieu of material
goods. A great dad, Rainey mused.

She heard Matt mention the name Cuchullainn,
and she knew the hero had come onto the scene.
Cuchullainn saved Derbhorgill from the terrible
clutches of the *Fomorii* through feats of fantastic daring, and naturally, Derbhorgill fell utterly in love
with him. But Derbhorgill had gone against her father's wishes, and her love for Cuchullainn had to
forever remain a secret. So she followed her handsome hero around each day in the form of a swan
so no one would suspect she was the one who was
his constant companion.

Fairy tales. What a sucker she had been for them
when she was little, Rainey thought to herself.

Knights in shining armor, princes who whisked you away to eternal happiness . . . Alan had been her chivalrous prince. But her shining hero had been slain. And happiness was a commodity she pursued now only for Sasha. Everything else was fleeting as fairy dust.

The name Laoghaire brought her attention back to the story, and she knew things were about to take an unhappy turn. Cuchullainn and his friend, Laoghaire, went on a hunting trip, and when a flock of swans flew overhead, Laoghaire brought one down with a stone from a slingshot. The swan was Derbhorgill. Cuchullainn sucked the stone from her wound and saved her life. But then they were united by blood and could no longer marry. With her heart broken, Derbhorgill married Laoghaire, the wrong man. Hardly a happy ending.

Emma gave a heartfelt sigh and muttered something softly in Gaelic as the legend drew to a close.

"Aye, dear lady," Matt replied, "a sad and familiar tale. But now let me relate one you may not have heard before. If you lose the thread of it, Sasha and I will catch the both of you up afterward."

He took the dagger and the other items he had brought and climbed up next to Sasha on the fallen tree. He then motioned for Emma to move closer to Rainey for purposes of translation. Apparently, this story hadn't been included on the preview sheet, and Rainey gave him a look of skepticism.

This time, the story was in Gaelic from the start, and Emma did her best to keep up with Matt's pace. But she could only retrieve a word or two here, a stray sentence there, and the heart of the story was lost to her and to Rainey.

The most they could fit together was that it was a love story about a princess who wore a light blue gown, a warrior who was blinded in battle when his enchanted dagger was stolen, and some kind of treachery against the king. They never could sift out the significance of the worn button.

But most of all, it was Matt's extraordinary skill with Gaelic that filled the night air. Whatever the legend was truly about, its magic wrapped around them all. It wasn't hard to imagine spirits from the past gathered in a circle as they had in Sasha's drawing, summoned forth by his words. In any language, he was an extraordinary storyteller.

At the end of the tale, a single tear slid down Sasha's cheek, and she touched the dagger with more than a sense of awe—she touched it with a sense of understanding. Matt patted her hand companionably, then gathered up his treasures and slid off the tree. He went down on his haunches behind Rainey and Emma as he tucked the visual aids back into his pack.

"So, how did you do, ladies?" he asked.

Emma smoothed the crease in her brown woolen slacks. "Not verra well, I'm afraid," she said with a note of regret. "I don't suppose ye could fill us in on the gist of it?"

"Here now, it was nothin' more than a wee bit of Macinnes geneology, Emma," he replied. "The blue gown belonged to a dear lady named Catriona on my mother's side of the family tree. The dirk belonged, not to her doddering old husband, but to Raibeart, the warrior prince she loved. And the wee button came from the shoe of their only child, Mairead, a daughter born in secret far from home on the Isle of Skye. Raibeart never saw her. He died in a dungeon, blind and abandoned, a political prisoner because of his forbidden love for Catriona."

"How sad," Rainey said. The story of a father and daughter separated from each other touched her heart, and she looked at the objects Matt had brought with fresh respect. "I'd gladly tell you the whole of the tale," Matt explained, "but it seems our wee queen of the fairies has other plans."

He inclined his head toward the tree where Sasha had been sitting. She was climbing down, and when she reached the ground, she started toward the trail by which they had come.

Rainey followed, convinced that Sasha was ready to leave. But just past the reach of the fire's light, Sasha sat down on the trail, her sight locked far beyond the trees overhead.

"What is it, Sash?" Rainey asked softly. "Do you want to go home?"

Sasha nodded in the darkness and pointed toward the sky. The fog parted, and a sea of stars pressed down on them. This far from the glow of the city, no small square of space was without a shimmering crowd of celestial light.

And in a whisper that was barely more than the breezes playing in the branches overhead, Sasha sent a single word toward the heavens.

"Glomach."

Chapter 7

"Glomach. Now we're gettin' somewhere," Matt said softly over Rainey's shoulder.

Rainey was still too surprised to move as she stared down into Sasha's expectant face. Even in a whisper, this was the first word she had come close to saying in three years.

"Tell me she's not claiming to be from some distant planet, okay?"

Matt chuckled at her softly. "If she is, Harvard, then yours truly has been on the mother ship as well."

"I wouldn't doubt it for an instant."

Matt sat down beside Sasha and took her hand in his.

"Tell me, if you will, Sasha, how many sisters are there?" he asked kindly.

Sasha frowned in concentration, but didn't answer.

"*A Sasha, cia mheud peathraichean a tha ann?*" he asked in Gaelic. After a moment's thought, she held up her open hand to indicate five, and Matt gave Rainey a thumbs-up sign.

"But she's an only child," Rainey replied.

"She's referrin' to a place. The Five Sisters is a set of munros, mountains not far from the Falls of Glomach."

"A waterfall."

"Oh, aye, one of the biggest. Bit by bit, she's givin' us a map to follow."

He smiled at Sasha, and she gave him an impish grin. Then she raised her thumb and forefinger to her lips and made a locking gesture to let him know he had gotten all he was going to out of her for the night. Matt rose and hoisted her easily over his shoulder as if she were a sack of flour.

Rainey was a bit taken aback at his exuberance, but Sasha squealed with delight and pounded on his back as if they had known each other for years. Matt moaned and groaned in comical fashion at her attack as they started merrily down the path.

Emma came up beside Rainey, with Angus at her heels and the picnic basket in her hand. "Did we make some progress, then, love?" she asked as Rainey took the basket. Matt had left them the flashlight, so they made their way gingerly along the trail, following the lead of Sasha's laughter. How Matt was finding his way was a mystery.

Rainey tripped over an exposed root and bit back a swear word. "What do you know about a place called the Falls of Glomach, Emma?" she asked as she sidestepped some fresh wild animal scat. Angus decided the new find was of great interest, and Emma had to attach his leash to pull him away.

"Come along, Angus," she said sternly. "It won't do to lag behind, ye wee rascal." Once Angus was back in motion, she was able to focus on Rainey's question. "Glomach, ye say? Aye, and there's a sight a body's not like to forget. They call it Hidden Falls because it's a five-mile hike just to get there from the road. Most folks settle for picture postcards of it. But my brothers and I did the trip a few times back when the earth was still coolin'. A hundred fourteen meters from top to bottom, Glomach. That's what, three hundred sixty? No three hundred seventy feet, ye ken. A fair drop, would ye no agree?"

"Right, a fair drop," Rainey said, her thoughts racing. She had to wonder if Glomach was the falls in Sasha's drawing, the one with the pool of blood beneath it.

Emma sensed her mood. "Did Matt say somethin' about Glomach, Rainey?"

"No, Sasha did."

"Sasha?" Emma grabbed Rainey's sleeve and turned her around. Her soft brown eyes were filled with hope. "Are ye sayin' our Sasha spoke at last?"

"A single word. A whisper, really."

"But it's a start. Nothin' short of a miracle, is it no? And we've the Macinnes to thank for it. He's bringin' her back to us, I'm that sure of it."

Rainey tucked her hair behind her ear and looked at Emma squarely. "Is he bringing her back to us, Emma? Or is he bringing her back to Glomach, a place of bloodshed? What kind of miracle is it to take her from the nightmares of the present and catapult her into the nightmares of the past, a past that isn't even hers?"

Emma pressed her lips together in thought, then cinched her scarf around her head against the chill. "Here's what we know, Rainey. Things could not have gone on the way they were, ye ken? What with Sasha sittin' atop filing cabinets and never speakin' a word. And Evanston and the state hot on her heels. Ye tried every way known to man to fix things by way of modern science. It only made matters worse."

Rainey glanced down the trail with concern, and Emma tucked a finger under her chin to bring her attention back to the conversation. "The way I see it, lass, the nightmares from the present and the ones from the past are connected somehow. Now figurin' out which came first is a job for one of those fancy talk show hosts with the thousand-dollar haircuts. But what truly matters, Rainey, is the fact that the wee lassie has been brought back to laughter, and by God, she's comin' around to speakin' to ye again. The rest we'll solve one crisis at a time. But for now, ye got to put it all in the bank for safekeepin' and let it collect what interest it can. There's no easy road left to us. But at least we've got ourselves a road."

"I can't go through this without you, Emma," Rainey said as she gave her a warm hug. "Promise you'll stand by me to translate everything that happens, not just the words, but everything else, too."

"You've got me, love," Emma assured her. "Although you and I are goin' to have to brush up on the Gaelic if we're not to look the fools."

"No kidding."

Sasha was sound asleep by the time they got home. Matt carried her into her bedroom and settled her gently on top of the covers, shoes and all, under Rainey's watchful eyes. Emma and Angus had gone home, and the house seemed unusually quiet as Rainey watched Matt head for the front door. His hair was wild from the damp air. He looked as though he was going to ask her something important, and she wasn't sure she wanted to hear the question. If he was courting the idea of going back on his crayon promise not to exploit his work with Sasha, she was going to nail him. He paused a few steps from her and rubbed his chin in thought.

"I'm goin' away," he said simply.

"Oh?" Rainey ran her hand along the back of the couch and focused her attention on the mantel portrait of Sasha. "I fully understand. You have your career to consider, of course."

"And you have yours," he said with half a smile. Something caught in the pit of her stomach at the reminder of all the work she hadn't done over the weekend. Monday morning was only a few hours away. But it was more than the unfinished work that gnawed at her. Familiar pangs of loss crept in around the edges of her heart, and she steeled her emotions. As she extended her hand to Matt formally, she actually wanted to punch him for putting her on this roller coaster.

"Thank you for all your time and effort, Dr. Macinnes. You've been very kind to Sasha, and I'm sure she'll always think of you fondly."

Matt rested his left palm over their joined hands, and Rainey squared her shoulders.

"All well and good, Harvard, but you'll not be rid of me that easily. I'll be back Wednesday."

"Wednesday?"

He let go of her hand reluctantly and set his backpack down on the edge of the couch. After a moment's rummaging, he withdrew a handheld tape recorder and ran through the buttons to illustrate how it worked.

"If she says anythin', anythin' at all in any language, put it on tape." He handed her the recorder, and she nodded her agreement. There was an uncomfortable silence. "I regret the unfortunate timin' of this trip, but I have some material I must hand deliver. More's the pity, it cannot be postponed." He ran his fingers through his hair out of restlessness. "I don't have my itinerary along, but if you need me, Rainey . . . I mean it. If for any reason . . . that is, if Sasha so much as sneezes, Phoebe will know how to get in touch with me." His eyes locked with hers. "Don't hesitate to call me if things change even a wee bit. I'll find a way to be here. For Sasha. For the both of you." He grabbed his pack and started toward the door.

"I want to know where all of your research with Sasha is leading, Matt. We have to talk this out."

He turned to her, but when she couldn't seem to find the right words to say, he gave her a reassuring smile.

"Aye, Harvard, we must talk, you and I. But not to worry," he said cheerfully. "The questions are gettin' easier to figure out, and before long, we'll have our answers as well. If it stings a bit, it's because we're curin' a pretty sizable hurt."

Rainey walked up beside him. "But what kind of a cure will it be, I wonder? Sometimes the truth is better left unsaid."

There was a small rip in his sweater she hadn't noticed before. It was hard to picture him sitting down to mend it with a needle and thread. But he was a university professor, after all. He could hire someone to do his mending for him, one of his more voluptuous and adoring students, perhaps. She could do a better job of it for him, she decided. A blush crept up her cheeks at the thought. Somehow, mending a man's clothing struck her as a very intimate thing, and she hoped he couldn't read her thoughts.

He frowned down at the rip, tsking to himself as he stuck his finger through it. With a sigh, he looked up at her and said, "The truth, *mo chridhe*, will always demand its due."

Something about the way he delved through her with his eyes made Rainey wonder if he had read her thoughts.

"Hidin' from the facts does not make them go away, Rainey. And facin' the truth head-on can sometimes turn a thorn into a rose." He laid his hand on her shoulder, then quickly let it fall away.

Which truth was he talking about? she wondered.

"The tape recorder," he said, tapping it in her

hand. "Use it, and tell Sasha I'll come by to the house to see her on Wednesday. That's a promise."

"I'll tell her," Rainey agreed. "But please keep in mind, promises, especially ones made by grown-ups, are very important things to little girls like Sasha."

"And to their mothers as well, I've a notion." He gave her a teasing wink. "I'll not forget. Keep the faith, love, and I'll see you come Wednesday. Promise."

Rainey watched him disappear into the darkness. Faith. There it was again. She hugged herself against the chill and lectured her heart for beating so fast.

A part of her breathed a sigh of relief that Matt Macinnes was going to be gone out of their lives for a day or two. She needed a break from the way he filled her thoughts, and the way he filled a room with his presence.

But another part of her felt a need to run after him in the hope he wouldn't leave her teetering on the brink of so many things she couldn't put a name to. As she stood alone in the doorway, she was forced to admit she was dangerously close to the hope Matt Macinnes might be an answer to some of her own troubles as well as Sasha's. But he was gone now, and despite what he had said, there was no guarantee she would ever see him again. In fact, she experienced a moment's doubt that he had ever truly existed.

"Oh, and one more thing, Harvard."

She started at the sound of his voice as he emerged into the small square of light the door afforded. He bounded up the steps toward her, and for an instant, her senses vibrated at the confusing possibility he might take her into his arms. How could she be so overwhelmingly joyful at seeing him again after only a few seconds?

But he didn't embrace her. Instead, he pressed a small, dark green velvet pouch into her hand.

"See that Sasha gets this, if you will," he said, his eyes intent on the pouch. "She may have no reaction to it whatsoever. But my guess is she'll find it of interest. Hasty back, *mo chridhe.*" With a smart salute, he bounded back down the steps and disappeared into the night as he had done before.

Rainey stared down at the pouch. If she concentrated could she bring him back yet again?

"Get some rest!" he called from the distance.

She ducked inside and shut the door. If he was really reading her thoughts, she better put a layer of wood between the two of them, because she couldn't trust her instincts right now.

She was just tired, she told herself. And tomorrow was another Monday. A workday. And, by law, a school day. Damn.

Her curiosity got the better of her, and she emptied the pouch in her hand. In it was an oval brooch the size of her palm, fashioned of countless twisted complex strands and knots of silver woven in an endless maze. The piece appeared to be extremely old, but it was warm to the touch and hypnotic to the eye. She would swear it vibrated in her hand. But what was more surprising, it was somehow familiar, and she felt the urge to keep it for her own. She closed her hand over it and absorbed its wondrous smooth feel.

If it affected her so strongly, she had to speculate what kind of effect it would have on Sasha. Tomorrow, she would find out.

"I need another twenty-four hours, Ted," Rainey told her boss as casually as she could. There was silence on the other end. "You know how Herman Baxter is about the copy. It's got to be perfect, and it's not easy to come up with a campaign palatable enough for the marketplace that still sounds like something crazy old Captain Peanut would say from his front porch rocker in Cow Pie Hollow."

"Rainey, before you go any further . . . ," Ted began.

She didn't like the sound of this. Ted was her division boss, but he was three years younger than she was. He was a divorced, egotistical fashion plate who was driven to be number one in the advertising industry on the West Coast, whatever the cost to those around him. And he was about twenty-four hours away from a heart attack from the pressure, as far as Rainey was concerned. Right now, however, it was the nagging echo over the phone lines that made the muscles at the back of her neck tighten and her mouth go dry.

"Ted, do you have me on the speakerphone, by any chance?" she asked cautiously.

"Mr. Baxter is here with me in the office, Rainey," Ted replied curtly. "You know how conscientious he is about keeping tabs on how things are progressing with his ads. Since you called while he was here in the office, I insisted he hear firsthand how you were doing. I don't think I need to tell you how appalled we both are by the tone of this call. I believe you owe my client an immediate apology."

"Of course," Rainey said. She tried to keep a lid on her anger. "Please tell Mr. Baxter that he has my sincerest apologies. I've been under a good deal of stress for the past few weeks, and I'm afraid I spoke thoughtlessly. I think he knows I have all the respect in the world for what he's accomplished in the peanut butter industry over the past forty-five years. And I think he understands I always have his best interest at heart." She waited.

"Nice, Rainey, very nice," Ted said, his voice dripping with sarcasm. "Baxter walked out. Thanks to your mouth, I have to go save the account for the company. You're a loose cannon, Nielson."

"That was a dirty trick with the speakerphone, and you know it, Ted," Rainey countered. "If you wanted the Baxter account, you should have said something to me. We could have worked it out. I didn't ask Mr. Townsend to assign him to me, if you'll recall. I was already booked solid when he added Baxter to my load. Of course, now I'm down to Baxter and the Frosty Freeze account."

"Correction, Nielson, you're down to zero."

She didn't need to see his smirk to know it was there. Her voice turned to ice. "What are you talking about, Ted?"

"Baxter's mine now. You're out of the picture. And Frosty Freeze just went under. The CEO absconded with five million dollars the day before yesterday. Don't you ever read the papers, honey?"

"I've been a bit pressed for time. And I'll thank you not to call me honey."

He gave her a snorting laugh. "Fine. Let's just call you unemployed, shall we? Well, you've got all the time in the world now, don't you, babe? I suggest you get a newspaper as soon as possible, something with a lot of classifieds. It's going to be a pleasure not to have to listen to all your pathetic tales of woe anymore, Nielson. Try to get a grip, okay? Gotta go." He hung up.

Rainey sat back in shock. She had been counting on those two accounts. Now she was out of a job.

Chapter 8

A heavy downpour beat against the house as Rainey watched Sasha finish her breakfast cereal. A part of her listened for distant thunder. That same part prayed she wouldn't hear it. It was the last thing they needed today.

She hadn't said anything to Sasha about being out of work. Mr. Townsend, Ted's superior, was overseas on business for two weeks, much to Ted's glee, she was sure. It was the only reason Ted could afford to be so high-handed. Townsend had always liked her work, though, so there was still a chance to save her job if Townsend ever got the message she had left with his secretary.

But the idea of two weeks without a penny coming in made her half-crazy. The insurance money from Alan's death was almost gone because of Sasha's special schools and the therapies they had tried. She had to get her job back or find a new one fast.

This would play right into Evanston's hands and give that woman from Child Welfare her final trump card. Rainey wasn't sure they could pack fast enough to make a getaway. And now that the government was involved, they would have to abandon their identities and invent new ones. How did you explain something like that to an eight-year-old?

Sasha made circles of her fingers and pressed them to her eyes.

"He'll come to see us in a few days, sweetheart," Rainey explained. "There were some things he had to take care of for his job."

Sasha slammed down her spoon in an uncustomary show of anger and stalked into the living room.

She should have expected this, Rainey told herself as she followed Sasha. Whatever strain all of this had put on her own heart, the frustration and the impact on Sasha's emotions had to be magnified a hundredfold. She found her kneeling beside the coffee table, scrubbing away at a piece of paper with a black crayon. A tear splashed against the drawing, but Sasha didn't pause in her work.

The picture showed the blackbirds and a hastily drawn version of the falls. Most of the birds lay on their sides, dead. Others looked to the falls with their wings outstretched and tears of despair streaming from their eyes. It was a scene of total devastation. Sasha quickly sketched an outline of the broadsword and pointed to it vehemently. Then she formed the shape of glasses with her fingers and pressed them to her tear-filled eyes.

"It's all right, Sash, Matt will be back," Rainey vowed in the hope she was right. Sasha pounded her fist on the coffee table. She caught the tears running down her cheeks with the tip of her tongue as she scribbled yet more of the dead birds.

"It's all right, Sasha. Really. He'll be here Wednesday, the day after tomorrow. He promised."

Something tightened in the pit of Rainey's stomach as she experienced a strong sensation of déjà vu. These were very close to the words of reassurance she had given Sasha shortly before Alan had died. She stared at the drawing. Whatever his destination might be, she hoped Macinnes was safe.

Rainey reached into the pocket of her slacks and pulled out the green velvet pouch Matt had left. It was a fifty-fifty gamble whether this would make things better. She placed it next to Sasha's picture and waited to see her reaction.

"Matt left it for you. It's a brooch, like a pin you wear. He thought you might like it." Even through the velvet, Rainey could see its glorious curves and knots in her mind's eye. It was as if the image of it had been branded on her heart.

Sasha remained focused on the bird she was drawing until it was finished. Then she set her crayon aside and considered the pouch before she picked it up. The worn velvet was plainly of interest to her as she investigated its soft plush with her fingertips. But when she emptied the silver brooch into her palm, she drew in a sharp breath, and her whole demeanor changed. She stood slowly and walked toward the window with the brooch at arm's length. Whether she feared it or adored it was unclear. But it had struck a chord. Rainey walked over to the window and stood beside her.

"What is it, Sash?" she asked gently. "Have you seen it before?" The question didn't seem nearly as ludicrous as it would have a few days ago. Sasha's answer came in the form of stars scattered across the crown she drew in the condensation on the window. The rain pelted against the glass, as if to wash away all her work before the world could see its secrets.

Beneath the crown, she duplicated the complex, tangled pattern of the brooch, knot for knot, without looking at the pin a second time. As she drew, she repeated a series of words in a soft whisper. They were unfamiliar to Rainey, and Gaelic, no doubt. But the moment was too fragile to use the tape recorder Matt had left, and she did her best to memorize them.

"Thrus do chinneadh ri chèile."

Rainey said it over and over to herself, concentrating on the rhythm and inflection of each syllable. It sounded so lovely, so tranquil. But for all she knew, it could just as easily be a declaration of war or a curse of some kind. Emma had gone to meet Robbie for lunch, so until dinner, there was no way to find out the words' meaning.

She thought about Matt's insistence that she get in touch with him if there was any change. Perhaps he knew Sasha would react to the brooch this way and thought nothing of it. Or maybe this constituted a development significant enough to warrant contacting him. She was quite sure Phoebe Givens wouldn't think so.

Sasha covered the window with stars and birds as she whispered the same phrase over and over. Then she walked solemnly to her bedroom.

Rainey dashed to the kitchen and grabbed her old Polaroid camera out of a cupboard. She couldn't remember the last time she had put film into it, and she prayed the flash would still work. There was only time for a single shot before she heard Sasha's bedroom door close. The flash had worked. She hurriedly stuffed the camera under the couch cushions before she could see if a photo developed.

Sasha returned with the pouch suspended around her neck by a long green satin hair ribbon. Rainey's eyes were drawn to the faint outline of the brooch inside. Her palm felt warm at the memory of holding it in her hand. Was Sasha through with it for now?

"I thought maybe we could make some sugar cookies for Emma today, Sash," Rainey said with a quick smile. "What do you think? We could use the star-shaped cookie cutters, if you like."

Sasha gave her a look that radiated wisdom and experience far beyond her years. She had an air of detachment, and it was almost as if the idea of something so menial as baking cookies was a mild insult. But her expression softened, and she gave a half-hearted nod as she walked over to the window and used the sleeve of her sweater to wipe away the images she had drawn.

Sasha was once again willing to participate in the customary activities of an eight-year-old, if it would make her mother happy. But things had definitely taken a turn. She was going through the motions, but there could be little question that it was a part she was playing now, and more than ever, her heart wasn't in it. When Rainey was able to retrieve the Polaroid from beneath the couch cushion, the print was blank.

They spent the day baking cookies, doing the laundry, and watching TV by the fire. But despite the casualness of all they did, there was a definite tension in the house. The storm refused to let up, and they both jumped at every gust of wind or creak of the rafters. A registered letter arrived with Evanston's return address on it. She refused it. She let the answering machine take a curt message from Mrs. Malinsky's office at Child Welfare. It was a thinly veiled order for Rainey to call immediately. After that, Rainey had shut off the machine.

By dinnertime, their nerves were frayed. So when Angus bounded into the kitchen from the outside, they nearly leaped out of their skins. The little Scottie shook the rain off his fur until he was staggering sideways, and Emma called a cheery hallo from the front door.

"We're all in the kitchen, Emma," Rainey called as she laughed at Angus's antics. "Don't bother to wipe your feet, neighbor. It's hopeless."

Emma walked in rubbing her arms for warmth. "Och, it's the Great Flood beyond that door, and that's a fact." She tested the air and smiled her approval at the aroma of roast chicken, potatoes, and freshly baked sugar cookies. "It seems we've timed it right, Angus, my lad. So, what can this poor old moocher lady do to help with the preparations, Rainey?"

Sasha was overjoyed at seeing Angus, and the two of them adjourned to the living room to make up for lost time. Rainey took the opportunity to speak privately to Emma.

"I'm probably not going to get this right, Emma, so forgive me for butchering the language. But what does '*Thrus do chinneadh ri chèile*' mean?"

Emma gave it some thought as she rolled the words around on her tongue. "It's verra old, ye ken?" She frowned in concentration. "It's havin' to do with family, or like souls, if ye stretch it a bit, mayhap. *Chinneadh.* 'Thy kindred gathered together.' Aye, that's pretty close. 'Thy kindred gathered together.'" The likely source of the words dawned on her. "Was it our wee Sasha said this to ye, love?"

Rainey broke open a baked potato and added a meager pat of butter to it. How much butter would they have after two weeks of unemployment? she wondered.

"She's still only communicating in whispers. But yes, Sasha said it. What do you think it signifies?" She grabbed a second potato and cut it open mechanically.

"Haven't a clue, dear. What brought it on, do ye suppose? Does the Macinnes have a notion?"

The knife slipped in Rainey's hand as she opened the third potato, and she muttered a curse as she walked to the sink to tend to the small cut on her finger.

"He's out of town until Wednesday," she said in exasperation as she rinsed her hand.

"Out of town, ye say?" Emma said in surprise. "After all that's happened the last coupla days, he's taken himself out of the picture?"

Rainey drew in a sharp breath as she splashed medication on the cut. It was something she'd like to be doing to Matt Macinnes at the moment, notwithstanding the fact that he had endured far worse cuts than hers in his lifetime, if that scar on his face was any testimony. She shuddered at the thought of what that wound must have looked like on the day it happened. She also experienced an unwelcome surge of sympathy.

"How many times do I have to say it? He's coming back!" She wrapped a Band-Aid around her finger and sighed. "I'm sorry, Emma. It's just that the air has smelled like thunder all day, if that makes any sense. And . . . I've lost my job." Emma took over the dishing up duties, and Rainey sat down gratefully on a kitchen chair.

"Yer job with the advert people, love? How did it happen?'

"It's a long story. There's a guy at work who wants my accounts. Hopefully, I'll be able to go over his head. But it's going to take some time. And as the good doctor keeps saying, time is yet another thing we're running short of. And he had the nerve to leave town after giving Sasha an heirloom of some kind," she said.

"What sort of heirloom?"

"It's a brooch. Sasha's wearing it in a velvet pouch around her neck at the moment. It's what prompted her to say that thing about gathering together."

"And what does the thing look like, Rainey?"

"Oh, I don't know, it's made of all these twisted lines and knots of old silver, like a maze. I probably can't remember it well enough to give you a real impression of it." She picked up the pen and message pad from next to the phone and started to draw. Within ninety seconds, she had replicated the brooch down to the finest detail.

Emma stared at it in awe. "I think I get the gist, love," she said in joking understatement. "I've seen other old pieces with similar themes in museums back home. I made a kind of a study of them back in my Edinburgh days. It was cheaper than the movies. But what ye've shown me here is far more complex than those others, ye ken."

She pointed to a perfect woven square of knots at the left of the design. "Ye see this part? O' course, somethin' this old, yer always guessin' at the meanin', but patterns like this are said to stand for the four winds, *gaoth à thuath, gaoth à deas, gaoth an ear, gaoth an iar*—the north, the south, the east, and the west. It's sometimes thought to be a man's symbol, masculine." She touched each intersection reverently.

"And this configuration to the right, the one major line curved free at the end, I'd bet a month's supply of jam that's a symbol for the sea, a totally feminine sign. See here how the silver's broken through this figure eight to the side, yet kept its own strength? Now what do ye suppose that signifies, lass?" She leaned back and crossed her arms over her chest, pressing her lips together like a seasoned schoolteacher.

Rainey stared at the place where the graceful silver arch curved through the small figure eight. The major line had a strength and integrity of its own, but passing through the smaller design had affected its arc, perhaps altering its original path.

"A child."

"Aye, most likely," Emma confirmed. "And only the one. But ye see how the line curves back upon itself at the end?" Rainey nodded, Emma's next words already echoing in her ears. "There's the possibility of another child. And these twisted lines around the periphery, see how they lead from the male symbol to the female, and then to the large figure eight at the center? It's a symbol for infinity, for heaven, if it suits ye. The thing is tellin' us a story, though whether it's history or a prediction, I've no notion."

Rainey tucked her hair behind her ears. "What are we really talking about here?"

Emma pressed her thumb to her mouth as she considered Rainey's drawing. "This is no bit of bric-a-brac, Rainey. If it has such meanin' to Sasha as ye say, she could most likely tell us the whole of the story. But whether or not she'd be willin' is another matter. The Macinnes could very probably give us a clue, but he's no here." She started to spoon gravy onto the chicken and potatoes, then looked at Rainey in all seriousness. "Do ye trust him, love?"

Rainey gave it some serious thought as she straightened the fork of her place setting. "I believe he has Sasha's best interests at heart. But I can never get a straight answer from him. He acts like he has some kind of grand design in all of this, like he knows where it's all going to lead somehow. But I feel so shut out; shut out of the language, of Celtic culture, of the places Sasha goes when he talks to her." She smoothed a loose edge of her bandage absently, then looked up at Emma. "I'm not used to being out of the loop. It hurts that I can't help Sasha myself."

"Aye, dear, I know," Emma said to comfort her. "It's hard to put yer faith in someone ye hardly know."

It was true she hardly knew Matt Macinnes, Rainey told herself. And yet, it seemed like he had been a part of their lives for a very long time. She touched the lines of the square design on the drawing. She would always think of them as masculine now.

"He doesn't know what it means to have someone he loves in jeopardy, Emma. And I get the feeling if there's a single word he doesn't know the meaning of, it's 'failure.' "

Emma wasn't smiling. "Shall I tell ye how he got that scar on his cheek, Rainey?"

"You know how it happened?" She had been curious about it since the first time she had seen him standing in her kitchen doorway.

"Aye, love. Robbie told me. Seems it's the kind of a thing one man confides in another. Male bonding, or some such nonsense."

Rainey looked over her shoulder toward the living room. Sasha and Angus were still happily at play. "I'd like to know."

Emma set about tossing the greens for the salad as she spoke.

"Are ye familiar with the Shetland Islands, by chance?" She gave the Italian dressing bottle an energetic shake.

"They're the ones off the northeast corner of Scotland, right?"

"The very same. They're magnificent. They're also rugged and mostly uninhabited, save for the ghosts of the ancient folk who dwelt there long before the days of recorded history."

"Have you ever been to the Shetlands, Emma?" Rainey pictured the islands with bands of wild Celts roaming across the countryside.

"Oh, aye, I took the ferryboats a time or two when I was young. But I didna fully appreciate the amazin' archaeological sites the way I might today. The islands are thick with old forts and the like. The last time I made a day of it, I was with a handsome young suitor, mind, so me brains were somewhere south of where they should've been. Had to marry that smooth talker strictly in the hope of gettin' my wits back. Didn't work." She gave Rainey a wink as she set the salad bowl on the table.

"One born every minute," Rainey said with a smile of sympathy.

"True enough. But I digress." She swiped a strand of hair out of her eyes with the back of her hand. "The Macinnes comes by his knowledge of the old ways quite naturally, ye see. His father was an archaeologist who specialized in Scottish history, and his mother was a professor of classical languages at Glasgow University. The senior Macinnes researched some of the ruins in the Shetlands near Mousa Broch on the big island. Matt and his mother often went along to the digs, I'm told, so his days were filled with historical places and such from a verra tender age. From what my Robbie tells me, what with Matt bein' an only child and all, he was verra close to both his parents."

Rainey plucked a chunk of carrot from the salad and considered it for a moment before she popped it into her mouth. "It's amazing, isn't it?" she said. "Matt, Alan, Sasha, and I were all only children. What are the odds of that, I wonder. So what became of Matt's parents?"

Emma refolded the napkin next to Sasha's place at the table.

"They drowned in the North Sea, lass, the pair of them."

"My God, how did it happen? Was Matt with them?"

"He tried to save them, our Matt. One of the Shetland ferryboats went down of a sudden when a storm blew up outta nowhere, as they sometimes do late in the year. Matt was eighteen at the time, on leave from the university for the weekend."

"The same age I was when my father died."

"It was a verra hard loss for ye both. The ship broke up quickly, and Matt's mother not being much of a swimmer, especially in those icy waters, Matt and his father spent their strength keepin' her afloat

on a bit of wreckage. But she'd hit her head on
somethin' when she fell into the water, and the poor
woman never regained consciousness.

"The two men swam toward one of the lifeboats
for all they were worth with the mother in tow. But
the waves were monstrous, and the shock of the accident and the cold was too much. The father's
strength gave out, and he purely passed away clinging to that bit of deck. And as Matt tried to haul the
three of them through those frigid waves, the boards
commenced to sink. Matt floated his body beneath
the wood to help keep it afloat, and as he did so, he
was battered by the wreckage, and a broken nail laid
open his cheek, addin' to his other injuries. Robbie
says Matt was so numb from the cold and the terror
by then, he didn't even feel it happen."

"How did he survive it?" Rainey asked.

"I don't know, love. The seas were the devil himself, and by the time help got to him, Matt was barely
alive. But he had taken the belt from around his
waist and tethered his parents, wrist to wrist, across
that shattered bit of board, in the barest hope they
were still clingin' to life. And when they were both
pronounced dead on the deck of the rescue ship, he
went a bit mad, I suppose. The man was entitled. He
took the wedding rings from their fingers and has
kept them safe ever since. It was a terrible tragedy
for a man the likes of our Matt."

Rainey swiped a tear from her cheek as she stood
up and walked over to the doorway to the living
room. She watched Sasha at play with Angus.

"Our Matt," she said sadly. "I told him he had no
understanding of what it felt like to lose someone he
loved—what it felt like to lose family. He must think
I'm cruel beyond belief."

"Ye had no way of knowin', Rainey."

"That's just the point. I thought I knew everything

I needed to know about him. Now I realize I know next to nothing." She paused to draw a deep breath. "I suppose, in a way, he's every bit the shining hero Sasha makes him out to be."

"You'll no hear it from himself, accordin' to Robbie. Buries himself in his work year-round, the Macinnes. Teachin', restorin' old automobiles in the wee hours of the night, and a game of golf whenever Robbie can drag him out, that's the lot. I take it Matt sees that day in the North Sea as a personal failure, ye ken, even after lo these many years. He canna let go of it, and somewhere in that stubborn heart of his, he still blames himself for his parents' deaths."

"But that's ridiculous," Rainey insisted as she dished salad onto each plate. "From what you've told me, he did everything humanly possible to save them."

"Oh, aye. You know it, and I know it. But ye could never prove it by him."

"Well, maybe someone should set him straight," Rainey said as she tossed another bit of carrot into her mouth.

"Anyone we know, perchance?" The sly look Emma gave her spoke volumes.

"Perchance."

Emma laid her hand on Rainey's. "There's one thing more ye should know. That storm that took the ferry down . . ."

"What about it?"

"It was the worst thunderstorm to come roarin' out of the north in a hundred years. *Mar leòghann fiadhaich.* Like a fierce lion, it came."

"A thunderstorm?" Rainey swallowed hard and turned to find Sasha standing in the doorway with fresh tears in her eyes. In her hand was the drawing of the dozens of lifeless birds.

"*Furtachd is fòir,*" Emma said under her breath. Help and deliverence.

Chapter 9

The power went out during dinner, and they adjourned to the living room for sugar cookies and milk by candlelight.

The storm worsened, and it was decided that Emma and Angus would spend the night on the sofa bed by the fire. They pulled the sofa mattress out and all sat snuggled together in blankets, contemplating the flames on the hearth. Angus burrowed between them and popped his head out of the covers in comical fashion, lifting the tension a bit. But the dark room was full of untold stories, and as they sat in silence, Matt Macinnes was very much in each of their thoughts.

"Here, now," Emma said cheerily as she shifted to get more comfortable. "What about we all sing a jolly song?" One glance at her companions dissuaded her from that notion. "Verra well, a wee fairy story, then, eh?" Sasha touched Emma's hand and gave her a slow smile.

"Only if it's in English, Emma, agreed?" Rainey insisted.

"In Lizzie's own," Emma assured her.

"Lizzie?"

"The queen, love. You know the one—enough jewels to feed the world's hungry for a month, philanderin' kids, terrible taste in hats?"

"Oh, right, that Lizzie."

"Now, then, if I may proceed." Emma pulled the blanket up around her shoulders as if it were a mantle of ermine. "There was a fairy tree in my family's backyard when I was a wee lass."

A frown of disbelief flickered across Rainey's face.

"Now, don't be givin' me that 'modern science says different' look of yers, Rainey, because I won't tolerate it in this matter. Trust me, that tree was the genuine article. 'Twas a fine old oak, the likes of which would have made any coven of druids proud. Oaks are sacred. In fact, some say the word druid first meant 'oak knowledge.' " She cleared her throat with great ceremony and got a faraway look in her eyes as she settled her thoughts into the past.

"As I look back at it now," she began, "I realize a goodly portion of what I saw at the tree may well've been my brothers havin' me on, me bein' the youngest and a lass, ye ken? But there were some happenin's went beyond even what that lot could conjure up." She gave Sasha a merry wink, and Sasha tried to wink back, without success.

"My strongest recollection is of a day much like this one, with the winds howlin' and the rains puttin' everythin' to sail. I couldna have been more than ten, I suppose, and all in a huff, I was, because my brother Edmond had broken one of my mother's best china plates with a rubber ball and pinned the blame on me. He was a spoilt brat, was Edmond, though I love him dearly now. He lives up in Canada. Five kids with families of their own. Anyway, Mama took his word over mine in the matter, like always, and I was banished to the upstairs in shame." She sat up a bit straighter and squared her shoulders.

"Och, there was a rare dose of miscarried justice, and if I'd known the proper way to piece together a wicked curse, I would've come up with a grand one to heap on Edmond's noggin, I guarantee ye. But a lassie's place in those days was to bear what was dished up to her with a demure smile and a buttoned lip. And though my mother was a kind and generous woman, God rest her, she had a blind spot the size of Aberdeen when it came to her precious Eddie. The wee snake." With a wave of her hand, she dismissed her anger of old.

"Be that as it may, bein' the only lass, as I say, I had a wee room of me own up in the attic. And I was in the practice of climbin' out my bedroom window and slidin' down the drainpipe to get a moment's peace away from the boys now and then. Most times, I went straight to the tree for comfort. It was a grand old lady, always willin' to listen to the prattle and dreams of a wee lassie in the midst of a jailbreak." Angus nestled a bit closer to her, and she cooed to him comfortingly.

"Well, on the day in question, I had such a mad on, I shinnied down that drainpipe like it was an Olympic event, mind, and made for the tree through the flood. And me without so much as a wrap or a scarf, ye ken?" She gave a delicate shudder and accepted the sugar cookie Rainey offered in comfort. "I sat there at the foot of my very own fairy tree, my young tears minglin' with the rain, and spilled out the tragedies of my heart, blow by blow."

Sasha took the pouch from around her neck and handed it to Emma to hold in a gesture of sympathy.

Emma glanced at Rainey. Rainey nodded, and Emma regarded the pouch reverently.

"I thank ye for lettin' me mind such a treasure, sweetheart." Sasha gave her a regal smile of acknowledgment.

"Once or twice, I'd got what ye might call answers from the tree, a fresh acorn dropped in my lap or a leaf landin' on the top of my head. To a lass of ten, it was direct communication, blessin's bestowed by the Wee Folk. I kept all my precious mementos tucked beneath my bed in an old cigar box. They were magic, those bits of bark and bracken. And though ye couldn've got a copper penny for the lot, to me they were right proper jewels. But none of it compared to the gift the fairies gave me that day."

A pine log popped and hissed loudly in the fireplace, and they all started. When they exchanged looks of surprise, all three of them burst into laughter. But a broken branch blew across the roof, sounding for all the world like a clumsy intruder, and they lost their good spirits. The storm wanted in. Emma smoothed a stray wisp of hair back into place.

"As I was sayin', shiverin' and soaked clear through, I was, but determined as stone not to go back into a house where I was persecuted so. After a time, though, I could see the lights come on in the house. It looked so warm and cozy, I could see my mother standin' at the kitchen sink, gettin' the supper ready. When I think back on it now, it was a pretty safe bet she could see me sittin' there from the kitchen window. But she never once let on she saw me, not in all her years, bless her.

"Over and over, I kept askin' the fairy tree what I should do. It was a matter of pride, ye see. I wanted to go back into that house in the worst way. It's a certainty I'd gone blue from the cold, and even through the rain, I could smell my mother's biscuits bakin'. But I'd been wronged, ye ken? It was a crime perpetrated against me, a symbol to guarantee that one day the wrong would be righted. It was the most important thing in the world to me that day." She gave a wistful sigh.

"I waited till it was nearly dark. And I have to admit, I was close to givin' up the cause. But I looked up into the tree one last time, askin' for a sign. And do ye know what I saw, Sasha?"

Sasha shook her head slowly, her attention rapt.

"There, buried deep in the bark not five feet above where I was sittin', was the end of a small piece of old metal. Now, mind you, yours truly had played on and climbed over every branch and leaf of that tree since she was old enough to toddle over to it, most especially the place where that metal was wedged. But I promise you, I never saw it before, not once. Well, let me tell ye, I scrambled up the trunk and wiggled my treasure loose in jig time. And what do ye think? It was the tip of an old arrow, left there from medieval times, so I'm told."

Rainey drew in a breath in surprise. "You're joking, Emma, it was really there all that time, and nobody knew about it?"

Emma pressed her lips together. "Call me daft, if it suits ye, but the fairies knew it was there. They knew it all along, and kept it well hidden till it was needed. It was the very thing I had hoped for, bein' it was a symbol of courage in battle. I wrapped it in my hand, marched back to the house, and skittered back up that slippery pipe just in time to hear my mother call me down for supper."

"That was a close one," Rainey said with a grin.

"Aye, that it was," Emma agreed. "I threw off my wet things and changed into dry ones as fast as I could, stuffin' the arrowhead into my pocket. And when I got to the table, I noticed Edmond wouldna look me in the eye. I thought perhaps he was sorry for what he'd done, but I suspected different. I touched the new talisman in my pocket, and my mother commenced to tellin' me how Edmond had confessed to his crime, and I was to have his dessert as well as my own after supper—spice cake, her specialty. She apologized for doubtin' me and kissed me on the cheek. Needless to say, I was flabbergasted.

"To this day, I don't know what made Edmond tell. Maybe one of my other brothers had somethin' on him. Most likely my mother thought Edmond was just trying to protect me, I imagine, him bein' Eddie and all. But he gave her such a thorough confession, she finally had to accept that her little darlin' was to blame.

"Of course, just before bedtime, I spied her sneakin' him a bit of cake in a napkin. But by then, it didn't matter. I'd won my victory." She reached inside the neckline of her blouse and pulled out a gold chain. At the end of it was a weathered arrowhead. Emma looked at it thoughtfully.

"I came that close to givin' it to Robbie's dad before he went off to war. But I was young and scart about the Nazis, and I thought its magic was only meant for me, ye know. Maybe if I'd sent it along with William . . ." She sighed. "Well, my Robbie gets it when the time comes. I've made certain sure of that, eh."

Rainey and Sasha both inspected the arrowhead with a sense of awe. Sasha rubbed it between her fingers as if to borrow some of its magic, then carefully accepted the green velvet pouch back from Emma. She settled the ribbon around her neck so the brooch was once again close to her heart.

"Okay, ladies, it's bedtime," Rainey announced. She looked down at Sasha. "Shall we set up sleeping bags out here, Sash, so we can all be near the fire?" So we can all be near each other for courage, she admitted to herself as the wind thrashed against the windows. Why were storms like this always twice as frightening in the dark? She had to wonder if the weather was a reflection of all Sasha was going through.

Sasha took one of the flashlights and headed toward the hall closet where the sleeping bags and air mattresses were kept. Alan had been planning a camping vacation in Europe for the three of them at the time of his death, and they had gotten to the point of buying some of the equipment.

Emma protested at being the only one with a bed, but by the time the mattresses were inflated side by side, everyone had a comfortable place to sleep. The fire died down to a warm glow, and Emma sang them all to sleep with the soft Gaelic lullabies of her childhood.

Rainey gazed up into the gray-green branches of the gnarled oak. Despite her wariness of high things, its great height didn't unnerve her in the least. The big tree was like an old friend. An immaculate white swan nestled high in the branches, its graceful head tucked beneath its wing in gentle repose. Tiny fairies dressed in bits of moss and fern darted in and out of its snowy feathers, a hundred downy games of hide-and-seek all going on at once. They were perfect little translucent beings, each with a glistening set of iridescent wings that came in very handy in avoiding an opponent's tag. The whole tree was aglow with the light of their magic as they flew about covering the swan with clouds of sparkling mist.

It quite simply made Rainey happy to watch the fairies' lightning-quick antics, but her laugh of delight caught their attention, and they froze. They stared at her with curiosity and perhaps a bit of suspicion, and the swan raised its noble head to regard her. There was a sadness in the swan's eyes, and unmistakable recognition.

"It's okay," Rainey assured them all with a smile. "I live very far away from here. I just want to watch." The dream lost its glow.

In a frenzy, the fairies pulled the oak's branches down to hide the swan from intruding eyes, and with astonishing swiftness, they all faded, then disappeared. The tree went from the verdant lushness of summer to the skeletal bleakness of winter. It was as if the magic had been stolen, and Rainey felt tears of anger and loss well up in her eyes.

"Come back!" she shouted. But the tree itself withered and crumbled into dust. She walked to where it had been and picked up a single fresh acorn, a gift left behind. As she held it in her hand, she became aware of a roaring sound behind her. It grew louder, until she had to cover her ears to keep it out. Her every instinct warned her she didn't want to learn what was making that thunderous noise, but its demand that she look was irresistible.

Someone called her name. Matt.

Like one in a trance, she turned. She couldn't see him anywhere, yet he kept calling her name. Before her, a monstrous falls plunged over jagged rock, reaching from where she stood to the roof of heaven. She staggered back from the sheer, crushing height of it as it careened down the cliff, emptying the sky.

"Glomach," she said in stunned awe. It could be no other. She felt Matt's presence all around her, but she was very much alone and at the mercy of the falls.

A flock of black birds circled overhead, cawing and strafing one another. But when they came to rest on the rocky cliff, they took on human form—men, women, and children from another time, all dressed in rags, all clinging to the rocks for dear life. To fall from such a height would guarantee death.

No one looked down. They all stared up to where a single slender woman stood on a ledge far higher than the rest.

Rainey reached out instinctively to catch her if she should fall. Though the gesture would be futile.

"It is Sirona. I can help her," Matt's voice said in her ear. He was beside her. But he was dressed as Sasha had portrayed him in her drawing, in the garb of an ancient warrior, and he was as translucent as the fairies had been.

"Sirona, the Queen," he shouted over the din of the falls. "I will save her, if you let me. And she will save us all. She waits above, as she has waited before. Others have failed her. I have failed others I have loved. But I will not fail her, if you put your faith in me. What is your decision?" He pointed to those clinging to the cliff. "*Thrus do chinneadh ri chèile.* Thy kindred gathered together. They can wait no longer."

Ominous black clouds gathered overhead, and lightning split the sky. Rainey looked to the highest point of the falls and felt the scream rise in her throat. But her cry was soundless over the pounding roar of the falls. Everything began to spin before he eyes, and she fell to the ground, desperate for anything to steady a world that was spinning out of control.

"Sasha!"

She sat bold upright in her sleeping bag. It was still dark. Had she failed Sasha? Had she failed Sirona?

The living room was freezing, and it took her a moment to get her bearings. In the dim glow from the fire, she looked down beside her to where Sasha had been. The sleeping bag was empty, and in a blinding flash of lightning Rainey saw that the front door stood open. The wind howled through the room as a tremendous explosion of thunder made the house tremble to its foundation. The storm had taken on biblical proportions.

Emma stirred and rubbed the sleep from her eyes to see Rainey struggling into her boots as she ran toward the front door.

"What is it, Rainey?" she called. But Rainey was already out the door and down the steps. Emma saw that Sasha's bed was empty. She said a quick prayer as rain splattered across the threshold. When she felt around on the floor for her shoes, Emma's fingers brushed against something small and smooth on Rainey's sleeping bag. She held it up between herself and the dying embers of the fire.

"Well, now, what do ye make of that, Angus? An acorn. The fairies must've paid us a visit," she said as she slid on her shoes. But Angus, too, was nowhere to be seen. "Ah, this night is goin' to drive me to drink," she muttered to herself as she threw on her coat and scarf. "Native Scotch, and nothin' less."

Chapter 10

Rainey trembled with cold and worry as she stood in the yard, calling to Sasha. Between the shattering blasts of thunder, she listened for any clue to which way Sasha might have gone. Each time lightning split the darkness, she whirled in every direction, desperate for any sign. She started when Emma came up beside her with a raincoat in her hand.

"It's all right, lass, 'tis only me," Emma said as she settled the coat around Rainey's shoulders. She looked at the roiling clouds overhead and pulled her lucky arrowhead out for courage. "What the devil is happenin' that we have weather the likes of this?" She handed the acorn she had found to Rainey. "I found it on your sleepin' bag."

Rainey could scarcely believe her eyes. Her dream had crossed over into reality.

"I don't know what any of this means, Emma. I had a dream about a waterfall." A shudder ran down her spine at the memory. "I have to find Sasha. I know she's in danger, but I don't know where to begin to look for her."

Emma gave her a thoughtful frown. "I've an idea." She waited for a break in the thunder and raised two fingers to her mouth in a loud whistle. Moments passed. Then, as a cataclysmic bolt of lightning raked across the sky, little Angus bounded out of a stand of trees twenty yards away. He trotted dutifully up to Emma, and she praised him no end.

"Take us to Sasha, lovey," she instructed him gently. He cocked his head at her in hopes of a biscuit bribe. But when it became clear she had none, he gave her a disgruntled look. "To it, ye wee villain, back to Sasha."

Angus shook himself vigorously, then trotted off in the direction from which he had come. Emma handed Rainey a flashlight, and the two of them raced after the little Scottie. Twigs scraped their faces, and the ground was slick beneath their feet as they forged their way through the wooded area. Much of the surrounding property hadn't been developed, and Rainey had always suspected Sasha had secret hiding places close to home.

The trees were a mixture of redwood, maple, and oak, and despite the nearness to civilization, the dense undergrowth and the darkness made progress slow. Twice, they lost sight of Angus, and he had to be called back. It was taking too long, and Rainey was beside herself with concern. The storm had become a dedicated enemy, and God knew what traumas Sasha was going through because of the relentless thunder.

Emma tugged at her sleeve. "I have to catch me breath, love," she said with regret. "Go on without me, and I'll catch you up in a bit."

The rain was torrential, and it would take some doing to find this place again. "Are you sure, Emma? I don't feel right about leaving you here by yourself."

As she wrapped her raincoat more securely around herself, Emma gave her a stalwart smile and pointed to the rumbling skies. "I've got me flashlight. Why, this is a shy mist where I hail from, lass. Mark the trail now and again like the Macinnes taught Sasha, and I'll find ye right enough." She waved Rainey on.

"Be off with ye, now, or Angus'll leave us both behind."

Rainey tucked her dripping hair behind her ears and gave Emma a quick hug.

"Sasha can't be far, Emma. Another hundred yards and you come to the road." She didn't want to think about what might have happened if Sasha had reached the road. And she prayed Angus wasn't simply following rabbit tracks. "I'll mark the trail as often as I can," she promised.

"Not to worry, love. I'll find the way. Go on with ye, now. That's an order."

Angus stopped and took a few hesitant steps back toward them. But Emma shooed him on his mission, and Rainey trudged after him. The rain punished her, and after each crash of thunder, she called out to Sasha in the fervent hope she would show herself. But storms like this tended to make Sasha silent and frozen. She could be two feet away, and Rainey might not see her in the undergrowth.

They were going around in circles, Rainey was convinced. This patch of wooded area couldn't be this large. There was no sign of Emma behind her, but she felt eyes watching her. It had to be Sasha. Who else could it be? She had heard stories of derelicts camping in the uninhabited woods in the area— convicts set free for lack of jail space, the mentally disturbed who had no government medical facility to go to. She was letting her imagination run away with her, she told herself. But it just made her more frantic to find Sasha.

Angus had disappeared. He didn't come running back to her when she called to him. She thought she heard him bark in the distance, but a crushing clap of thunder left her ears ringing. Which way now? When she called out Sasha's name, the thunder cracked again, drowning her out. All of nature was stacked against her. Her knees were close to buckling, she was shaking so hard from the strain and the cold, and the tiny hairs at the back of her neck prickled in warning.

"Who's there?" she shouted into the dark. "Sasha?"

Lightning split the sky again, and Rainey saw the outline of a large man walking toward her—or away from her—she couldn't be sure. She was truly afraid now. He was carrying something . . . someone. She couldn't get her legs to move as the lightning stopped and everything went dark. Then it dawned on her what she had seen in that flash of raw electricity. The man was carrying Sasha. Rainey pointed her flashlight in the direction where she had seen them, but the light wouldn't work.

She shouted to Sasha, but she could hear nothing over the wind as it pinned her against a tree. She felt her way, inch by inch, through the dark, calling out, threatening and promising in turn. A branch caught her hard in the shin, and she crumpled to her knees in the mud. A sob of anger and frustration choked her.

Lightning tore across the sky once more, and he was there, not three feet away, towering above her. Sasha was wrapped in his arms and Angus panted at his heels. He was the power and majesty of the storm personified, the knight from Sasha's drawing and the dream. Yet his clothing was of the here and now, and he was most definitely flesh and bone. Sasha smiled out at her distantly from inside the protection of his long raincoat. Tucked in her arms was what appeared to be a new teddy bear. Total blackout returned, and Rainey felt a moment of doubt that she had truly seen them.

"So tell me, Harvard, is your passport in order?"

"Macinnes!" she said hoarsely as she struggled to her feet.

He took the flashlight from her hand and smacked it sharply against his thigh. It snapped to life, and he gave it back to her.

"It's not Wednesday," was all Rainey could think to say.

"Rumor had it I was needed here. I finished what had to be done." He tucked a dripping curl behind Rainey's ear for her and frowned at the coat she had dropped a short distance away. *"Rèitich gnothaichean a' freagairt an luchd as fainne,"* he said fondly.

"What?" Rainey swiped the tears of relief from her cheeks and laid her trembling fingers over Sasha's hand.

Emma chimed in from a few yards away, " 'Temper the wind to the shorn lamb,' that's what it means," she provided. "Bless us all, that can only be the Macinnes. And just in the nick of time."

The thin beam from Emma's flashlight drew nearer, and Rainey felt her heartbeat begin to return to normal. She wanted to check Sasha for bruises and scratches, but more than anything, she wanted her home out of the storm.

"Where were you, young lady?" she asked Sasha. Her voice cracked with emotion, and Matt offered her his elbow in gentlemanly fashion. She was too shaken for pride, and Matt smiled down at her when she accepted his offer.

"She was meditatin' in the branches of an old oak. Now, there was a fairy playground if ever I saw one," Matt provided.

"But how did you know where to look for her?" Rainey had to ask.

"She told me."

Rainey pulled him to a stop. "What are you saying? She knew where to phone you in the middle of the night?"

"Hardly." He started them walking again. "By way of conversation, that first night in the kitchen I asked her if there was a fairy tree close by. Through one thing and another, I found out where it was. When I saw your front door open, I suspected she'd gone out to chase down the thunder. The tree was the logical place to look."

"Right, a fairy tree," Rainey said with a touch of irony as she slipped on a muddy patch. Matt's hand was instantly there on her arm to lend support. His father's gold band shone on his finger in the receding glow of the storm, and she felt a tug at her heart. How full of cold reminders storms like this must be for him.

Not trusting her own sense of direction at the moment, she let him lead the way. He seemed to have no need for a flashlight as he carried Sasha through the woods with total confidence. The storm, so overpowering in its impact only moments before, withdrew toward the hills, leaving calmer skies. She had to wonder if Matt and Sasha had commanded it away.

When they reached the house, it felt to Rainey as if they had been away for a week. Emma had had enough for one night, so she and Angus found their way home. The power was still out, so Rainey took the flashlight and led Sasha into her bedroom so she could change into her pj's while Matt banked the fire. She toweled Sasha's hair dry with such fervor Sasha groaned in exasperation.

By the time they went back into the living room, a warming blaze crackled and popped on the hearth. When Matt rose to greet them, he raised one eyebrow toward Rainey in silent inquiry about Sasha's well-being. And now that they were safely home, she granted him a reserved smile of thanks.

She settled Sasha into her sleeping bag and kissed her forehead tenderly. Sasha held the new teddy up for Rainey to hug. Tied around the brown plush at his neck was a big plaid bow.

"He's a beauty, sweetheart," Rainey said softly. She hugged the bear, then nestled it in beside Sasha. "It was nice of Matt to give him to you." Tears of relief welled up in her throat. "I love you, Sash. Now, tomorrow, and always. No matter what. Never forget that."

Sasha kissed her cheek and gave her a shy smile. Then she whispered, *"Tha a t-àm a bhith falbh, Mama. Glomach."*

Rainey sat back on her heels. "I'm sorry, Sash, I'm trying, but I don't understand."

"She says it's time to be goin'," Matt provided. "It's time we went to Glomach." He focused his attention on the fire, suspecting what Rainey's reaction might be.

The dream came flooding back to her. "We'll discuss it tomorrow," she said to close the subject.

Sasha looked to Matt for support, and when he gave her a wink, Rainey stood up abruptly and went into the kitchen.

Matt followed her, a candle in his hand. "We must talk now, Rainey."

She stood by the sink, staring out the window into the night. "I don't like the way this is going. Don't ask me to take her to the falls, Macinnes. I can't do it. The expense . . . the risk . . . And what if it's all something you've inadvertently put into her head, suggestions so the things she does make sense?" Her hands were trembling so badly, she had to clasp them together.

"You're soaked to the bone, Harvard." Matt

wrapped his coat around her shoulders and leaned against the sink beside her. "There's no question but that she must go to Glomach."

"Why, for godsakes? I don't understand. Why can't we just work it out here, on American soil where she'll be safe?"

He caught a droplet from the faucet on his fingertip, then let it fall to the drain with a tiny splash. "Do you honestly believe she's safe here, Rainey? She climbed that tree tonight to get closer to the storm. The thunder carries the sound of the falls to her, and she longs to be near it. Thunder can be a very powerful messenger. Each time she hears it, it reminds her that she's got work to be done. She can't be truly free and whole until it's finished. And there is so little time."

Rainey turned to him slowly. "So little time. There are those words again. What aren't you telling me?"

He sighed from the depth of his soul and pushed his glasses a bit further up the bridge of his nose. "The time of the Winter Solstice is drawing near. Traditionally, it's a time of great legends and magic. And with regard to the particular legend I have referred to more than once, it's pivotal."

"What happens?" Rainey asked cautiously.

Matt made the outline of a crown in the drops of water in the sink. "You know that crown Sasha draws?" Rainey nodded with a look of open trepidation. "The legend dictates that the crown must be returned to the Falls of Glomach at the time of the Winter Solstice."

Rainey gave a humorless laugh. "The crown. The crown from a fairy tale?"

"Legend."

"Legend. So you're saying this crown that may or may not exist in the real world needs to be taken to the falls on the day of the Winter Solstice. Well, I

wish you all the luck in your search for the thing."
She folded her arms across her chest, mildly relieved
that the task had turned out to be an impossible one.
After all, Macinnes couldn't reasonably expect them
to look the world over for the crown in hopes of
finding it before the Solstice. They didn't have the
manpower or the resources for such a wild-goose
chase. They would just have to come up with another
solution to Sasha's problems.

"You're not goin' to like this, Harvard, but I know
where Sasha's crown is."

A knot tightened in the pit of Rainey's stomach.
"What do you mean? Are you saying you have the
thing in your possession?"

"No. It's part of the well-guarded private collection
in Castle MacDonnaugh in the north of Scotland. It's
not been seen out of its wooden chest for centuries.
And whenever the reigning chieftain of the Clan
MacDonnaugh dies, his body lies in state beside the
open chest in bold defiance of the crown's powers.
The next in line must perform the ritual opening and
closing of the chest blindfolded, or face a life of
blindness."

Rainey turned to him, her nerves on edge. "Then
how do you know it's still there, for godsakes, or that
it even exists? The thing probably crumbled from old
age long ago, assuming it ever existed in the first
place. If nobody's seen it in all that time, what's to
say the owner isn't lying? Somebody probably sold
it to pay their back taxes a couple of hundred years
ago. And besides, how do you know it's the right
crown?"

"It's the one, all right. And I did some checking.
It's still there." He walked over to the kitchen table
and took a star-shaped sugar cookie from a plate
piled high with them. He cradled the five-pointed
shape in his hand, then held it up to her in the

candlelight, just as she had done for him with Sasha's bread.

"I had my suspicions all along, mind. I was quite certain we were on the right track because the story was so familiar to me. But I needed confirmation, so I inquired of a friend who is an expert in the origins of old legends."

"A friend." Her defenses rose. "And what precisely did you tell this 'friend' of yours, may I ask?"

He took a healthy bite of the cookie. "I told him I knew the crown's rightful owner. And that she wanted it back."

"You what? We had a bargain, remember? You weren't supposed to tell anyone about what Sasha's going through right now."

He reached for a second cookie, then thought better of it. "Not to worry," he said calmly, "I gave no pertinent names or addresses. You're safe. Besides, old Edgar is that deep into his research on the Roman occupation of the Isles, he hardly took any notice of my questions. I'm certain he has no interest in Sasha."

"How can you be so sure?" Rainey insisted. "Maybe his grant money is about to run out, and he needs new material to keep the financial ball rolling. You may have given him an inspiration. This could be the end of everything. Sasha was to be protected. She's more at risk than ever, and how do we know what the next storm will make her do?" She gripped the back of the kitchen chair. "We can't take any more chances. We can't move away again. We can't afford to run. The insurance settlement is nearly gone. Evanston will be on us in a heartbeat. The state will take her away from me. I have no money. And now my job . . ."

Her knees turned to water, and the blood drained

from her head. She was going to hit the floor, and there was nothing she could do to prevent it.

"What about your job, Rainey?"

"Lost it. Fired. I've got to get it back."

To her surprise, she didn't fall, and Matt's voice was next to her ear as it had been in the dream. The room tipped sideways, and she most definitely wasn't on her feet. Matt had lifted her into his arms, she realized, and they were in motion toward the living room. It might have been a romantic gesture, had it been anyone but him. Most likely, he was concerned for the safety of his jacket around her shoulders, she told herself in a daze.

He was strong, she'd give him that. But she wasn't in control of the situation, and that could be a mistake, she warned herself. Somehow, she just didn't have the strength to let it all get to her at the moment. Besides, he smelled of rain-soaked forest and woodsmoke. It was reassuring. And he was warm.

"Sacked, eh?" Matt whispered in her ear. "Naw, lass, it's only an opportunity for a fine holiday abroad, eh? Let someone else share the burden, Rainey. It's time."

The fire had gone down, and the living room was close to darkness, as, with efficient care, he removed his coat from her shoulder and set her down on the sofa bed. She didn't protest when he slipped off her wet boots, sweatshirt, and jeans and settled her snugly beneath the covers. She was still decent. More or less. And if he settled in beside her, she would go for the kitchen knife.

But she felt the mattress lift as he rose. She waited to hear the front door close behind him. But what she heard was him humming softly to himself as he stoked the fire. He was still close by. She didn't want to admit it, but his presence made her feel warmer than a dozen blankets.

"The crown," she said drowsily as she rolled over onto her side to watch him tend the hearth. "Do we really need it?"

He continued his task. "Aye, love, that we do. It's essential. The crown is the key to it all. The queen must have it totally in her possession."

"Maybe you could just borrow it for a little while."

"Borrow the Crown of Glomach?" he exclaimed in a whisper. His burr was suddenly thick as the walls of one of those old Scottish castles he loved to talk about.

"The crown canna be borroit, lassie. There's the grand tr-r-radition must be upheeled. As it has been since it was created, the Starry Crown must be won by stealth. It must be stolen."

Chapter 11

Stolen. The word was very much on Rainey's mind as she awoke to the aroma of fresh coffee and toast. As was so often the case lately, she had to wonder if what Matt had told her the night before had been part of a dream. Thankfully, she couldn't remember anything specific from her sleep this morning. But the message that the crown must be stolen remained loud and clear.

She did remember shivering at some point long after Matt had put her to bed. It had felt like there weren't enough blankets in the world to make her warm. She had been too aching from the cold to get up in search of more covers, but even half-asleep, she had been miserable.

Then, all at once, the cold had begun to go away. Her backbone and the backs of her thighs had started to warm up. Alan must have come to bed at last, it had occurred to her through the mists of sleep. But no, that was wrong. Alan was gone. . . . She hadn't had the energy to work it all out in her head, and sleep had called to her. But the sensations had been very real.

She turned over slowly and ran her hand over the space beside her. It was empty and gave back no warmth. But as she settled her head against the other pillow, she thought she detected the faintest hint of a familiar scent. A wave of warmth spun around the core of her, and she pulled the blanket a bit higher at the realization she was in her underwear.

Sasha stirred in her sleep, and Rainey felt a blush warm her cheeks. What if Matt had actually lain beside her at some point during the night? And what if Sasha had seen?

Sasha was still very young. Her conclusions would be limited. But it might raise difficult questions. Of course, she had no real proof. Just like she had no real proof of anything Matt Macinnes had told her to date.

The bed made her feel claustrophobic. So she wrapped the sheet around herself and padded quietly toward her bedroom to get dressed.

"You look grand just as you are, Harvard," Matt said softly from the kitchen. He walked over to the doorway and watched her openly. "Can I tempt you with a bit o' brekkie, then?"

"Not hungry," she lied as she smoothed her hair self-consciously. As usual, he looked like he had been up and about for hours, and it made her wonder if he had been watching her as she slept.

He tsked at her. "Not hungry, is it? It's a ways till lunch." When he glanced at his watch, he expressed surprise. "I stand corrected. Lunch is in twenty minutes."

Rainey looked at the small crystal clock next to Sasha's picture on the mantel. It was twenty to twelve. She had slept half the day. No wonder Matt gave the impression he had been up for a while.

"I have to shower," she explained as she gathered the trailing sheet into her arms. "Help yourself to whatever's in the kitchen. But I guess you've already taken care of that." She nodded toward the coffee cup in his hand. "I'll be out in a minute."

"Rainey," he said, "that business about your passport being in order . . ."

"Yes?"

"Is it? And what about Sasha's?"

"Alan scheduled a trip to Europe for us all shortly before he died. I'd never been overseas, and Sasha was old enough to handle the flight. It was supposed to be the first real vacation the three of us had taken as a family." She plucked at a stray thread on the sheet, lost for the moment in memories.

"Rainey?" Matt said gently.

She squared her shoulders and gave him a look that was all business. "Our passports will work."

"Good. Can you be packed by four?"

"Four, as in four hours from now?"

"I took the liberty of booking us a six o'clock flight out of San Francisco. Emma said she could be ready by three when I spoke to her this mornin'. But then, she's only packin' for one. Robbie's comin' by to pick Angus up for the duration. It'll do the pair of them good, though Emma was ready to smuggle them both into her luggage. You'd best not let the dear lady down by makin' us all late, now. It's quite the sacrifice she's makin', givin' up her beastly familiar this way."

Rainey could do little more than stare at him. "You booked us a flight?"

"A boat would take too long, don't you think?" He took a healthy gulp of his coffee and grinned at her surprise. "It's my treat."

She gave him a dubious look. "Your treat. You mean you're charging it to the university."

He returned her look evenly. "Naw, lass, to do that I'd have to account to the powers that be the reason for the expenditures, now, wouldn't I? You and I know I can't be doin' that. I'd be betrayin' my promise. Instead, I took a wee bit of personal leave.

I'm dealin' with a family crisis, you see. Seems they've forgotten I've got no family to speak of." He waved the point away. "The lesson plans are all set, and I've got a couple of half-daft understudies purely slatherin' to give my pulpit a go. There's plenty of time for damage control when I get back. And anyway, the break for the holidays comes at the end of the week."

"If we go, it will have to be with the understanding that the expense will be a loan. I will find a way to pay you back every penny. Are we agreed?"

Matt walked over to the coffee table and picked up a piece of Sasha's drawing paper and the well-worn red crayon so Rainey could put their agreement in writing. He gave the items to her, and as their hands brushed, the attraction between them was undeniable.

Rainey pulled her hand away, and for the second time in five minutes, she blushed. She was forever close to disaster with him. Matt backed away, his hands raised in a gesture of peace.

"Now, now, Harvard, I was only playin' the gentleman."

"Right. I'll try to remember that. Just answer one question for me, Macinnes."

He bowed to her formally.

"What happens if we get the crown?"

He rubbed his chin thoughtfully. "When we get the crown—and we will, I promise you—all will be right with the world."

"Meaning?"

"Meanin' the curse will be lifted."

"Curse? What curse? You never said anything about any curse."

He folded his arms across his chest, unshaken by her questions.

"Well, now, it would hardly be a proper legend without the obligatory curse for good measure."

"Tell me, damn it." She shivered when a cold wave of premonition prickled her spine.

"It has to do with the secret of the falls, you see. Before the time of recorded history, when the Picts, the Vikings, and the Celts were all vying for the north of Scotland, there was one powerful king by the name of Nynniaw. He had a brother by the name of Peibaw, who was also a king, and the two of them warred with each other regularly. Each brother had a daughter, but no sons. Peibaw's daughter was Beairteas, the name meaning riches. She was beautiful, but her beauty was soured by her greed for wealth and power. Nynniaw, by contrast, had a lovely daughter by the name of Sirona, who was known for her strength of character and magical wisdom far beyond her years."

"Sirona?" Rainey said softly. It was the name she had heard in her dream. Sasha stirred in her sleep.

"Aye, the name means star, as it happens. There was a Gaulish goddess by that name, and many claimed the young princess was the same being, so enchanting she was with her dark curls and her eyes the blue of a Highland loch in spring. Sirona's mother had been stolen away by Viking raiders soon after her birth. Though it was thought her mother was still alive, she was lost to them. While Beairteas grew lazy and selfish under her father's spoiling care, Sirona was raised to fight with a sword by her father."

"She was a female warrior?"

"Sirona was as brave in battle as any a seasoned warrior. More than by lineage, she had earned the right to rule. Sirona was destined to wear Nynniaw's crown, a crown he had fashioned with his own hands.

"She was betrothed to a warrior prince from a neighboring clan. His name was Stalcair, which means hunter, and their marriage was to be an alliance to strengthen Sirona's clan. But more than that, though they had known each other only briefly, it was also to be an alliance of love."

Rainey sat down on a nearby chair. "The same crown that waits for us in Scotland?"

"Aye, the same. It was stolen from that fair queen in the far distant past, an injustice that lives in legend to this day."

"Who stole it?"

"The first time? It was her uncle, Peibaw." He swirled the last of his coffee in his cup as if to read his fortune there. "As the story goes, Peibaw heard a rumor that the bonnie Sirona had found a way to charm the stars out of the skies and turn them into jewels to swell her father's coffers. She was the namesake of a goddess, after all, and such sorcery would be a simple task for her.

"Naturally, Peibaw concluded his brother was amassing this magical fortune in order to mount a massive war against him. He ordered the petulant Beairteas to bring jewels down from the sky as her cousin had done, and when she failed to do so, he had her beaten and banished from his sight. She lurked about on the edges of the camps, clutching at charity and stealing outright from her own kin whenever the opportunity arose. Needless to say, Nynniaw blamed all of this catastrophe on his brother and decided to declare war before Peibaw got the chance to do it first."

"A lovely family," Rainey commented.

"Ah, well, families can be a problem to this day." Something flickered through his eyes briefly, a memory, an old wound never healed. But he shuttered it all quickly.

"Sirona's treasure was said to be hidden somewhere within the cliff behind the falls. Only the king and Sirona herself knew where, and they had sworn themselves to secrecy. Indeed, if one of them should be killed, the other was bound to a vow of silence until vengeance could be won."

Rainey glanced over to where Sasha slept with her new teddy bear clutched close to her heart. "Sasha's silence began when she learned her father had been killed."

"Aye. It was an old promise lit like a candle in her heart."

"So, you're telling me you're hoping to find a missing treasure out of all of this?"

Matt gave her a sly grin. "I had a feelin' you'd jump on that one. But not to worry. Treasure is hardly a motivation here. I'm far from the only one in the world to know about the legend, and fortune hunters from every corner of the globe have scoured those cliffs for hundreds of years with everything from their fingernails to be the latest high-tech equipment. If anything was ever there, and as I say, there was always some doubt, it's either long since gone or forever a secret in the heart of the falls. You must remember, tales of jewels and the like were often grossly exaggerated to give the storyteller status."

Rainey nodded her understanding. "So this Sirona's father was killed over some jewels that may not have existed."

"Quite true. Sirona's father was taken by force to the top of the falls where he and his followers were ordered to reveal where the treasure was. The wars between the two brothers had gone on for so many years, for reasons large and small, they were probably both a bit wrong in the head. It would not have been beyond Sirona's father to remain stubborn on the matter even if there were no jewels, you understand."

"A pigheaded Scotsman, what a concept," Rainey couldn't resist saying. It only got her a wink.

"Aye, well then, that nasty Peibaw fellow brought the rest of Nynniaw's clan to the top of the falls. And one by one, he ordered his brother's followers to climb down the cliff in search of the treasure. Men, women, even small children were commanded over the side as their king watched in angry silence. And one by one, they fell to their deaths. Only a very few remained alive at the top of the falls."

"My god, what a story."

"Aye. Sirona cried bitter tears for those who lost their lives, and she called out to her father, saying she would fetch more stars from the sky for him that very night if they could reveal the location of the treasure of Peibaw. Out of pity for his people and his daughter's sorrow, Nynniaw reluctantly agreed."

"Not much of a bargain."

"Not a bargain at all. Peibaw was so lathered with triumph that for a moment, he forgot his goal of getting the jewels. As his brother started down the cliff to the treasure's hiding place, Peibaw snatched the Crown of Glomach from Nynniaw's head and waved it in the air. He shouted, 'You won't be needin' this anymore, brother, because you no longer have any subjects.' And with that, he ordered all of Nynniaw's followers thrown from the top of the falls. They fell against the rocks and into the deep pool below. The pool flowed red with their blood. Nynniaw witnessed it in horror as he clung to a thin ledge.

" 'I curse you, brother,' he shouted. 'I curse your eyes to blindness and the eyes of all who behold my crown who are not of my clan from this day forth that you may never again see the beauty of the jewels you so covet nor the celestial places from which they came.'

"Needless to say, this promptly set Peibaw off, and he hurled Nynniaw's own sword deep into his brother's heart. Nynniaw fell to the pool below, dead. And at the same moment, Peibaw was struck totally sightless."

"The curse was a little slow, I'd say," Rainey said.

"Yes, well, once Peibaw stopped carrying on from the shock of his blindness, he turned his attention to Sirona. She was totally alone now. Peibaw had eliminated one source of information about where the treasure was, but he still had a second one. And what was more, he had the goose who laid the golden egg, so to speak, still at his disposal. If he couldn't get her to talk, he'd just get her to make fresh jewels, a mountain of them. All was not lost, though you have to suppose groping around in the dark had to put a bit of a damper on his glee."

"I imagine." Rainey envisioned that young woman of so long ago facing death alone, a pool of blood waiting for her below. Where did one find such courage?

"Peibaw had Sirona placed on a narrow precipice at the head of the falls," Matt explained. "Below her lay only carnage, including the body of her father, so she sat down cross-legged and locked her eyes on the horizon, refusing to look down.

"Her uncle, the man who had grown up under the same roof with her father, gave her a simple choice. Produce the old treasure, manufacture a better one, or die.

"She held her head high, so the story goes, and said, 'As rightful queen of this place, I decree that the souls of my beloved father and his loyal subjects shall remain here until such time as my crown is restored to me. Then they shall be set free from this infamy. Until that day, at the time of the Winter Solstice, none shall see treasure from this place.' And with that, she rose to her feet and dove over the edge of the cliff. Some say she disappeared altogether. Others say she transformed into a swan and flew away to a magical oak tree where she is kept safe by the fairies until her crown is returned to her."

Rainey blinked in surprise. "You said the swan lived in a fairy tree?" She must have heard this story somewhere when she was little. How else could she explain the tree and the swan being in her dreams so vividly?

"Aye, a holy oak, so the story goes, hidden away from the world," Matt said. "Her beloved Stalcair came upon the terrible scene at the falls the next day. He had received warning of the attack too late, and so great was his sorrow at his failure to save Sirona and her clan, he fell to his knees at the top of the falls and swore by the hilt of his sword that he would spend all eternity guarding the spirits of Glomach until her rule was restored.

"The next day, Peibaw and Beairteas were discovered dead at the bottom of a gorge. Their bodies were still locked in mortal combat, but neither of them had succeeded in achieving sole ownership of the crown. It was nowhere to be found.

"For four decades, Stalcair stood watch over the falls while his clansmen searched for Peibaw's clan and the crown. He engraved the image of a swan onto the handle of his sword, and for each Winter Solstice that passed, he carved a single notch into the hilt.

"But Peibaw's followers were nowhere to be found. Some say they all lost their power of sight. That they were unable to resist the temptation of gazing upon the crown's splendor just once. And as they wandered blindly through the wilderness, they each became separated from the group, one by one, and were devoured by wild animals. Some say they fled to Wales where rumors of the crown abounded.

"At last, out of sorrow and old age, Stalcair could keep his watch no longer. And on the day of the coldest Winter Solstice anyone could remember, he hurled his sword over the falls and dove after it into the deadly pool below in hopes of being closer to his beloved Sirona. Several private collections boast of havin' Stalcair's sword, but to date, they've all been proven to be false copies."

"And the crown?"

"Tradition says it lay buried in the ground for hundreds of years, away from men's eyes. Until the day a nobleman's mount stumbled over it during a hunting expedition. They were hunting for swan for the supper table, as the story goes, but when the nobleman stopped to investigate the obstacle in his path, he was struck blind where he stood. Still, having seen it for only an instant, the nobleman was so captivated by the crown's beauty, he ordered that it be wrapped in his cloak and taken back to his castle. It was placed into a wooden chest to protect the sight of anyone who came in contact with it, and the crown's legend spread and flourished.

"Clan MacDonnaugh, er, confiscated it from Clan Cameron in the early 1600s. The Camerons stole it by night from Clan Mackinnon the century before, and Clan Buchanan brags of havin' it prior to that. The list goes on. But what matters is the MacDonnaugh claims to have it now."

"The MacDonnaugh?"

"The laird, the head of the MacDonnaugh clan. And it's said when Sirona's crown is restored to her, Stalcair will return to guard her with his sword. Until that time, their souls can only touch once each year, at the time of the Winter Solstice. To this day, there are sightings of a mated pair of swans in the pool at the time of the Solstice, one as white as snow upon the heather, the other as black as sorrow." He pushed his glasses up on the bridge of his nose in academic fashion. "But these are mostly the embellishments of incurable romantics."

"Romantics like yourself, I take it?"

He shrugged.

Rainey stood up and started toward the bedroom. The story had definitely gotten to her, and the cold was playing havoc with her in more ways than one. "Are you trying to tell me you've actually seen those two swans?"

He nodded curtly. "Indeed I have. And what's more, I've seen Queen Sirona herself. She's curled up in a sleepin' bag there by the fire."

"Right. And who does that make me, pray tell?"

As he grabbed his jacket, he gave her a courtier's bow. "Why, the Queen Mother, of course."

"Great, again with the silly hats," she said with a sigh.

"Maybe we'll fetch a crown for you as well, Harvard. How would that suit your fancy?"

She grew serious. "I don't need any crowns or jewels to make me happy. All I want is for Sasha to be a regular little girl and for things to return to normal."

Matt gave her a long look. "It's what I want for her, too, Rainey. But first, we must return things to normal for that lady from so long ago. It must happen, and it must happen quickly. We can do it, you and I. But it's going to require a one hundred percent commitment from you. I can't ease your doubts any more than I have, and for that I'm sorry." He shook his head slowly. "I'm askin' you to do this as an act of faith, pure and simple."

"Faith."

"Aye." He paused at the front door. "There was a phone call for you earlier."

"A phone call?" The tension returned to the pit of Rainey's stomach.

"It was a Mrs. Malinsky." He saw her anxiety, and it made his heart ache. But perhaps this would help to motivate her toward their ultimate goal. "You needed your rest, so I told her you were in the middle of an important business call. It's a wee dodge I learned from Phoebe. This Malinsky person says you're to call her so the two of you can arrange to have a meetin' at her office. She says you're to bring Sasha with you, and you'll need to bring proof of employment and current paid receipts from Sasha's school and therapy sessions."

"I see." A numbness spread to Rainey's extremities. "I guess I better call her."

Matt rubbed his chin thoughtfully. "As it happens, she said she'd be in the field for the remainder of the day, and ye should call her tomorrow." The look of tenuous relief she gave him nearly melted him on the spot. "But of course, that won't be possible because you'll be solidly on Scottish soil by then. And British currency is a bloody hassle to use for long distance in a phone booth."

"I imagine." Rainey hardly heard his words. This Malinsky woman was closing in so fast. And there was no guarantee she would accept last month's pay stubs and receipts. One simple phone call to the agency about the status of her job would blow her cover completely.

"If they try, they'll figure out Sasha and I went overseas," she said, more to herself than to Matt. "I hope this won't make matters worse."

"Ah, well, in point of fact, I took the liberty of listin' you and Sasha under my name for the tickets. There was purely because of the family rate break, you see. I should have checked with you first, I know, and you'll have to show proper ID at the check-in. But you can just say you've kept your maiden name for business purposes, and I'm sure it'll be fine. The boardin' passes won't say Nielson. It'll be a clean getaway." He gave her a wink.

"Four o'clock sharp, Harvard. Pack warm. The Highlands have no patience for rookies. Ask Sasha, she'll tell you." With a smart salute, he let himself out.

Rainey caught sight of her rain-soaked leather boots near the foot of the sofa bed. They were ruined. Matt had taken them off for her last night, and no doubt that was one of the things he had in mind when he warned her about being a rookie.

They were going to Scotland. The whole idea was absurd and incredibly elating. They could leave Evanston and Child Welfare behind. They could simply jump on a plane and leave everything behind.

But she wasn't really leaving things behind, she reminded herself. Sasha's problem was coming with them, and her troubles with the state of Evanston would be waiting for her when they returned, compounded a hundredfold. Still, the trip was a chance to help Sasha, the last chance.

It was noon, and she had to be ready for the airport at four. She had no spending money, and no idea what to buy, anyway. When she glanced over at Sasha, she found her wide-awake and looking back at her, the new teddy wrapped securely in her arms.

"Hello, sleepyhead, how long have you been awake?"

Sasha held up four fingers.

"Four hours?"

With a shake of her head, Sasha raised her circled fingers to her eyes to indicate Matt. She then held up four fingers again.

"Gotcha. Four o'clock sharp," Rainey groaned. "For somebody who's the Queen Mother, I certainly get ordered around a lot. I think I better take another look at the job description before I sign on for another hitch."

Sasha gave her a doubtful look, then dashed off to her room to start packing.

Swans, fairy trees, and vows of love that transcend death—she had never been a sucker for such things before, Rainey assured herself. But she was becoming a believer. It wouldn't surprise her a bit to find a pair of swans camped on the front porch. She would even know how to call them by name, Sirona and Stalcair. As she glanced down at the sheet she still had wrapped around herself, she had a giddy thought that maybe it was all she would pack.

The phone rang about two o'clock. She suspected it was Matt making sure she was taking care of business, and she was ready to tell him in no uncertain terms that she had matters well under control. There didn't seem to be any point in mentioning she still had all her clothing possibilities spread out across her bed in a state of anarchy. But the answering machine picked up the call before she had a chance to get to it, and her hand froze on the receiver when she heard the message coming in. It was Evanston.

"Pick up the phone this instant, Mrs. Nielson," he ordered. His voice scraped across the line, harsh and dictatorial. Age had not been kind to him, and his quest for immortality hinged upon coming up with a headline-making research breakthrough that would bear his name. His health was failing, and the lack of time remaining to him only speeded the death of his conscience.

"I don't have the time or the inclination to play games with you, Mrs. Nielson," he contended with a wheeze that turned into a hacking cough. "You're out of the picture at any rate."

Rainey couldn't bring herself to pick up the phone. To speak to Evanston would only lend him more power and assure him of Sasha's location. He thrived on confrontation. It was an elixir to him. But his statement that she was somehow out of Sasha's life now petrified her to the bones. What had the old bastard accomplished behind her back?

"The child is mine now, Mrs. Nielson. I'm sure a Mrs. Malinsky from the Child Protection Department has been in touch with you by now regarding the question of Sasha's custody. Certain complaints have been filed. It may be of interest to you to know, parties other than myself have questioned your right to the child. Seems you've been making quite a public spectacle of my latest acquisition. Now, haven't I always told you you were that child's worst enemy?

"Well, now it's come home to roost, Mrs. Nielson. Certain legally binding forms have been signed. I make this call to you only to caution you against making any move to leave the area. The official records testify to your rampant instability and to your inability to remain at one address. It's all there in black and white. You really are a pathetic specimen of motherhood.

"But rest assured, Mrs. Nielson, Sasha is no longer your concern. We'll see that she's scrubbed regularly and that her weight is maintained, of course. After all, it's in our best interest to keep her free of infection until the research is completed. History will be made, Mrs. Nielson. History. On that you may depend."

He began to cough again, and an ugly taste rose in Rainey's throat. She felt sick to her stomach as she picked up the receiver, ready to give Evanston every kind of hell there was, regardless of the cost. But the line was dead. The worst of her nightmares was fast becoming reality, and she was shaking from head to foot.

There was a tug at her sleeve, and she turned to find Sasha standing beside her. Rainey knelt down next to her and took her into her arms, desperate to protect Sasha any way she could. Sasha pointed to the phone and made a mean face.

"Don't worry, Sash," Rainey said with as much confidence as she could muster. "I'll keep you safe, sweetheart, I swear it. We're going to get out of here for a while." She put Sasha at arm's length so their eyes met. "Let's get our things packed right away, fast, so Matt won't have to wait for us, okay? Everything's going to be fine." Sasha nodded solemnly, and Rainey watched as she walked dutifully to her room.

Rainey returned to her own packing duties, but as she stared at the piles of lightweight California clothing she wanted to weep. Evanston's threats cut back and forth through her mind, and concentration was impossible. She wanted to nail him for the unscrupulous bastard he was. She wanted to see him put away where he wouldn't have the power to destroy anyone's life.

But it was too big a job, and there was far too much at stake. They had to get out of here now. Any second thoughts or hesitation of an hour ago no longer had any meaning. They had to get to Scotland with Matt. In fact, Timbuktu might be an even better destination.

When the phone rang an hour or so later, Rainey nearly jumped out of her skin. She thanked God when she heard Emma on the answering machine and picked up the receiver quickly. But Emma's voice was filled with warning.

"Take Sasha and go to one of the back rooms,

love," she said urgently. "Hurry! And don't come out or make a sound till I ring ye again. Understood? I'll ring three times and hang up. Then call ye again. Got it?"

"Emma, what's happening?" Sasha was standing beside her, and she took her hand quickly.

"No time, love, do as yer told!"

She hung up, and Rainey raced to Sasha's bedroom with Sasha in tow. They dashed into Sasha's closet and waited among the broken shelves, utterly still. There was a loud knock on the front door. Then another. And a third.

"We are here for Sasha, Mrs. Nielson!" a voice shouted. "Let's keep this simple, shall we?"

Rainey and Sasha started when there was a harsh knock at the back door. The sound of footsteps stopped outside Sasha's window, and Rainey swallowed a curse. Sasha's curtains were covered with bright dancing stars and teddy bears, and she had let Sasha put playful stickers on the glass. It was obvious this was a little girls' bedroom. And all the shrubs at the side of the house made it so no one would see if there was a break-in. It had never been an issue until now.

Someone was trying the window to see if it was locked. Luckily it was. But the adrenaline rushing through Rainey's veins pushed her past fear. From where she stood, she could see Sasha's softball bat. The temptation to lunge for it and break the glass in the bastard's face made her blood pound. She was being forced to hide in her own home, and it was intolerable.

But when she looked down into Sasha's concerned face, she knew this was not the time for heroism. She had her suspicions about who was out there, but she didn't know how many of them there were. If they overpowered her, Sasha would have no protection at all. And Sasha's safety had to come first.

She heard a distant whistle, and the footsteps receded. They waited like statues, hardly daring to breathe. At long last, the phone rang three times, then stopped. Rainey was almost afraid to pick it up when it began to ring again, for fear someone else had learned Emma's secret code.

"It was a black late-model van, love," Emma explained. "I'd never seen it before, and it just didna look right to me parked down the road like that. Pulled up about twenty minutes ago. So I got out my sportin' glasses for a better look, ye ken. In tiny gold letters on the door, it said ERI."

"Evanston Research Institute." Rainey could hardly bring herself to say the words.

"Aye, lass, the villain. There were three of the bullies. All dressed in their fine suits and ties and wearin' gloves. I've watched enough of yer crime dramas on the telly to know they were up to a dirty business, Rainey."

"Dear God."

"When I saw the one go 'round by the side of the house, I came out into the yard and let 'em see me plain. The one at the front door walked over to me, bold as ye please, and asked if ye were to home. He pointed to yer car like I was a witness on the stand or somethin'. But I told him yer car was broke down, and you and Sasha had taken the bus to the local market. Well, he took one look at yer car, love, and took me at my word. He whistled to the others, and they all piled into the van and left. All except one. He's lurkin' out front by yer redwood tree."

"I can't believe this." Rainey sat down on the chair next to the phone. Was Evanston really crazy enough to try to kidnap Sasha?

"Aye, and they'll be back for the straggler. I'll go

out and keep him busy, love. Go 'round by the back way and bring yer things over here. Stay low. I've called the Macinnes. He'll be comin' in a fresh vehicle to throw 'em off the scent. We'll have him pull into the garage. Have a care, love. I dunna like the way things are goin'."

"Neither do I. Thanks, Emma." She hung up the phone and jammed the rest of their clothes into two small suitcases. She saw the man in the suit having a cigarette next to her redwood tree as she peeked between the living room curtains. Seconds later, Emma joined him with a plate of scones in her hand. He was distracted for the moment, so she and Sasha stealthily made their way through the bushes to Emma's house.

For Evanston to be this bold, it could well mean Child Protection was on his side. With budget cuts and overworked staff, it wouldn't be hard to understand how someone like this Mrs. Malinsky would be only too happy to turn a case over to a prominent professional—one less headache. A government agency couldn't openly condone child abduction, certainly. But it wasn't impossible that they might be persuaded to overlook questionable tactics if they could be convinced it was for the sake of Sasha's health and safety. And Evanston could be a very persuasive man.

No place was safe now.

Chapter 12

Once they were through customs in Glasgow, Rainey let Matt carry their bags. They were weighed down with half a dozen borrowed sweaters. She and Sasha had had to duck down in the backseat of Matt's classic old Ford station wagon when they left for the airport because Evanston's van was once again lying in wait down the street. Fortunately, it didn't look like the van tried to follow them, but Matt took a complex, roundabout route to the airport as an added precaution.

Rainey had eyed everyone in the terminal with suspicion, never letting go of Sasha's hand for fear they might have to run from danger. It had made her feel like a criminal, and she promised herself it was going to end. Stress and jet lag were taking their toll on her. She had been too keyed up to sleep on the long flight.

Jet lag didn't dampen Emma's spirits in the least, however. When Rainey recounted the story of Sirona and Stalcair to her, it opened a floodgate of stories and memories for her. Sirona's legend was one she had heard once or twice as a young girl, and she had spent much of the flight recounting fairy tales of her youth and expounding upon places she wanted to show them all, if time allowed. From the sound of it, they would have to allow most of a century.

It was ten o'clock in the morning, Glasgow time, but Rainey couldn't keep her eyes open as Matt chauffeured their rented car on the drive from the airport. She was desperate for sleep. So she curled up against Sasha's shoulder in the backseat, and made Emma promise to fill her in on any important scenery she missed.

It wasn't a very long nap, but when Sasha nudged her awake, she felt like a new person. Her dreams had been overrun with fairies, fairies of her own. They had whispered secrets in her ears and covered her with that same glowing dust of enchantment she had seen in her dream of the swan. This time, instead of being wary of her, they had run to her in warm welcome and treated her like royalty. She had experienced such a strong sense of homecoming, she had wept sweet tears of relief.

There would be help for them now. Somehow, the puzzle pieces were starting to fit into place. The answers were waiting for them. And just before she awoke, they gave her an important gift of some kind, though her memory of what it was was foggy. Now, in the waking world, a kind of euphoria wrapped around her at the realization she was truly in Scotland. It felt absolutely natural, like she had been inexcusably out of place until now.

But when she saw the grand facade of their hotel, the euphoria ebbed and she was torn between utter joy at the luxury of the place and the hard reality that she would never be able to reimburse Matt for the cost. The Devonshire—even the name sounded out of her financial reach. She didn't want to have to be the grouchy, practical one. But the fact was, she had no guarantees about the future.

As she started to piece together a speech to explain why she and Sasha would have to find another hotel on the cheaper side of town, Sasha let go of her hand

and bounded into the lobby after Matt. Rainey started after her, but Emma caught her arm.

"Let her go, Rainey," she said kindly. "It's only for the one night, eh? It canna do so very much harm to let the Macinnes do this for ye. I get the feelin' he takes pleasure from doin' nice things for the pair of ye. It's more than a gift to you, ye ken? It's a gift to himself as well. So let the man have his fun. Goodness only knows what the next few days'll hold in store for us all. Enjoy the party, love. That's an order."

"What if we're wrong?" Rainey glanced up at the hotel's elegant town house exterior and the gray clouds gathering overhead. She didn't want to face any thunder right now.

Emma shrugged. "And what if we are wrong? Sasha's been nothin' but grins and gratitude since we touched down. She's in her element, and a change of scene will do us all good."

"I can't afford a gamble like this, and I don't want to be indebted to Macinnes."

"Financially? Or otherwise . . . ?"

Rainey gave Emma a suspicious look. "What do you mean by 'otherwise'?"

"Well, now, I may be in me dotage, love, but I know a fair-and-square come-hither dance when I see one. And the two of you are jiggin' to beat the band."

"You're crazy." Rainey turned away to hide her embarrassment. "This is about Sasha, nothing more."

Emma touched her arm. "Ah, listen, darlin', I've said it before, and I'll say it again, nobody doubts you're one hundred percent committed to Sasha. But, by god, you're only human, lassie. Shuttin' yourself off from the possibility of real happiness is a disservice to you and Sasha both."

"Macinnes is Sasha's shining knight, not mine. What if it's the treasure of the falls he's really after?

He's known about the possibility of the jewels all along."

Emma gave her a long look. "Oh, it's the treasure of the falls he's after, right enough. And you and Sasha are it. What's to say he can't be your shining knight as well, Rainey?"

There was no time for a reply as Sasha came running out of the hotel's front doors, a jubilant smile on her face. She gestured for the two of them to come in.

Rainey started toward her. "I can't deal with any other possibilities right now, Emma. We have to stick to business."

"It's that strong, is it?" Emma chuckled at Rainey's dirty look as they followed Sasha inside.

Matt was waiting for them next to the elevator.

"I've sent the luggage ahead with the bellboy," he said, pointing toward the heavens with his thumb. Rainey's dubious look didn't escape him. It said she would have preferred to save the expense by carrying her own bags.

"The lad's only tryin' to make an honest livin' in a harsh world, Harvard. You mustn't begrudge him." He gave her a mischievous wink and herded them forward. He sensed a moment of hesitation on Rainey's part about getting into the elevator, but he tucked her arm through his and didn't give her the chance to balk.

When they reached the rooms, Emma stifled a gasp, and Rainey could only stare in awe. A huge oak four-poster bed was the center focus of the suite. It was piled high with lace-trimmed pillows and elegantly canopied and curtained in heavy mauve brocade in medieval fashion. A fire danced merrily on the marble hearth, and all around the room there were lovely arrangements of holly, brightly colored ribbons, and poinsettias.

A second, smaller bed, with layer upon layer of colorful handmade quilts, waited on the other side of the fireplace. It was like a fantastic holiday dream come true, and Rainey didn't dare step inside for fear it would dissolve. With all that had been going on, she had forgotten Christmas was only a few days away.

"I haven't shopped for a single present," she groaned.

"Not to worry, love. Christmas has a way of comin' all on its own," Matt said as he breezed past her to tip the bellboy.

Rainey watched him handle the situation with utter confidence. He was easily a head taller than the bellboy, and even in his travel-worn slacks and sweater and with his hair in anarchy from the weather, he looked . . . The only word that came to her mind was heroic. A strange word to choose. Maybe the fairies had sprinkled a bit too much of that magic stuff in her eyes. Or maybe it was just the way Sasha idolized him. But it did seem impossible she had only known him for a few days.

A crazy notion occurred to her that maybe she had known him before somehow. He was so very different from Alan, except in his devotion to Sasha. It wasn't fair to compare the two men. They were so dissimilar. But there was no question Matt inspired that same feeling of familiarity she had experienced when she saw the fairies in her dreams. It should have been unsettling, but somehow, it wasn't.

"Right, ladies," Matt said, "let's get Emma to her quarters and me to mine and perhaps meet in the lobby in an hour to go in search of some lunch. Does that sound agreeable?"

Rainey turned to Sasha, who nodded vigorously.

"We'll need to shower and change," Rainey said. "Yes, an hour should be sufficient."

Matt gave her a teasing grin. "A shower, is it? I'll be certain to have housekeeping provide an extra sheet or two. I wouldn't have your lingerie wardrobe go lacking."

"I don't always wear a sheet when I come out of the shower, Macinnes," she informed him. She hefted her suitcase onto the bed and opened it for his benefit. Nothing was visible but sweaters.

"My wardrobe is quite sufficient, thank you," she said lightly.

He gave her a dubious look. "Ah, I quite prefer you in linen, you know. But to each her own."

Emma cleared her throat in stern chaperon style.

"All right, you two," she said. "Matt, I'll thank ye to get this parade back on the road. The pair of ye can moon over each other out among the heather, if ye must. But I, for one, am ready to try out me own pallet of straw for a tick. Just a wee lie-down to catch my breath, mind you. I don't want to miss any of this city." She grabbed her suitcase and started to drag it down the hallway.

"I'm not mooning over anybody," Rainey called after her.

Matt sighed and shook his head. "I'd best go after her. I promised Robbie I'd see to it she didn't come to any harm. No doubt she'll have herself settled in the royal suite before I can catch her up." He paused in the doorway and turned his attention to Sasha. With a tip of his head toward Rainey, he said, *"Bi iriosal,"* and Sasha giggled softly.

He had said something about her pride, she was sure, and when she gave him a disgruntled look, he provided, "I told her to get you to put your pride in your pocket, Harvard."

Rainey squared her shoulders. "My pride's just fine where it is."

"Aye, just a bit swollen from the plane ride, I expect."

She tossed a pillow at his head, but he managed to duck out of the door in time. His good-natured laughter could be heard all the way down the hall.

Sasha closed the door and picked up the pillow to hand it to her mother. She made the familiar circles of her hands and pressed them to her eyes. Then she drew the outline of a heart on her chest with her fingertip and pointed at Rainey.

"I may not understand Scottish Gaelic, Sash, but I get what you're trying to say to me. I know you like Matt, sweetheart. I like him, too. He's doing his best to help us. We all know that. But please don't read more into it, Sasha. Things between grown-ups just aren't that simple, and I don't want you to get your hopes up."

Sasha shrugged, then flashed her a brilliant, knowing smile.

"Fine, have it your own way, Sash. But don't be disappointed if when all of this is over, he says, 'So long, see you in the funny papers.' "

A newspaper lay on the glass coffee table. Sasha picked it up and turned to the comics, then handed it to her mother.

"Right, everybody's a comedian." Rainey managed a smile as she tousled Sasha's hair.

The phone rang, and they both jumped, memories of Evanston's chilling call still very much in their minds.

Rainey picked up the receiver slowly. "Yes?"

It was the clerk at the main desk. "Long-distance call from the States, mum. Sounds pretty official, like. Shall I patch it through, then?"

"No," Rainey said quickly, her voice hardly more than a rasping whisper. "No calls, please. Are you sure you have to right room?"

"Why, yes, mum, Room 311."

Rainey glanced down at the key on the bed. "You have the wrong room. This is 211."

"Oh, sorry to disturb you, Mrs. . . . er, Macinnes. It won't happen again, I assure you. Enjoy your stay, mum."

"Thank you." Rainey hung up and sat down on the bed, her heart still in her throat. She glanced over at Sasha. "If it rings again, we're not going to answer it, okay? My heart can't take it." Sasha nodded in agreement.

"Emma, if I might have a moment of your time," Matt called as he caught up to her outside her room.

Emma let the pair of them in. Her room was just as pleasing as the other one had been, and she smiled her approval at Matt.

"What is it, love," she said with a hint of tease, "are ye after needin' a bit of advice to the lovelorn, lad?" She sat down on the bed to test its firmness and seemed satisfied.

Matt walked over to a window and looked out at the quaint streets below. The mists sprayed against the glass, turning everything into an impressionist's tableau. "It's got that bold a face to it, has it?" he said softly. "I suppose when a person wears his heart's desires on his sleeve so foolishly, grand theft would no be the wisest profession to pursue." He traced a pattern in the condensation on the window. It was the design of Sasha's brooch.

Emma unwrapped the elegant mint left on her pillow and popped it into her mouth. "So which dilemma has ye more in a know at the moment, Matthew, love or thievery?"

He turned to her with a look of genuine worry. "They're one and the same, then, are they not? Those two precious ladies are countin' on me to save the day. And all I can give them is a fairy tale."

"Legend, Macinnes. A legend," Emma corrected him.

"Fine, throw it back in my face. I deserve it." He began to pace the room. "I've brought them all this way. And why? Because I want to solve Sasha's problems and bring her back whole into the real world?" He stopped in the middle of the room. "By God, I don't know if I truly want to bring her back to the present day. There it is. The way she is now, there is so much to be learned from her. She's like a glorious wee time-travel machine. I find myself wanting to take her aside and question her for days about Sirona's time, how they lived, how they died. She could reveal so much that is lost to us. Who can say if all that knowledge, all that memory will disappear when the Solstice is over? A chance of a lifetime may be over when it's barely begun."

He threw himself down in a chair. "Thoughts like these make me no better than that bloody Evanston bastard. We both want to use Sasha for our own selfish purposes, regardless of the cost to her and to Rainey.

"God, when I think of Rainey . . ." He leaned forward and ran his hand through his hair. "It's hard as swingin' an elephant over my head, gettin' her to trust me enough just to hold Sasha's hand. If she heard the way I'm talking right now, I'd never see the pair of them again."

Emma unwrapped the mint from the other pillow on her bed and slid it into her mouth. "Ye're no Evanston. Ye havna got that kind of poison in ye, no matter how deep ye look. And well Rainey knows it. God's truth now, Matthew," she said as she chewed, "are ye a believer, young man?"

He raised his eyes to her, a man in turmoil. "What?"

"Ye heard the question. It's simple enough for a university professor, ye ken. I'm about askin' ye if ye're a believer. Ye've told Rainey the bare bones of Sirona's legend. But I'm no so sure ye've educated her to the rest, man. She must be told about the fairies' part in all of this. I promise ye, Sasha knows. And if ye're the fella I judge ye to be, ye'll do right and tell Rainey the whole of it."

"She's not the type to accept such things," he said with a shake of his head. "I shouldn't be either, of course. I quite nearly got thrown out for trying to convince her about the first part of the tale. If I go on about how getting the crown to the falls at the Solstice is pivotal not only to Sasha's well-being, but to the survival of a lot of mystical little beings as well, I'll lose her for good. And if I frost the cake by telling her I believe it all to be true, she'll probably turn me over to Evanston in chains for research purposes, and rightly so."

Emma folded the foil candy wrappers into neat, tiny squares and placed them on the nightstand. "Rainey has her back pressed up against the wall right now, no mistake, but she's found good reason in her heart to trust ye, laddie. And ye can count on one hand the number of people in the world she trusts. She must be told. If she adjusts herself to the idea now, things will go a lot smoother. Spring it on her later, and we may well suffer for it. Take it from me, ye don't have the capacity to let her down, my boy."

He stood up and walked back to the window. "You have a lot more faith in me than I do, Emma," he said. "I have a history of failing those I love."

"Och, listen here, ye wee scamp, I for one won't tolerate another word from ye about failure," Emma said with an edge of anger. "I know the particulars of how ye came by that scar on yer cheek. And I know ye still harbor far more guilt than a man's entitled to over such a thing.

He wiped the patterns from the windowpane. "You weren't there. No one else was there. One minute, they were both alive. A few minutes later, their lives were over. No gentle journey into old age, no passionate words of farewell. Only cold and brutal death. I watched it happen like someone trapped in a dream. I never really woke up from that horrible dream. I'm still walking in the middle of it, Emma. I go through the day like anyone else, but I find myself shiverin' for no reason sometimes, you know, even in the summer. It's because I'm still there, floatin' helpless in those cold waters."

"Ye've been entrusted with a new task, laddie, a way to make a fresh start for yerself," Emma said kindly. "Whether ye volunteered for the duty or it was thrust upon ye, ye got to see it through. Ye know full well how many are dependin' on ye. And as to all that information Sasha knows about the old times, I suspect she'll always have it in that precious heart of hers. She'll share it with ye one day, have no fear, because she knows she can trust it to yer keepin'. Just like I know I can trust Rainey to yer keepin'. There's more than enough doubt floatin' around out there already, Macinnes. I'll hear no more of it from you. It ain't befittin'. And if ye don't make Rainey yer own out of all of this, I'll hang ye by yer heels with my own two hands, because the poor lass is wearin' her heart on the same sleeve as yerself, if ye haven't bothered to notice."

He knelt down in front of Emma and took her hand in his. "Did anyone ever tell you you're one hell of a fighter, Emma Ferguson?"

She blushed at his flattery. "Och, aye, mostly my

wee brother Edmond, right after he'd go for my throat. I taught him a thing or two when we were young. And the day he tried to chop down my fairy tree with his new carvin' knife, I took off a piece of his ear."

"*Dia gar teàrnadh!*" Matt exclaimed in mock terror.

"Aye, lad, may God have mercy on ye indeed if ye make the mistake of gettin' on me wrong side." She tidied his hair with maternal concern.

Chapter 13

"Christmas fairies," Rainey muttered to herself. She stared at the menu of local Scottish dishes without seeing it.

"What's all this about fairies, then, Harvard?" Matt asked. He exchanged a quick glance with Emma as he drew the menu from Rainey's hands to turn it right side up. Rainey gave him a mildly perturbed look.

Emma had insisted they visit Ubiquitous Chips, a long-established favorite of Glaswegians, for their first meal on native soil, and even the relaxed, covered courtyard atmosphere did little to improve Rainey's concentration.

"Fairies, Rainey," he reiterated. "You were sayin' somethin' about fairies. Have you got one whisperin' mischief in your ear, by chance?"

"Hardly. It's just that Emma mentioned Scotland had Christmas fairies instead of elves. I just found it to be an interesting variation on the old theme."

Matt gave her a grin as he cleaned his glasses with his napkin. "Ah, now there's that stiff Boston clip I'm ever so fond of. Give it both barrels, lass."

Rainey slowly sipped her water. "I only meant I'd like to learn more about fairies someday. They seem to be very important to Scottish mythology."

He settled his glasses back onto the bridge of his

nose. "Mythology. Aye, they are important indeed. But in point of fact, Scots tend to brush over Christmas a bit because it's considered more a Papist holiday, an unpopular notion since the crush of the rebellions in the 1700s."

"So Scottish people don't like Christmas?"

Emma set her menu down. "Not so, love. A Scot businessman knows an opportunity for increased profits when he sees one. We just don't go mad for it like they do in the States. Hogmanay is the favorite holiday this time of year."

"Hog which?"

"Hogmanay," Matt provided. "It's said the word comes from the French expression *'au geux menez,'* which means bring gifts to beggars. Most people celebrate it on the thirty-first of December, but the purists hold to the eleventh of January in keepin' with the ancient calendar. It's one of those celebrations left over from the time of the holy oaks."

"A fire ceremony, I suppose."

"Aye, to be sure."

He arched one eyebrow at her in what Rainey interpreted as a challenge.

Emma cleared her throat. "So we're to take it you're no so much for Christmas, then, Matt?" she proposed. She pressed her lips together to let him know he better give his answer some careful thought.

Matt leaned forward and picked up a spoon for closer examination. "On the contrary, dear lady, I'm one of its biggest fans. My mother kept Christmas in a grand way, and I feel her presence very strongly this time of year." He was lost in thought for a moment, then his eyes rose to Rainey. "Besides which, any holiday that propounds peace on earth and goodwill to men is more than worthy of support."

"Gnothach miadhail," Emma said reverently.

Matt's eyes were still intent on Rainey. "Aye, Emma, a most precious thing."

Rainey tried to resume her study of the menu. But images of the four-poster bed waiting for her at the hotel kept coming to mind. The visions had Matt Macinnes waiting for her there with the covers turned back. Those bedroom images were getting to her, and she gave a little shiver.

"I hope you're not takin' a chill, Rainey," Matt said as he motioned to the waiter. "Perhaps I should call the hotel and have them put the warmin' stones between the sheets a bit early."

Emma cleared her throat to the point of pain in maternal warning.

"No, I'm fine," Rainey said quickly. Did nothing escape his attention?

"Still and all, a healthy dose of feather fowlie and stovies will put you to rights," he contended. "That and a cup of tea."

"I don't know about feather fowlie," she said as she looked over the menu. "Don't they have something simple, like chicken soup?" Everyone else at the table laughed, and she felt the color rise in her cheeks.

Emma took pity on her. "Feather fowlie *is* chicken soup, love," she explained.

"Oh, well I guess I'll try some, then." Rainey closed her menu for fear she would inadvertently order squid with a side of snails.

Emma raised her water glass in a salute, with Sasha and Matt following suit. "To Rainey, a true Scot," she declared. "*Ceud mile fàilte!* A hundred thousand welcomes!"

Rainey raised her glass in an answering salute. "And to feather fowlie—I hope it tastes like chicken!" She gave them all a slow smile.

"To feather fowlie," Matt and Emma chimed in.

Stovies turned out to be potatoes cooked with onions. To this, Emma added Loch Fyne toasts with kippers, while Rainey and Sasha settled on the more familiar fish and chips. Matt satisfied his craving for Aberdeen beef with a hefty steak, claiming he had had more than his fill of "California Cuisine" in the last few years. And they all finished off with sweet scones and marmalade. No one went away hungry.

They spent the afternoon wandering through the shopping areas of the Merchant City, perusing all the sophisticated shops without buying anything. But then, at Emma's insistence, they took the long walk down Sauchiehall Street to a shop that specialized in authentic Highland knits and tweeds, in search of a memento for Robbie back home. The shop smelled of fine wools and candle wax, and the shelves were piled high with exquisite sweaters, tartan shawls, jackets, and scarves, each more beautiful than the last. But Emma had no problem choosing a neck scarf done in the traditional Ferguson tartan. And for Angus, she selected a Ferguson plaid coat with brass buckles, tailor-made for a dapper Scottie.

Matt watched with a pang of regret as Rainey ran her hand over the soft wool of a beautifully crafted tartan shawl. The dark blues and forest-greens of the rich piece suited her. It could easily have been made for her, and the temptation to walk up and wrap it around her shoulders was a strong one. Never mind that out of this entire mad collage of color she had inadvertently latched on to the Macinnes clan tartan.

He could tell how much she wanted it. And he wanted it for her. But pride was a formidable adversary—almost as daunting as the ever-present ghost of a loving husband. It was irrational, he knew, but he found himself burning with jealousy toward Alan. He had seen the handsome family photo on the mantel and the birthday video of Sasha and her father more than once. He had also seen the covert flirtation going on between Rainey and Alan as she ran the video camera. And that first night out on the back porch, Rainey had made it very clear how much she remained devoted to her husband's memory. Their relationship had been a genuine one. There was no mistaking the love that little family had shared.

If Alan were simply another man, he would find a way to compete, Matt assured himself. It nagged at his conscience that, had he met her under other circumstances, he most probably would have tried to steal Rainey away from Alan, even if they were already married. Just how far he would have gotten, he would never know. The question remained, could he compete against Alan's memory?

There was something to be said, he decided, for the ancient notion of stealing a wife and making her your own out among the heather before she had a chance to protest. Of course, not only was that politically incorrect and a shameless travesty of a woman's rights, it had been known to lead to castration in the dead of night.

No wonder men went to war. It was a far simpler proposition.

Still, he was anxious to get her to the Highlands. It was where he pictured her in the dreams that kept him tossing and tearing at the sheets all night. It was where they were both meant to be with Sasha. He was so convinced of it, it had become a religion in his heart.

He walked over to Rainey. She was so engrossed in the marvelous texture of the shawl's weave, she didn't sense him behind her.

"It costs nothing to try it on, Harvard," he said.

She started, and when she turned, she was so close, it was only natural to enclose her in his arms. The shawl fell to the ground as he looked down into her dark blue eyes. He rejoiced that she didn't pull away from him.

"It's used goods now," he said with a smile as he inclined his head toward the floor. "I'll have to buy it for you, *mo chridhe*." The way she looked at him made him want to kneel at her feet. "Besides which, we make for the Highlands tomorrow. You and Sasha will be in need of proper wraps and decent pairs of boots, as well. The snows are comin', and there'll be hazards enough without neglectin' the things we can control."

Control. The word cut through the pleasant fog in Rainey's head, and she stepped back out of Matt's arms. She was dangerously close to losing her perspective, and her resistance to him was definitely running low. Sasha and Emma were both smiling at her knowingly.

"We have to take care of business," she said, more to herself than to him. "I can't get it out of my mind, what's waiting for us when we go home. I'm sorry. I don't mean to rain on anybody's parade. This place is wonderful, really. And the shawl? Well, it's about the most amazing thing I've ever seen. But I have the sweaters Emma loaned me. They'll be warm. And I'm sure there must be a drugstore or a hardware store where they sell inexpensive rubber boots. There's no point investing all of our travel budget on things we'll only need for a few days."

Matt picked up the fallen shawl and held it lightly in his hands. "Those few days are the reason we're here, love. The crown must still be won, and it waits far to the north of here where there are no drugstores, no hardware stores. Conditions will be harsh. We have to be properly prepared."

Rainey looked at the shawl with longing. It was as if it had always been hers, as if it could protect her from far more than the chill of the mists. He was right, she and Sasha were ill-prepared for the rigors of the Highlands, and she had to do something about it before they left the city.

Matt wrapped the shawl around her shoulders. "Merry Christmas," he said kindly.

She ran her hand lovingly over the soft wool. "But I don't have anything for you in return."

"Seeing it on you is gift enough, *mo chridhe*."

If she accepted it now, Matt told himself, he could be satisfied that he had made some small progress with her. If she refused it, remained stubborn in her total independence, he would have to chalk it up as another small failure.

Rainey draped one end of the shawl over her shoulder as if she had been doing it all her life and gave him a reserved smile. "Thank you, Matt," she said. "It's very thoughtful of you. I know it will come in very handy."

Triumph. The temptation to jump for joy was nearly overpowering, but Matt did his best to contain his jubilation. He caught Emma's eye, and she gave him a subtle thumbs-up sign.

"Now," he said rather breathlessly, "we must find you and Sasha some sturdy boots and more cold-weather attire." He took the price tag from her shawl to the cashier.

Emma admired the fine wool of Rainey's new shawl. "It's ever so fetchin' on ye, Rainey," she said for Matt's benefit. Then, more softly, she added, "He's gettin' to ye, isn't he, lass?"

Rainey glanced at Matt. He and Sasha were sorting through a stack of blue cable-knit sweaters in Sasha's size, and she could hear portions of his fluent Gaelic. No doubt he was telling her glorious stories about fairies and the dangerous beauty of the Highlands.

"He's getting to us all, Emma," Rainey said with a sigh. "He's going home. He said as much. He's going to a sanctuary where he feels safe, a place that belongs to him. Our home is in California. And by now, it's probably overrun with government officials and Evanston's goons. You're our friend, so your place will be off-limits now, too. Don't you see, Emma, Sasha and I no longer have a home. Whatever happens, after the Solstice we have nowhere to go. Matt can't answer all our problems for us. Sasha and I have to answer them for ourselves."

Emma squeezed her hand. "Ah, love, I wish I had solutions. All I can say is, I'll always be there for ye, whether it's this side of the pond or the other. We'll work somethin' out. I promise ye."

Rainey gave her a heartfelt hug. "You're one amazing lady, Emma Ferguson. I hope you realize how much Sasha and I need you and love you."

Emma patted her arm. "Posh, lassie, we're a team, 'tis all, you, Sasha, and me. The Three Musketeers." She cast a look at Matt, and he turned to flash a grin at the pair of them. "And D'Artagnon as well, o' course," Emma was quick to add.

Rainey caressed the lovely shawl around her shoulders. "Since you're the expert, wasn't D'Artagnon the one who almost got them all killed because of his reckless impetuousness?"

"Was he the one?" Emma asked, her face a picture of innocence. "Och, no, I dunna think so. Anyway, I know things will be fine when all of this is over." She hurried off toward the cashier, her own purchases in hand.

Sasha smiled up into Matt's eyes, and Rainey felt a fresh tug at her heart. How lucky Matt was to be going home. At the moment, the notion seemed like a luxury beyond price to Rainey.

By the time they returned to the hotel, everyone was ready to relax. Sasha curled up on her warm bed and fell asleep instantly. The dark mists danced against the windows, making the fire's glow all the more welcome, but Rainey seemed reluctant to take off her new shawl.

Emma settled herself into an overstuffed chair and gave Rainey and Matt a doting look as the pair of them stood in the center of the room.

"Be off with ye, then," she said with a dismissive wave of her hand. "Tip a pint for me, ye wee treasures, whilst I mind the fort."

Rainey gave her a scolding look. Matt gave her one of quiet thanks.

"We really should discuss our plans for the next few days, Harvard," he said in all seriousness. "And it might be wisest to talk while Sasha rests."

"I suppose," Rainey conceded. Sasha was sleeping so deeply, the teddy bear Matt had given her clutched beside her, that it was doubtful she would wake up anytime soon. And Rainey's curiosity wouldn't allow her to pass up a chance to find out what Matt's big plan was. After all, he was proposing they borrow the crown out from under some clan chieftain's nose. No, she had to face it, he had said they were going to have to steal it. His plan better be mighty good. The last thing Sasha needed was to have her mother doing time for robbery in some dank Scottish dungeon.

Matt got the phone number of the place they would be from the phone book, and Emma gave their destination the nod.

"Not to worriet," she said as she patted the chair's cushions into a more comfortable shape. "You're only a phone call away, and little Sasha and I have the charms around our necks to lend us protection." She touched the arrowhead beneath her sweater and regarded them with a mischievous twinkle in her eye. "It's to be hoped the two of ye have protection of yer own."

Rainey blushed from head to toe at Emma's provocative double meaning.

"Now, don't ye be lookin' at me like I'm the one who's taken to speakin' in tongues, lassie," Emma insisted. "I'm a cosmopolitan woman of the world these days, a California surfer girl if ever there was one, ye ken? I'm verra up-to-date."

"We'll have a little talk about this later," Rainey said. She raised one eyebrow tentatively at Matt, and he bowed toward the door. "We won't be long, Emma, I promise. Don't hesitate to call if you need anything, or if Sasha wakes up and needs me."

Emma shooed them off. "Go. Have fun while yer still young. And yers truly will have to settle for givin' a lesson or two to that muscle-bound room service laddie I saw in the hall." She tidied her hair with great ceremony.

Matt gave her a thumbs-up. "Do your worst to the poor fella, Emma. Who knows? You might even persuade him to try the straight life."

Emma gave him a look of surprise. "Straight life? Yer jokin'. That lovely hunk of male?"

He held the door for Rainey, and as he followed her out, he called to Emma, "Have a grand evening, Gidget. Hasty back."

Emma kicked off her shoes. "Hmmph. Gidget, indeed! Such cheek in the face of his elders." But she smiled to herself as she watched the fire play on the hearth. And as the time slipped by, she saw images of her own young love dancing among the flames. All thoughts of room service gave way to sweet memories of her own heroic Scot.

Chapter 14

Fatigue stung Rainey's eyes as she looked over the evening's specials on a blackboard above their cozy booth at the Drum and Monkey. She had thought she would never be hungry again after so huge a lunch, but the delicious aromas from the kitchen along with the notion of potato leek soup served with roasted salmon struck a strong chord. The rich old wood-paneled walls and brass fixtures gave the pub a warm, welcoming atmosphere, and she felt very much at home. The only thing that made her a bit uncomfortable was the way Matt kept studying her as if she were the object of some volatile scientific experiment.

"I suppose it's the Scottish air that's given me such an appetite," she said to make conversation. Matt gave her another of those unsettling looks.

"Aye, most certainly the air. That and the fact you've been in an emotional whirlwind for the past three years."

She folded her shawl neatly beside her. "It's not really something you get used to, I guess."

He sighed from the depths of his soul. "You know, Rainey, I'm fluent in a dozen languages. I know a million and two wise sayings and proverbs from the world over. I should be able to speak my mind to you with perfect accuracy, you understand. But when it comes to sayin' the things I want to communicate to you, even the simplest things, it all fails me." He ran his finger over a double set of initials carved into the wall beside him. Countless coats of varnish had dulled them, but they still remained as testimony to a couple's commitment to one another decades ago.

Rainey felt the familiar warmth rise in her cheeks. They were wandering onto dangerous ground. She knew his not being able to speak his mind wasn't intended as a complaint. He was opening doors between them, doors she wasn't sure she was ready to open.

It might have been easier if he hadn't been wearing the sweater that needed mending. And even though she had seen him run his hand through his hair to smooth it before they came in, the russet length of it was in disarray from the mists outside. She found herself wanting to tame it for him, and the thought of touching him with such intimacy wrapped a velvet glove around her heart. Even conjuring up Alan's handsome face failed to loosen its hold. Worse still, she found it difficult to remember the little things about Alan that had always made him so dear. She had counted on his memory as a shield for so long. Now, with a few humble words, Matt had reduced her defenses to tatters.

"Tell me about your family, Rainey. Are you close?"

The question took her by surprise, and the image of her father's smile flashed into her mind. With it came a strong sense of things left unsaid and unfinished. This wasn't her favorite subject. "My father died years ago."

Matt sensed her hesitancy, but he was compelled to pursue the subject.

"If I may be so bold, how did your father leave this world?"

"He had heart trouble. He was under a lot of stress at his job, the overachieving type. It was all quite sudden. One Sunday, he decided it was time to clean the gutters on our house. He should have hired someone to do it, but once William Grant took a notion, there was no stopping him. His heart gave out and he fell to his death." She shifted uncomfortably. "I've had this thing about heights ever since."

"Your fear of heights began with your father's death? It wasn't present before that?"

"No, not that I remember." She gave a small shiver at the memory of how difficult it had been to say good-bye to her father.

"And what of your mother?"

"My mother is very old school. She lived for my father. How she acted, what she wore, everything she did was with him in mind. I warned her she should develop some outside interests, a hobby or a bridge club. But she wouldn't listen.

"When my father died, in a way, she died, too. Most of the time, it's like she's living somewhere else in her mind. She withdraws. There are medications she takes for the depression, but nothing seems to do much good. I helped the best I could for the first years. But then I had troubles of my own."

Matt nodded solemnly. "The loss of your husband. He must have been an exceptional man to deserve two such miraculous women in his life. I'm certain you must still feel his loss very deeply."

"Alan and I understood each other." Rainey toyed with the salt shaker, unprepared to look Matt in the eye just then. "We both knew what we wanted out of life and how we were going to accomplish it together. Everything was straightforward. Things were simpler. And of course we had Sasha. He worshipped her. He spent every free moment with her, playing with her, telling her bedtime stories, and tak-

ing her for long walks when I had deadlines to meet
for the agency. He was sensitive, caring, and support-
ive. He was a godsend in so many ways. And even
when his career started to demand more and more
of his time . . . even when it started to feel like he
was slipping away from us sometimes . . ." She
blinked her stubborn tears away and made a study
of her silverware.

"I know it sounds ridiculous," she said, "but I
can't help feeling that Alan let us down. Our lives
were clearly mapped out. The future was secure. And
in a split second, that stability was gone forever.
When I'm thinking rationally, I know I can't blame
him. It makes no sense. But when I see what his
going on that one damn business flight has done to
Sasha . . ."

"It's only natural to feel as you do, Rainey," Matt
said kindly. "It helps to have someone to blame, even
if it's unfair to do so. But you are not your mother.
You have so much strength, love, so much determination. You will always have what it takes to move
on with your life. And Sasha has every bit of her
mother's substance. The two of you are so much the
same, a formidable pair, two grand ladies of extraordinary courage."

In his heart, Matt felt a tiny flicker of hope burst
into flame. Never once had she used the word love
in connection with Alan. Understanding, stability,
goals—with these memories he could do battle. He
didn't doubt for a moment that she had held a kind
of love for the man. He was the one she had thought
to spend her whole life with, and he was the father
of her only child. But love, heart and soul, was quite
a different matter. There was hope.

Rainey looked at him with genuine interest. "Do
you ever wonder why you make the decisions you
do? I mean, you decided to stay unmarried. You de-

cided to come to America. What do you suppose inspired you to do those things? And if you say the fairies made you do it, I'm going to walk out of here right now."

He gave it some careful thought. "I'd like to boast that it was all part of some grand design I'd set for my life, a blueprint for success as you might call it," he said in all seriousness. Then he gave her half a smile. "But the fact of the matter is, I follow my own whims. However the mood strikes me, that's the letter and number of my day."

"Right. You are a very tall child, Matt Macinnes. So what am I doing hanging around with you?"

"Solving a mystery and having a bit of an adventure, as it happens. Totally out of character for you, wouldn't you say?"

"Totally. But since you brought it up, just what exactly is the plan?"

"The plan?"

"The plan to get Sasha's crown. Work with me here, Macinnes, because if what you have in mind is a danger to any of us, including yourself, you'll have to come up with some other way to resolve the problem about the waterfall."

Yet another look. *"An eas roceach,"* he said softly.

She didn't know what that meant, but it sounded very much like a line from a love song. It made her think of that first night on the back porch at home when he had pointed to the moon and asked her what she saw. She wasn't sure what she would see if she looked at that same moon right now. Certainly more than she had seen then.

"Like I said, just exactly what is the plan?" She leaned forward and rested her chin on her hand.

He studied his ale. "There is no plan, per se."

"No plan?" she demanded.

Fortunately, a local fiddle band struck up a rousing

jig next to the bar, so only a few heads turned at her anger.

Matt raised his hands to quiet her. "I'm sayin' we'll have to play it by ear, Rainey. We'll have to follow our instincts."

"So you don't have the vaguest idea how we're going to pull this off." She picked up her purse and shawl and started to slide out of the booth. "We'll find a plan of our own."

He grabbed her arm. "Sit down, Rainey. Please, hear me out. It's goin' to work."

She sat down reluctantly on the edge of the seat. "What is, some fairy-tale happy ending you've just remembered?"

"This fairy tale has yet to find its happy ending, love. We just make it come to pass. But justice is on our side."

"Justice? You're in the wrong century, Macinnes. How are we supposed to pull this off? None of us has ever stolen anything. Alarms, security systems, we don't know the first thing about how to get past obstacles like that. We'll all end up in jail. And I for one can't bail us out."

A waiter approached their table, and Matt squeezed her arm gently.

"Order somethin', Rainey. Do me that favor."

She gave the waiter a dark look. "Soup."

"The same, and fresh ale." Matt held up two fingers to indicate ale for them both, and the waiter left.

"You must understand," he implored her, "this pipeline to the past we have is absolutely real. Sasha will lead us where we must go."

Rainey twisted her napkin. "At what cost, her life? I won't put her in jeopardy. If something goes wrong, aside from all the other risks, I might lose her forever. I can't live with that possibility."

Matt laid his hand over hers, his mood very

earnest. "Sasha's in jeopardy every minute we don't resolve this. The Solstice is almost upon us, and to wait . . . She must go to the falls with the crown in her possession. Sirona's mission and Sasha's future have become one. At the falls, they will come together. It's the only way Sasha will know any peace."

"It's all so dangerous. There must be another way."

"The danger to her physical and emotional well-being as things stand is very real, love. You've seen the evidence of it more than once. To say she will die trying to complete her mission without our help is no exaggeration. With our help, there is a strong chance of success. Her time has come, and no amount of delay or denial will deter her in her cause. There are so many doors leading her to the old time now, so many triggers. She can never go back to the way she was, even a year ago. She can only go forward."

To her sorrow, everything he said rang true in Rainey's heart. She tucked her hair behind her ear and looked him straight in the eye.

"I've said this before, but I've never meant it more than I do at this moment. Sasha is all I've got. Can you understand that? There is nothing left for me anywhere in the world but right here. I can't go back any more than Sasha can. Prove to me it's all worth the gamble."

Matt leaned closer so she alone would hear his words. "I've no wish to be cruel, but if we don't try this, Rainey, how long will it be before Sasha plunges from the highest branch of a tree? How long before she breaks away from you one afternoon and perches herself on top of the tallest skyscraper in town? How long before she sneaks herself aboard a Greyhound bus headed for the falls at Yosemite, or better yet, Niagara? How long before the government authorities take her from you permanently—ten minutes after you return to the States? An unemployed single mother with an emotionally disturbed child, a child who displays antisocial and often schizophrenic behavior in public—it's pure candy for dull-witted social workers.

"And what about Evanston? From what you've told me, he's got the machinery in place to grab her from you on sight."

"I won't let that happen." Rainey's voice broke with emotion. "We'll move again. I'll find another job."

Matt enclosed her hand between his own. "What, you'll bleach her lovely hair and your own and teach her to wear colored contacts to hide her looks and every essence of who she truly is? And by and by, you'll still have to get her to speak English, or someone will blow the whistle on you."

Rainey tried to pull her hand away, but Matt kept a firm hold. "It's too late to run, *mo chridhe*. If you move a hundred times, it will be of no help to Sasha. And it would destroy the pair of you. You can't treat her symptoms on your own any longer. We must find the cure together.

"Whatever you decide to do, Rainey, I'll support you, whether it's here on Scottish soil or stateside. I'm in this for the duration if you'll let me stay after all I've said. You know only too well where I stand on the matter, and needless to say, Sasha has very strong opinions about it. But in the end, it's you, love, who will say whether or not we go to the falls."

Rainey struggled with the decision. For a hundred different reasons, she didn't want to make it at all. "And you promise me you can get us all there and back alive?" she asked cautiously.

Matt raised his right hand, but kept his hold on her hand with his left. "I promise to protect everyone's safety as long as there is breath in my body," he vowed.

"Brave words, Stanford, but it doesn't answer my question."

He brought his hand beck to hers. "It's an ambitious climb when the weather is fine, Rainey. In the dead of winter, it will be a very real challenge. I can't guarantee what fate has in store for us. There are hazards I can't anticipate. But I'll do everything in my power to keep you all safe from harm. It's the best I can do."

"The best you can do. I can't ask for anything more," Rainey concluded. "I'll probably regret this for the rest of my life, but we have to try it."

"*Glè mhath!* Excellent, *mo chridhe!*" he said in a jubilant whisper. "Nothing can stand in our way now."

Rainey gave him half a smile. "I'm glad one of us is so sure."

The soup arrived. Matt let go of her hand, and it felt to Rainey as if her only lifeline had been cut. Here was the harsh reality of their goal. No more running. She had to accept that the crown was their only hope. It went against everything in her nature to leap into all of this without a set agenda.

As she stirred her soup, the rising steam made her think of the mists of a waterfall. There was a roaring in her ears, and her heart began to pound almost to the point of pain. She was stressed, she told herself. It was her blood pressure, or a bus must have gone by outside. But the fact was, she felt a strong yearning to go north, not just for Sasha, but for herself. It was wrong that she wasn't there now, this very instant.

"This is all very difficult for me," she said.

"A jewel of understatement," Matt replied with a world-weary smile. "I wish I could lay it all out for you in neat rows, love. But it's simply not the nature of the thing. It's goin' to require all our wits and a healthy dose of faith."

"There's that word again," Rainey said softly.

"Aye, *creideamh*, it's a fine one, that. It can also be defined as somethin' you choose to believe in." He savored a spoonful of his soup. "Eat up, now. You're goin' to need your strength."

She looked across at him. Something in the way he had said she would need her strength made her wonder if he was saying more to her than it appeared on the surface.

"What do you know about this man, this chieftain who has possession of the crown?" she asked.

"He was a neighbor when I was a lad."

"A neighbor? Why didn't you say so before?"

"In point of fact, I've never met the man." He pushed her ale closer to her hand in an encouraging way. "The Highlands are vast. He wasn't far away by local standards, mind, bein' only a two-kilometer hike. But my parents forbade me to go anywhere near the place, seein' it was the haunted castle of the neighborhood. So, I tended to give it a wide berth when I had my senses about me."

Rainey looked up from her soup. "And when you didn't have your senses about you?"

He gave her a wink. "Let's just say I was never adverse to gettin' to know the lay of the land. And as a youth, I was possessed of far more curiosity than sense."

"But I thought your parents' work for the university kept you all in town."

"I see I'm not the only one doin' research these days." His smile faded when he realized how much of his history she might actually know. "We all went north to the Highlands for the summer in the early days. It was our real home. Of course, in later years, expeditions for the university took us all to the islands much of the time. In a way, my parents seemed to grow cool toward the Highlands. We saw very little of home in the end, more's the pity." He rubbed the scar on his cheek, then caught himself doing so and folded his hands in front of him.

"But in my younger years, I prowled the heather like one of Rob Roy's own, and the legend that's grown so close to all our hearts was as basic to my daily life as bread and milk. That and a hundred other tales my parents recited from their own youth filled the cool summer evenings with a magic and wonderment you don't find anywhere but in the Highlands."

Rainey dipped a corner of freshly baked potato bread into her soup. "So what happened to your parents' home? I mean, you teach in the States now." She wondered for the first time if he planned to stay on in America. He was so obviously enamored of the Highlands, why had he chosen to leave them so far behind?

"Everything is still as it was, to the best of my knowledge. We'll stay there the night tomorrow."

"Are you all right with that?"

He gave her a look full of mischief. "Are you? As I've told you, the nearest neighbor is a hefty walk away, and he's most likely going to try to do us damage before we're done. I've asked you before, and I'll ask you again, are you game for it, Harvard? Because from here on, there's no turnin' back."

"I—"

"Mrs. Nielson?"

Rainey turned with a start when the young waiter touched her shoulder.

"I'm Lorraine Nielson."

"A call for you, missus." The waiter handed her a telephone and went on about his business.

With a worried glance at Matt, Rainey pressed the receiver to her ear. Clearly, the news was not good.

"We're on our way, Emma. Tell her we're coming. It's not your fault. See if Gaelic helps. We'll be right there." She slammed down the receiver and grabbed her things. "Come on, Macinnes!" she called over her shoulder. "Sasha's on the balcony railing, and Emma can't get her to come in."

"To it, lass!" he said as he raced after her. "The time is too near. We never should have left."

When they arrived at the hotel, an icy wind was whipping through the room from the balcony. They found Emma outside, shivering from the cold. But she refused to let go of the tail of Sasha's shirt. Sasha had removed a group of flowerpots from a corner of the balcony railing and seated herself there cross-legged, two stories above the street. Her eyes were locked on the rolling mists overhead.

Emma's face was filled with worry. "Can ye ever forgive me for fallin' asleep that way, Rainey? She was dreamin' soundly. I'd swear to it. And the next thing I know, I wake to find the curtains blowin' and the wee lassie gone entirely. My heart will never be the same."

"It's all right, Emma. We should have seen it coming. It's too near the Solstice." She looked to Matt. "Tell me what to say."

"Tell her to come in, love, *thig a-steach.*"

Rainey walked up behind Sasha. *"Thig a-steach,"* she said softly. It felt absolutely natural to ask Sasha to come inside in Gaelic.

Matt wrapped his jacket around Emma's shoulders. "Our Rainey has a way with the words, does she no, Mrs. Ferguson?"

Emma gave him a sideward glance. "Aye, that she does. And with a marked Highland accent like Sasha, did ye notice?"

"True enough. No one would ever mistake the pair of them for Glaswegians, I expect." He went out onto the balcony and took Rainey's hand.

Rainey felt the weight lift from her as Matt reeled off an impressive speech to Sasha. The sound of his voice gave her comfort.

Sasha turned to them, her expression still distant. Her face was bravely set and angelic in the pale light as she accepted Matt's hand and slid to safety on the balcony.

Something had changed. There was nothing of Sasha the child about her demeanor any longer. She was cool and strong. The soul of a woman shone through her dark blue eyes. And when Matt asked her if she would like a cup of hot chocolate to dispel the chill, she merely regarded him without emotion and walked back to her bed. She withdrew the silver brooch from its pouch around her neck, and with the tip of her finger, traced and retraced the complex maze of knots and curves reverently.

Rainey pulled the balcony doors shut with relief, then sat down next to Sasha. Perhaps Sasha had heard that same roaring noise she had experienced in the pub. Or perhaps she no longer needed triggers to hear the summoning of the falls. Maybe it rang in her ears all the time.

The brooch was mesmerizing in its complex beauty, and to Rainey's surprise, Sasha handed it to her. It was warm to the touch, and it felt very right in her palm. Without thinking, Rainey started to trace the lines as she had seen Sasha do. It gave her a peaceful feeling, and at the same time, a restless sense of anticipation. She would swear she could feel some kind of power flowing from the silver. The word magic came to mind. Reluctantly, she gave it back to Sasha. Sasha smiled up into her eyes with knowing grace.

Matt banked the fire on the hearth. "It's a kind of road map," he provided. "The brooch there. It's a road map to paradise. It was discovered near the falls by my mother's great-great-great-grandmother. Tradition has it it must be passed on solely to female members of the family. And since the family is sadly lacking in females at the moment, it's best it be entrusted to Sasha."

Rainey watched as Sasha continued her tracing journey with utter familiarity. Was it simply a traditional pattern?

"It has a very strong Scandinavian influence, of course," Matt continued, "so we're lookin' in the vicinity of a thousand years ago, most likely."

Emma clucked her tongue. "A thousand years, just think of it."

"I'm not sure I can," Rainey said as she looked down at the brooch with new respect. Its edges were well worn, but the silver and the design were as pure and true as the day it had been made so very long ago.

"The way my mother told it," Matt explained, "if you are pure of heart and follow the curves in the proper fashion, you'll find the road to heaven." He turned toward the three of them. "It's hard to say if it's a useful tool when you're adrift on a hostile sea. Perhaps if my mother had remembered to take it with her that day, her journey to paradise might have been a smoother one."

"They've found peace," Rainey said softly. In her heart, she knew it to be true. The question was, what would it take for Matt to find peace of his own?

Rainey looked into the eyes of each person in turn. Everyone was exhausted. But no one was ready to sleep. The lovely four-poster bed stood warm and waiting for her, but she knew she would do nothing but fight the soft sheets. It would be an inexcusable waste of precious hours. She turned to Matt.

"Do you know the way to the Highlands in the dark?" she asked.

"It's the road home, love. I'm not likely to forget it."

Rainey's eyes misted. "Then take us there, Matt. We're running out of time."

Chapter 15

"Behold the Three Sisters, ladies," Matt announced from the driver's seat of their snug rental car.

The sun couldn't shoulder its way through the heavy rolling mists of dawn, and as gray light rose over the barren, snow-dusted peaks of the Three Sisters of Glen Coe, it might have been a hundred years ago, or a thousand. For that matter, the massive buttresses of black stone could have been war-hardened sentries from another world, stoic soldiers sworn fast to their watch. Only the narrow curves of the West Highland Highway gave a clue to the century, and this thin evidence was easily overshadowed by the heart-stopping impact of the glen.

Rainey couldn't take her eyes off the forbidding slopes. They seemed to bear down on the car, despite their haunting beauty.

"This is where the massacre took place," she said reverently.

"Aye, it is," Matt confirmed.

He and Emma had given her a history lesson as they traveled from Glasgow, and now this very real reminder of how forty members of the Jacobite Clan Macdonald had been murdered in 1692 by their "guests," the pro-English Campbells, sent a hard shiver down Rainey's back. Somewhere inside, she could hear the three-hundred-year-old cries of battle and betrayal from that monstrous day.

This time, the seating arrangements had landed Rainey next to Matt, and she watched for signs of fatigue from him as he drove. So far, his stamina was boundless.

She was pleased with herself, too, because the journey north had done nothing but fortify her with fresh energy. History had never been her best subject in school, but even as the miles flew by in the dark, she could feel the tales of each glen and loch take up permanent residence in her heart. She vowed to see them all in the daylight on the way back.

The way back. What would have happened to them all by then, she wondered? Sasha hadn't so much as whispered a word since the incident on the balcony. It was possible that there would be no more middle ground of communication with her from here on in.

"Didn't you once say there were five sisters rather than three, Matt?" she asked, to get her mind on other things.

"You've a sterling memory, Harvard," he said. "The five lie to the north."

"Kintail, Glen Shiel," Emma provided. "We're a goodly portion of the way there." She rolled down her window to breathe in the heady, crisp scent of Highland mist and heather, then leaned toward the front seat. "Is there any hope of such a thing as a scone and a cup of tea on this grand safari, Macinnes? No so much for myself, ye ken."

"I understand your sentiments well, dear lady," Matt replied. "We're not far out of Fort William, and I know of a little spot where we can catch our breath."

The "little spot" he had in mind turned out to be the imposing Castle Inverlochy, which looked out over its own private loch. The waters were a restless, gunmetal gray, like the skies, and the flag above the castle's tallest turret snapped in the rising wind. The luxurious country house hotel provided such a lavish breakfast of hearty Scottish favorites that by the end of the meal, they were all rejuvenated and ready to face the day.

Rainey had cringed at the absence of prices on the menu. But, as it happened, she never had a chance to reach for her purse to pay. The waiter explained their tab had already been taken care of by an elderly gentleman and his lovely blond companion seated at the far side of the room. Matt nodded his thanks to their benefactors formally, then rose from the table.

"Don't hurry your tea, ladies," he said, his attention focused across the room. "It seems I have a social obligation."

They all watched him shake hands and sit down with the two at the other table. The woman, though outwardly polite, had an air of cold disdain, even at a distance. She was dressed in powder blue, which emphasized the extraordinary paleness of her hair and complexion.

"What do you make of it, Emma?" Rainey asked quietly.

Emma pulled her glasses from her purse, and as she pretended to study the lunch menu, she in fact studied the pair at the other table.

"Blue bloods, if ye want my own personal opinion," she said with distaste.

"You mean royalty? I've never seen either of those two in the tabloids." Rainey stirred her tea vigorously, even though there had been nothing added to it.

Emma squinted over the top of the menu. "The attitude, love. Ye can smell it a mile away. Bred to privilege, the both of 'em. Not our kind of folk."

Rainey tried not to stare openly. "So how do you suppose Matt knows them?"

"Through his parents' connections, most like. We're no that far from where he spent his summers. Mayhap they're locals. Or maybe the old man thought we three lassies so bonnie, he was fair overcome with generosity." She folded her arms across her chest and sat back with satisfaction.

Rainey didn't have time to respond to that notion because Matt was up and headed back in their direction.

"If you will do me the honor, dear ladies, I would ask you to accompany me. There are some people you should meet."

"Who, some old girlfriend you jilted in your callow youth?" Rainey offered.

Matt grinned at her over his shoulder. "Ah, jealousy is very becomin', Harvard."

"Jealousy?" she replied in a harsh whisper. "Let me know when you're done flattering yourself, Macinnes."

"Only if it's to give you a turn, love," he replied with a wink.

She groaned her exasperation. They reached the table, and Rainey noticed for the first time that the man was in a wheelchair. He didn't look up at them as Matt began the introductions.

"Emma Ferguson, Lorraine and Sasha Nielson, permit me to introduce you to Lord Carlyle MacDonnaugh and his lovely daughter, Cassandra, the Countess Golarti. Lord MacDonnaugh has been generous enough to make a gift of our breakfast." He nudged Rainey when she couldn't seem to find her voice, and Cassandra gave her a smile that said nothing at all.

Rainey felt her hackles rise. What did one say to thieving aristocrats? "How nice to meet you both," she heard herself say politely. "Thank you for our breakfast."

Emma added her thanks, and Lord MacDonnaugh mumbled something to Cassandra.

"Yes, Poppy, Americans," Cassandra responded. "All decked out in their denim dungarees." Her eyes held on Sasha for a moment as if there might be a flicker of something disturbing there. She dismissed the notion and gestured for everyone to be seated at the table.

"You'll have to forgive Lord MacDonnaugh, I'm afraid," she offered as if her father were not present beside her. "He lost his eyesight many years ago, and now he's quite dependent on me, aren't you, dear heart?" She patted her father's withered hand condescendingly as Rainey and Matt exchanged a look over the lord's loss of his eyesight.

Lord MacDonnaugh jerked his hand away. "Shut up, girl! You're livin' off of my charity, I'll remind ye. And I'll thank ye to keep a civil tongue in yer head, or ye'll be beddin' in the kennels in the company of yer betters. That Roman bastard left ye destitute, just as I predicted. So ye best be tender to me, or yer out on yer gold-plated arse!" He lapsed into a coughing spell.

As Cassandra leaned closer to Matt, her perfect pageboy hairdo fell sensuously over her shoulders. "This isn't one of Poppy's better days. Actually, he no longer has any better days. It takes all my time and energy just to keep him from wasting away before my eyes," she said with a pout calculated to elicit sympathy. "We're the last of this branch of the Clan MacDonnaugh, I'm afraid, Poppy and I. Quite honestly, our line hasn't thrived in the modern world. There was a time, of course, when nothing could be denied us." She glanced at her father, who had apparently fallen asleep. He hardly fit the profile of mighty conqueror at the moment.

"I sincerely doubt there is much denied to a lovely woman like yourself, Countess," Matt replied.

Cassandra gave him a bitter smile. "You'd be amazed at the appalling life of austerity I've been reduced to now that I'm obliged to be Poppy's constant nursemaid." Lord Carlyle blustered in his sleep, and Cassandra gave him a dark glance. "We're just back from the specialists in Edinburgh, you see," she explained with a delicate sigh. "I shudder at the fortune he's squandered merely to hear the same news over and over. Incurable. He will never see again. It's that simple." She lifted one shoulder in a gesture that was more come-hither than shrug of dismay.

"A pity," Matt said. "Nothin' hereditary, it's to be hoped."

Cassandra leaned closer still, ignoring the other women at the table. "Only on the male side of the family, I'm certain. You know what's really a pity, Matthew?" she asked in a breathy whisper. "It's a pity I didn't grab you and lock you away for my own on one of those misty nights when I saw you prowling among the heather outside my bedroom window. Quite the brawn savage you were in those days, like a lion in search of a mate, all wild and woolly." She gave him a smile of open invitation and laid her hand on his arm with an air of possession.

Matt returned her smile indulgently. "I doubt I could have maintained pace with you, Countess. Though my imagination was undeniably rich in those days, my grasp of the ways of the world was rather small. You would have been disappointed with your catch."

"Somehow, I doubt that," Cassandra replied. "I kept up with your illustrious career in the States, you know. It's how I recognized you across the room. I have a scrapbook full of newspaper and magazine clippings raving about your professional triumphs. It was a silly little hobby I pursued while my dear departed husband was away on his endless trips to all the great gambling capitals of the world."

She pressed her lips together in distaste at the reminder of her husband's philandering and neglectful ways, then forced a smile.

"The photos hardly did you justice, I must say, Matthew. I knew you'd be back. No California beach bunny could ever hold a candle to a true Highland woman."

Emma cleared her throat in warning.

Cassandra straightened in her seat. "Forgive me," she said lightly, "I have this perfectly awful habit of speaking the truth without the sugar. I hope I haven't offended our dear little visitors from foreign shores."

Rainey returned Cassandra's look of boredom. "Not at all. The truth has never been a problem for us. Just the absence of it."

"Indeed."

Cassandra narrowed her gray eyes, and Matt jumped into the conversation.

"We'll be stayin' the night at the house," he said brightly. "I hope the caretakers have been doin' the place justice."

"It's not wise to let the wolves mind the hens, Matthew," Cassandra said with a note of maternal scolding. She slapped the back of his hand teasingly. "Chances are, the help has stolen you to ruin." She dismissed the matter with a wave of her manicured hand, then had an inspiration.

"But you must come for cocktails tomorrow night," she insisted. "I won't take no for an answer." With a cursory glance at Sasha, she added, "Of course, it would probably be past little Sandy's bedtime, so I'll understand perfectly if the ladies wish to beg off. Motherhood plays havoc with the social calendar, I'm certain—to say nothing of the complexion."

Rainey caught the mischievous gleam in Matt's eyes. "We manage," she replied levelly. "And as a matter of fact, Sasha is quite the night owl. We wouldn't think of turning down such a special invitation, would we, Sasha?"

Sasha shook her head slowly when Rainey smiled down at her. But to Rainey's shock, she saw Sasha was holding a steak knife in deadly fashion under the table. Sasha's eyes were intent on Lord MacDonnaugh's every shoring breath, and Rainey touched Matt's sleeve to subtly draw his attention to the knife.

Sasha whispered the words, *"Cuir às dha,"* meaning, "Destroy him." Rainey laid her hand over Sasha's. She was half-tempted to pick up a knife as well.

"What did that dear wee thing say?" Cassandra inquired coolly. "I could have sworn she spoke in Gaelic." She tapped her long nails on the linen tablecloth impatiently. "Gaelic has no place outside of the barnyard, to my way of thinking. I'm proud to say I don't understand a word of it, and all this fuss the locals make about bringing it back, for godsakes, is a crime against all modern intelligence." She took a slow sip of her orange juice, which was laced with champagne. "It's a badge of ignorance and shame only to be worn by the poor, as far as I'm concerned. I did my level best to get away from such backward thinking permanently. I've had enough heath and heather to choke me for a lifetime.

"I was to be a woman of the world, you see. But thanks to my Carlo's untimely death, here I am back among the bumpkins and the bonnie lochs once more. I warned Carlo these Highland roads could be treacherous at night. He was a fool to be driving at such speeds. When his brakes failed, he had no hope of slowing down." She turned her juice glass slowly between her fingers. "They told me he died instantly, you know. Though of necessity, the funeral was closed-casket. The remains were found scattered all over the road."

A cold possibility struck her for the first time, and she gave her father a hard, accusing look. He gave no hint of rousing from his thick slumber, and her voice was pure ice as she spoke.

"Now I'm a prisoner here, and the mere sound of Gaelic makes me physically ill."

Emma was first to answer. "Not a word of Gaelic, ye say? *Bi taingeil!*" she said, meaning thank the lucky stars. Undaunted by Cassandra's glare, she was quick to add, "Sasha was only commentin' on what an uncommon shade of gold yer hair is, Countess. And I have to say, I've never seen the like of it myself outside of a magazine or maybe a pinup calendar."

Matt quickly took Cassandra's hand into his own. "I can't begin to tell you how wonderful it is to truly meet you at last, Countess Golarti," he said smoothly. "But now, we must be on our way. Please extend our thanks and our good-byes to your dear father, and we'll look forward to seeing you both tomorrow night."

"You must call me Cassandra," she insisted as she let her hand linger in his. "After all, we were practically raised together. Kissing cousins, I believe they call it." She kissed his scarred cheek, leaving a telltale lipstick mark there.

"Until tomorrow, then, Cassandra." Matt withdrew tactfully from her grip as Rainey and Emma ushered Sasha toward the door. The knife was back on the table, but Sasha tossed deadly looks over her shoulder at Lord MacDonnaugh and Cassandra.

Once they were outside, Matt rubbed away the lipstick with distaste and gave them all a hearty laugh. "Now my dear ladies, we have a plan."

Rainey herded Sasha toward the car. "What plan? Sasha's ready to slit both their throats, and I have to say, I was close to using the cutlery on them myself. What a hateful pair. I don't know how we're going to stand being around them."

Matt held the car door open as Rainey and Sasha slid into the backseat. "Precisely my point, Harvard—you won't have to be around them. Cassandra is goin' to do everything in her power to stay away from all three of you and keep me away from you in the process."

She gave him a skeptical look. "I think your ego is out of control, Macinnes."

"Naw, lass, purely a statement of fact. The Mac-Donnaughs are notorious for their poor eyesight, are they not? Perhaps if Cassandra's vanity would loosen far enough to permit her a simple pair of spectacles, she'd see the error of her ways." He pushed his own glasses a little further up on his nose and squinted at her like a mole in bright sunlight. "We must use her weaknesses, love. While I keep her . . . amused, you will have the perfect opportunity to find the crown without all that unsavory breakin' and enterin' business. We're invited guests, no less."

"And you don't think Cassandra will be suspicious if we're unaccounted for?" Rainey asked. "She doesn't strike me as the trusting type. And I wouldn't begin to know where to look for the family jewels."

Matt raised his eyebrow at her from the front seat. "I won't be touchin' that line just now. But I will remind you the item in question rightfully belongs to Sasha, not the MacDonnaughs."

"Right. I keep forgetting. Probably because it's locked away in someone else's attic."

Emma took her place in the front seat. "The dungeon, more likely," she said casually.

"The place has a dungeon?" Rainey gave Matt a dubious look in the rearview mirror.

"Aye, well, 'tis a proper castle, after all," he replied. "But if boyhood memory serves, the crown is most commonly kept sealed away in a chest in the laird's bedchamber."

"You mean we have to get into that old man's bedroom?" Rainey demanded.

Matt smiled at the road ahead. "I think the MacDonnaugh took a likin' to you, Harvard. I'd swear he snored in your direction there for a bit. At your knock, he'll probably open the bedroom door for you personally. I only ask that you be gentle with the man, love, regardless of your prejudices. He's got to be pushin' a hundred, if he's a day."

"He's blind, remember?" she replied. "It would be a little tough for him to 'take a likin' ' to me, as you so cleverly put it, when he's never even seen me."

"Ah, but there are the other senses, love," he countered. "In the absence of one, the others intensify, so I'm told. And there's that marvelous scent you always have about you, fresh-picked lavender with a hint of citrus . . ." He inhaled deeply and sighed.

"Bargain hand soap and fabric softener, Macinnes," Rainey said, though the color rose in her cheeks at his flattery.

"Yes, well, it makes you smell like a goddess, *mo chridhe*, and I haven't a doubt Lord Iron Britches picked up on it as well, the sly old dog. You're probably the only thing could drag him out of that chair."

Rainey stared out at the bleak, wintry hills beyond the frosted car window. "I'll bet if he knew we were planning to rob him, it might get a rise out of him," she said with a sigh of worry.

"Look at it this way," Matt offered, "it's only proper for the crown to be retrieved this way. It's how it's always been done. And you've got to figure, whatever happens, we won't be stealin' the old man blind."

At Emma's chuckle, Rainey stifled a smile rather than give him encouragement.

"I think we've all gone crazy to even think of trying this," she said. "And I just pray the Mother Ship picks us up before the SWAT team arrives."

Sasha stared out the window on her side. A shaft of pale winter sun shot through the rolling mists, making the new shawl of snow on one of the hills shimmer and glow. She reached forward and lightly touched Matt's shoulder. Without a word, he pulled the car over to the side of the road.

When Sasha started to get out of the car, Rainey made a move to stop her, but Matt's cautioning glance warned her against it. Together, they all hiked to the top of the hill. The frozen ground crunched beneath their feet, and the air crackled with ice. The snow was only a few inches deep, but the wind was frigid and unforgiving. Somehow, the narrow spire of sunlight maintained its position until their arrival.

Sasha took up a handful of snow and held it toward the break in the clouds in solemn, heartfelt homage. The icy flakes sifted through her hand in a sparkling cascade.

"*Mar theine speur*," she whispered.

"Like starlight," Matt said softly.

Then, Sasha traced the pattern of her brooch into the snow, followed by the sword, and the starry crown. And, as she stood, she raised her arms toward the heavens.

"*Is e seo m' uair-sa!*"

"It's my time, my turn!" Matt translated quietly.

Her whispers grew harsh. *"Chan eil uainn ach an ceartas. Na beò is na mairbh."*

"We want only justice," Emma provided. "For the living and the dead."

Sasha fell to her knees, and the mists swirled and churned in madness overhead, sealing out the rays of light once more. Whether it was a promise of help or a refusal of it was unclear. Sasha looked up into Matt's eyes imploringly.

"I'm here for you, lassie," he said with total dedication. "I swear by God, I won't fail you."

"Labhair an dubh armach," Sasha answered in a soft whisper as her eyes met her mother's.

" 'The dark warrior spoke,' is what she said to ye, Rainey," Emma explained.

Without another thought, Matt swept Sasha into his arms and carried her back toward the car.

As Rainey scrambled down the hill, a terrifying revelation came to her. She turned toward Emma, her eyes filled with urgency.

"Emma, do you think she was talking about some communication from the spirit world? Or is she talking about Matt?"

Emma wrapped her coat around herself more securely against the cruelty of the wind. "I canna say, love. But my guess is the truth will be clear to us verra soon now. We're that close to the time of the Solstice, once we have the crown in our possession, it'll all come together like tea and scones."

Rainey shivered to her bones, dissatisfied with Emma's answer. "But what if the plan doesn't work? In the legend, when Sirona realized she couldn't get her crown back, when she knew justice couldn't be served, she chose death over dishonor."

Emma had a problem looking her in the eye. "Oh, aye, lass, but that was long ago, in another time, ye ken? It's only in the story. Sasha's in the here and now. I dunna think it would ever go so far. Besides which, we won't let it. We're a determined team. We're all kin here now. The crown will be hers, so that other matter is no a problem. Ye set yer mind on victory, love. We must succeed." She waved her fist in the air and set off down the hill.

Rainey sat down on the cold hillside, her eyes focused on the gathering of hills on the far side of the road. She looked down to see Sasha, Emma, and Matt watching her from the bottom of the slope. They were all so convinced about this. There was indeed a kinship about the three of them, a common bond of belief. It made perfect sense to them that Sasha was living out the requirements of an ancient fairy tale. Correction—legend. But what if it all went wrong? What if they couldn't actually get the crown? Or, worse yet, what if it didn't exist? How was she going to keep Sasha alive?

Chapter 16

Rainey kept a watchful eye on Matt as he strode up the frosty hill toward her. Was he Sasha's dark warrior? There were her drawings of him to consider and his absolute devotion to her. A vivid image of two swans, one white and one black, came to mind.

The steep climb was nothing to him. After all, he had grown up roaming these wild hills, she reminded herself, the way she had roamed her safe, suburban Connecticut neighborhood. He was probably going to try to persuade her to come along quietly. It wasn't going to happen.

She was frozen to the bone, but she couldn't make herself move. It felt like she had been racing at a dead run ever since Matt Macinnes came into her life, and there was this crazy notion in her head that if she stayed exactly where she was, the madness would slow down to a manageable speed. She just wanted to forget about Lord MacDonnaugh and Sirona's damned crown. And later on, when everyone had really thought things through and regained their senses, they could all go out for a nice dinner and fly home. Well, maybe not home . . .

Her mental circuits were on overload. She felt at odds with the whole world. It wasn't a feeling she was willing to get used to. With each passing moment, Sasha slipped further into Sirona's world. If they went on as they had been, Sasha might die. They might all end up dead. Couldn't anyone else see that?

Matt sat down beside her and slid a thin blade of dry grass between his teeth, chewing on it thoughtfully. His sigh rose in a cloud of icy vapor.

"I'm glad we have this opportunity to talk, Rainey," he said calmly.

"You're glad we're sitting here on this frozen hill in the middle of nowhere?" As usual, this was not at all what she had expected from him.

"Aye, I am." He stared down at the car, where Emma and Sasha waited patiently in the front seat. "I may have a problem."

Rainey rocked herself for warmth. "What kind of a problem?"

He took the blade of grass from his mouth and studied it. "What has Emma told you of my parents?"

"I know they were killed in a ferryboat accident some years ago," she said in an effort to stick to neutral ground.

"What else do you know?" The words were not without pain.

It felt very natural to put her hand on his shoulder. He stiffened slightly at the gesture, but something told her he didn't wish her to take her hand away. In that instant, she realized he was fighting his feelings for her as hard as she was fighting hers for him.

"I'm sorry about how it happened, Matt."

He cleared his throat roughly. "So you know it all."

"I know the facts. What it did to you, heart and soul, I can only imagine."

Though he didn't move or make a sound, it felt to her as if he might shatter before her eyes. Without a word, she promised him shelter if he let down his defenses. And in answer, he laid his scarred cheek against her hand, a world-weary plea for trust and salvation. She wanted to weep for him.

"Do you know how it feels to be afraid, Rainey? To be so bloody afraid it feels like your heart is goin' to crumble from the helpless sorrow of it all? When you've done everythin' you can think to do, and it's not half enough? I don't ever want that feelin' back again." He sat up and tossed a stone down the hillside.

Rainey felt every ounce of his pain. She experienced that same sense of helplessness over Sasha.

"You expect too much of yourself," she said. "There will always be things you can't control. We all get cornered sometimes. For me, it happens on a daily basis. You can't blame yourself for having human limitations."

"Those damnable limitations can rob you of the ones you love. That kind of thievery can destroy a man."

"You can't let it get to you, Matt. There's far too much at stake."

He threw a second rock with a vengeance. "That's precisely my point! Each time I see Sasha trace the path to paradise on the silver brooch, or as she was just now on the hilltop, I feel the weight of responsibility press down on my shoulders. She's countin' on me. You're countin' on me. Christ, a hundred ghosts are countin' on me. And what if I fail them all? What if I fail you, Rainey?" His eyes were dark with uncertainty as they locked with hers. He closed her cold hands between his own. "I've failed before, as you know. If it happens again, it will be the end for me, you understand?"

He had done it again. She had been fully prepared to stop their lunatic journey here and now. She had been ready with a whole arsenal of reasons why they should not go any further with their quest for the Starry Crown. Now, here she was about to turn into a cheerleader for the cause. There wasn't a particle of doubt in her mind that his concerns were heartfelt and genuine.

"You have to understand something, Matt," she began cautiously. "At times, all I want to do is get as far away from you as I can." She saw his grim smile. "You are forever leading us into danger with your pursuit of stolen crowns and fairy tales, Macinnes. Sometimes . . . most of the time, I'm convinced you're crazy. But I don't believe you will ever let any of us down. And that will always be good enough for me."

He kissed her hand reverently. "Do you know you are my redeemer, Rainey? It's a nasty job, and one not of your own choosin'. But there it is. And I can't seem to stop abusin' the gift. I know I can't help the past. Nothing will bring back the ones we've lost. It's the ghosts I have to lay to rest, yours, mine, and Sasha's."

"You don't have to do it alone, Matt," she said as she returned Sasha's wave. "Emma says we're all kin in this now."

"And what do you say, Rainey?"

She sighed. "I think we're all a little short on family at the moment, so we might as well declare ourselves one."

Matt pressed her hand to his cheek. "More than anything in this world, I'm afraid of losing you and Sasha," he said humbly. "I'm a fool to confess such a thing, I have no doubt. But I cannot bring myself to be anything less than honest, come what may. It is a simple fact that I dedicated myself to you the first time we met. It's a gamble I'm takin' by tellin' you this. And I'll thank you not to slap my face for my boldness."

She patted his cheek. "That mouth of yours is going to get you into trouble you can't get out of one of these days, Stanford."

"Aye, done and done."

As she had longed to do from the first time she saw him, she ran her hand behind his ear to smooth his hair. It curled silken around her fingers, and when he closed his eyes slowly at her touch, she no longer felt the cold.

Alan had never been the wild and passionate type. She hadn't wanted that from him. It had always struck her as dangerous to lose control of herself to another person. Alan hadn't asked it of her. He had been her first and only lover, and he had been a gentle and caring husband. She had always felt comfortable with him, and he had given her Sasha.

What would Matt Macinnes give her? He was taller, broader through the shoulders, and more athletic than Alan. And far more impulsive. She lowered her eyes quickly as a bolt of vivid imagination gave her a tantalizing hint of what he would feel like inside her.

"You are a hopeless romantic, Macinnes," she said awkwardly.

"Hopeless?"

She gave his hair a tug. "Maybe not so hopeless. Maybe just incurable."

"So you're sayin' there is hope for us, but no cure?"

"Don't put words into my mouth, smart guy." She started to take her hand away, but he returned it to the nape of his neck.

"Ah, but the words in people's mouths are what I'm about, *mo chridhe*. And if they aren't already there, I'm goin' to do everythin' in my power to put them there."

The wind whipped around them. "You have to

know, I'm not the romantic type. But I do know something about loyalty. I admire it. And I would like to thank you for the loyalty you show toward Sasha. It means a great deal to us both."

"Loyalty, is that what I've been showin'? I suppose that's a part of it. I don't imagine it would be wise to put another name to it just yet."

"Not at all wise," she said. "But what are we going to do about that problem of yours?"

He looked away from her, toward the horizon. "I'll handle it. We must be goin' now. The weather's about to close in on us."

Rainey caught his sleeve as he started to rise. "I'm not buying the macho bit, Matt. What's going on?"

He trained his sight on the car. "I haven't been back to the Highland house since they perished, Rainey," he explained. "It must be faced, to be sure. I've put it off far too long. I'm no longer the wayward, irresponsible youth who fled to Edinburgh, then to America, only to find it wasn't far enough. All these years, I've been waitin' for the Mother Ship to take me further away still." He looked at her at last.

"The thing of it is," he said, almost shyly, "all this time, deep down, I've been lookin' for a strong enough reason to come back, a reason to truly say good-bye to them in the place where I knew them best. You and Sasha are that glorious reason. I can't imagine a better one. You're givin' me the strength to return home, Rainey. And I thank you for that."

"I give you strength?" she said in amazement.

He brought her hand to his lips and kissed it cherishingly. "*Carraig mo neairt*. The rock of my strength. Aye, *mo chridhe*, and a very precious rock."

He tucked her hair behind her ear. "I confess I'm in dread of seeing the house again, though I so dearly loved it once. Until now, I thought it was beyond me to go back. A thousand nights, but one nightmare . . . I'm of the mind it'll never truly be over and done. Will you help me break the curse, Rainey, just as I will help you break the hold of the falls? I will stand beside you, by God, I swear it. Will you stand beside me when the time comes as well? Perhaps we can save each other." He rose to his feet and offered her his hand.

As she took it, she smiled at him and said, "Tell me how to say, 'Hero in distress, take heart.' "

"*Saoidh na airc, gabh misneachd,*" he said smoothly.

She chewed her lower lip over the complexity of the words. "Right," she said, "well, you get the idea."

"Indeed I do, *mo chridhe*. But the fact remains, my heart is no longer my own. It's in your care."

"I'm not sure I'm up to that kind of responsibility," she said as she picked her way cautiously toward the bottom of the hill.

He caught her in his arms as she slipped on an icy patch, and she relaxed instantly in his embrace. "Oh, you're up to it, my sweet Rainey," he assured her. "What remains to be seen is if you're willin'."

"I can't answer that right now, Matt," she said. The truth was, she didn't dare answer while she was wrapped securely in his arms, because she wasn't sure she could say no to anything he proposed at this moment. And if she did find the presence of mind to say no, he would just find a way to talk her into it anyway.

"We both know the time will come for your answer, love," he said as he tugged her forward down the hill at a much faster clip than she would have chosen for safety's sake. But she didn't stumble again, and by the time they reached the car, she felt rather proud of herself.

"It always comes down to time, doesn't it?" she said.

He held the car door open for her. "Aye, that it does. Time and the courage to face the risk in hopes of winning the prize."

Rainey ducked into the warmth of the car. "I hope Sirona has enough courage to loan some to the rest of us."

The weather closed around them with a vengeance. They had driven the length of Loch Lochy and most of Loch Garry and Loch Loyne before passing through the forest of Bunloinn. Now, they were skirting the shores of yet another loch, Loch Cluanie. Though it was still the afternoon, darkness was already falling, and a curtain of sleet pummeled the windshield. Visibility was almost nil.

When they turned off the main road, Rainey felt compelled to ask, "You're sure this is the way, right, Matt? I mean there isn't exactly a gas station on every corner where you can ask directions." She doubted he would be the type to ask anyway. "There might be a map in the glove compartment," she offered.

He winked at her from the driver's seat. "No need, love. It's not far now. We'll be there directly."

They drove for what seemed to Rainey to be hours, crawling along within the limitations of the headlights. The sleet deteriorated into heavy Highland mists that pressed against the windows, blocking all else from view. So, when Matt stopped the car, Rainey came to the conclusion they had gone as far as they could safely go. He indicated they should all get out, but she couldn't see the sense in it. If they so much as wandered a few feet from the car, it would be very easy to become disoriented.

"Come along, Harvard," Matt instructed, "unless you plan to spend the night in the car." He started to unload their baggage.

"Are you saying we have to hike the rest of the way to the house?"

He gave her a dubious frown. "I understand you're no so much for hikin', love, but I think we might create a wee bit of a stir if I should have to carry you over the threshold at this stage of the game."

"Threshold?" She swiped her hand across the window to clear away the condensation. A short distance from them stood a dark, squarish shape. She saw now that there was a stone fence covered with ivy and an iron gate beside the car. A set of wide, round stepping stones led toward what she decided was a house. There were no lights on inside it, but the mists parted just enough so she could see an old-fashioned, gabled cottage with a thatched roof. The walls were covered with bare vines, but despite the bleakness of the day, it wasn't hard to imagine the place bedecked in the colorful splendor of roses in more temperate weather. She took an instant liking to it.

"Come along, then," Matt insisted. "I'm afraid there's work to be done before things could be considered hospitable. It seems it was decided I was never coming back. But not to worry. I'll put a fire on the hearth first thing to drive away the chill. It's not so very large a place, mind you, but we'll make it cozy." Sasha followed after him dutifully, the stuffed bear tucked under her arm. She treated the bear more as a valued keepsake than a companion now.

Emma tugged at Rainey's sleeve as she started to follow Matt up the walk. It was the first chance they had had to talk in quite a while without Matt's immediate presence.

"What was all that on the hill between you and the Macinnes, lassie?" she asked in a quick whisper.

"The two of ye looked mighty chummy, if ye were to ask me."

Rainey made a study of a bit of lint on her jacket sleeve. "He was just having a little self-esteem problem," she said with a shrug.

Emma gave her a narrow look. "Ye mind translatin' that for an old woman who's no so verra famous for her patience, miss?"

Matt disappeared inside the cottage with Sasha in tow.

"It's hard for him to come back here, Emma. This is the first time since his parents died, and, understandably, it's bringing back a lot of unpleasant memories. He just wasn't sure how he was going to be able to handle it, that's all. I simply did what I could to reassure him that we had every confidence in him. I told him we'd help him through this, and I let him know we were as committed to getting Sasha's crown as he is."

"And holdin' his hand and pettin' his head like he was your favorite spaniel, that was the reassurin' part, I take it. And if the man has another spasm of self-doubt, I'm to rest assured ye'll be out in the barn givin' him a comfortin' that'll curl the man's toes, I imagine." She gave Rainey a sly wink. "It seems he's made prodigious progress. I canna say I'm disappointed."

Rainey blushed in spite of herself. "Don't read so much into this, Emma," she cautioned. "He's a poet, for godsakes. He traps me with my own words half the time, and I end up saying and doing things I would never do under normal conditions. We're all thrown together by circumstances here, and I'm trying my best to keep a level head."

"A level head, is it?" Emma said with a snort. "Yer head's the least of it. It's the rest of ye goin' to be leveled right proper before he's done. No point in fightin' it so, dear. Little Sasha told me so herself, you and the Macinnes were an item. She says it's destiny, pure and simple. She ought to know. Besides which, there's no a one of us can't see it dancin' pretty between the pair of ye, save for yer own sweet self, of course. Open yer eyes, Rainey, and take a good long look. There's more than destiny at work here. It's the fairies."

Chapter 17

Fairies.

Rainey warmed her hands above the merry blaze Matt had built on the old hearth. She didn't doubt the possibility of fairies being nearby. The mists off the loch and the trees around the cottage were probably alive with them. After all, this was their native territory.

How far she had come in her thinking, it dawned on her.

Once the old-fashioned kerosene lamps had been lit and the covers pulled off the few pieces of furniture, the inside of the cottage looked very much as she had imagined it would, with a low, wide-beamed ceiling and a dormered loft for sleeping. Granted, her house in California was small, but how a family of three could have lived under these confined circumstances was a mystery to her. It felt like they had slipped back in time a hundred years.

The main room was piled high with ancient Celtic artifacts and memorabilia collected on the countless expeditions Matt and his family had taken to the northern islands. Glass display cases and open shelves were stacked to bulging with miscellaneous antiquities and reference books. There was hardly enough room to walk because of the dozens of cardboard boxes everywhere.

Sasha was undaunted by the clutter. In fact, her eyes danced with excitement over each new find.

"Be careful, sweetheart," Rainey cautioned gently as Sasha studied the delicate piece of broken pottery in her hand.

Matt nurtured the fire with an experienced hand, but there was a restlessness about him. "She's welcome to it," he said curtly. "There are a million more in the box just like it, for godsakes."

Rainey looked down at the priceless bit of pottery with a thoughtful frown. "Should you be giving it to her? I mean, shouldn't all of this be in a museum or a university somewhere?"

Her question made Matt's attention stray, and a log rolled out of balance. The wood had to be wrestled back into place. "If it gives Sasha some small happiness, she's welcome to every bloody box and bit of broken crockery in this place. The museums are full to bursting with things that rightfully belong in caves and in the ground. Warehouses are stacked to the roof with the broken remains of all our past lives."

He gestured about the room. "This is the very reason I chose language over archaeology. Language lives wherever a human being has the knowledge and tenacity to use it. It demands no turning over of a man's grave to study his burial robes, no crates of broken crockery to make itself understood.

"The only arguments my father and I had were over the fundamental ethics of his life's work. I was a headstrong idealist testing the edges of manhood, and my father always encouraged me to speak my mind plainly. I'm sure I did so to a fault.

"There was one dig in particular, an island location dating back well before the time of the Roman Empire. My father had an unbridled passion for the place, but I was convinced that disturbing the spirits who rested there was sacrilege of the first order. As hard as I tried to convince him to leave that one place alone, I could make no progress with him. It was our destination the day my parents were killed."

"It must have been very hard for you, Matt," Rainey said as she looked about the room. How offensive all of the carefully stacked specimens and boxes must be to someone with Matt's convictions.

"Aye, well, it was far harder on them, then, wasn't it? I suspect my mother would have sided with my point of view under other circumstances. In her heart, she was more partial to language than to artifacts. But her loyalty to my father was rock solid, and above all, she wanted to maintain the peace between my father and me. There was no swaying them when they stood as a united front, and I could always tell by my mother's expression when it would be pointless to argue my stand further. In fact, my father and I argued about the dig the morning of the disaster. My mother came to his defense instead of mine, and I was sulking in my quarters below when the storm gained the upper hand." He stoked the fire with more force than was necessary. "My opinions haven't changed in all these years. But perhaps if I'd acted more like a man that morning and less like a sullen child, things would have worked out quite differently."

Sasha walked up to him with a glass jar she had found among the stacks. A tear ran down her cheek as she held it up for his inspection, and all the blood seemed to drain from his face at the sight of it. In the jar was a bed of dried moss and a spray of very old heather. Hanging from one small branch of the heather was a paper-thin gossamer wing. Its iridescent surface was ripped to tatters, robbed of its natural tensile strength by time and captivity.

Rainey came closer to see her find. "What is it,

Sash?" she asked. "It looks like a dragonfly's wing, doesn't it? I'll bet the owner was sorry to lose it."

But Sasha paid no attention to her mother. Instead, she thrust the jar toward Matt. *"A bheil cuimhne agad air an là sin?"* she demanded in a cold whisper.

Rainey glanced over her shoulder at Emma.

"She asked him if he remembered the day the wing was found."

Matt's eyes grew dark with tortured memory. "Aye, Sasha, I do. Winter Solstice, the year before all was lost to me. And may God forgive me, it was the one specimen I collected myself. There can be no forgiveness for such an act of blasphemy. And I've paid a wicked price ever since. But the debt has still to be satisfied."

Without another word, he took the jar from Sasha and walked out the front door.

Sasha watched him go, then turned to her mother with a questioning look. *"Ciod e an damacraich a tha ort?"* she asked in a fervent whisper.

Rainey glanced at Emma.

"The lass asks what makes ye hesitate? Go on with ye, lass," Emma insisted. "He's havin' himself a tough time of it."

Rainey considered the door for only a moment before she went out in search of Matt.

Emma sat down beside Sasha. Sasha handed her a small disk of polished metal which Emma automatically used to check her own appearance. "Ah, they were that vain a lot even back then, don't ye know, Sasha. Some things don't ever change." She looked at Sasha thoughtfully. "I'm wonderin' if there's a barn nearby. If so, we'll catch yer mother up there by and by, I expect."

Sasha gave her a knowing smile. She made circles of her fingers and held them up to her eyes to indicate Matt. Then she hugged herself as she mouthed the word Mama.

"Aye, lassie, they're quite the bonnie pair, those two. And both stubborn as Highland rain."

The dark mists danced in a tight circle around Rainey as she walked through the winter-bare garden behind the cottage. From what little she could see, everything had gone to seed years ago. She loved to garden, though she never really had time to dedicate to it, and she had some notion of how much work it would take to bring the neglected little garden back into production.

The thorn of a neglected rosebush caught her finger, staining the branch with her blood and sending a sad shower of brown leaves to the ground. She wrapped a Kleenex around her finger quickly. Restoring this place would require a genuine labor of love.

She felt a bit light-headed from the mists and a lack of sleep. It was a temptation to call out to Matt. But she didn't want him to think she had come chasing after him. His pride was already raw from the strain of being on home ground again. Perhaps he wanted to be left alone to gather himself. He had hardly asked for her company as he stalked out the door. It was even possible he had gone in the opposite direction, toward the loch. But pure instinct told her he had not. And right now, whether he liked it or not, she felt a compelling need to see his face.

She reached the end of the garden and strained her eyes to make out shapes in the fog. Her sore finger throbbed from the cold, and she shoved her hand into her jacket pocket. The mists lifted slightly, and she found herself at the edge of a wall of trees. Was Matt somewhere in the heart of the forest, she wondered? She glanced over her shoulder toward the cottage to be certain of her bearings, but she could no longer see its comforting lights. The mists had even closed over the end of the path.

The garden was only a few steps away, she assured herself. Now was the time to go back to the safety of the cottage, before total darkness fell. If she got lost, it would only make matters worse. Common sense demanded that she turn around and go back. But a pull far stronger demanded that she go forward.

She considered the woods. There was a narrow path visible through the trees where before there had been none. And somewhere in the distance, she saw a glowing light. Surely, if she took the path and never strayed from it, she would be able to find her way back. She would mark the trail as they had done in the woods at home, big markers she would be able to find even in the dark.

The moment she stepped into the forest, real darkness closed in around her, and a light snow began to fall. The flakes were large and soft as they landed in her hair and on her sleeves. They stuck to the path and to the pine boughs above her, so she was careful to mark her trail every few yards.

But as time went by, the way ahead became obscured, as did the markers behind her. She had nothing to guide her forward but the light that shone persistently through the trees. Chances were, it was a caretaker's home or a neighbor who might have seen Matt. If nothing else, whoever lived there could probably draw her a map of how to get back to the cottage. There was no reason for concern.

The light ahead had a peculiar quality. One moment it was large. The next, it narrowed and nearly disappeared, giving her good cause for worry. But it never went away entirely as she stepped over fallen trees and bare roots. Strangely, she didn't notice the cold as she shook the snow from her shoulders. She had walked a long way, yet she seemed to be no closer to her goal. The hike and the strain of the day were taking their toll on her, so she decided to sit down for a moment on the stump of a fallen tree. She took her hands out of her pockets and was surprised to find that her finger was no longer sore. It had been nothing, after all. She stuffed the Kleenex back into her coat pocket.

It felt warmer, sitting down, and as she looked about her, she realized her eyes had adjusted to the darkness. She could see individual trees and rocks. The forest struck her as very old, with its gnarled oaks and ancient mosses. It dawned on her the reason she could see these things was because the glowing light was beside her. As she turned toward it, she saw that it was in fact an enormous fairy tree. In the dead of winter, it was alive with smooth summer foliage. Warm breezes teased through the leaves, and a wide circle of green grass and brightly colored wildflowers surrounded its base.

It made sense now, why at times the light had been strong, while at other times dim. A thousand tiny, magical beings were engaged in mad games of hide-and-seek. The females wore gowns of fern, lily of the valley, or huckleberry leaves and crowns of marguerite, morning glory, or forget-me-nots. The males wore tunics of moss and bracken with comical hats of acorn shells.

In one instant, the tree was utterly dark as everyone hid except for a single fairy dressed in a lily leaf. Her iridescent wings opened and closed in rhythm with her counting. The next moment, the whole tree was aflutter with light as the rest raced to touch base before they were tagged.

Rainey rubbed her eyes in amazement when she saw the design of Sasha's brooch carved into the juncture of the tree's massive branches. These things were only supposed to happen when she was asleep. Yet she was wide-awake, as far as she could tell, and it all felt very real. She must be far more lost than she'd thought, she decided.

The fairies watched her with open interest. They made no effort to conceal themselves, and it was apparent they had no intention of leaving her as they had in the first dream. In fact, they bowed as one in greeting to her. She wasn't even sure they were the same fairies from her dream, or if this was the same tree.

The white swan was nowhere to be seen, although it wasn't completely out of the realm of possibility that it was there and she wasn't being allowed to see it. Her brain was starting to run in tight little circles, and she experienced the same light-headedness she had felt earlier. The small portion of her that still clung to reality defined what she saw as a bout of low blood sugar or the onset of a migraine headache. But the rest of her knew better. This was something she was going to have to come to terms with without the definitions of modern science.

In small groups, the fairies started to climb down out of the tree and venture toward her cautiously. She wasn't afraid. Somehow, she knew they meant her no harm, though there was certainly a gleam of playful mischief in their light green eyes. They were each no bigger than her hand as they gathered about her, and they all had hair of one shade of red or another. But there were so many of them. Even gentle mischief from a mob this size was going to be hard to handle. There was only one thing she could think to do.

"Matt?" she called softly. "Matt, I need you."

The fairies looked at her, cocking their heads to one side in unison at her words.

"Matt?" one of them said in a voice no bigger than a cricket's.

"Matt?" they all shouted as one. "Matt! Matt! Matt!" It became a rousing cheer as they all locked elbows and danced around merrily. A cloud of sparkling dust rose from their wings, glowing phosphorescent as they did their boisterous jig.

Then, just as swiftly as they had started, the fairies froze, staring beyond where Rainey sat. A whispered word here, a nudge there, and suddenly there was a fresh explosion of cheering, though this time it was disorganized and unintelligible.

"May anyone attend this party, Harvard?"

Rainey turned with a start to find Matt standing behind her. He smiled down benevolently at her shining throng.

"You can see them?" she asked in an urgent whisper. "Thank God I'm not the only crazy one!"

He swung his leg over her tree stump and settled his weight down beside her. "See what, *mo chridhe*?"

The fairies gathered around them both now. A particularly bold pair started to climb up Matt's pant leg.

Rainey worried her lip as she watched the fairies' antics. One was about to dive into Matt's pants pocket.

"I was asking if you could see the . . . um, fairies," she said tentatively.

"Och, come now, lass, fairies is it? You're havin' me on."

She noticed the glass jar from the cottage on the ground nearby. It was empty now.

Matt pushed his glasses a bit further up the bridge of his nose and rubbed his chin in careful thought. The fairy, a male smaller than the rest, took this opportunity to jump into Matt's pocket. An instant later, he emerged in triumph, dragging an English penny behind him.

Tsking loudly, Matt reached down and picked the little fairy up by the collar, penny and all. Shamefacedly, the fairy offered the coin to him as if it had been his intention all along. Matt accepted the penny, but seemed to be in no hurry to set the little fellow down.

"You're that keen, Master Suim Mhaith. You've earned the name Pretty Penny once again, my friend. I see you have not changed your villainous ways," he said scoldingly. "It's a penny saved is a penny earned, man, not a penny stolen, if memory serves. And I see you're still leading others astray."

The little fairy shrugged and tipped his acorn hat in apology, and Matt set him down with the others. Suim Mhaith's peers immediately jostled him about in a collective tease over being so easily caught, and his partner in crime slid down Matt's pant leg unobtrusively.

Matt turned to Rainey. "Now then, you were sayin' somethin' about fairies, love. It's common knowledge there's no such a thing, you understand."

He set his hand down beside the heel of his boot and a particularly exquisite female fairy, dressed in a gown of shiny green rose leaves, stepped daintily onto his palm. Her auburn curls reached to her waist between her gossamer wings, and she wore a wreath of tiny violets. Matt brought her up close to his ear, and she whispered something to him shyly. Matt nodded sagely, then brought her up before Rainey. The fairy curtsied low in a shower of sparkle, then raised her eyes with a knowing smile.

"This is Mar a' Ghealach, Rainey," Matt said.

"It's from your poem on the back porch at home. 'Like the moon,' " Rainey translated easily. But more than just remembering the words, she understood them as if they had always been a part of her.

Matt lifted one eyebrow at this development, but

seemed unshaken by it. It was almost as if he had been expecting it. "Aye, love, the name suits her, does it not?" The little fairy wrapped her shining wings across her face to hide her becoming blush at Matt's praise. He chuckled at her show of shyness and carefully placed his little finger between her fragile wings to bring her chin up. "Mar a' Ghealach is asking how our Sasha is faring. She also says she knows you, *mo chridhe*. What do you say?"

Rainey looked into the fairy's clear green eyes. She couldn't answer the question. It should have been easy. She was a stranger to Scotland, a stranger to these woods, and certainly a stranger to anything like fairies.

These were Sasha's friends. Or more properly, Sirona's friends. But as Mar a' Ghealach held her gaze, something new rose inside Rainey. Like the memory of a bedtime story she had been told only once as a very small child, thin wisps of imagery began to wrap around her heart, imagery of fairies and swans and a sword drenched in blood.

It almost felt as if she had been given a drug of some kind, although she was sure she had not. The tree, the fairies, how she had gotten there were a jumble in her mind. Reality and fairy tale swirled together. Her fingers and toes tingled with numbness, and she experienced a kind of elation at being in Mar a' Ghealach's presence.

The idea of remaining among the fairies forever didn't seem at all preposterous. In fact, it was hard to imagine that the rest of the world existed any longer. It was of no importance if it did, because this was heaven on earth. She found herself saying over and over in her mind that she must bring Sasha here so the two of them could be secure from all the Evanstons and Malinskys of the world. Here there would be sanctuary and peace. Of course, in a way, it would be a kind of death. She understood that. But they would be safe. A kind of death. Her thoughts had ventured too far. She was trembling violently as she pulled her eyes away from the persuasiveness of Mar a' Ghealach's inquisitive gaze.

"I'm not sure I understand what she means when she says she knows me, Matt," she said, her attention back on the empty glass jar. It was the only thing present from the world beyond the fairy tree.

Mar a' Ghealach whispered something more in Matt's ear. "She says the question no longer matters, love, because the answer is in your eyes." He saw that her attention had gone to the jar. "I understood the fairies in my heart, you see," he said with a sad smile for Mar a' Ghealach. "But I felt I had to understand them with my brain as well.

"I was a young student, bright enough in my own way, I suppose. And of course, there was the family tradition of removal for the purpose of academic study. The concept was basic to my upbringing, even though my heart rebelled at the notion. They are quite a phenomenon, after all, and I studied them as best I could here at the tree. But in the end, I felt the need for more extensive research into what makes them as they are."

Words failed him as he fought with hard memories. Mar a' Ghealach wrapped her slender arms around his thumb and laid her head against him to give him comfort. Tears rose in Rainey's eyes at the sight of the two of them.

Matt sighed from the depths of his soul. "Mar a' Ghealach had a beautiful twin sister, Mar a' Ghrian."

"Like the sun," Rainey translated. It no longer surprised her that the Gaelic was there. In fact, it dawned on her now that they had all been speaking it since her arrival at the tree.

Matt's eyes grew distant as he slipped into memories. "She was as warm and shining as the sun on the heather. And as impossible as it sounds, there was a kind of love between us. A love that pushed aside the folly of her leaving the safety of the tree at my insistence. It was madness on my part. The madness of youth, curiosity, and misplaced pride.

"I didn't understand then that the powers of all the fairies had been so badly hindered by the length of time the crown had been away from the falls. Sirona is one of their own, and the fact that the injustices done to her have not been righted for all these centuries drained them all of their strength. Mar a' Ghrian was no exception. But her desire to make me happy overshadowed her sense of self-preservation."

He ran his hand through his hair. "Just one harmless night of scientific method, one night of collecting data in the proper way. Simple measurements, perhaps a brief recording of her glorious voice, I managed none of them. We simply spoke to one another half the night, there in the cottage. She felt tired, she said, so I placed her in among the heather and moss we had brought from the tree so she could get an hour's rest. There was plenty of time, I was sure. But I, too, felt the need of rest, and I fell asleep beside the jar, her shining face lost in dreams the last thing I saw."

The fairy crowd gave a collective mournful sigh. It was clear that the story was very familiar to them. Mar a' Ghealach pressed her finger to her lips and smiled down upon them all sadly. It was almost as if it was unnecessary for Matt to complete the story. But Rainey needed to hear.

"What happened, Matt?" she asked softly. Unshed tears shone in his eyes as he looked to her.

"She was destroyed. When I awoke, it was already daylight. Nothing remained of my lovely Mar a' Ghrian but a single tattered wing. A thing so precious, a being so miraculous had perished while trusting in my care. I didn't eat or sleep for days afterward. It was the beginning of a downward spiral in my life that led to the loss of my parents. I thank God I've been forgiven enough to be permitted to return to the tree."

Mar a' Ghealach patted his thumb and kissed it lightly.

"But it wasn't your fault, Matt," Rainey insisted. "You had no way of knowing." She looked down at the gathering of tiny fairies at her feet. There were looks of concern and expectation on their faces.

Matt held his hand up so he and Mar a' Ghealach were on the same level. "But that's the point, my love. If research had been my true goal, I would have gone in far smaller stages in order to protect the subject of my studies.

"The truth of it is, I tried to transform Mar a' Ghrian into a part of my own harsh world. I had spent time in her domain, but more than anything, I wanted her magical purity to be a part of my real world. It was never meant to be, and somewhere in my heart, I knew it. The fairies are far more forgiving than I am. As far as I am concerned, I still owe them a life."

"A life?"

"Aye."

Something constricted inside Rainey's chest as she experienced renewed waves of longing to bring Sasha here. Her limbs felt numb again, and she had a sudden pang of doubt that the desire to bring Sasha to the tree was her own idea. Maybe the thought was being put into her head by Matt and the fairies. Matt owed them a life. What if the life he had decided to provide was Sasha's? What if Sasha chose to cross over into this enchanting, magical world, never to return?

Who could blame a little girl for wanting to play among the fairies till the end of time? At the promise of returning to this lovely, ethereal world, why not leap from the falls as she had done before as a way to find a greater happiness, a place better than the real world, a place where she felt she belonged?

The risk. She was being asked to accept too much. She couldn't do it. None of this was possible. It was a dream of some sort, pure hallucination.

The beauty of the tree began to fade. The fairies' colorful clothes began to wither and turn to brown. Their faces, so young and full of energy before, looked old, sick, and tired. And the tree itself began to gnarl and lose its shiny leaves. It had the quality of an evil nightmare, and Rainey wanted no more of it.

"You can't have her. Sasha is mine!" she said coldly.

The fairies began to back away in confusion, and when a single tear of sorrow glistened down Mar a' Ghealach's fair cheek, Rainey could bear it no more.

"I have to leave here!" she cried. She broke for the forest, desperate for solid reality.

Matt rose to stop her. "Rainey, wait, you misunderstand! There's no danger!" he called to her as he set Mar a' Ghealach down among the fairies. She was so weak now, she had to lean against the others for support. Matt gave her a quick look of apology before he ran after Rainey.

The raw cold assaulted her senses now, and without the fairy light to guide her, she ran blindly. She had to get back to Sasha for fear the fairies were calling to her, calling her away forever.

The forest was no longer welcoming. Jagged branches snagged her clothing, and the snow turned to hard sleet as she plunged forward. Her sense of direction was gone, and as she looked over her shoulder to get her bearings, there was only darkness.

She was on the edge of panic. If she kept going, surely she would come to the edge of the forest soon. But there was no guarantee how big the forest was or if she was even going in a straight line. If she was running in circles, it would be dawn before she could begin to see her way.

Perhaps the fairies were intentionally keeping her lost, it occurred to her. Was that their nature? She knew noting of their ways. Maybe eliminating her from the picture would clear the path to Sasha for them.

She didn't want to think in these terms. In her heart, she didn't honestly believe the fairies meant her any ill will. She wanted to understand it all, but it was beyond her capabilities at the moment.

The thought of Mar a' Ghealach perched so trustingly on Matt's hand filled her mind. "Somehow, you're one of them, Matt, and you're pulling Sasha away from me." His solution to Sasha's problems was going to be to return her not solely to the falls, but to the fairies. She wasn't going to let that happen.

The sleet stung her face as she forced herself to trudge on. Her fingers and toes burned from the cold. The night had turned so hostile, she might freeze, she knew. Then she would be no help to Sasha at all.

"Do you want to be helped, Sasha?" she asked herself as she fought her way between the tangled oaks.

The question settled like a massive stone between her shoulder blades, and the temptation to simply lie down and be done with the whole problem was an overwhelming one. She had never been this tired in all her life. If she only sat down to catch her breath and kept a close watch on herself to be sure she didn't rest too long or fall asleep, she would be all right. Resting would give her the strength to go on. It would be to her benefit, she assured herself. It would make it so she could get back to Sasha. That was all that mattered. Sasha.

Chapter 18

Warmth. The sleet had stopped.

Rainey opened her eyes to find she was no longer in the forest, but in a room she had never seen before. Had the forest been a dream, or was this room the dream?

She was sitting in a winged-back chair of heavy blue brocade beside the biggest stone fireplace she had ever seen. Even in the dim light, she could see it was large enough to walk into. And on the broad expanse above the mantel was a fan-shaped display of old spears and swords.

A fire burned before her, but it did little to fight back the darkness and there was still an icy nighttime chill in the room, indicating the blaze was young. There was a downy woolen blanket wrapped around her. It smelled mildly of cedar, and at first she thought it was somehow the shawl Matt had bought for her in Glasgow. But only the design of the tartan was the same. She nestled deeper into its warmth.

"You gave us all quite a scare, Harvard."

She started at the sound of Matt's voice. There was strong emotion in his voice, although she couldn't be sure if it was concern or irritation. Perhaps a mixture of both. She stood up to face him. It felt like her knees were going to give out beneath her, and she grabbed the back of the chair for support.

"Where are we? How did I get here?" she demanded. Now that she saw the antiquities in the room, she was tempted to ask what century it was, as well.

"This is home," Matt said with a simple shrug. "It was the closest place to bring you." He ran his fingers along the top of an exquisitely inlaid sideboard and frowned at the thick layer of dust that came up.

"Whose home?" Rainey insisted. She was getting that light-headed feeling again.

"My parents' home. Or more properly, mine in terms of current ownership," he replied without enthusiasm.

Rainey frowned at him. From what she could see, the place was a castle.

"What about the cottage?" she asked as she wrapped the blanket around her shoulders more securely.

Matt walked to the hearth and leaned his forearm against the ornately carved mantel. The pattern was a dense Celtic profusion of curves and knots, and he traced the familiar designs absently. The firelight touched his hair with burnished copper, and there was an unbending Highlander set to his jaw.

"The cottage was originally the gardener's quarters. MacPherson was the man's name. But, as the years went by, we were never home enough of the year to justify the keepin' of gardens. The MacPhersons moved on, and the cottage came to be used for additional storage. I hadn't been inside since I was a lad. My father . . ." He gazed into the fire, gathering himself. "My father used to take me for walks down by the loch of a Sunday when the weather was fine. We'd stop by the cottage on the way, you see, because Tildy, the gardener's wife, always had a batch of scones fresh out of the oven for us. Much like your Emma, Tildy MacPherson.

"It was a father-and-son ritual, like, goin' to the loch. Silly, sentimental nonsense, and no mistake." He turned to Rainey, the pain of loss riding just under the surface. "It's over and done, lo these many years. And yet, bein' inside that cottage again was a hard reminder. I thought it would be easier than to face comin' here. But it was no easier, just a side gate to the same empty valley." His fingers trembled slightly as he pushed his glasses up to the bridge of his nose and gave her half a smile. It failed to reach his eyes. A thin veil of moisture gathered across his brow, despite the cold.

Rainey could see it was a torture for him to be in this house.

"I'm sorry you were forced to come here because of me. But we have to talk."

"No need for apologies, Rainey. As I told you, it's my problem. And if the truth be told, you've already been of help. Because of you, I'm inside. Nothing has been touched since the day the three of us left as a family."

The fire's light sent shadows dancing wildly across the dust-coated portraits on the wall. The men were dressed in elaborate Highland kilts and regalia, their hair one shade of red or another, their eyes as riveting a blue-gray color as those of their living counterpart. The women, without exception, were dark-haired, blue-eyed beauties with an unmistakable look of intelligence. All were portrayed with handsome children and hunting dogs clustered at their feet, with the loch as a backdrop. To a one, they looked out on the world, their backs straight with pride, their hearts demanding unswerving courage. Matt's parents were not the only ghosts residing in this place.

One woman's portrait in particular caught her eye. Dressed in an impeccably tailored suit of Scottish tweed, the young beauty with ebony hair stared at her with a serene smile. The eyes were unquestionably Matt's.

Rainey inclined her head toward the painting. "Your mother?"

Matt was reluctant to look at it. "Aye."

"And your father?"

"Far wall, third from the right."

The breath caught in her throat when she saw it. At first, it appeared to be a portrait of Matt. But the man in the painting, dressed in classic Macinnes tartans, was thinner through the face, more intense, and perhaps a bit lacking in Matt's wry sense of humor. Still, he had been a strikingly handsome man, a man she suspected she would have liked. She could easily picture father and son strolling beside the loch with the sun breaking through the mists.

It occurred to her the quality of the painting that appealed to her so much was the framework of Matt's spirit she saw there. Matt had turned back toward the fire, but in her heart, she could see his features as clearly as if he were inches away from her. It would always be there now, that marvelous face with its scar of failed bravery. There was no point denying it to herself.

"Tell me about the fairies, Matt. I have to understand."

He turned to her slowly, his face unreadable.

Rainey pulled the blanket a bit higher around her shoulders against that look. "Don't bother to deny it all, Macinnes. I know that damn fairy tree is out there somewhere in the woods. Although I wouldn't bet my life I could find it a second time." She stepped nearer to the fire. "They wanted me to find them, didn't they? That's the only reason it was so easy. But why me? It's Sasha . . ." She concentrated on the flames. "It's Sasha they want."

Matt took her hand. "It was an attempt to communicate with you. But I'm not certain you're ready to accept it just yet, Rainey."

She pulled her hand away and retreated into the cold shadows away from the fire. "They want her back, don't they? The fairies plan to keep her. They need her. Well, I won't allow it! I remember hearing stories when I was little about fairies who stole children, stories about changelings. She's my daughter, for godsakes, Matt!"

The blanket she wore brushed against a table and a porcelain vase crashed to the floor. She whirled toward the source of the noise, then flashed her attention back to Matt.

"Listen to the way I'm talking, will you?" she marveled. "When I hear myself carry on this way about fairies, I think I belong in a mental ward. But you and I both know they're real. And Sasha knows it best of all. I won't lose her, I promise you that. The whole purpose of this business with the crown was to bring her back to me. To me, Matt. I can't solve Sirona's problems, and if you care about us as you say you do, you won't let the fairies steal Sasha from me."

Matt made no effort to approach her. "They won't steal her, Rainey. It was never their intention."

She tucked her hair behind her ear with a vengeance. "And if she wants to go with them, to stay with them, what then? Will they send her back to me?"

He shook his head slowly, and she took it as his answer. She walked purposefully toward the door. "If I'm the only one who will protect her, so be it. I'm used to it. If the fairies haven't made the cottage disappear off the face of the earth by now, I'm going to take Sasha away from here tonight. There has to be somewhere safe in the world." Tears glistened in her eyes, but she swiped them away. "I never heard of any fairies in South America. Maybe we'll try living there for a while."

Matt stepped between her and the door. "You can't go out there right now, Rainey," he said firmly. "It's not safe."

She gave him an accusing look. "Will the fairies come after me for opposing them? Tell me."

"They have no thought of causing you any harm, *mo chridhe*, regardless of your low opinion of them. Nor do they plan to keep Sasha, as hard as that is for you to believe. Their only purpose is to return the crown to its rightful place.

"For as long as memory records, there has been no true spring in the woods between here and the falls. The falls themselves are barren of trees. No wildflowers bloom, and the birds pass us by. The fairies must have the promise of spring to survive. It's their way. They have clung to hope for so long that now their magic can sustain only the immediate area around a few of the blessed trees. If they venture too far from home, they will wither and cease to be, just as Mar a' Ghrian did. When the crown is returned to Sirona at the falls, the balance of nature will be restored. The fairies will be freed of their captivity of sorrow and the forests will flower. It will be a day of miracles.

"If you listen to your heart, you'll know the truth of it, Rainey. Sirona was a spirit sister to the fairies. She visited them as a young girl and learned their ways. They want only peace and happiness for her. They want the crown for her sake. It was a precious gift, revealin' themselves to you as they did. They were bestowin' their last best trust in you. It was a rare thing. The trouble was, with so little time, it was a gamble to try the introductions so early on. It was a gamble we all lost."

Rainey looked up into his eyes. "They trust in you completely, though, don't they?"

"Aye. I'm an incurable dreamer, remember? They knew I was a safe candidate for contact from the day I was born into this house. It's only the weather that's a danger to you, Rainey. The snow is blowin' in monstrous drifts. We have no working phones here, no working vehicles. With no electricity, none of the caretakers stay the night, and the path back through the wood is a circuitous one at best. It would be unwise to try it in the dark."

She considered his words. "So we're a long way from the cottage?"

"Not so very far by daylight. But as it is out there now, it might as well be from here to Glasgow."

"If it meant Sasha's safety, I'd crawl from here to Glasgow on my hands and knees."

He gave her a grim smile. "And well I know it, lass. But all I have told you is the truth. I'll swear it on my mother's grave, if it will reassure you. You can see her marker from the window. It lies next to my father's stone."

She instinctively glanced toward the shuttered window he had indicated, and something caught in her chest. His parents' graves were so near.

"And you promise Sasha is safe at the cottage with Emma at this moment? The fairies won't call her out into the cold?"

He moved aside from the door. "You have my word of honor." He laid his hand on her shoulder lightly, then made a sweeping gesture to take in the entire gathering of his ancestors. "I hardly think this is the place to jeopardize my honor carelessly."

Rainey looked at the door for a long moment. "Then we're here for the night," she said, as much to herself as to him.

"Aye, though in point of fact, the night is half

gone." He walked back to the fire. "You must be weary. I thought perhaps . . ." He kept his sight trained on the flames. "There are a number of blankets in the cedar chest there next to the hearth. I'm not so ready for sleep just yet, but I can make you a pallet near the fire, if you like. You'll be warm. And undisturbed. If it would be more of a comfort to you, I can take myself to one of the other rooms. There are a couple of dozen."

Rainey joined him beside the fire, her sight, too, focused on the dancing flames. "If we had stayed at the cottage tonight, we would have slept in the same room, right?" He nodded. "So what's the difference? If you're satisfied with the arrangements, so am I."

"So be it." Without looking at her, he went to the cedar chest and withdrew an armload of neatly folded blankets. He spread them out a short distance from the hearth and rolled up a hand-stitched quilt for her pillow.

"They're a bit musty from bein' in storage, mind," he said as he smoothed a thick blue-plaid lap blanket across his creation. "But they'll do till mornin', most like. If you should take a chill . . ." He looked to her at last, his eyes speaking volumes, but quickly turned his attention back to tending the fire. "That is, I'll see to it you don't feel the cold."

"Matt?"

"Aye?" He went down on his haunches and stoked the fire with a vengeance. When she didn't speak, he rose to face her. "I'd best go in search of more wood. What is it, Rainey?"

Her eyes were trained on the portrait of his mother. "I don't think I can sleep just yet, either. Will you keep me company for a little while? I can't seem to stop shaking."

He drew her down to sit on the blankets and wrapped another quilt lightly across her shoulders.

"It's all too new, lass, the fairies and all. I know it's hard to accept. I keep forgettin' how strange it must be. The fairy trees are second nature to me, ye ken? They were always there. I've never questioned them."

Rainey started to tuck her hands under the blankets, but Matt took them between his own warm palms. The iciness left them at once, and she smiled at him gratefully. They sat, side by side, each lost in thought as they stared into the comforting fire.

"Where do you see us all a month from now, Matt?" Rainey asked. "I mean, if all goes well and we return the crown to the falls, what happens next?" She had thought it was a fairly simple question, but he gave it a good deal of careful consideration.

"A month from now, *mo chridhe*? I see a world of possibilities. One, you and Sasha return to your everyday lives in California, none the worse for wear. You get your job back by use of your marvelous powers of persuasion, and Sasha develops a crush on the lad who sits next to her at the local public elementary school. I go back to my dreary lesson plans, and at long last, leave the two of you the hell alone, as you have so eloquently requested from the start. A perfect future for us all, wouldn't you say?"

He let go of her hands and leaned forward to reposition a log on the fire. For a moment, he was between her and the only source of warmth, and combining this with his vision for the future left Rainey feeling colder than she had ever felt in her life.

It was, above all else, clinical for him. Fairies, legendary queens, and hand-holding aside, this was a project of study for him. She was glad for the reminder, she told herself. Somehow, she had managed to braid other emotions into his actions, emotions that were more of the fairy-tale variety than little Pretty Penny. This was good. This would help her combat her own vulnerability toward him. She had to lock onto this feeling of desertion. It was a positive step. A gift, as he was so fond of saying.

When he returned to her side, she kept her hands from him. "I'm feeling very tired all of a sudden," she said without feeling. It was true. She was physically and emotionally exhausted. "I'm going to try to get some sleep now." She didn't wait for his response, but curled herself up under the quilt, being careful not to make contact with him in any way.

"Understood," he replied. "But you only heard one of my glowing visions for the future. There are others, you know."

She pulled the quilt up around her ears to block out the sight and sound of him. "I don't want to hear any more of your damned predictions, Macinnes. I'll deal with the future as it comes. No more guesswork."

He tsked at her scoldingly. "My glowin' career as a soothsayer, cut short in its prime. A pity. I'm goin' to fetch us some more wood. I won't be long. Sleep well, Rainey. Tomorrow is a big day for us all."

"Just go. And give the spirits my regards."

"Fuel, lass. I'm only goin' after fuel. Damned if you're not a mistrustful soul at times."

"Not mistrustful, just realistic," she countered.

"God save us all from realists, *mo chridhe.*"

She heard the door latch behind him, and felt the full impact of the bleak loneliness of the room. She felt like a prisoner of the walls now. The paintings blurred into ghoulish shapes as her stubborn tears came, one after another, until the quilt beneath her head was damp.

"I don't need you, Matt Macinnes," she ground out against the delicately stitched cloth. And if she hadn't been so tired, lonely, and cold to the bone, she might have been able to convince herself it was the truth.

What seemed like only a few seconds later, she opened her eyes to find the little fairy Mar a' Ghealach curtseying before her on the hearth. The fire's glow shone through the fairy's gossamer wings as she spread them to absorb the welcome warmth. There was a tentativeness about her, a readiness to take flight if the danger became too great. The violet wreath around her head was wilted with snow, and the dark green rose leaves of her gown were tinged with brown. For her to come so far from the safety of the tree must have taken a great deal of courage, Rainey knew. Time was of the essence. She sat up, and Mar a' Ghealach took a step back.

"Hello, Mar a' Ghealach. I'm a bit surprised to see you," she said cautiously. She had automatically spoken in Gaelic, and Mar a' Ghealach responded softly in the same language.

"Only those who truly believe can see us," she said with a shiver that sent sparkling dust from her wings shimmering to the hearth. "Do my words sound familiar to you?"

"Familiar?" Rainey frowned in concentration as she fought against light-headedness.

"You have heard them before. I have come to give you warning. He is in danger of perishing from sorrow. You are the only one who can rescue him. Without purity of love in your heart, all will be lost." She bowed her head in anguish, and a single purple blossom fell from her wreath.

Rainey felt a great heaviness in her chest. "Tell me, Mar a' Ghealach, am I dreaming at this moment?"

The fairy raised her head. "If it is all a dream, or if none of it is a dream, my lady, it matters not. What matters is his survival and the restoration of the crown to its rightful place. These things are our only hope. I can do no more than to swear to you that the cause is right and just.

"He is calling to you in his own way, my lady. He mourns for Mar a' Ghrian and his parents. You will hear him soon. And then you must rise up and go to him. His parents are at peace. And Mar a' Ghrian lives again in another time. He must be made to believe these things. You alone can accomplish this."

"How can I help him, Mar a' Ghealach? I'm sorry for the loss of Mar a' Ghrian. And I never knew his parents, but I firmly believe they understood he did his best to save them."

"Do you have faith in the healing powers of love, my lady?" the fairy asked with a flutter of her wings.

Did she have faith, Rainey asked herself? Images of Matt and Sasha playing tag in Emma's yard raced through her mind. Matt had a deep devotion for Sasha, there was no doubt of it in her mind. And Sasha had come so far, thriving on that nurturing love. It had proven to be more effective than anything science or technology had offered. She, herself, had come a long way, too, thanks to Matt.

She met Mar a' Ghealach's steady gaze. "Yes, I understand what love can do."

"And you love him, my lady, honestly, with all your heart, as a woman loves the one man she chooses for herself?"

Rainey knew it was pointless to deny it to the little fairy. "Yes."

Mar a' Ghealach's face shone with relief. "Then give him his miracle, my lady. Show him what truly lives in your heart. It will save us all, and we will sing your praises among the oaks."

Rainey gave her a shy smile. "I'll do whatever I

can, Mar a' Ghealach. Whether he likes it or not, I'll give Matt his miracle."

Mar a' Ghealach smiled in return. "Then it will be your miracle as well, my lady." She floated upward and wrapped her arms around Rainey's index finger, hugging it lightly.

"I apologize for my brashness in the garden, my lady," she said humbly. "I reached out to you, in hopes of speaking to you alone before you entered the forest. But I had been away from the tree too long, and thorns had grown where my hands should be. In my haste, I fear I brought you pain," she said. "I am glad to see the damage has healed. Our mutual friend saved my life by returning me to the sanctuary of the oak. It is not the first time he has saved one of us from ceasing to be."

"Saving lives seems to come naturally to him."

"It is his gift. This is why he suffers so when the miracles die within him. You and your beloved daughter will bring his faith back to life."

"I hope you're right, Mar a' Ghealach."

"I have faith in you, my lady."

The fairy's dress had turned entirely to brown, and the wreath around her head was as withered and dry as any other remnant of spring in December. She appeared to be very worn from her efforts to communicate as she floated toward the hearth.

"I must go," she said, barely above a whisper. "Sleep, my lady, but in your dreams, listen for his call. It will come soon."

Rainy suddenly felt very weary. She lay down among the blankets and closed her eyes. Whether or not she slept, she would never be sure, but there was a new warmth in her heart, a warmth kindled by a fairy whose spirit was so like the moon.

Chapter 19

Rainey opened her eyes slowly, wondering what she would see. The room was still dark, and it was a struggle to breathe, she was shaking so hard. The fire was little more than a glow on the big hearth, and her breath made clouds of white in the frigid night air. If she moved, she would lose the small pocket of warmth her body had generated. But she remembered Mar a' Ghealach's words and instinctively listened for Matt's voice.

"Matt, are you here?" she called softly.

There was no answer. Either he was a very sound sleeper, or she was still alone in the room. Reluctantly, she sat up, taking the quilt with her.

A hint of color on the hearth caught her eye. There was a single violet blossom on one of the stones. It rested on a scattering of sparkling dust. But when she reached out to touch it, the flower withered and dissolved before her eyes, and the bright dust melted like frost in the midday sun. She felt a sense of loss. Mar a' Ghealach had been real, but all proof of her was gone. Even so, now she had an absolute trust in the idea of the fairy's existence, in her mind as well as her heart. Hopefully, Mar a' Ghealach had returned to the protection of the oak in time to stop the damaging effects of the winter cold.

"So help me, Macinnes, if you're out there somewhere warm and snug, hugging some fairy tree, you're going to pay dearly for a long time to come. You're not the only one who can make sacred oaths."

She thought she heard him. She glanced around the room, but other than the portraits staring back at her from the walls, she was utterly alone. This wasn't right. Regardless of how intellectually detached he might be, she didn't think he would intentionally subject her to this kind of cold. He had promised he wouldn't.

There was a pair of very old torches in holders on the wall, one on either side of the hearth. She took one down and when she dipped it into the fire's glowing embers, it burst into flame.

With the quilt still wrapped tightly around her shoulders, she ventured out of the room to find herself in a large foyer with a series of heavy wooden doors like the one she had just come through. There was also a broad stone staircase which led to the next floor. It was a Pandora's box of possible directions.

She heard a distant crash from above, and against her better judgment, she considered the stairs. The stone stairway was worn in the middle beneath the faded paisley carpet, but she didn't doubt its strength. She wasn't fond of its height, however.

Keeping a firm grip on the sturdy wooden banister, she started upward. The torch popped and sizzled in her hand, and she held it a little further from her face. The crashing grew louder and more frequent as she concentrated all of her attention on her feet. She groaned with relief when she reached the second-floor landing.

"Matt?" she called out. The sound of furniture and porcelain landing against solid surfaces was the only reply. If it wasn't Matt, she might be about to come face-to-face with an angry member of the Scottish spirit world. She hoped her Gaelic would be up to it.

As she edged her way along the dark hall, she saw a pale light coming from a partly open door at the end of the hallway. She didn't call Matt's name this time because whoever or whatever was in there was effectively trashing the place.

It occurred to her that if it were thieves, she was going to take the torch to them. And if it were kids vandalizing because the house was thought to be empty, she was going to throw them out bodily, no matter how many of them there were. Why she felt so savagely protective of this house was beyond her, but she had heard enough destruction for one night.

Mustering her courage, she held the torch out like a sword and flung the door open hard against the wall. Half-blinded by the torch's raw light, she planted herself squarely in the doorway.

"Okay, punks, you're out of here!" she shouted like a street-hardened cop.

She held the torch to one side and let her eyes adjust to the pale candlelight in the room. It was a bedroom. Or more correctly, it had been a bedroom. Now it was a shambles. Piles of shattered furniture and clothing lay strewn everywhere. A broken whiskey bottle lay in shards in the fireplace. And in the middle of the room stood the most shattered thing of all.

Matt stared at her through grim, red-rimmed eyes like she was an apparition. His hair and clothing were wet, probably from the snows outside. He had lost his glasses, and he looked very different to her without them. He was every male portrait on those walls downstairs. And he was a man in pain. He rubbed his eyes mercilessly in an effort to clear them.

"Sirona?" he said hoarsely.

Rainey ventured a cautious step forward. "Get a grip, Matt. It's me, Rainey. What's wrong?"

"Rainey. What's wrong, you ask?" he demanded

with a bitter twist. His laugh was touched with nervous breakdown, and she withdrew her brave step forward. "Why, whatever could be wrong?" he insisted. "We need firewood. Am I wrong here?" He didn't wait for her reply, but threw an antique stool against the far wall. It landed in a pile of broken joints.

"Stick by bloody stick, I'm goin' to reduce this place to kindlin'. I'm goin' to purge it from my heart." He hefted a sports trophy in his hand, then tossed it to join the stool.

"You make it look so damned easy, Rainey, this shuttin' off of your heart. How difficult could it be for me to do the same? Tell me the secret of your success." He started toward her, but she stood her ground.

"You're drunk, Macinnes. It doesn't become you."

He grabbed the torch from her hand and tossed it onto the cold hearth. "There's no enough whiskey in all the world to let me forget, Rainey. I canna get warm, ye ken? There's a cold well inside me that grows deeper with each breath I take. Damn me if I haven't tried to fill it—with teachin', with poetry, with Sasha's troubles, with you, by God. I should be dead. Do you understand what I'm sayin' to you? Where's the justice of it?

"I was young. I had nothin' to lose. They had everythin' to lose. They had so much to give to the world, so much love and knowledge. It should have been me. I was expendable. At least in death, I might have found a wee bit of bloody peace. But the sea stole 'em from me, and now all that's left is squares of marble on the hill."

"You're forgetting something very important, Matt," Rainey said calmly. "*You* are their greatest accomplishment. Your parents live on through you. Who they were, what they believed in, you carry it inside you each day. They made you who you are. You're their legacy. You can't go on blaming yourself for their deaths, any more than I can go on blaming Alan for Sasha's troubles."

He kicked the rubble aside as he paced. "Alan! Christ, Rainey, don't curse me with that ghost as well. How am I to do battle against this almighty dead hero of yours? I have no weapons to fight him. The perfect husband, the perfect father . . . I saw the video, remember? You and Sasha worshipped the bastard. It tears me apart. I have no right to feel as I do. I have no right to desire you." He stopped in front of her and started to put his hands on her shoulders. But he thought better of it, and let his hands fall into fists at his sides. "I have no right."

Desire. How drunk was he that he would use that particular word? Rainey wondered. He was a pro with language. Was it possible she didn't know all the word's meanings? Like a lightning strike, she was suddenly acutely aware of the heat of him, and her body instantly produced an answering heat. The word desire was very much in her mind as well. She had spoken of Alan, but Alan was not the man she ached for at the moment.

"Alan is gone," she said, speaking her thoughts aloud. It gave her a kind of freedom to say it. "He gave me the greatest gift he had to give. He gave me Sasha. She was always the absolute focus of both our lives. And I'll be forever grateful to him for her."

Matt tried to absorb what she was saying. Was she saying there was a chance for him?

"Listen to me, Matt." She touched his arm, and he stared at her hand as if it had magical powers. "In your own way, you're giving me Sasha, too. You and I are here for her. We need each other, and she needs us both. We can't undo the past. It's time to take care of the living."

He shook his head slowly. "In my head, I know you're right. But my heart . . . that empty hole in my heart is killin' me like cold, slow poison. You're killin' me, Rainey." He was shivering violently from head to foot as his eyes met hers.

There was a war raging inside him as surely as there had been one going on in her. Her heart went out to him, not solely because of his sorrow, but because she could no longer deny that, right or wrong, she wanted to give her heart to him. She couldn't think now why it had taken her so long to realize the simple sense of it.

To trust him was more than a commitment of her own future. It was a commitment of Sasha's future as well. Until now, it had seemed like an impossible decision to make. There was the terrible risk that she would lose Matt one day as she had lost Alan. She should keep a part of herself isolated, detached from all he was asking of her without a word at this moment. But there was no part of her willing to volunteer for so black a watch.

"We've only known each other a few days," she said. "But somehow, it feels like you've always been beside me. Even when I was little, you were watching over me with your heart, weren't you? You knew something would lead me to you. And that something was Sasha."

She reached up and lightly traced the scar on his cheek. In return, he pressed her palm to his lips, and she experienced a wave of pleasurable shock that flashed to her extremities. This was more than simple attraction. This one small gesture bonded their souls.

"Take me out of the cold, Rainey," he said tenderly. "Take my heart away from this misery for one night, *mo chridhe*, and I'll never ask another thing of you." He waited.

"It can't be that way, Matt."

He dropped to his knees before her, a beaten man, and she laid her hand on his head. She knelt in front of him and took his face between her hands. He looked as if she had shot an arrow through him, and it nearly broke her heart.

"When you look at me right now, Macinnes, what do you see?"

He couldn't find any words.

"What, no shining moon, no silver dreams, no ancient verses?" She smiled through her tears. "When you look at me now, what you see is a believer. I can't fight it anymore. I'm buying it all, the man in the moon, fairies, starry crowns, and sad poets. But you have to understand, I can't give you just one night, Matt. The only way I can do this is if I give you them all." She held her breath from the dangerous importance of her own words and stared at that damnable tear in his sweater. "Are you game for it, Stanford, for all the nights to come?"

He tucked his finger under her chin and raised her eyes to his. "Tonight and for all the lifetimes to come, *mo chridhe.*"

The gentle but possessive pressure of his lips against hers was like the answer to a prayer she hadn't even been aware she had been saying since he had come into her life. His scent was that of snow on wool, exertion, and the barest hint of fine Scottish whiskey as her lips parted beneath the explorations of his kiss. She wanted him there. What was more, as he molded her body to him, she felt a hunger inside as she had never felt before. There was something between them she could only liken to a mating call. It was a bond no amount of time or interference from the outside world could shake.

He kissed her until her head was reeling, then led her to the hearth, where he tossed a few of the closest pieces of broken furniture onto the smoldering torch.

In the better light, the full extent of the damage he had done to the room could be seen. There was a large, swirling Celtic pattern that looked like a pair of swans carved into the mantelpiece. It was spectacular.

Matt hauled a bare mattress over to the hearth, then stripped off his wet sweater. The wool was thick and his shirt underneath was only a little damp. He glanced back at the room, marveling at his own handiwork.

Rainey leaned into his embrace and felt herself relax instantly. She heard the strong beating of his heart, and contentment washed over her. But she wanted to be kissed again. When she looked up at him, she saw he was minding the progress of the fire like a Highlander of old among the heather. His heart was still unsettled.

"You must understand, Rainey, how I feel about you has nothin' to do with swords or legends. I need you like I need the air I breathe. If we had met under other circumstances, I would have felt the same. I would have known you, *mo chridhe*. It's never been this way for me. I want you and Sasha in my life for all the years to come. I can no longer imagine my future without the pair of you." He smiled at her, his face filled with hope. "If you like, I'll take that red crayon you always seem to have about your person and pledge my faith to you across these walls for all to see."

Rainey grinned up at him, and to his surprise, she produced the crayon from her pants pocket. "It's becoming kind of a good luck charm for me," she said with a shrug.

He kissed her soundly, then stood up and scrawled his declaration of love and fidelity in old Gaelic across the wall. She read it aloud as he wrote.

" 'I hereby pledge my life and my love for all time

to the fair Lorraine. I will abide with her, care for her, and cherish her. I will be a loyal husband and father, forsaking all others, for all the days to come, so help me God.' "

The crayon was nearly gone by the time he had signed his name. But Rainey took it from him and wrote, "My life, my love I will share with Matthew Macinnes for all time." She signed her name and turned to him with pride. "That's pretty official, I'd say."

Matt wrapped her in his arms as they stood, side by side, next to their written vows. He tilted her chin up and searched her soul with his eyes. "Will you lie with me, Rainey?"

She wrapped a stray lock of his hair around her finger and went up on tiptoes to whisper in his ear, "Aye."

He closed his eyes slowly, absorbing her decision, then swept her into his arms. *"Glè' mhath, mo chridhe!* Wonderful!" he shouted for every person and fairy within a square mile to hear. He carried her to the mattress with ease and set her down there as if she were fashioned of glass. After tossing more chunks of broken furniture onto the fire, he dragged over an armload of the bedclothes he had scattered earlier. There seemed little point in trying to sort them out, so he wrapped whatever was useful around the two of them. There was enough warmth between them at this moment to stave off the night's stubborn chill.

Rainey snuggled close to him as she watched the fire gain strength. "Remember that first night on the back porch at home when you asked me what I saw when I looked up at the moon?" she asked.

"Aye, love, I remember it well," he replied with a kiss to the top of her head. "I was a bit rough on you, I'm afraid."

"You were smug and incredibly full of yourself, as

I recall." She persuaded one of his shirt buttons open and relished the sound of his deep laughter close up. She glanced up at him, her eyes full of mischief. "Of course, I've gotten used to that."

He slid his finger down the bridge of her nose. "Have you, now?"

She caught his hand in her own, her mood suddenly serious. "I was just thinking about how cold I felt that night. I don't know how to explain it, but it was like I was sharing the need for warmth with every living creature who had ever existed. It was a connection, an empathy. As long as you feel the need for warmth every now and then, you know you're alive. Maybe I was foreseeing tonight. I didn't know it at the time, but you were the warmth I needed. Why couldn't I see it then?"

In the fire's glow, her eyes dilated almost into blackness as her lips parted with another, unspoken question. He smiled down at her with total devotion.

"It had to happen here, *mo chridhe.* I don't understand why myself, but this is where you and I were meant to truly find one another. Perhaps there are forces at work beyond our understanding. But there is one force at work here I understand very well."

He kissed her to within an inch of her soul, and she responded like a desert wanderer given a cool drink at last. With gentle hands, he cupped her mouth to his, capturing her breath, savoring her sweet taste, her scent. He leaned her back among the blankets and settled beside her, propping himself on one elbow. As he smoothed her hair, he smiled at her and took the opportunity to run his fingertips down to where the pulse beat rapidly at the base of her throat. She sighed contentedly as he slid his hand down her arm. Though she was fully clothed, his hand was poised very near her breast, and she shivered with anticipation.

"With your kind permission, my love," he said, his voice rough with desire.

Her eyes misted as she looked up at him. "What I have is yours," she said softly.

He kissed the bridge of her nose. "On the contrary, what you have is yours, *mo chridhe*. All I ask is that you share it with me from time to time," he said with an enticing grin. "Or perhaps every minute of the day and night, if I continue to feel as I do at this moment."

She gave a delicious sigh as she undid the remaining buttons on his shirt. "Every minute of the day and night, huh? What a slave driver. So much for making a living. I guess I have a future of food stamps ahead of me after all. Maybe I better think this through." She raised one eyebrow at the reddish brown hair on his chest and gave his ribs a playful tickle. He caught her hand and pressed it against his heart.

"I am far more the slave than the slave driver," he said lovingly.

She took his hand and slid it beneath her sweater to where her own heart beat at breakneck speed. He savored its rhythm, then persuaded her bra strap down and brushed the warmth of his palm across her tightening nipple. The breath caught in her throat as he took the weight of her breast into his hand and held it as he would a nesting dove.

"You are so rare a jewel, Rainey," he whispered in her ear.

"Still after treasure, are you, Macinnes?" she tossed at him, even as she kissed his cheek.

"Indeed I am," he replied as he shifted her into a sitting position on top of him.

She pulled her sweater over her head and tossed her bra aside, mindless of the cold now as she explored the strong dimensions of his chest with her hands. From the start, she had sensed his strength, but now the reality of his marvelous build was no longer a mystery. It was there for her to see in the fire's glow. He was pleasing to her eyes as well as to her touch.

But to her surprise, there were three more scars she had not seen until now. One was long and jagged where his collarbone met his shoulder. The second one ran across his solar plexus in a single four-inch gash. The third was as cruel as the first, running the length of the ribs on his left side. The wounds were old, but the marks remained as vivid reminders. She kissed each one in turn.

"The storm," she said with a sad kind of awe.

"Aye. Let's not speak of it." He took her hands into his own and pulled her down to him. "There's only the one scar for the world to see. The rest I show only to you, Rainey."

She felt an overwhelming longing to ease his sorrow. "You never have to hide anything from me, Matt. I can take it. We can take it together. You told me it was time to share the burden of caring for Sasha. Well, it doesn't stop there. We have to share it all. It's the only way it'll work."

"For now, my wee Queen Mother," he said, "we shall concentrate on nothin' but the good." She squealed with delight when, in one swift move, he rolled her neatly beneath him.

Her dark curls fanned out across the sheets, and she gave him a Mae West roll of her eyes. "Is this how they treated royalty in the old days?" she asked flirtatiously.

"Oh, aye, royalty was forever between the sheets. It was all they were good at. Of course, for Highland royalty, a strip of plaid was all a person needed to strike up a warm acquaintance. You'd best get used to the notion of sheddin' all this California denim."

He undid the top button of her jeans and slid the zipper down, letting his hand linger there.

Rainey closed her eyes and drank in the warm sensation of his hand on her skin. "We're going to be savages out among the heather, I take it."

"Savages here and now, *mo chridhe*."

His kiss challenged her to hold nothing back, and she was glad to oblige him. As he slipped off her shoes and the last of her clothing, she loosened his belt buckle and eased his pants down over his lean hips. He kicked his clothing aside as if he might never use it again. There was no hiding his desire for her now.

He ran the backs of his fingers down her cheek and gave her a look of hunger barely held in check. "I must ask the question, Rainey. In my wallet . . . That is to say, if you wish for protection . . . I swear to you I would never put you in danger. But if it's too soon for you to make this kind of commitment, I will understand."

She took his face between her hands. "I'm not afraid of the future, Matt, our future. I trust what lies ahead for us. I trust you. So much has happened to bring us together, it's time we put our faith in each other to work."

Matt rested his hands on her arms. She gave a small shiver at the contact, and his eyes rose to hers in silent question of whether she was cold. She shook her head to assure him she was not, and he smiled in return as he took in the sleek curves of her anatomy.

"Have you always been so bonnie?" he asked.

"Bonnie? These days I only seem to answer to the name Harvard." She traced a light circle around his left nipple and grinned in triumph when it responded immediately to her attention. "Do you mean have I been bonnie for the last twenty minutes?"

"I mean for the last twenty lifetimes."

He didn't wait for her reply, but enfolded her within his arms. His kiss was a passionate promise of total devotion, because what he would do next would bond them to one another for all their lives.

The moon's soft glow through a break in the shutters surrounded them as Rainey eagerly answered his call for joining. She had only been with one other man in her life. Alan had been sweet and considerate toward her, and she had loved him dearly for all he had given her. But Matt knew the secrets of her heart better than she knew them herself. And as his gentle fingers explored the dark pathway between her legs and coaxed her quickly into readiness, she welcomed him. She was ravenous for him.

It had been a very long time since she had known a man's intimate touch, and she knew she would rush over the threshold of climax against his hand if he didn't give her a chance to catch her breath. She groaned softly as she struggled to maintain control over her body's heated tremors when he rubbed the little knot of her tenderest flesh lightly between his thumb and forefinger. He praised the resulting honey with stroke after gentle stroke of his palm.

He wasn't about to give her a chance to catch her breath. The second time, the hundredth time, they could take leisurely excursions into more complex sensual pleasure. But this first mating of their souls would be as it would have been among the heather, an urgent and wild thing with but one purpose.

A mist of perspiration formed across his back. "I cannot survive another breath without bein' inside you, Rainey," he said with an edge of pain. "Take me in from the cold."

A single tear slid down her cheek as she looked into his eyes. "Welcome home, Matt."

She reached down and guided the hard strength of him deep inside her. He filled her so, it seemed impossible he could move. But with a single bold stroke to the very heart of her, she cried out his name and climaxed around him with such force that she was certain she must have caused him pain. But he showed no signs of damage, and she wrapped her legs high across his back and took him deeper with each powerful drive of his hips. She answered his every move with an animal energy.

But when she reached down and caressed him where they were joined, his head jerked up, and he froze. He pulled back to within an inch of leaving her, the sweat glistening across his shoulders, his eyes intent on the swans above the fire. But there was no thought in his mind of truly withdrawing from her.

"*Ionad-naomha*," he said like a prayer. Sanctuary.

He whispered her name. Then, with a shout that might have otherwise been saved for the battlefield, he thrust so deeply into her very soul, she cried out in revelation. The time was upon them. He delivered a river of renewed life into her, keeping with such singleness of purpose that she ended up with her back on the hearthstones. Her sloe-eyed smile told him it wasn't a cause for concern.

Chapter 20

In the cold darkness before dawn, Rainey awoke with a shiver. She reached over beneath the blankets to borrow warmth from Matt. But his place beside her was empty. She turned over to find him staring into the fire with nothing to protect him from the frigid air but a blanket draped across his shoulders.

She had no regrets about the glorious hours they had spent wrapped in each other's arms. Hopefully, he had none either. But his demeanor was one of desolation, and she prayed she wasn't the cause. She pulled a thick woolen blanket around herself and laid her hand gently on his shoulder. He had been so utterly lost, half in though, half in a dream, that he turned to her with a start, hardly aware of what was going on around him.

"I'll protect you!" he cried.

"It's all right, Matt," Rainey said soothingly. "Everything's fine."

"Is it, love?" He took up her hand and kissed it tenderly. His eyes warmed to her when he saw her skin still glowed from their lovemaking.

"Well, if it isn't right now, it soon will be," she said with conviction.

He was so tense, she automatically started to massage his shoulders. She wasn't used to this mood of his. She was the one who always had the doubts.

And especially now, after their night together, she was relying on his unswerving optimism to carry them all through the things to come. There had to be something she could say to lift his spirits.

"I'd like to bring Sasha here, Matt," she said quietly. "I'd like to show her your home."

"This place is no longer mine, Rainey," he said firmly. "I don't belong here. It's their place. I don't think I'm so very welcome here anymore."

She sat down beside him and wrapped part of her blanket around his back. "Well, maybe not when you're trashing the place," she said with a glance over her shoulder at the mess behind them. "I was ready to toss you out myself."

"Were you now?" He tried to grin, but the smile failed to reach his eyes.

"I very definitely was," she insisted. "I haven't seen much of this house, but what I have seen is pretty amazing, you know." He pressed his lips together in stubborn resistance, but she was determined to be just as stubborn.

"Look," she continued, "you saw how Sasha reacted to those bits of broken pottery at the cottage, right?" He nodded. "Well, if she could stay in this place, she'd be in seventh heaven." She gestured about her.

Matt surveyed the rubble in his room with doubt. "So there are seven heavens as far as you're concerned?"

Rainey sighed. "I wonder if Mar a' Ghealach knew how difficult this particular little miracle was going to be," she muttered to herself.

The fairy's name caught Matt's attention. "What about Mar a' Ghealach?"

She was sorely tempted to say the little fairy had left strict orders for him to snap out of this guilt nonsense over the loss of his parents. But chances were, Mar a' Ghealach had already tried to talk him out of it in her own way.

"I was just thinking about her. I'm convinced she wants you to stay here in the Highlands."

"Mar a' Ghealach has more important things to worry about."

Rainey set about braiding the fringe on her blanket. "Well, I'd like to bring Sasha here. And maybe for a little while, I'd like this to be our home, yours, mine, and hers."

Matt stood up abruptly and strode a few paces from the fire. He wrapped his blanket around himself like a tartan of old and looked every bit the fierce Highland warrior in the firelight.

"It can't happen, Rainey," he said, his emotions on edge. "I know what you're tryin' to do. And I know your heart's in the right place. But you can't force a thing like this. The scars don't vanish so easily as that."

Rainey stared into the fire, seeing the image of Matt's face there as clearly as if she were looking directly at him. She knew what she had to do. But it was like standing at the top of that waterfall in her dreams. There was no turning back, but going forward was going to be very dangerous.

"When the head of the Macinnes clan marries, he brings his wife here, am I right? It's the tradition, almost the law."

"Aye."

He hadn't moved, but his answer had seemed to come from very far away. Rainey kept her eyes focused on the flames and hoped her courage would hold.

"When we get married, I want you to bring us here. This is where we all belong."

He groaned as if she had struck him a very low blow, and in the heavy silence that followed, Rainey decided that she had overplayed her hand. She stood up, and without looking at him, she started toward the door. It had been the only plan to come into her head. What was more, she wanted nothing more.

Matt caught her as she passed.

"Rainey," he said raggedly. "I love you as I've never loved anyone or anything in my entire life, and if moving into this house is what you desire, it will be my wedding gift to you."

She couldn't stand the thought of what this was doing to him. He was willing to make this sacrifice for her, but she wasn't willing to let him do it. She grabbed him by the arms.

"Listen to me, Macinnes, they're at peace! They want us here. Can't you get it through that thick Highland skull of yours? They want you to move on with your life. What will it take to convince you? Do you need a sign from them? Fine, that should be easy enough."

She had no idea where it was coming from, but a voice in her head was telling her precisely what to do. Without waiting for Matt's reply, she took his hand and hauled him into the hallway. She didn't have the help of the torch this time, but there was no question in her mind where she should go.

At the far end of the hall, she pulled open a door. The room beyond was dark except for the dim outline of two tall, arched windows. The snow must have subsided because the pale glow of the moon shone through onto the massive, four-poster bed and the Oriental rugs.

Matt paused outside the door, but Rainey wouldn't let him lag behind. She was driven to do this. Though even now, she wasn't sure what she was doing. It seemed inevitable that she would stumble over something in the dark. But it didn't happen.

Between the two windows stood a dressing table.

The large oval mirror above it gave her a start when she unexpectedly caught the motion of her own reflection. It would not have surprised her to see Matt's mother's reflection there. She sat down on the small low-backed chair. Matt stood beside her, saying not a word. She felt a tingle of anticipation flash up her spine.

"Left drawer, toward the back," she heard herself say. She opened the drawer and eased her hand through the dense network of cobwebs to a small book with a lock and a little square box. It felt like the box was covered in velvet.

"Were you in this room earlier tonight, Rainey?" Matt asked.

"I've never been in here before," she replied. "Unless I was walking in my sleep." Not a complete impossibility, as far as she was concerned. But she had no recollection of ever being in the room. "These are things your mother wants you to have," she said with absolute conviction as she handed them to him. "The key to the diary is behind the third brick down on the right side of the fireplace, the one with the triangular notch."

She rose from the chair and crossed to where a tall bureau stood. Without another thought, she pulled open the heavy bottom drawer and reached under the neatly folded trousers still stored there. For a moment, she thought her instincts had been wrong when she found nothing unusual. Then her fingers brushed against a smooth object. She withdrew the palm-sized leather box and handed it to Matt.

"A communication from my father, you're tellin' me," he said in amazement.

"Aye, Stanford, that's precisely what I'm telling you."

They returned to Matt's bedroom, where he tossed more broken bits of furniture onto the fire to offer them better light. He and Rainey sat down side by side on the mattress, the three treasures and the diary's key between them.

"I can't bring myself to open it," Matt said of the diary.

Rainey took the small key and slid it into the diary's lock. It turned easily, and the latch released. The diary fell open to an elegantly penned entry near the back. While the installment before it had filled an entire page, this one took up only half. It was the last entry. Rainey handed the book to Matt. There was anguish on his face as he began to read aloud.

" 'Only time for a few words. We're all off to the islands again this morning. We dare not chance staying at the house too long. The skies look fretful, but my darling Andrew has never let the threat of dirty weather hold us back. Needless to say, if that were the case, we should never leave the city.' " He could read no further, and Rainey took the diary into her own lap.

" 'I have thoughts of wearing Nana's paradise brooch from Glomach today for our safekeeping,' " Rainey read. " 'I often think of the courageous Sirona on days like this and wonder if our own dear Matt may someday be the one to put things to rights for that miraculous lady of old. I am a silly romantic. But goodness knows, old Lord MacDonnaugh and that snippy daughter of his could use a good bit of comeuppance in their lives.

" 'Perhaps that pair of swans from the Book of Kells on Matthew's mantelpiece will in time give him inspiration—two souls joined as one beyond time and separation. They were always my favorite. I am reminded that the day of the Winter Solstice Swan will soon be upon us again. How the days do fly! Sincerest apologies for so weak an attempt at humor!

" 'My heart fairly bursts with pride each time I

look at that handsome son Andrew and I have managed to raise to manhood. I know he and his father are sometimes at odds over the methods required by field archaeology. But it's only natural, I feel, for men to test their strengths of will against one another. They are so alike and so dear.

" 'I often see the best parts of myself in Matt. It's pure vanity, to be sure, but he is my one wee pinch of immortality, the swan who guards my soul for all the generations to come.

" 'But I am waxing far too poetic, and my beloved Andrew is calling from below. More concerning our perilous adventures at sea upon my return.' "

Rainey set the diary in front of Matt.

He stood up and laid his hand over the swan emblem on the mantel as he kicked a piece of wood deeper into the fire. "She never got the opportunity to add more."

The little box was still unopened, and Rainey picked it up, cradling it in her hand. It was covered in dark blue velvet, and it looked to be very old. She started to give it to Matt, but he indicated for her to open it.

She pulled back the lid slowly to find a small piece of meticulously folded paper. Written in his mother's neat hand were the words, "For Matt's bride, that she may always carry the Highlands in her heart." When she drew the paper out of the box, beneath it she discovered a lovely gold locket and chain. Engraved at the center of the heart were the words *Creideamh, Gradhaich, Siorruidheachd,* meaning faith, love, and eternity. She took it out of the box and let the firelight play off the words and the Celtic knots and roses pattern etched around the edges.

"Oh, Matt, it's glorious!" she exclaimed. "I can't image how old it must be. How could your mother even think of parting with it?"

With tender care, she slipped her thumbnail under the locket's latch and persuaded it open. Inside was a tiny spray of Highland heather crowned with a single pressed violet.

Matt saw her joy at the piece. "She meant for you to have it, Rainey. It seems she knew you were there on my horizon. Who can say, perhaps she oversaw our comin' together." He took the locket from her hand and placed it around her neck so it rested next to her heart. "It looks very natural on you, *mo chridhe*. She always thought of everythin', my dear mother."

Rainey touched the locket reverently. "She must have been an amazing lady."

"Aye, she was all of that." He smiled at her sadly, and Rainey pushed the leather box from his father's bureau toward him. He opened it slowly. Inside was a very old and worn key with a paper disk attached to it. On the disk it said in a masculine scrawl, "For Matt's 21st." Matt frowned at the key, deep in thought.

"Do you know what it goes to?" Rainey asked. He didn't seem to hear her question as he turned the key over in his palm.

She touched his sleeve, bursting with curiosity. "Come on, Macinnes, spill it. What do you think it is?"

"I wonder if it's possible," was all he said as he set the key back into its box and closed the lid. He stared into the fire for a moment, then sprang to his feet and raced toward the door, the box in hand. "We'll have need of the torch, Harvard," he called over his shoulder.

Rainey fished the handle of the torch out of the fire and ran after him in the hope he hadn't left her too far behind. He had taken the stairs, and she stopped cold on the landing.

"The torch, Harvard!" she heard Matt call.

"Coming!" she called back. The dark steps stretched out before her, and perspiration gathered at her temples as she fought with the idea of such a descent. She had to take it very slowly, concentrating all her energy on reaching Matt rather than focusing on the height.

She found Matt in the room with the portraits. After hastily dipping the second torch into the meager embers of the fire, he took the first torch from Rainey's hand and set it into its holder. Though far from bright, the torches provided a small degree of light to the entire room.

Matt headed directly toward a set of three tall wood cabinets that stood against the back wall. They looked like rifle storage closets, and Rainey approached them with caution as Matt withdrew the key from the leather box.

It wasn't until the third cabinet that the key slid home. Taller and plainer than the other two, this cabinet resisted opening. The key had done its work, but no amount of tugging and jostling could make the door budge.

Matt was cursing in four different languages by the time Rainey walked up to him and laid her hand gently over his on the handle. Instantly, there was a satisfying scrape, and the door began to move.

"I guess you must have loosened it up," she said with a grin.

"Aye, to be sure." Impressed, Matt gave her a sideward glance as they joined forces to slide the door open. It was heavily lined and insulated on the inside.

The cabinet housed a single object, an exquisitely crafted broadsword of the old school. Matt instantly went down on one knee at the very sight of it, and Rainey could only stare in awe. The air was heavily charged as they beheld the sword's clean, lethal power. On the oak handle was the elegantly carved head of a swan much like the ones on the mantel in Matt's room. And all along the hilt were dozens of evenly placed notches.

Rainey reached out to touch the sheer majesty of it. But the impact of what it might be made her hesitate. "It's the sword from the falls, isn't it?" she said reverently.

Matt lifted the weapon free of the simple pegs of wood from which it had been hanging and stepped back a few paces before he swung it in a swift and skillful series of figure eights. The air sang with the magic of finely honed metal cleaving through years of secret captivity. With a look of pure masculine elation, Matt nodded in answer to her question.

Rainey watched as he hefted the balanced weight of the weapon in his hand, and was surprised to find she felt a real sense of pride in his natural abilities with the sword.

"It's absolute perfection," Matt announced as he examined the blade. "When I was no higher than his knee, my father took me aside and defined every piece of family heritage in this house. Nothin' was overlooked. But when I pointed my wee finger at this cabinet, he said, 'Not until you've reached your majority, my son. That's the family tradition.'

"I remember he did tell me the story, though, how in the eighth century, my ancestor risked his life to retrieve a trophy from its watery restin' place." He pressed his hand against the sword's hilt. "The Viking hordes had got wind of the possibility of a treasure in a waterfall where our family lived, so the story went. Nothin' could hold back the men of the north sniffin' out riches. They cut down everythin' and everyone who got in their way. But by no means was a man of Macinnes blood goin' to let such a thing as this fall into invadin' hands.

"As it was, my ancestor, Aedan by name, had to perform his act of bravery under the cloak of darkness. All the more courageous because it was believed in those days that spirits would steal your soul if you wandered abroad at night. And Glomach was overrun with spirits. My father said to me, 'There will come a day when the care and protection of this precious secret will pass to you, Matthew. There are many who would take it from us in the name of profit or posterity. We cannot let this happen. You cannot let this happen. The contents of the cabinet must always remain with a Macinnes.'"

Matt shook his head at the memory. "After that one day, we never spoke of the cabinet again. But it was always somewhere in the back of my mind. I'm amazed how well I recollect every word my father said to me about it. I couldn't have been more than Sasha's age at the time. I never knew what waited inside the case until now. The family has been guardin' the safety of this marvelous creation for well over a thousand years."

A surge of emotion raced through Rainey's heart as she watched Matt turn the sword's handle in his hand. "The legend is real. And you're sure it's not a forgery or a replica of some kind? I mean, you read about fake paintings that fool the experts all the time. They can do amazing things with phonies these days." There was a tightening in her chest as she questioned the sword's authenticity. There was no need to wait for Matt's answer to know in her heart the sword was genuine.

"Oh, it's the true article, and no mistake." He looked at Rainey with fresh eyes. "I'm the last of the line, ye ken, the last of the sword's rightful protectors. It's an obligation of the blood. I cannot remain the last, *mo chridhe*."

Rainey touched the locket that rose and fell lightly

with the beating of her heart. She understood very well what he was saying to her. The discovery of the sword gave them both a new sense of urgency. It was another link in the chain leading them all closer to the Winter Solstice. The crown couldn't be far behind. This night had already been one of vows, fairies, and magic. Now, here was a fresh connection.

"It was Sasha's voice I heard guiding me to the things your parents wanted you to have," she explained. "It's all tied to Sirona. And even though she's not here, Sasha knew what direction we had to take. It's what you've been trying to tell me all along. Sasha has a gift of understanding. I've been worried about her tonight with the Solstice so near. But I know now that all her energy is being channeled toward us. She's okay. We're going to make all of this happen."

Chapter 21

"Wake up, *mo chridhe.*"

Rainey smiled as Matt ran his finger along the curve of her ear. The warm contact of his chest and hips against her skin mixed with the earthy musk of their lovemaking made her sigh with contentment. She kept her eyes closed for just a while longer as she stretched. Her whole body felt weary and tender, but in a very pleasant way. And now, here he was waking her yet again.

"You're an insatiable sex fiend, Matthew Macinnes," she said with a throaty laugh. "And I wouldn't have it any other way."

He gave a self-conscious cough. "Have a care, love, we've got company."

Her eyes flew open and she turned over, cautious to keep the bedding wrapped around herself. She wasn't sure whether to expect fairies or The Ghost of Christmas Past.

"Sasha?" she exclaimed in surprise.

Sasha stood in the doorway. Her shoes were wet, and she was wearing one of Emma's sweaters with the sleeves rolled up. But most strikingly, she held the broadsword firmly in her hands. The tip of the blade rested between her feet and the handle was taller than she was. But she seemed perfectly at home with the enormous weapon as she gave them both a benevolent smile. It wasn't difficult to imagine what Sirona might have looked like as a young girl.

Rainey felt for her clothing among the bedding. "Good morning, Sash. Be careful with that thing, now, sweetheart. Where's Emma?" She gave Matt a nudge in hopes of getting him to look for her things from his vantage point. He gave her a mischievous wink and shrugged in reply, to her complete exasperation.

Emma came puffing up behind Sasha. The stairs had taken their toll, and she averted her eyes quickly when she saw Rainey and Matt on the mattress together. She grabbed Sasha's shoulders and turned her around in matronly fashion.

"It looks as if we've found the barn, darlin'," she said to Sasha as she fought for breath. "However did ye manage to drag that monstrous weapon all this way up the steps, lassie?"

The blankets flew in all directions as Rainey searched frantically for her clothes. To her disgust, Matt found his easily and slipped into them in leisurely fashion. As usual, he seemed to enjoy watching her struggle to stay decent.

"Help me, Macinnes!" she insisted in a harsh whisper.

He sighed in disappointment and dug her things out from under the mattress. It looked likely that he had hidden them there, and Rainey gave him a scolding frown. When she yanked her sweater on over her head, he pointed significantly to a point at the base of his own throat, and she automatically touched the place on herself. It felt bruised, and she realized he was warning her to cover up a telltale badge of his passion for her. She pulled her collar up quickly, blushing from head to foot.

Matt went down on his haunches behind her and kissed the back of her neck enticingly. "I believe the word of the day is insatiable, Harvard," he whispered against her untidy curls. She nudged him hard with her elbow, and he toppled backward with a satisfying snort of surprise. With a sheepish grin, he put his attention to the fire.

Emma cleared her throat uncomfortably. "Perhaps Sasha and I should wait for the pair of ye below."

Rainey scrambled into her jeans. "Not a problem. You can turn around now. How did the two of you find this place?" she asked in hopes of changing the focus of everyone's attention. She realized for the first time that pale morning light filtered through the curtains.

Emma took in the disaster area that was Matt's bedroom as she and Sasha came in. "Some things could no be salvaged after the Nazi Blitz in World War II, Sasha," she said, furrowing her brow at Rainey. "I had no notion the damage was so heavy this far north." She picked up one of Rainey's shoes and tossed it to her.

"Er, we didn't have much light," Rainey was quick to say. "I guess we knocked a few things over by accident."

"Quite a few things, by the look of it," Emma replied as she ran a smoothing hand across her hair. She dismissed the matter with a shrug. "Be that as it may, Sasha woke me to let me know in no uncertain terms there was somewhere we had to go. I'll admit I had a moment's pause when you and the good doctor didna return from your, er, walk. But I figured the two of ye were safe enough. And as it wasna a worry to Sasha, we settled ourselves in satisfactorily against the weather.

"But came the dawn, she was up and haulin' me out the door. I wanted to keep to the road, ye ken, but she'd have none of it. So, we tramped our way through the woods, with our own Sasha here takin' the lead." She tousled Sasha's dark curls affectionately, but Sasha's attention was focused on the hilt of the sword. "I had no notion where she was takin' us. The lassie was so dead sure of the way, though, I couldna see holdin' her back. As it happens, she was comin' here."

Sasha nodded in stately fashion, then dragged the broadsword over to the hearth where Matt was banking the fire. He gave her a warm smile of welcome, and in return, she reached into her pants pocket and brought forth his glasses.

He laid his hand lightly on her shoulder. "There's a clever lass. I thank you for giving me back my eyesight, Sasha. Now I have the pleasure of seeing your dear mother for the true beauty she is."

He gave Rainey a wink, then straightened the frames a bit and settled the glasses onto the bridge of his nose. The professorial facade returned, but since everyone in the room had just seen him among the tangled sheets with Rainey, it was doubtful the words "academic snob" would ever come to mind again.

Emma warmed her hands by the fire. "Ah, yes, yer spectacles. Sasha came by them near an old oak in the woods. We paused there during our journey. A grand auld fairy tree if ever there was one, that fine oak. Sasha knew it was special right off. Burdened down with snow, it was. But it was one of the magical royal guard, I'm that sure."

Sasha leaned the broadsword's carved handle reverently against the mantel swans and threw her arms around Matt's neck, a look of worry on her young face. *"Tha a' chraobh mhaol, gun duilleach,"* she whispered in his ear. *The tree is bare, leafless.*

"Aye, lassie, it's a sorrow, I know. But we're goin' to fix it." He set her back to arm's length. "You knew exactly where the sword was, didn't you, sweetheart?

And if I'd taken the trouble to lock the cabinet, you would have found a way to get to it." She nodded. "You know, together with your beloved mother and our dear Emma, we're goin' to get the crown as well, are we not?" Sasha smiled at her mother and Emma, looking very grateful for coconspirators.

Emma tidied what could be salvaged of the bric-a-brac in the room. "Och, well now, I hate to be the one to always be bringin' the subject up, but I wonder if there's such a thing as a bowl of parritch or a heel of bread to be had on the premises. I know that hike gave Sasha and me quite an appetite, and I imagine . . . the walk the two of ye had last night has given ye reason enough to want to renew yer strength."

Matt chuckled as Emma and Rainey blushed simultaneously. "It's unlikely there's anything about in the cupboards," he explained. "But I might be able to search out some fishing poles."

His speculations were interrupted by a resounding knock on the main door downstairs. Everyone exchanged glances.

"Wait here, if you will, ladies," Matt said as he headed for the stairs. He paused in the doorway, rubbing his chin in thought. "Feel free to toss whatever's handy onto the fire if you're still taken with the chill. I'll return directly." They all listened to his receding footsteps.

"Emma, have you got a comb or a hairbrush with you?" Rainey asked as she tried to smooth her hair.

"Aye, I do, lassie," Emma replied as she pulled a plastic comb from her handbag.

Rainey took it gratefully. "I must look like a bad horror movie," she said with a groan as she forced the comb through her tangled curls.

"Naw, lass, ye have the look of a woman in love, if I may be so bold. And I, for one, couldna be happier for the pair of ye." She withdrew some lip balm from her bag. "You'll have need of this as well, by the look of it," she said with a sideward smile.

"Thanks, Emma, you're a lifesaver." She glanced at Sasha to see her reaction to all of this.

But Sasha's attention was focused on the locket around Rainey's neck. She brought her palms together slowly, like the joining of two souls, and smiled at her mother. Nodding toward the crayon pledges on the wall, she then threw herself into her mother's welcoming arms.

"*Seud-suirghe, gu cian nan cian,*" she whispered in Rainey's ear, meaning a love token for all eternity.

"*Tha, tha sin ceart,*" Rainey replied, meaning you are right. A surge of love and loyalty rose in her heart.

"Rainey, love," Emma exclaimed, "that was the Gaelic! Do ye have it now as well?"

Rainey nodded. "Since last night. Since going to the fairy tree."

"The fairy tree? *Ceart gu lèor!* Then ye're a believer now." Emma crossed her arms and settled back on her heels with satisfaction.

"I suppose I am."

Sasha touched the locket lightly and looked into Rainey's eyes with a silent request for permission to open it. Rainey nodded her consent. The locket parted easily, and Sasha was amazed at its contents. She pressed a kiss to her fingertip and brushed it lightly against the violet.

"Mar a' Ghealach." Sasha whispered the fairy's name with tears in her eyes. "*Mheath a' chraobh,*" she sobbed, meaning the tree faded.

Rainey tucked a finger under Sasha's chin and brought her eyes up. "You know about Mar a' Ghealach, Sash?" Sasha nodded. "And Pretty Penny?"

"Suim Mhaith." Sasha whispered his name in

Gaelic softly. Then she promptly recited a swift roll
call of a dozen more fairy names, each one reflecting
a trait or propensity of its bearer: Rag-tag, who was
devil-may-care about his appearance; porcelain-
skinned Snowdrop; and Nectar Child, a youngster
who had a taste for sweets. The list went on, and as
she whispered each name, Sasha smiled or shook her
head at remembered antics as if she were talking
about well-loved cousins and playmates.

Emma walked over to the pair of them. "What's
all this about, then?" she asked.

Rainey turned to her slowly with a faraway look
in her eyes. "Fairies. It's all about fairies."

Emma rocked on her heels and tapped her chin
with her forefinger thoughtfully. "Och, and what is
it ye need to know about 'em? Go on with ye, ask
me anythin'."

Matt cleared his throat from the doorway. He held
a huge wicker basket. "Breakfast is served, dear ladies," he announced with an elaborate bow.

"You're kidding," Rainey said in surprise. "Who
was nice enough to send us a meal?"

"Why, the very queen of largesse, *mo chridhe*,"
Matt replied with a lopsided grin.

He brought the basket over to the hearth and lifted
the lid. Inside was a perfume-soaked card with
Matt's name on it. There was no mention of anyone
else. At the bottom, the words, "Can't wait to be
with you tonight!" and, "With all my love," were
boldly underlined, along with Cassandra MacDonnaugh's enormous, exaggerated signature.

Emma gave a derisive snort. "She's the queen of
somethin', all right, that one. But I'm thinkin' it has
more to do with animal husbandry."

Rainey ran her hand over the expensive bottle of
champagne enclosed. "Hmm, do you suppose arsenic
is detectable with the naked eye?"

Matt caressed her shoulder lightly. "I'll thank you not to use such provocative language, my love, or I cannot be responsible for the consequences," he said out of the corner of his mouth. "As you well know, I am obsessed with your beauty. Even a sneeze from your fair face may send me careening out of control. I say this only out of concern for your welfare, you understand."

Rainey rolled her eyes at him. "Talk about animal husbandry . . . Or maybe animal by-products would be a better description."

Matt clutched his shirt as if she had mortally wounded him, then joined in the merry digging to see what bounty Cassandra had sent. Fresh soda bread, scones and butter, four kinds of jam, kippers, ham, smoked trout and sausages, fruit, tea and shortbread squares—it seemed they would never reach the bottom. But everyone was famished, and they managed to put a healthy dent in the supplies before they were done.

Emma sighed contentedly, a plastic cup of champagne in her hand. "Well, if Blondie is after doin' us all in, I'd say she's done a fair brilliant job of it. And I, for one, can think of far worse ways to go." She saluted them all with her cup and downed the contents.

Rainey was not quite so ready to sing Cassandra's praises. She swirled the last sip of her champagne in her cup. "I'm not looking forward to tonight," she said.

Matt took a bite of a shortbread square and handed the rest to Rainey with a smile. "Personally, there are certain aspects of tonight I'm lookin' forward to very much."

"Oh, really? Suddenly you're a big Cassandra Mac-Donnaugh fan?" Rainey gave him a look of warning.

"I mean comin' back home, Harvard. Comin' home with you."

"Home?"

He covered her hand with his own. "Aye, *mo chridhe*, home."

Emma rose to her feet. "Well, that's remedied, then," she said, nodding to Matt and Rainey. She lifted the corners of her skirt just enough to transport her crumbs safely to the hearth and scattered most of them into the fire. But the largest ones she set in a tiny circle on the hearthstones.

"Ye never know but what we might have a few guests when we aren't lookin'," she explained. "This way the wee ones will know they're welcome, even if we're busy elsewhere when they come. It's only common courtesy, ye ken? Now who's for a walk along the loch? There's no a one of ye doesn't need to peel away a pound or two of sausage and short-bread, now. It'll do us all a world of good to clear our heads with a bit of heath and heather."

Rainey leaned against Matt's shoulder. When the two of them exchanged wistful looks and seemed in no great hurry to go anywhere, Emma wadded up a gold-embossed paper napkin and tossed it at Rainey's head.

"None of yer moonin' and come-hithers now, you two," she insisted. "If we're to win this war, we'd best put our minds on how it's to be done. Are we in agreement here?"

Matt stood up, bringing Rainey with him. "We're in complete agreement, aren't we, love?"

"Right, sure," Rainey said. The meal had made her sleepy, and what she wanted more than anything was to curl up with Matt and take a nice long winter's nap. She wasn't going to do them any good if she couldn't keep her eyes open, and the possibility of letting everyone down made her flinch inwardly.

Emma took her by the hand. "No slackers now, surfer girl. We'll all take the stairs together, arm in arm, dear. No need to fret. Let's be off. By now the mists should be liftin' nicely."

Once down the stairs and out the door, the winds off the loch whipped icy crystals across Rainey's cheeks, doing away with any notions of sleep. The scent of clean, cold water, moss, and marsh grass cleared her senses. It wasn't easy to keep up with Matt's swift hiking pace, but Sasha skipped along the shore beside him, flinging stones into the ruffling waves as if she had been doing it every day of her young life. She looked very much at home, and her delighted laughter echoed like a lilting song across the water to the barren, snow-crowned hills on the far side.

Matt joined in her good-spirited sports, dispelling Rainey's worries that this stroll beside the loch might trigger too many memories for him. He and Sasha looked absolutely natural together as they tossed stones for distance. It was hard to imagine Sasha hadn't known him all her life. Emma came up beside Rainey, locking arms with her.

"Are ye happy, then, lassie?" she asked.

Rainey considered all they had yet to accomplish. Somehow, it didn't seem as insurmountable now. Up until very recently, she could not have honestly said she was happy. But at this moment in time, with the silvery veils of Scottish mist rising slowly off the deep, blue-gray waters of the loch and the sounds of Sasha's laughter mixing with that of the man she loved, she could say it with all her heart.

"I am happy, Emma, happier than I've ever been." She took in a deep breath of the chilled Highland air and let it out with slow satisfaction.

Emma leaned over and picked up a tossing stone of her own. "Och, I was afraid of that," she said with feigned dismay. "Ye'll be walkin' around moonstruck from here on out, I suppose."

Rainey glanced to where Matt stood, and he instinctively turned to smile at her as if she were his own personal angel sent from heaven. The locket felt warm against her heart, and she thought of the tiny violet safely tucked inside. Mar a' Ghealach's spirit was all around them.

"You're right, Emma," she said, "moonstruck is exactly what I am."

Chapter 22

Rainey adjusted the collar of her green silk blouse nervously as they all waited outside the massive wooden doors to Castle MacDonnaugh. It was a nice blouse, one she wore when she had to make presentations of her work. But it had a tiny stain next to the third button, and there were several wrinkles across the back she hadn't been able to remove. It would have been far more practical to wear one of Emma's sweaters against the cold night breezes whipping around them at the moment, but her vanity had gotten the better of her.

The heavy iron gate across the driveway had opened for them automatically, and now a security camera stared down at them in an intimidating way. In the dark, the black silhouette of the castle was every bit as cold and imposing as she had envisioned, with its stone turrets and spires. She hadn't even seen Cassandra MacDonnaugh yet, but she was on edge. On the one hand, she wanted nothing to do with the woman. On the other, she wanted to deck her just on general principles.

But there was more to it than a simple dislike of spoiled snobs and a burgeoning jealousy over Cassandra's attentions toward Matt. She could hardly say she really knew Cassandra, yet there was something there, a wicked chemistry that made her hackles rise and her adrenaline shoot through the roof. It was hard to reconcile, but for Sasha's sake and for her own, she wanted the woman's blood.

It was a new sensation, maybe something akin to what soldiers in the heat of battle felt toward the enemy, she supposed. But as footsteps sounded from the other side of the door, Rainey felt the little hairs on her arms stand on end, and even in the frigid air, she felt too warm. Her hands closed into fists.

"Gently, my dove," Matt whispered in her ear. He took her hand into his, forcing her fingers to relax. "Shall I make her dance at the end of the sword, or is that women's work?" He chuckled at her look of surprise because he had read her thoughts so easily. "Be patient with the charade for only one night, *mo chridhe*, and the treasures of heaven will be ours."

"The only treasure I want is to see that crown in Sasha's hands and Cassandra's conceited smile wiped off her face."

Matt kissed the back of her hand quickly. "Your wish is my command. But one thing I may have neglected to mention, the crown and all the MacDonnaugh fortune used to belong to Lord Carlyle's older brother, Douglas. The two were always competing with one another, as brothers are wont to do. But of course, as the elder son, Douglas inherited the family fortune, and Carlyle was left with the scraps."

The footsteps behind the door drew dangerously near, and Matt continued in a hurried whisper.

"Douglas died rather mysteriously some years ago during a rock climbing expedition the two brothers took. It was ruled an accident at the time, the family bein' so prominent. Seems the climb was all done on Carlyle's dare. It was all to be nothing more than a day's lark for just the two of them. But Douglas ended up at the bottom of a cliff with a hikin' pick buried deep in his chest."

The similarity between the MacDonnaugh story and Sirona's story did not escape her. "Why did you wait until now to tell me all of this?" she demanded in a shocked whisper.

"If I'd told you before that the old man was very comfortable with the notion of murder, would you have come?"

She didn't have time to absorb the implications of Douglas's suspicious death because the door swung open. It was a momentary relief to see a scowling butler rather than Cassandra herself. The butler's white hair stood up like a scrub brush, and his eyebrows were bushy to the point of obscuring his eyesight. There was an air of world-weariness about him as he turned off a long series of switches on the alarm box just inside the door. He squinted at the intruders on the porch with no sign of welcome as they stood shivering under the polished brass sconces. Then he promptly started to close the door in their faces. Matt stepped forward and thrust his foot strategically in the door, while the butler grumbled something about calling the local constabulary.

"You never had a problem lettin' me in the door in the old days, Malcolm MacPherson," Matt said jovially. "Could it be you've forgotten the lad who toiled beside you in the garden, ferretin' out the fattest fishin' worms in all of Glens Shiel as you worked your magic with a spade?"

The old man stopped in his tracks, his brow furrowed in the painful process of recollection. His eyes were focused on the foyer's garish portrait of Cassandra as he spoke.

"I told ye a hundred times, Matty Mac, the fat ones are too slow and lazy. The hungry ones, lad, the ones all wiggle and wriggle, they're the ones ye want. They'll do ye a fair jig an' fill yer pan in the blink of an eye." He seemed to snap free of a dream as he turned to them. His eyes misted as he truly looked at Matt for the first time. "Is that you, Matty, or is this old digger havin' another of his blood pressure spells?"

Matt embraced him warmly, patting him on the back. "It's me all right, Malcolm, returned from the Colonies."

"Och, and yer a sight, Matty," Malcolm declared. He straightened and squared his shoulders. "So, ye've come home to stay, then? That house has been like a great ghost ship without a Macinnes at the helm. It's time ye took yer rightful place, laddie. Yer kin would have wanted it that way. It's expected of ye."

Matt caught Rainey's eye and gave her a slow smile. "Aye, man, it looks as though I'm here for good."

Sasha pulled on her mother's sleeve. Rainey saw her point first to her head, then to the second floor, indicating that the crown was in the house. Rainey nodded her understanding.

Malcolm laid a hand on Matt's shoulder. "That's grand, Matty, simply grand." The smile dissolved from his weathered face. "We lost our Tildy five years back, ye know. She tried to keep at the workin', and her heart give out." He looked to Matt as if he half-expected the miracle of Tildy's return from him.

"I'm sorry, Malcolm. I didn't know," Matt said with heartfelt sympathy. "She was a fine, dear woman, and I'll miss her."

"Aye, well, she loved ye like a son, Matty Mac. But the years wear on, do they no, and there's no bringin' her back, I suppose." His attention went to the others.

"I have three very special ladies with me, Malcolm," Matt provided.

"I'm no blind as the MacDonnaugh, Matty. I can

see her beauty for meself, can I no?" Malcolm insisted, his eyes locked on Emma. Emma blushed becomingly and put her attention to the silver letter tray on the foyer table.

A cloud of expensive perfume assaulted them, and they turned as one to find Cassandra regarding them with mild interest. She was dressed in a pink angora sweater and a white slim skirt, which gave her the appearance of cotton candy.

"Quite the bonnie wee family reunion," she said coolly. She came forward and offered a limp hand to Matt. He accepted it, kissing it with gentlemanly grace. Without taking her eyes from Matt's genteel smile, Cassandra inclined her head toward Malcolm. "I believe you have been assigned duties elsewhere, MacPherson. You have not forgotten your probationary status, it's to be hoped."

"No, mum," Malcolm replied swiftly. "I'll be about my duties straight away. It was good to see ye, Master Macinnes, ladies." He bobbed a quick bow and forged his way up the sweeping double staircase to the next floor.

Cassandra sighed. "I really must give him the sack," she said with an air of distaste. "Poppy insists on keeping him. It seems they discuss fishing, or some such nonsense."

There was a loud rapping noise from the main hall, and Matt let Cassandra lead him there while everyone else followed behind. Lord MacDonnaugh was seated in his wheelchair beside an enormous stone fireplace. He was thrashing a cane against a mahogany coffee table with such force that both cane and table were splintered. His face was expressionless as he stared sightlessly into the flames, but pure anger radiated from him.

"Get out!" he shouted when he sensed others in

the room. He smacked the cane down so hard, it shattered, and the table collapsed to its knees.

Matt took in the situation warily. "Have we come at an inopportune time, Cassandra?" he asked.

She gave him a honeyed smile. "Not at all, Matthew," she replied as she drew him nearer the fire. "Poppy's just in one of his black moods, aren't you, dearest?" she said as she ran her finger along her father's ear.

The old man recoiled at her touch and whipped the stump of the cane around in her direction. But Matt caught his move in time and stopped the cane firmly in his hand. Lord MacDonnaugh tugged to free it, but he was no match for Matt's youth and strength. His pale, clouded eyes shone unnaturally in the firelight.

"You'd best behave yourself, Poppy," Cassandra said. "The Macinnes is in the house."

The old man drew in a ragged breath. He leaned forward, squinting his eyes, though it did nothing to help his vision. "Yer a liar, girl. The Macinnes was planted good and proper."

Cassandra rolled her eyes and gave Matt a long-suffering look of apology. "Macinnes, the son, Poppy. Remember, I explained it to you yesterday. This is Matthew Macinnes. He's been away in America."

"What's he doin' in my house? Who told ye to let him in?" Lord MacDonnaugh demanded.

"I invited him, Poppy. I have the right to bring anyone I choose into this mausoleum. Matthew is my personal guest. For that matter, if I decide to invite Jack the Ripper for high tea, you'll hold your tongue."

"I'll show you who's in charge here, girl," he growled as he struggled to rise out of his chair. He hadn't the strength, and he fell back heavily into his seat.

Cassandra warmed to a fresh battle in this vicious little war without end. "He really is pathetic, isn't he, Matthew? Carlyle MacDonnaugh, noble laird of the clan, last remaining hope of the line, thanks to a bit of well-aimed rock climbing equipment."

"You shut up, girl!" Lord MacDonnaugh commanded.

"And here he is, the mighty laird, reduced to the state of a sickly old badger hoarding his fortune in the dark. Useless." She kicked his chair, and it lurched dangerously near the fire.

"Curse your greedy heart, daughter!" he grumbled as he tried to wheel his chair back from the heat.

Emma pressed her lips together in concern. "If ye'll pardon my sayin' so, countess, ye should give yer father a wee bit more respect."

Cassandra turned on her. "To what end? He has no one but me. And he's honor bound to preserve the family, aren't you, Poppy? All that sewage about Highland pride and duty to the clan." She ruffled his thinning hair, and he swung uselessly at her hand.

"By God, I'll disown you and leave the lot to charity!" he vowed.

"Brilliant!" Cassandra said with sweet venom. "I'll have my solicitor bring by the papers for you to sign." She gave Matt a Cheshire smile and a subversive wink. "I'll even read the documents to you so you'll know just what you're signing away. Or will you? For that matter, who's to say it will actually be my solicitor? It could just be that gorgeous Welsh garage mechanic I hired last week. All beef and bulge, that one. But you'd never know the difference, would you, Poppy?"

"I'll see you get not one penny, daughter!" he pledged.

"See me? I think not." She turned to find her guests staring at her with something less than admiration. Her demeanor underwent a dizzying transformation. "But I'm forgetting our lovely guests," she said smoothly. "I'm sure Matthew cares nothing for all this legal wrangling."

"You get that Macinnes bastard out of my house this instant!" Lord MacDonnaugh demanded. "He'll ruin me. His kind is never content to leave well enough alone. He's a thief, just like his sire. You'll see. He'll try to take the crown. It's what they all want. But no one will be gettin' it from me, do you understand? The crown will never leave this house so long as I draw breath."

Matt and Rainey exchanged a quick glance as Cassandra grabbed the handles of Lord Carlyle's wheelchair and propelled him toward the foyer. He tried to set the brake, but Cassandra slapped his hands away as she sped him toward the door.

"What's the matter, Poppy, the brake of no use to you? Is your vehicle racing out of control? Certainly you're no stranger to such things." She snorted at his rage. "You're obsessed with that damned crown, old man. It's a disease in your feeble heart. Who would want the Glomach when they could have all those Renaissance masterpieces collecting dust upstairs?" she said curtly. "You keep this up, and I'm going to see to it you're declared mentally incompetent so I can sell that bloody crown and all the rest to the highest bidder."

"Cassandra?" Matt ventured tactfully. But Cassandra was still stoking her own inferno. Sasha's hands were balled into fists at her sides, and Emma's color was high. Rainey, he noticed, was paying little attention. She stared into the fire as if the flames were imparting vital information to her.

"*Tha an choron an seo,*" she said softly.

Matt didn't dare draw attention to her by answering her statement that she, too, sensed the crown's presence nearby.

"It's a waste of capital to let all those treasures sit up there century after century," Cassandra persisted. "Sell them on the open market, for godsakes. I could put the profits to good use."

"You so much as go near the Glomach, Cassandra, and I'll put your eyes out myself, do you hear me?" Lord MacDonnaugh vowed. "You are a disgrace to your name!" he shouted.

Cassandra gave him a dark smile. "I'm precisely what you made of me, Poppy." The old laird went very still, and she gave his chair a hard shove toward the library. Then, she glided back toward her guests, neatly slamming the door behind her.

Cassandra dusted off her hands as if she had just removed a week's worth of rubbish. She gave Matt a sultry look. "Fathers can be so trying at times. Don't you agree?" She pouted against her fingertips. "A wise move on your part, Matthew, setting your parents adrift on a stormy sea."

Rainey felt Matt tense at her side. Was there any way on earth all of this was worth it, she wondered?

"I'm quite free of family entanglements, Cassandra," Matt replied evenly.

"Quite. Well, now that that unpleasantness is over, shall I ring for MacPherson to bring us the refreshments?" She glanced at the women. "I only hope there will be enough. I hadn't counted on so many hungry mouths for supper."

Rainey wrapped her arm around Sasha's shoulders. "Not a problem, Cassandra. I don't imagine we have much of an appetite at the moment."

"I'm certain we'll all do just fine, Cassandra," Matt replied in an effort to diffuse the tension between the women. "It's so very kind of you to entertain us on such short notice."

If bashing her father about could be considered entertainment, he thought to himself. He fought back the urge to dive out of the nearest window when she wrapped her arm through his and laid her head against his shoulder.

Cassandra pulled the servant bell and looked up into Matt's eyes as if they were alone in the room. "Perhaps you'll find a way to share a bit of hospitality in return," she proposed as she ran her hand down his arm.

"It would be my pleasure, I'm sure."

"I'd see to it, Matthew." Her smile was openly carnal, and his look told her she understood her offer.

They all sat down on the two couches in front of the fire, with Cassandra nearly in Matt's lap. Everyone was ill at ease except the hostess. Rainey judged it would be best to say nothing rather than risk betraying her true feelings about the evening.

Matt patted Cassandra's roving hand companionably. "So, my dear, whatever is this obsession your father has about a crown?" he asked lightly as Mac-Pherson entered the room with hors d'oeuvres and drinks for everyone. Malcolm frowned at Matt's mention of the crown, almost going as far as a glance of warning, but he withdrew from the room without a word.

"The Glomach?" Cassandra said casually as she lit a cigarette. "I'd toss the foolish thing in the nearest ditch just to irritate Poppy if it weren't for the fact it's said to be carved of pure silver and every inch encrusted with precious gems."

"You've never seen it, then?" Matt asked.

"Poppy wouldn't allow it. But I know it must be worth millions. You've seen all the absurdly expensive security measures Poppy's taken. He's put bars on all the windows, for godsakes. It took a healthy bite out of our net worth, I'll tell you. I could understand it in terms of the da Vincis, of course. But he did it all to safeguard the Glomach."

Matt made a study of the portrait of Lord MacDonnaugh as a boy that hung opposite Cassandra's painting. "But I thought the Glomach was all just a local fairy tale."

"Legend," Rainey said out of habit.

Cassandra ignored her comment as she drew in a long breath of smoke and then exhaled it slowly. "Well, all I can tell you is that Poppy has it, and it's the only piece up there that old man really cares about anymore—clan pride and all that. He killed my uncle Douglas over the thing, you know. It's hardly a secret. Oh, they never bothered to pursue it in the courts, but Poppy brags about it when he's in his cups, how he got Uncle Douglas up there on the side of that cliff and saw to it that the 'accident' was carried out with military precision. He'd have found a way to get me out rock climbing as well by now, I haven't a doubt, if he wasn't pieced together these days with string and sealing wax." She brooded over her anger with her father for a moment as she drew in smoke from her cigarette. "Now, he's the one who should worry about staying alive."

"Of course, the years do catch up to one," Matt said calmly. He understood all too well that they needed to accomplish their mission and get out of this house as quickly as possible. There was a powder keg with a very short fuse lit between the MacDonnaughs, and he didn't want any of the people he loved to be in the vicinity when it went off.

Cassandra was all smiles. "You wouldn't happen to know of anyone with a million pounds sterling who would want to buy a silly old crown, would you, Matthew?"

"A million, you say?" Matt said, rubbing his chin in consideration. "As it happens, I might be interested in such a proposition myself, Cassandra."

Rainey gave him a sideward glance. Was there a change in plan? Then it struck her. If Matt could convince Cassandra to give him the crown in return for a check, say, he could keep the crown and put a stop payment on the funds. Officially, the crown's tradition would have been upheld. It would have in fact been stolen. Of course, they might all still end up in jail.

Cassandra blinked in surprise at Matt's offer. "Are you saying you have that kind of money to spend, Matthew?" Her eyes were aglow with avarice.

"Aye, well, I have a wee coin or two."

"Of course, the ferryboat disaster. On top of your inheritance, there was the insurance money. It's brilliant. Why, you must have gotten millions. What clever planning, Matthew!" Cassandra kissed him soundly on the mouth, but got nothing in return.

"Actually, I feel the crown may be an excellent object of study at the university where I teach," Matt said. "I don't foresee any problems with the deal, so long as your father doesn't stand in our way."

"Don't you worry about Poppy," Cassandra said with absolute surety. "I'm taking this out of his hands." She slid a canapé into her mouth and washed it down quickly with champagne.

Matt picked up a cracker and placed a square of cheese on it. "Only one thing concerns me," he said. Cassandra swallowed a second canapé hard. "I remember from my childhood that there is supposed to be a curse of some kind attached to the crown. Something to do with blindness, if I'm not mistaken. Now, you must admit, what with your father's unfortunate affliction, I would need some kind of assurance from you that no harm would befall me or my students while looking at the crown."

Sasha squirmed in her seat, impatient with all these questions and delays. She was fully prepared to storm up the stairs and take the crown all on her own right now. But Rainey squeezed her hand lightly in warning. They were getting very close to their goal.

Cassandra emptied her champagne glass. "The curse?" she said with an uncomfortable laugh. "You're a man of learning, Matthew. How could you even broach the subject of curses?"

She frowned when Sasha leaned forward to take a cracker. "Those are for the grown-ups, Sandy," she said icily. Sasha crumbled the cracker in her hand and let the crumbs fall into a pile on the floor.

Rainey stiffened. "We normally eat dinner a bit earlier than this."

Cassandra narrowed her eyes at Sasha. "Then perhaps you should take her out of here and give her her bottle elsewhere."

Emma rose to the occasion. "Now see here . . ."

Matt knew the situation was rapidly getting out of hand. "We're losing track of the point of our conversation, ladies," he said with pointed looks at Rainey and Emma. Every woman in the room glared at him as one, then each regained her composure. "As I was sayin', on a capital investment of this size, I'd have to have some kind of guarantee of safety."

Cassandra considered the problem, then rose to her feet. "Wait here. I'll have MacPherson bring the chest down, and we'll open it up. I'll prove to you the thing is harmless." She rang the servant bell, and when Malcolm arrived, she told him to bring the chest downstairs. The color drained from his ruddy cheeks.

"Is my father currently in his bedchamber?" Cassandra asked, her voice a bit higher pitched than usual. She was clearly feeling the strain of treading on very dangerous ground.

Malcolm gave Matt a quick glance. "No, mum, his lordship is in the library with the doors securely locked. He asked that the fire be lit, then gave orders that he was not to be disturbed for any reason."

"Good, then you should have no problem with your assignment."

"No, mum, no trouble a tall." He didn't move.

"Well?" Cassandra snapped.

Matt stepped forward. "Perhaps I should assist him in getting it down the stairs," he offered. But Cassandra waved him back.

"MacPherson is well paid to do his work. I'm certain he can handle it on his own."

Matt shrugged an apology, and Malcolm trudged off to his duties.

"So, Matthew, you must tell me all about your fabulous adventures abroad," Cassandra insisted. "It's been so very long since I was in the States. Do tell me Tiffany's is still going strong. I couldn't bear any bad news from that front."

"To the best of my knowledge, they're still in business," Matt supplied.

"How grand! Well, I assure you, I plan to go on quite an international shopping spree come spring."

"What about Lord MacDonnaugh?" Matt inquired. "Will he be up to such an extensive journey?"

Cassandra gave an ironic little laugh. "The winters are bitter here, and he grows weaker by the hour. I sincerely doubt he will survive till the spring." She made it sound as if she were discussing the fate of an easily replaced plant in the garden.

Matt took a small sip of his champagne. "You have always struck me as a woman who gets exactly what she wants, Cassandra."

She snuggled nearer to him, pressing her breast against his arm provocatively. "You're quite right, Matthew," she replied as she closed her eyes with a dreamy expression.

Matt kept his gaze carefully trained on the fire as Cassandra ran her hand boldly down his inner thigh. Her scarlet thumbnail grazed a vulnerable male part, and Rainey choked on the sip of champagne she had taken. Emma patted Rainey's back as she gasped for air, and in the confusion, Sasha rose from the couch and started to wander around the room.

She appeared to be merely a bored child curious about her new surroundings. But she was, in fact, easing her way out into the hall. While Matt dealt with Cassandra and Emma dealt with Rainey, Sasha slipped out into the foyer. There, she saw Malcolm sitting in the shadows at the top of the stairs. He sighed and rested his chin in his hands as he watched Sasha come up to where he sat.

"Ye shouldna be out here, lassie," he said kindly. "Yer mother will be missin' ye in a tick."

Sasha looked around the landing for any signs of the chest, but she could see none. She took Malcolm's hand and smiled at him through worried eyes.

Malcolm shook his head. "I canna do it, love," he said in despair. "I tried to lift the bloody t'ing, but it's too heavy for an old man the likes of me. That harpy's goin' to sack me anyhow. There's no point in cripplin' meself over it all."

Sasha pulled him to his feet and instinctively started toward Lord MacDonnaugh's bedchamber. Malcolm resisted.

"Ye dunna understand, lassie," he insisted in a desperate whisper. "It canna be budged, ye ken? His lordship's got it nailed down or some such. Do ye no understand what I'm sayin' to ye? Do ye never speak?"

Sasha turned to him, her lips pressed together in determination. She tugged on his hand, unwilling to brook his resistance. He walked forward, one reluctant step after another until they came to Lord Carlyle's door. Malcolm withdrew a massive key from his pocket, but Sasha waved it away. She turned the old iron knob firmly, and the room opened up to them.

"By god, I musta forgot to lock it again when I come out," Malcolm reasoned. But he knew for a certainty he would never forget to do something so important. Cassandra might take him to task every five minutes, but the truth was, he was very thorough in his responsibilities.

Inside, there was an enormous canopy bed, draped with ancient black velvet and gold brocade, and all around the room were stacks of priceless paintings and countless other works of art. Against the far wall stood a huge safe.

Malcolm knew next to nothing about art, except what he liked and disliked. But he knew some of the names on his lordship's art collection, famous old Italian, Dutch, and French fellows, very popular with the upper crust.

Sasha had no interest in the paintings and statues. She dragged Malcolm over to the antique nightstand that stood next to his lordship's tidily made bed. On the stand rested the chest. It was relatively small, considering the importance of its probable contents, with brass fittings and worn leather handles. It had no formal locks, the curse being sufficient security. Only a piece of stag's horn through an iron latch held it closed. On the lid was the Pathway to Paradise symbol from Sasha's brooch.

Sasha went to her knees at the sight of it and began to whisper to herself in Gaelic. Malcolm wasn't sure what to do, but he was certain he was in line for another brow-beating from Cassandra. He tried to lift the chest again in hopes he could get both it and Sasha downstairs as quickly as possible, but the chest wouldn't budge.

Sasha rose slowly and nudged Malcolm out of the way. She wrapped her small hands around the chest's leather handles and lifted it as if it were fashioned of feathers. Malcolm backed away a step, hardly able to believe his own eyes.

"Set it down, lassie! It'll fair break yer wee back."

Sasha shook her head at the idea and headed for the stairs. She carried the chest down into the foyer with ease, but instead of heading for the hall, she started toward the front door.

"No, no, Sasha!" Malcolm said in a frantic whisper. "Ye must take it to Cassandra."

Sasha kept walking toward the door, heedless of Malcolm's instructions.

"Well, well, so there's a wee thief in our midst after all." Cassandra's voice slithered across the room at Sasha as if it were wrapped in scales.

Chapter 23

"Sasha, sweetheart, come over here to me," Rainey was quick to say. Cassandra's mood was volatile, and it was imperative that she not be given the opportunity to direct her poison at Sasha.

For a moment, Sasha stared at the front door, the chest securely in her hands. Then, she turned and walked up to Cassandra, her face unreadable. Cassandra thrust her hands out in exasperation, but as she took the handles of the chest, she was instantly thrown to the stone floor by the overwhelming weight of the wooden box. Her knees were badly bruised, her white skirt streaked, and a telltale patch of blood pooled at the pushed-up sleeve of her pink sweater where she had scraped her elbow. She didn't try to lift the chest again, but rose painfully, her eyes intent on Sasha. Her gaze held the promise of violence.

"What the bloody hell is going on?" Lord MacDonnaugh shouted from the library door. In his haste to wheel himself toward the others, the chair lurched forward, and a vintage long-barreled revolver clattered out of his lap blanket to the floor.

Malcolm caught Matt's sleeve. "His lordship had me clean and load his gun collection this mornin', Matty," he said in a concerned whisper. "That ain't no rusted-over antique himself is jugglin' with over there. It's a Colt in prime condition and slick as a whistle. Have a care for the ladies, my boy. One thing more—that revolver's got a twin."

Matt gave Rainey a cautioning glance. The danger had become very real. They would have to come back later for the crown. There was no choice now. It was time to get out. "I think it would be best if we continued our discussion another time, Cassandra," he said tactfully.

She grabbed his arm with an iron grip as Lord Carlyle started toward them. "No, nobody's going anywhere." She glared daggers, first at her father, then at the chest. "We'll have an end to this here and now." She limped over and picked up the fallen gun. In one smooth motion, she aimed it straight at her father's heart. The sound of her pulling back the hammer made him freeze.

He knew it was his daughter by her lavish perfume. "What are you about, girl?" he demanded harshly.

Cassandra gave him a frigid smile as she steadied her aim at his chest. "I'm closing an important business deal, Poppy."

"What're ye talkin' about, daughter? What business deal? Ye haven't a shilling to yer name, save what I see fit to give ye. And yer even more destitute when it comes to a brain."

Cassandra backed away slowly, never taking her eyes off her father as she walked over to the chest. "That's where you're wrong, Poppy," she said sweetly.

"You're daft, girl, you've got nothin'," Lord Carlyle said with a snort as he wheeled himself in her direction.

Cassandra glanced at Sasha. Sasha's eyes were cold and determined beyond her years as she returned Cassandra's threatening gaze.

"There's only one thing left to be done before the transaction can be completed." Cassandra laid a hand on Sasha's shoulder and drew her away from Rainey.

Rainey reached out to bring her back, but Cassandra flashed the gun down against Sasha's ear, and Rainey didn't dare move.

"Stay back, surfer girl," Cassandra said in deadly earnest.

Matt pulled Rainey over to his side, and Emma took her hand. Rainey was shaking miserably, but Matt sensed a monumental anger in her. All hell was about to break loose. "What are you trying to accomplish by all of this, Cassandra?" he asked firmly.

The smile she gave him was that of a woman slipping into madness. "You want proof that the crown will cause no harm, don't you, Matthew? That was the bargain. Well, I'm about to prove to you that it's as impotent as that shriveled old sod in the wheelchair there." With the gun still pressed to Sasha's temple, she led her to stand in front of the chest. With a single nudge from the toe of her Italian pump, Cassandra removed the bit of horn that served as the lock on the chest. All that remained to be done now was to lift the lid and expose the crown.

"I demand to know what's happenin' here!" Lord Carlyle shouted. "I won't allow this. All you people, get out of my house this instant!"

Cassandra smiled. "It's all over for you, you murderous old bugger. Now, shut your mouth, or I'll close it for you permanently and blame it on burglars."

Lord Carlyle clamped his mouth shut.

"Cassandra," Matt said calmly, "there's no need to prove anything about the crown. I'll take it as it is. The university can run tests to make sure it's safe for study. If you'd like, I can give you my personal check right now without further delay."

Cassandra shook her head. "No, no, Matthew, the deal was that I'd prove to you the crown had no power." She looked down at Sasha. "And now, little Malibu Barbie here is going to do the job for us."

"No!" Rainey shouted. "Sasha, come away from there. If you want someone to be your volunteer, Cassandra, let me do it. Sasha's just a child. She has her whole life ahead of her. Let me take the risk."

Cassandra tightened her grip on Sasha's shoulder. "I think not." She pressed Sasha to her knees in front of the chest. "You know, when I was a wee lassie, I used to dream about this chest. It was forbidden to me, and I dreamed it was full of ghosts and poisonous snakes and spiders. What do you think it's full of? Go on, little girl, open the chest. That's right. Be a good little sweetie now, so Auntie Cassandra won't have to blow your brains across the floor."

A slow smile lit Sasha's face as she laid her hands on the chest. She showed no hint of fear. But in the split second when Cassandra averted her eyes from the danger of seeing the crown, Rainey dove toward Sasha. Matt shouted a warning as Rainey covered Sasha's eyes with her hand and closed her own eyes tightly when the chest overturned. Malcolm grabbed Emma's shoulders and turned the pair of them around quickly as the contents of the chest spilled at Cassandra's feet. Out of reflex, Cassandra glanced down at it in awe and terror.

"The crown! Get it off me! It's scalding me! It's twisted and ugly! No, this can't be happening! Oh, God, it hurts!" she cried as she back away. Her eyes began to cloud and turn to scarlet, and with the revolver still held loosely in her hand, she rubbed at them until they bled.

Lord Carlyle's vindictive laughter rang to the rafters as he pulled the second Colt from beneath his lap robe and aimed it in the direction of Cassandra's cries of agony. "So you've learned your lesson at last, have you, daughter?" he said in triumph as she stumbled back painfully against a chair. "Who'll have you now, eh? You're nothin' but a blind, penniless circus freak. I don't have to see your face to know how hideous it's become. You have no eyes, girl. Nothing but burnt, cracked marbles to take to your grave as proof of your greed."

Cassandra gasped for air between sobs as blood and tears streamed down her face. She blinked uncontrollably. "That's where you're wrong, old man," she promised. "I'll have it all. I don't need anyone else!" Her eyes were useless, but she trained the revolver in her father's direction. Lord Carlyle only chuckled at her words, and Cassandra thrust the gun out to arm's length in hopes of improving her aim at him.

"You'll get nothing," he said, his voice like granite.

With the two of them locked in an impasse, Sasha pulled away from Rainey's protective hand and reached out toward the crown.

"No, Sash, don't look at it!" Rainey whispered. But before she could stop her, Sasha scooped the crown back into the chest and closed the lid silently.

"*Tha sin glèidhteach,*" she whispered, meaning the crown was in safekeeping once more.

Rainey opened her eyes cautiously to see Cassandra and Lord Carlyle squared off against each other in a deadly standoff. Matt grabbed her by the arm and hauled her to her feet as Sasha lifted the chest with ease. He nodded toward the library where flames were licking away at the furniture and the draperies. Lord Carlyle's threat had not been an idle one. He was burning the place down, rather than have his daughter inherit the castle and all its treasures.

Without a sound, Matt directed them all toward the front door as the air hung heavy with what might come next for Lord Carlyle and Cassandra. The door creaked as they eased it open, and everyone froze.

As if she were awakening from a trance, Cassandra turned the gun on them, her eyes lightless and ghoulish, her sweater stained with blood. She caught the scent of the smoke coming from the library, and for an instant, she tensed as she realized her father's suicidal plan. Then, a sense of deadly calm descended over her.

"Leaving the party so soon, Matthew?" she asked with demented sweetness. "I'm afraid I can't allow that. If you and I can't be an item, I simply cannot allow anyone else to have you."

Rainey clutched at Matt's arm, dreading that he might stay and play the noble knight. "No, Matt," she whispered. "You have to come with us now. Come on, we'll make a run for it!"

A shot rang out, missing their heads by mere inches, and Matt shoved everyone else outside as Cassandra came at them with a vengeance.

"Where's the goddamned door?" she cried.

A second shot echoed through the foyer as smoke billowed out of the library. Cassandra fell forward into Matt's arms. A trickle of blood trailed from her lips as her torn eyes stared up at him.

"Matthew?" she asked in a rasping whisper. She was dying as she spoke.

"Aye, Cassandra, I'm here."

"You didn't leave me here all alone this time. I want to go to America with you. Take me away from this place, Matthew, I beg of you!"

Matt felt the life slipping from her. It was pointless

to deny her anything now. "We'll go together, Cassandra, and spend the day at Tiffany's, if you like."

Her tortured face brightened for an instant, then pain and reality twisted her features.

"Poppy killed my Carlo," she ground out against the blood rising in her throat. "And now he's killed me, hasn't he?"

"Aye, lass, he has."

The stinging tears streamed down her cheeks. "I used to dream about you, Matthew. But you always ran to someone else, even in my dreams." She collapsed in death as a river of blood drained from the bullet hole in her back.

"You've murdered your daughter, Lord MacDonnaugh," Matt said as he set Cassandra's body down.

"Always was a crack shot," Lord Carlyle replied as he cocked the hammer on the Colt again. "It's a matter of timing as well as aim, you see? Eyes are a luxury. They spoil a man's true instincts for the kill. Had it comin' to her, that girl. She was a pathetic example of the breed. Her mother's fault. The blood was weakened from that quarter. A cullin' was called for. A disgrace to the MacDonnaugh name. Totally unfit to inherit. I've been meaning to do this for years. The Glomach stays in this house."

Matt glanced down at Cassandra's crumpled body. He felt no love for her, but a surge of pity filled his heart, knowing that she had lived and died at this bastard's hand.

"The crown is lost to you forever, old man. You're finished. At tomorrow's solstice, the Glomach returns to the falls. It's already gone."

"Lies! It's mine for all time! No one's ever had the courage to take it from a MacDonnaugh. I'll drop you where you stand, Macinnes!" The truth settled over him like a shroud as he sensed a new emptiness in the house. He was forced to believe Matt's words, and it turned his heart to stone. The only joy left to him now was bitter vengeance.

"My eyes may have burned to ashes, boy, but my other senses are quite keen, I promise you. Could have dropped your whole bloody family from half a kilometer away in the old days, if it suited me. And who is to say it didn't suit me to be rid of the lot of you?"

Matt's instincts grew very keen, and the hair prickled at the back of his neck. Smoke filled the room. "Just what are you tellin' me, Lord Carlyle?"

"Expediency, laddie. Easy enough to arrange a wee disaster at sea, eh? Oh, not the storm, to be sure. That was a gift from the devil. Even the laird of the MacDonnaughs hasn't mastered that one yet. But your father was in the way of my plans to drill for petroleum here in the Highlands, you see? Goddamned liberal do-gooder. Always whining his opposition to my plans in high places. 'Pollution,' he said. 'Wholesale destruction of the Highlands,' he said. We couldn't allow that kind of negative propaganda to continue, now, could we?"

"I don't suppose a man like you could ever allow opposition, Lord Carlyle." Matt closed his right hand as he would around the hilt of the broadsword. The war with his own guilt over his parents' deaths was over. Here was the true battle.

"Why do you think your family came to the Highlands so seldom in the end, boy? Love of their work?" Lord Carlyle said with smirk. "Hardly. It was because I told them I'd find a way to crush your bones and set you afire if they didn't leave off with their bleeding heart protests. Always go for the soft underbelly, ye see, lad? You were their Achilles' heel. It shut 'em right up for a while.

"They tried to keep you safe from me, the fools. And eventually, they got bold again. Now, they're of no trouble to me and no help to you whatsoever. Best of all, I can still see to it that your bones are burned to dust."

"Little wonder they warned me away from this place."

This was what his mother had meant in her diary about it being unwise to stay at the house the day of the storm, Matt realized.

"Little wonder, indeed. But then, forbidden fruit is always the sweeter. And from what I understand, you were seen peerin' about the grounds now and again in the old days, sniffin' up my girl's rump, no doubt. I would have skewered you for my breakfast, had I been given the opportunity. But you were a slippery one, young Macinnes. Not like my big brother. Douglas was the first of my generation to possess the crown, you know. He wanted everything for himself. But I couldn't have that, now, could I? I deserved it far more than that ineffectual sod. I should have had it all from the start.

"Douglas made it all far too easy. Of course, he had the privilege of watching my hiking pick bore a hole in his chest with the clearest of vision. Douglas always followed the rules. I make my own rules." He blinked his scalded eyes vacantly. "I should have taken a rock to his skull and tossed him down a well when we were children."

Lord MacDonnaugh ran his hand along the barrel of the gun lovingly. "Who says money can't buy happiness? It made short work of that Italian pig my daughter married. And if I'd had the foresight to pay the captain of the rescue ship as much as I parted with to bribe the engine crew on that ferryboat, I'd have truly gotten my money's worth. Your parents were no longer a concern, at any rate. And you had the good sense to crawl off and lick your wounds elsewhere. I've been drilling where I please to the north for fifteen years with hardly a whimper of protest from anyone who counts. I've won approval for strip-mining in the coming year as well. Marvelous." His self-satisfied chuckle turned into a cough from the thick smoke rolling into the foyer. "But see here, now I have you, and my triumph is complete. You and I have unfinished business, laddie."

Matt said nothing. No point in giving Lord Carlyle an easier target. Sabotage. The word screamed through his brain. It had been murder, cold, intentional, and calculated. Lord Carlyle had arranged it all. And the dozens of other innocents who had perished in those hostile north seas had been of no consequence to him whatsoever. It had been an exercise of the power of wealth without conscience. And he had been sent to die at sea with his parents.

But it hadn't been a fate ordained by Providence. It had been a murderous plot manufactured by Lord Carlyle MacDonnaugh. They might have survived the storm. Lord Carlyle's explosion had sealed their fate. It had all been a cruel waste of human life for the sake of an old man's avarice. An anger like he had never known before burned inside Matt. It was an anger that gave him permission to kill in return.

The flames were roaring up the walls toward the second story. In another thirty seconds, the entire interior would be engulfed.

Lord Carlyle smiled through the clouds of smoke, reading Matt's mood with no difficulty. "Would it give you pleasure to murder a blind old man in a wheelchair, Macinnes? Yes, I think it would. Come closer, laddie, and I'll give you the opportunity. I've nothing to live for. Come and put me out of my misery, boy. You'd be doing me a favor. It's like fine sex, is it not, putting a spark to the lead and feeling it gather up all hot and deadly before it plunges through to the heart. Sex and murder, it's all the same." He turned the revolver around so the handle was toward Matt in open invitation.

"You're dyin' of your own poison, old man." Matt stared at the handle of the revolver, sorely tempted to take it. The old bastard owned him everything—family, happiness, peace of mind. How easy it would be to collect in full.

"Aye, I'm dying of it all, right enough, and the pure joy of it all is I get to take you with me." He flexed his fingers around the revolver. "They haunt you, don't they, boy, those pathetic graves on the hill? Robbed of your dear father's guidance at such a vulnerable age." He snorted at the notion of Matt's father's wisdom. "And your mother, now there was a choice piece of ass I fancied. Always so neighborly, so close at hand. Big blue eyes and all those dark gypsy curls. Ones like that are best kept on all fours with a strap, mind you. Once you bring 'em to heel, though, by god, they'll grunt out a good breedin' like any raw sow in the yard. Drain a man dry, a lovely mouth like your mother's. Smack her lips, rub her wee belly, and say, 'Oh, thank you, your lordship. I beg of you, more cream, please. More cream.' "

"One of us is not going to leave this room alive, old man."

"You're already dead, boy. And so am I. The fire will incinerate us both in a matter of minutes. It's all part of the plan. But tell me, that bit of tail you brought with you tonight has the look of your dead mother about her, from what my girl told me. And when that one's filling her mouth with you, panting for your seed upon her tongue, I have no doubt you cry bitter tears and shout, 'Mama, oh, yes, Mama, squeeze your baby boy hard! That's it. Here it comes. Little Matty has a present for his poor dead mama. Oh, Christ, he needs his mama's love, but Lord Mac-Donnaugh has made a worm's feast of her lovely face.' " He lifted the gun toward Matt. "Have I got your attention yet, laddie?"

Matt's heart had gone utterly cold. "Aye, I hear you. And this place is but a spoonful of the sea of fire I have in mind for you!"

Matt grabbed the Colt and didn't hesitate to wrap his finger around the trigger. But one look down at the chambers told him they were empty. The gun was useless. And what was more, he saw now that Lord Carlyle had a double-barreled, saw-off shotgun aimed straight at him. It had been under the blanket beside him all along. It would scatter shot two yards wide. There was no way he could miss his target. Lord Carlyle sniffed the air and smiled.

"Ah, we have a visitor, scent of lavender and lemon soap. The more the merrier. Pull her close now, boy. Make it easy for me. And I'll remember you to your sweet-mouthed mother as I hump her in hell for all eternity!"

"Rainey?" Matt whirled as the shotgun blasted. But the next thing he knew, he was on the floor. Rainey was at his side like an angel of redemption, her finger pressed against his lips to keep him quiet. He had no idea how long she had been in the room, but she had managed to throw him down out of harm's way in time. And as he started to rise, she signaled for him to stay down. He frowned at her, aching to put an end to Lord Carlyle.

The old man wheeled over to his victim, the shotgun still in his hand. One wheel bumped into Matt's shoulder, and Lord Carlyle hit him a second time to assure himself his shot had hit true. Matt winced, but remained still for the sake of Rainey's safety.

"A crack shot to this day," Lord Carlyle gloated to himself. He coughed hard from the killing smoke. "Fools, all of them. I was always their better." He wheeled himself back toward the library, and an instant later, the second barrel of the shotgun reported. Lord Carlyle slumped over in his chair, one side of his head cleanly blown away.

"Damn and damn, he's robbed me again!" Matt shouted. He started toward Lord Carlyle, prepared to do he knew not what.

Rainey grabbed his arm. "No, Matt, leave it. He's set you free. If he had had the power to get you to do his killing for him, he would have won again. He would have gotten what he wanted. Now, it's over, and that last victory was taken away from him. We're alive, Matt, but not for long if we don't get out of here now."

He stared at her, trying to absorb what she was saying. She was right, and he kissed her tenderly just as the staircase collapsed in a horrific wall of flame. He took her hand and raced for the door.

"Why the hell did you come back in here, Rainey? You could have been killed in half a dozen ways!"

Rainey raised her arm to her face against the smoke. "Oh, and I suppose I should have let that monster blow a hole in your head the size of Boston and wipe out the Macinnes clan entirely? Great plan. I promised I'd be there for you, Matt. And I keep my promises. Besides which, you're no good to any of us dead. And with that stupid chest out there, we certainly all have enough to carry without having to haul you as well."

"I'll keep that in mind, Harvard," he said over a brutal cough as they stepped gingerly over Cassandra's crumpled body. "If I decide to get myself killed, I'll try to arrange for my own transportation."

"Good," she said. "Matt, I heard what he said about your parents and about me. I'm so sorry. I wanted to grab that revolver myself." She shuddered as she realized how close she had come to losing him.

Matt swung the door open at last. "It's over.

Nothin' can bring my parents back. But perhaps they have a new kind of freedom now. Perhaps I do as well. One more thing, Mrs. Nielson," he said formally.

"What now?"

"Thank you."

"You're welcome."

Their hair and clothing were scorched from the tremendous heat, and the rush of cool night air that met them when they opened the door was like a blessing from heaven. Everyone clustered around them as the fire took full possession of the interior of the castle.

Emma gave Rainey and Matt a heartfelt hug. From the looks of the two of them, she didn't think it best to ask what had happened inside. They were all alive, and the MacDonnaughs were out of the picture permanently. That's all that mattered. "Thank God, it's over," she said with a sigh of relief.

Sasha sat down beside the chest and laid her hand on it affectionately. *"Chan eil, tha e fìor thoiseach,"* she whispered to the stars overhead.

Malcolm tapped Emma's shoulder. "My hearin' is no so verra good. What did the lassie say?"

Emma grabbed Malcolm's ear playfully. "She said it's not over yet, ye ken? In fact, it's just beginnin'."

Malcolm pressed his lips together and rolled his eyes. "I'd best get a new bottle of iron tonic then, if this sort of thing is goin' to be everyday fare from here on out."

"Aye," Emma agreed. "Best to make it a barrel, and the two of us'll share."

Chapter 24

The Winter Solstice dawned cold and foreboding. Ice-laden mists rolled off the loch, scattering sprays of frost across the windowpanes and sending chilly drafts chasing around the room. It was the perfect day to stay indoors beside the fire. Unfortunately, no one would be afforded that luxury.

Sasha was the first one up, and she made sure everyone knew daylight was upon them. She wore one of Emma's heavy sweaters over her jacket for extra warmth, which made her look more like a woolly snowman than exiled royalty. But her spirits were high when at last they were ready. She tugged her mother toward the front door.

"Tha an là a' tarraing air," she whispered as she stood in the doorway with Rainey. Her words meant the day shows signs of a storm, but she seemed undaunted by the prospect. In fact, Sasha took in a deep breath of the frigid air and smiled at the dark clouds twisting in turmoil overhead. It was a smile of welcome.

Matt and Malcolm loaded the hiking supplies, the sword, and the chest into the car's trunk with no difficulty. With the deaths of the MacDonnaughs, the chest had lost its excessive weight. It had been the weight of the sorrow of the fairies, Sasha had told them. And now that the crown was going home, that one misery was behind them.

The road was slick, and the mists closed in around them as Matt drove cautiously along the loch. In time, the Five Sisters of Glenshiel loomed down on them to the right. The sight of the five barren peaks caused a single tear to slide down Sasha's cheek, and Rainey felt emotion rise in her heart as well. The mists cloaked the Sisters in mystery once again. Rainey wanted to see more. She felt a sense of loss.

Matt saw Rainey's look of regret. He knew how hard all of this was on her. "We'll stop for food at Shiel Bridge. Nothin' fancy, to be sure. But we should be able to stock up on a portable feast."

Rainey's sigh made a cloud of mist against the windshield. She was shaking to her toes from the cold and the stress of the day. But when she looked down at Sasha on the front seat next to her, she was struck by her total serenity. There was no hint of worry or uncertainty on that lovely little face as Sasha watched the bleak winter landscape go by.

"Maybe I just need protein," Rainey said.

But it was far more than that. Her insides ached, and the blood pounded in her ears. Under other circumstances, she would have told herself she was coming down with the flu. But this wasn't the flu. Something was eating away at her soul, something she couldn't name. She was seeing spots before her eyes, and all the strength was ebbing out of her limbs. How on earth was she going to make the climb to the falls? she wondered.

She steeled herself against the symptoms. If the others suspected her condition, they might be tempted to make her stay behind. That wasn't going to happen. She would probably have to crawl on her hands and knees with her eyes squeezed shut, but she was going to make the climb to that damn waterfall, for Sasha's sake and for her own. It was the only way she would ever get the place out of her dreams.

There was an information booth at the lot where they parked the car. Aside from the elderly attendant's car, the place was empty. Matt conversed with the man briefly and returned to the car with a collection of canned drinks and packaged snacks. Sasha trailed along behind him with welcome cups of hot cocoa for everyone. Moments later, the attendant closed the booth and drove away. It was unlikely he would have any more business on a day like this one.

Rainey sipped her cocoa gratefully. It gave her a bit of comfort, but she still experienced an overriding dizziness and a sense of profound premonition. While the others sat down at a picnic table, Matt came up beside her as she leaned against the side of the car. He stirred his cocoa thoughtfully with a little wooden stick.

"The booth attendant asked me if I'd heard the news about the fire at Castle MacDonnaugh," he said calmly.

"Did he say anything about victims?"

"The coroner's still bein' tight-lipped. But rumor has it, it was a double suicide since they both died with guns in their hands. The old man tossed priceless first editions into the fire on the hearth so the flames would spread. That much was certain. It was common knowledge how the two of them were with each other, so nobody's askin' too many questions. The MacDonnaugh fortune in the laird's bedchamber was a total loss. A pity, I suppose, because it's said MacDonnaugh willed the lot to research on improving the fight in Highland brown trout."

Rainey sighed from her soul. "Then it's true, there are no more MacDonnaughs."

"My conscience is clear. How about yours?" She nodded as he crumpled his empty cup and tossed it into a nearby receptacle. "How do you fair, *mo chridhe*?" he asked with gentle concern. He tucked a stray curl behind her ear and realized it was damp with perspiration.

She smiled nervously, but her eyes didn't meet his. "I'm fine. This is the big day. By tomorrow, everything will be back to normal. It will all be over. Sasha will be her old self. The fairies will be safe. And we'll all live happily ever after, right?" Her knees buckled, and Matt caught her in his arms.

"You're not up to this," he insisted. "You're pale as a ghost, and you haven't the strength to stand. There's your problem with heights to consider. It's a devilish hike, and the booth man said much of the trail has been washed out by winter storms. I'm goin' to recommend that Emma and Malcolm stay behind. It's best if you stay with them. It's too great a danger for you to go."

He tucked a finger under her chin and brought her attention to him. Her eyes were filled with unshed tears of worry and trepidation. "I'll not risk losin' you, Harvard," he told her firmly. There was an edge of steel to his words, as if they were a warning to himself, more than to her. He cupped her face between his hands.

"I've lost others this time of year, as you well know, and I'm not of a mind to let it happen again, Rainey. I swear to you, I won't let you down. It can't happen. Sasha and I have climbed together before. Remember the wee falls near your house? We can communicate beautifully, and the fact of the matter is, havin' anyone else along will only hold us back." Rainey turned her head away.

"I'm going," she said simply.

Matt sighed. "I can see you're goin' to be stubborn about this. But hear me out. You'll have to carry your own weight. Even with the chest as light as it is now, it's goin' to take everythin' we've got to get it to the falls, never mind to the top once there. I'll help you as best I can, but my hands are goin' to be full, love."

Rainey looked over to where Sasha sat drinking her cocoa. Sasha cocked her head to one side and smiled at her. There was absolute faith in Sasha's eyes. Absolute faith.

"If I hold you back or feel like I can't go on, you can finish it without me," Rainey conceded. "But I'm going. No more discussion." She freed herself from Matt's embrace and stood on her own. Nothing had changed. She still felt like she was made of straw. But there was no way she was going to stay behind with no knowledge of what was happening up the trail.

"Very well," Matt said as he folded his arms across his chest. "But you're a damned fool for it."

She managed half a smile. "Not the first time," she said. "After all, I fell in love with you, Stanford, didn't I?"

His stern expression melted, and he took her back into his arms, kissing the top of her head tenderly. "We're makin' a Scot of you, one foolish mistake at a time, surfer girl."

Despite Matt's best diplomatic efforts, Emma and Malcolm were equally determined to finish the trip. So, as a strange and wonderful army, they began their arduous march to the falls. The trail was worn and slick as a steady, bone-chilling rain began to fall. There were few trees, and the further they went, the more determined the rain became in its efforts to stop them.

Matt had wrapped the sword in thick, waterproof canvas. He wore it slung over his back so he could dedicate both hands to the chest. As Rainey trudged along behind him, she remembered that day in the woods near her house, when it had struck her how like a Highlander of old he seemed when he was away from civilization. She remembered, too, how he had held up a small spray of redwood covered with cobwebs to illustrate the magical nature of their goal. That much was still a mystery to her, and if she had had the breath to spare, she would have asked him about it. Certainly on that day, which now seemed like years ago, she never could have pictured herself hiking toward a treacherous waterfall in the wilds of Scotland. It all had a very dreamlike quality about it.

She knew her cheeks were burning from exertion and what she had decided had to be a virus she was fighting. Her legs felt like rubber, and why they kept climbing, one impossible step after another, was more than she cared to figure out. The bottom line was that she was still moving. If she concentrated on Matt's back instead of the steep, seemingly endless trail before them, somehow she would make it.

"How far have we come?" she asked, hoping for good news.

"About a mile, love," Matt said over his shoulder.

It felt to Rainey like it had been fifty. She swallowed hard over her dry throat. "H-how much further?"

He took another half a dozen strides before answering. "A ways, Harvard. One step at a time, love."

She didn't like the sound of that.

The rain was coming down in sheets by the time Matt brought them all to a halt for a brief rest. They huddled together among the ferns beneath a tarp and shared the shortbread cookies Matt had purchased in the parking lot. It was cozy and secluded, and under other, drier circumstances, it might have been the perfect picnic spot.

Sasha appeared well-rested and full of energy. And even Emma and Malcolm seemed none the worse for wear, which made Rainey feel all the more inadequate. It was plain to her and to everyone else in the small circle that she needed more time to rest, precious time they could little afford. Emma nudged Malcolm, and he cleared his throat.

"Did I ever tell ye the tale of the creature of our loch when ye were a lad, Matty Mac?" Malcolm asked.

Matt understood immediately what was afoot. "Aye, Malcolm, that you did. But only a thousand and one times. And I'm sure there are some here besides myself who would love to hear it told again." He winked at Rainey, and she did her best to smile.

Malcolm rubbed his chin thoughtfully, much as Matt had been seen to do. "Och, well, some say it was the work of smugglers, mind ye, pirates settin' up a rare decoy to scare away those would do mischief to their moneymakin' schemes. But my kin has lived on that loch since before the time of the first uprisin's, ye ken? And I'm here to tell ye, there's a thing lives in that loch that's got nothin' to do with money nor men. And it's got that Loch Ness minnow beat by a long sight."

"*Mar uile-bheist mhì-chiallach?*" Sasha whispered. Like a bad monster?

"Och, no, lassie," Malcolm was quick to say. "In the first place, it's a she, I'm that convinced. And she only makes herself known to those who are worthy of heart. They say William Wallace himself petted the thing on the head for luck before he sacked York. And I believe it." He sat back and folded his arms across his chest, defying anyone to contradict him. Then, he leaned forward with a smile on his weathered face for Sasha. "When we go back home, Sasha, I'll introduce ye to her myself. Would ye like that, lassie?" Sasha nodded eagerly.

Matt took Rainey's icy hand into his own. "Aye, well, we shall all look forward to that, Malcolm," he said. "But we must be goin' now. The weather's dirtier by the minute, and the day is short. Are you with us, Harvard?"

The thought of standing up was enough to make Rainey shudder, but she let Matt pull her to her feet. Emma and Malcolm walked up beside her and locked their arms through hers for support. She smiled her thanks. As much as she hated the thought of being a burden to everyone, the thought of remaining behind was far worse. Sasha gestured for her to follow as they broke into the rain again. The clouds were piled directly above them, malevolent and unforgiving, shutting out all hope of the sun.

As the time wore on, Rainey lost focus on her surroundings. Her legs no longer felt like they were connected to her. If they had been, they would have stopped long ago. So obviously they had minds of their own.

Scenes from her childhood began to wander through her mind as her subconscious took over what her conscious mind could no longer accept as sensible. She saw her mother smiling from the kitchen window, watching her as she played in the backyard of her home in Connecticut. She saw the neighbor's brown-and-white cocker spaniel sneak through the fence to come and play with her.

So long ago.

She saw her father climb the ladder to clean out the gutters. And in a nightmare of remembrance, she watched him clutch the killing pain in his chest and fall for what seemed like an eternity. Her father was dead. People fell from the tops of things and they died.

"No!" she cried as the rain and tears streamed down her face. She froze, unable to move another step.

Matt turned to her with great concern. "What is it, Rainey? What's wrong?" Her cheeks were bright with unhealthy color, and her eyes were dilated with fear. He handed the chest to Malcolm and hugged her to him.

Rainey sobbed, trying desperately to hold back her tears. She looked down at Sasha, close to hysteria. "She'll fall! We can't help her. The fairies can't help her. I can't let it happen again. Everyone I love falls from the sky." Sasha wrapped her arms around Rainey's waist to help comfort her.

Matt stroked her hair soothingly. "It will be all right, Rainey. I swear it to you. I'll be there for her. I won't fail you. No more failures for any of us."

Emma came forward and wiped the tears from Rainey's face with a handkerchief from her pocket. "Ye've had enough, Rainey," she said kindly. "Maybe the two of us should wait here."

Rainey fought back her desperation and did her best to regain control. "No, I'm sorry," she said as she swayed on her feet. "It's just that there's too much noise in my head. I can't hear myself think." She covered her ears with her hands, but the monstrous roaring sound continued. It was the way it had been in her dream of the falls. She stared at the others with a look of revelation. "We're there."

Matt gave her a grim smile and inclined his head up the trail. "Just around that bend, love. You've come this far. The time has come to see it through." He took the chest back from Malcolm. "We're only minutes from the time of the true Solstice." Emma and Malcolm took Rainey by the arm, and together they came around the last bend.

The gorge was breathtakingly deep and narrow, carved by thousands of years of rushing water. The falls plunged almost four hundred feet in two cascading sections separated by a projecting rock. At the bottom, where they now stood, was a deep chasm that pooled briefly before continuing toward the sea.

It was just as it had been in Rainey's dreams and Sasha's crayon drawings.

The pool itself was empty of life, but the sides of the gorge were populated with flocks of ravens. They huddled beneath the crowded ferns, silently eyeing the humans below and shaking the rain from their black wings. This, too, was just as Sasha had portrayed it.

Sasha pointed to the birds. *"An dream a bha diùth don bhàs,"* she whispered sadly, meaning the people who were near to death. The flocks rose as one into the air, circling the falls three times before they floated down to cluster around Sasha and Rainey. Unlike the rest of their kind, they showed no interest in the possibility of food. They merely gathered around in welcome as the fairies had done.

Matt, Emma, and Malcolm watched in awe as Rainey and Sasha sat down among the birds. One by one, the ravens approached them, then retreated to the flock.

Emma pressed her hand to her forehead. "I wouldna have believed it if I hadna seen it with my own eyes," she said softly. "Those birds are swearin' allegiance to the pair of 'em."

The flocks rose on the air and resumed their places on the walls of the gorge. It was an invitation to join them there. Rainey looked to Matt for their next move. He shifted the chest in his hands.

"To the top, love," he said simply. "And we'd best be quick about it. The time is very near. Come along, Sasha."

Rainey struggled to her feet. "I'm coming, too." She nearly lost her balance and had to grab Sasha's shoulder for support. Matt set his jaw. "If you go without me, Matt, I'll follow on my own. There's too much at stake. I won't sit by and watch." She was trembling so badly Sasha looked up at her with worry. "I'm okay, Sash," Rainey assured her. "You just lead the way, and I'll be right behind you." Sasha nodded reluctantly.

Matt grumbled a curse in Gaelic. "In the old days, a man was encouraged to beat a woman for such stubborn behavior."

Rainey swiped the dripping hair back off her face. She felt wretched. "Take a look at me, Macinnes," she insisted. "I've already had my beating for the day. Now, let's get on with it." She was seeing red and black spots before her eyes again, and it felt like her whole body was on fire. But she refused to give in to it.

Short of lashing her to a tree, Matt could see no alternative to letting her come. But tying her to a tree was sounding better and better to him. The feeling of impending loss rose inside him like the blade of a dagger being drawn up his spine. It was a feeling he had had before, and it shook him to his soul.

"If you kill yourself doin' this, Harvard, I personally will never forgive you," he warned. Under other circumstances, it might have been taken as a joke. But there was no humor in his words. And it would not be her he would never forgive.

"Duly noted," Rainey said over a rasping cough.

Malcolm helped Matt rig a sling for the chest so his hands could be free for the treacherous climb. Emma and Malcolm wisely stayed behind for this leg of the journey, although their hearts went out to the three who struggled up the last of the path leading to the top of the falls. Few people attempted the climb in the best of weather. But as the clouds tumbled and collided overhead, dumping a torrent nearly as heavy as the falls themselves, the steep trail looked utterly impossible. Ropes were secured around everyone's waists for safety's sake. They were halfway to the top when the first explosion of thunder tore down the gorge.

Chapter 25

Sasha froze as the thunder crashed against the walls of the gorge. For an instant, she was confused as the years of anticipation of this event and the reality of it became one. She gripped the rocks at the side of the vertical trail and tried to gather herself.

Rainey was directly behind her. She felt like she was aboard a ship at sea as the ground beneath her feet seemed to buckle and sway. The impact of the thunder and the sound of the falls made her head ache miserably. It was going to hurt to talk, but she had no alternative.

"You have to keep going, sweetheart," she said to Sasha. She didn't dare look up at her. "We're almost there."

Matt extended his hand to Sasha, and Rainey unclipped the safety rope around her own waist so he could pull Sasha up in front of him. Sasha started to climb again, and Rainey said a little prayer of thanks. Matt looked at her with very real concern as he fed a new length of rope to her.

"Reclip it around you, Rainey," he shouted. "You must use it."

The clip landed near her head, but she couldn't focus on it, and she didn't dare let go again to try and secure it around herself. She felt drained of her strength, her will.

The fear was a raw, living thing inside her, a demon gnawing at her soul. It dared her to look down with every aching breath she took. If she did look down, she would fall, just as she feared she would, and all of her worries and responsibilities would be over. She could sleep for an eternity. But something outside of herself was driving her on, something that wouldn't let her stop, wouldn't let the fear win.

"This is madness, Rainey," Matt called to her over the storm. "Go back, *mo chridhe!*"

"No." To say she was going to do this or die trying was no longer an offhanded expression. It was a fact.

Lightning ripped across the sky, and the thunder that followed was monstrous in its intensity. The last twenty feet were straight up, and the cliff pitched and whirled before Rainey's eyes. Rocks seemed to dissolve beneath her fingers, and the earth washed away beneath her feet. She couldn't get her bearings, and her hand slipped away from a supporting rock. She started to slide. Her foot caught on a thick root that protruded from the cliff, and she clawed at loose rocks and branches to gain any kind of a real hold.

"Matt!" she cried.

Matt had reached the top with Sasha. He shot a glance over the side of the cliff at Rainey's desperate face and hauled on the safety rope. It was slack.

For an instant, Rainey's face became his mother's, and he had to blink back the paralyzing terror. He couldn't help her. She clung to life by barest inches. It was too late, he told himself with punishing simplicity. She would slip away. She was going to die, and there was nothing in the world he could do to save her. He would try, but he would fail. She should never have trusted him. It was costing her her life. He cried out in anguish, and the sound of his sorrow echoed the distance of the gorge.

Tears of frustration blurred his sight, and his hands

shook. It was his destiny to watch everyone he truly loved die. He whirled toward Sasha, his mind locked in helpless rage, his soul as desperate for an answer as Rainey.

Sasha held her hands out urgently, her palms up. As she raised her right hand slightly, she whispered, *"Buiadh!"* meaning victory. When she raised her left hand, she said, *"Fuar ghlac a' bhàis,"* which meant the cold embrace of death. The choice was clearly his. But Sasha's look of utter hope and faith cut him free from the chains that crippled his heart.

"It will not happen this time!" he shouted. A barrage of thunder picked up his cry, challenging him to defy the odds and his past. He shed the slings from his back and knotted them to the ropes. Once they were swiftly secured around a sturdy outcropping of rock, he dove over the edge of the cliff.

"I'm comin', Rainey!" The fear in her eyes lashed away at his heart, and visions of her slipping to her death before he could reach her were a waking nightmare. He wanted to plunge headlong down to her, the risk be damned. She would be safe. It could be no other way.

"I-I can't hold on," Rainey whispered against the storm. There was a war going on inside her. A war that was tearing her apart. She had nothing more to give. Sasha had reached the top. It was all that mattered. The fever could take her now.

"You must have faith, Rainey!" Matt shouted. "We must all do this together, *mo chridhe.* Sasha needs you! I need you!"

Sasha lay down at the edge of the cliff, her blue eyes bright with tears as she looked down at her mother. *"Thoir suas ort, Mama!"* she called down. Up with you!

Matt was coming. Rainey knew it in her heart, even though she couldn't look up to see his progress.

But the fever was burning her alive, and there was no strength left in her arms. She was going to fall. Strangely, her greatest concern was what her death would do to Matt. It was so sad. She didn't want him to suffer.

Her fingers began to slip, and she could no longer prevent herself from looking down. It had been inevitable from the start. All of her fears of high places had led to this. She would force herself to face it bravely.

"I love you, Sasha," she said as she started to turn her head toward the pool hundreds of feet below.

"None to spare for your knight in shining armor, *mo chridhe?*"

A strong arm wrapped around her waist, and she sobbed with relief. Matt laced the rope around her securely and started the slow, upward pull that would take them both safely to the top. It required pure muscle to fight against the mud and the unrelenting downpour. But he took the task on like a man possessed. Rainey was still alive, and as Sasha helped them both over the top of the cliff, it felt very much like they were a true family.

Rainey sat down on solid ground and breathlessly accepted the hugs of her rescuers. She didn't dare look at Emma and Malcolm below, even to show them she was okay.

Matt smoothed the hair from her face. "You're all right, then, love?" he asked as he looked into her weary eyes. He was so thankful for the solid feel of her securely in his arms, he hardly noticed how weak her response was.

"The time is very near," was all she could say as she laid her head against his shoulder.

"Yes, love."

The winter rains had swollen the falls to the extreme. Water roared over the cliff, leaving only the barest tip of the center rock exposed. Dense clouds of mist rose to engulf the gorge.

Matt set the sword and the chest by Rainey. He sat next to her and brought Sasha down beside him. The three of them sat together in silence, catching their breath and absorbing for one short minute the fact of where they were. Rainey closed her eyes to stop the spinning in her head.

Sasha patted her mother's hand, then turned her attention to the chest. She ran her hand along the smooth wood with interest.

"Gliocas nam mnà sìthe," she said reverently, meaning the wisdom of the fairy women. Then, without warning, she stood up and kicked the chest over the falls. *"Chan fheumar."* No longer necessary, she explained with a shake of her dark curls.

"No, Sasha! What have you done, lass?" Matt shouted. He lunged for the edge, but it was too late. Rainey hardly stirred. She curled up and covered her ears against his shouts as the chest tumbled end over end into the chasm. Emma and Malcolm could only watch is dismay.

Matt turned to Sasha in disbelief. "Why, Sasha?" he cried. "We've come so far! What are we to do now, love? The crown is lost to us below."

Sasha only smiled and crooked her finger at him. In stunned silence, Matt went to her. She took his hand and led him to the outcropping of rock where the ropes still rested. There, she wrapped his arms around the stone so his back was to the falls and ran her hand over her own eyes to indicate to him that he should close his.

"You mustn't try to do anythin' on your own, Sasha," he said urgently. "Without the crown, there's nothin' to be accomplished. I don't understand, lassie."

"Na bitheadh iomagain ort," she said. She had said

for him not to worry. What was more, she had said it not in a whisper, but loudly enough to be heard over the storm and the noise of the falls. It was the first thing she had spoken aloud since her father's death.

"Sasha?" Rainey called. Somewhere in her fevered brain it registered that she had heard Sasha's voice. She forced herself to sit up, but the effort exhausted her. "We have to take care of the crown, honey. Where's the chest?" Sasha pointed to the falls and shrugged.

"She kicked it over the falls, Rainey," Matt provided. "I think we're finished before we could begin."

Rainey tried to focus on Sasha. "What about the crown, sweetheart? What are we going to do now?" Sasha sat down and patted her tummy. "You're hungry, Sash? I'm not sure I can deal with that right now."

She closed her eyes and held her aching head in her hands. When she opened her eyes, there was a narrow crown of silver in her lap. It was a simple circlet, free of stones. Yet, it was unmistakably a crown. All around the base was an exquisitely engraved tangle of Celtic knots and symbols. And at the center was a raised oval carved in the Path to Paradise design.

It showed no hint of tarnish, probably due to the airtight nature of the chest's seals. And at each of three evenly spaced intervals, there rose a tapered spire about four inches in height. Each spire ended in a different small silver filigree disk fashioned of a Celtic knot pattern. Rainey knew immediately that the three stood for faith, love, and eternity.

She was looking directly at the Starry Crown of Glomach. It could be nothing else, and yet she couldn't take her eyes from it. Where was the priceless crust of jewels? How long before her sight went forever to blackness?

Matt started to turn away from the safety of the tree. "What in God's name is going on, Rainey?" he demanded.

"Don't look at me, Matt! I have the crown. Somehow Sasha got it out of the chest, and she's given it to me."

"Christ, Rainey, your eyes! You saw what it did to Cassandra! Cover your eyes!"

"I'm all right, so far," she explained. "But I don't know for how long. Just don't look for now, until I can make some sense out of all of this." With no small effort, she brought her sight up to Sasha. "What's going on, Sash? The crown belongs to you, sweetheart, not to me." To her surprise, she felt stronger.

Sasha picked up the crown. But instead of taking it for her own, she set it lightly on her mother's head. Rainey drew in a sharp breath as a wave of euphoria rushed through her veins. She rose to her feet effortlessly, her stamina and courage restored a hundredfold. This was her place. She was where she needed to be.

"It has always been yours, Mama," Sasha said clearly in English. "I was only the messenger."

Rainey looked down at her with the light of revelation and gratitude in her eyes. She was home. Sirona's spirit was her own. The circle had been completed at last. The crown was hers. She glanced down to where Emma and Malcolm stood. Emma was frantically pointing to the chest where it bobbed among the waves of the pool. But it didn't matter now. The thunder stopped, and the storm subsided. Rainey drew the cold mists of the falls deeply into her lungs. They were life itself.

"Rainey?" Matt could resist no longer. He turned

to where she stood serenely at the edge of the falls. There was no longer any fear in her demeanor. His sight was unharmed, which could only mean the crown was in its rightful place. Instantly, he fell to his knees beside her. Unable to speak, he looked to Sasha. She only giggled at his confusion.

"Mama is the queen, Matt," she said matter-of-factly. She came over to him and laid her small hand on his shoulder. "In your heart, you knew it all along. You just forgot. I just waited for you to come to us, Matt." Her frown was a scolding one. "You took a very long time." The frown dissolved, and she kissed him on the cheek. "The crown didn't belong in that old wooden box. It belonged to Mama. So I took it out last night and carried it under my sweater. We didn't need the box anymore."

"But you let me carry it all the way up the falls?"

"I lifted it. It wasn't very heavy. And you seemed to like to keep it with you. At least you won't have to carry it back."

"True."

"Now," she said with a note of authority, "you must take up the sword and stand with Mama on the rock where it divides the falls. Then, all will be well. Every year, when the Solstice comes, you and Mama must bring the crown and the sword here." She tucked her hair behind her ear. "And next year, you must bring Creideamh here, so she will understand about the falls from the very start."

Matt ran his hand through his hair, his mind on overload. "Creideamh?"

"My new little sister."

"You'll have a new sister by then, eh?"

She curled a bit of his hair around her finger with interest. "Uh-huh. She has hair the color of yours."

"We'll name her Faith, then?"

Sasha drew the sword from its canvas wrapper and

handed it to him. He rose from his knees and accepted it proudly.

"I think I'm going to call her Carrie," Sasha said with conviction.

Matt chuckled at her in amazement and took Rainey's hand. He was unsure what effect all of this had had on her. In fact, he wasn't sure how to address her. But one look into her dark blue eyes told him she was still the woman he knew and loved. Only now, their ties to one another went far deeper than either of them could have ever imagined.

"Will you join me on the Solstice Rock?" he asked.

"Aye," she replied with ushed tears of love and joy shining in her eyes.

They stepped to the water's edge, and as they watched, the half of the river closest to them altered its own path, diverting to the far side of the Solstice Rock. A set of smooth boulders led straight to their goal, and as they stood over the cliff together, looking out at Sirona's rightful domain, the clouds parted. Shafts of sunlight streamed down on them, turning the falls into a bridal veil of rainbow color as Matt went down on one knee before Rainey. He raised the hilt of Stalcair's sword in homage to her, just as it had been in Sasha's drawing. Each notch shone in the sun, and the blade sent off mirror flashes of polished light.

"My family has guarded the sword for you all these many centuries," Matt said humbly, his voice rough with emotion. "The crown is now restored to its rightful place and its rightful owner. I have seen these things come to pass. I pledge you my love, my faith, my eternity."

She drew Matt to his feet and brought his hand to her cheek. "You already have these things from me," she said in return.

In that moment, as she turned to the falls, she saw

her father's face smiling at her lovingly through the mists. Beside him was the face of another man, a father she recognized from another, long-ago time— a warrior, a king. The two images merged as one before her eyes, and a sense of triumph welled up inside her.

"I have kept my promise," she shouted, her arms raised to the heavens. "My father, we have brought you peace. We have followed the path to this paradise. And now we free you to a paradise of your own. The crown has been returned to its rightful place, and justice has been served. There will be no more killing, no more thievery. Anger and greed have no place here. Love and faith have defeated all our enemies. Victory is ours!"

He nodded his understanding with pride, and as the peaceful vision of her father dissolved, a new image appeared. It was a pair of swans.

Matt took her hand, and as the mists rose, blanketing them with sparkling webs of moisture, the sun struck the countless droplets on the crown. It blazed with the fire of a thousand perfect stars. Here was the true glory of the Starry Crown.

Observing its brilliance, the ravens took to the air and circled the falls three times before they began to fly upward. Their circle tightened until the tips of their wings touched with each downward sweep. Faster and faster the ravens flew until they had achieved an impossible speed. They flew so fast, their forms were lost, setting free the spirits from Sasha's drawings. The ravens were no more.

Men, women, children, they spun toward the heavens. Soon they had gained such altitude, they could no longer be seen. They had been given their liberty, and in their place, though it was the middle of winter, the walls of the gorge bloomed forth in crowds of violets, heather, and forget-me-nots. It was the fulfillment of a promise.

Rainey saw Emma and Malcolm pointing to something in the pool at the base of the falls. She knew what she would see. There, floating tranquilly on the ruffling waters, was a mated pair of swans. One was purest white. The other was black. Before their eyes, the male's plumage gradually shed its darkness and turned to snowy white. No sign remained of its former color. The pair swam contentedly, side by side in the sun's warmth.

Matt gave Rainey's hand a gentle squeeze as he smiled down at the swans. "The souls of Sirona and Stalcair are at peace now. You've done well, *mo chridhe*. The falls have worked their magic. We have two homes now, you and I. One of them is here."

A fresh spray of mist doubled the crown's shimmering glow, until it was almost too bright to look upon.

"I never knew," Rainey said softly. "I always believed the crown was Sasha's. She was the one who knew what was happening. I still don't understand completely."

"Some things have no need of explanation, I think," Matt said reverently. "They are purely a gift." He watched as a series of breathtaking rainbows rose on the breeze.

Sasha plucked a bright blue sprig of forget-me-nots and tucked them behind her ear. She then picked a single violet and stared at it intently. "Don't you want the treasure, Mama?" she asked lightly.

"The treasure?" Rainey looked at the massive stone beneath her feet. It was warm, but from far more than the sunlight. Sirona's treasure lay under the stone. She was certain of it.

The waters retreated to the far shore, providing her with the perfect opportunity to retrieve the bur-

ied gems of old easily if it was her wish. Little wonder no one had found them. When she looked into
Matt's eyes, she knew he shared her feelings on the
matter.

"I have enough treasure," she said with a smile
for Sasha. With a deafening roar, the falls returned
to their half course.

"Lift your hands toward the sky, Mama," Sasha
said. She illustrated by holding her own palms up at
arm's length. "If you ever want the beautiful stones,
this is all you have to do."

Rainey did as she was told, and her hands soon
filled with the rainbow mists.

"Now, close your hands over the water and bring
them down. You'll see a surprise, Mama."

Rainey closed her hands and brought them down.
Water no longer dripped through her fingers. And
when she opened her hands, they were filled with
gems of every color—rubies, diamonds, sapphires,
emeralds, and amethyst. She drew in a sharp breath
as they sparkled and danced with light.

Sasha stepped across the boulders to the Solstice
Rock. She looked at the stones in her mother's hands
with a considering eye. "They're little. But it's your
first time. Next year, they'll be bigger." She brushed
the stones from her mother's hands and watched
them cascade down the clear waters.

Rainey glanced at Matt. "I'll do better next year,"
she said with a twinkle in her eye.

He gave her wink. "I have no doubt of it, *mo
chridhe.*"

"It's time to go to Mar a' Ghealach's party, Mama,"
Sasha said with a note of impatience. "The fairies are
waiting for us."

"I understand, Sash," Rainey said. She took another moment to look out over the shining falls, Sirona's kingdom. "We'll come back here often," she

promised. "Who knows, you might make a hiker out of me yet."

Matt kissed her tenderly. "My thoughts precisely, your majesty."

She smiled at him lovingly. "You, my loyal knight, have my royal permission to call me Harvard."

He bowed to her with a hint of mischief in his eyes. "Your wish is my command."

When they rejoined Emma and Malcolm at the base of the falls, Emma threw her arms around Rainey and Sasha.

"It's a miracle, Rainey, pure and simple," she sobbed. "I saw it all with my own two eyes, mind ye, but I still can't believe it. The crown, the swans, the lost souls flyin' up, it's more than a body could ever imagine. You and Sasha, and the Macinnes, why, ye've done what no one else could. Yer regular heroes, and I'm proud to say I know the lot of ye. But then, I always was proud." There was a fresh round of hugs.

Malcolm, in turn, shook Matt's hand vigorously. "Well done, Matty Mac," he said. "I always knew ye were a cut above. But damned if ye ain't a magician on top of the rest."

"Not a magician, Malcolm," Matt corrected. "Just a man who would do anythin' in this world for the two women he loves."

Malcolm slapped him on the back companionably. "Aye, Matty, and we're all a wee bit besotted at the moment," he said as he gave Emma a hearty wink. She tsked at him in reply, but there was most definitely a smile playing at the corner of her mouth. "Must be the altitude," Malcolm concluded.

The Solstice Swans swam behind the veil of the falls, their time at an end until the next Solstice. Rainey gazed up at the top of the falls. The flowers on the sides of the gorge nodded merrily in the springlike air as both halves of the stream resumed their normal rushing course.

She no longer feared Glomach. In a sense, the falls would always belong to her now. She felt a strong kinship with them and an understanding of this place. In fact, she was reluctant to leave. But darkness would close in soon, and she felt Mar a' Ghealach's happy call in her heart.

The sword was placed in its canvas carrier on Matt's back for safekeeping, and the crown was returned to Sasha's sweater for the journey to the car. The weather held, and the trail burst forth at their feet with a lush kaleidoscope of wildflowers that bloomed with all their hearts through the gray, frozen ground.

Chapter 26

The glow of the fairy tree lit the forest long before they reached it. Sounds of music and joyous celebration filled the night air, even at a distance. As Rainey and the others approached, cheers and cries of delight greeted them, and the fairy crowd rushed out from the protection of the oak to surround them. Each fairy carried a morning glory with a firefly at its center to help illuminate the way for their guests. There was a tiny ocean of light at their feet.

Matt leaned down to pick up Pretty Penny from among the throng. The little fairy doffed his acorn hat and bowed humbly to each human. Then the mischief returned to his bright green eyes, and he set his hands on his hips. "Will ye be needin' help to carry all that treasure, then?" he inquired in rapid Gaelic.

"No, thank you," Matt replied. "The treasure stays where it is." He brought his finger behind Pretty Penny's head and flipped the fairy's hat forward over his eyes. Pretty Penny blustered as those below howled with laughter. But once his hat was firmly back in place, the red-faced fairy laughed along with the rest. There was plenty of playful teasing and jostling as Matt set him back among his own kind.

The oak was covered with shining new leaves, and its bark was the rich, deep color of thriving health.

Mar a' Ghealach sat on a small throne of gleaming silver where the tree forked at the Path to Paradise symbol. Her flowing red hair was covered in a veil of fresh violets, and her gown of rose leaves was now thick with tiny burgundy roses in full bloom. She smiled warmly at her guests as they came forward, and she extended her hand to Rainey. Rainey accepted it gladly.

"Sirona's spirit has returned to her rightful place. You have saved us, my lady," Mar a' Ghealach said with genuine thanks. She glanced down at Sasha and smiled. "And I think perhaps we have done some saving of our own, as well."

Rainey exchanged a knowing smile with Sasha. "We're all doing better now."

"It's but the first night of a century of celebration, my lady. You and Sasha have our thanks for all the lifetimes to come. Please accept our humble gifts."

"We would be honored," Rainey said with an elegant curtsy.

Mar a' Ghealach clapped her hands three times, and an elaborate procession emerged from behind the tree. It took dozens of fairies to carry the five heroic crowns. The first two were fashioned of red roses and forget-me-nots, one for Rainey and one for Sasha. The next was a crown of forest laurel for Matt. And for Emma and Malcolm, there were crowns of fern and lily of the valley.

The celebration continued well into the night as everyone feasted on nuts and berries and nasturtium nectar. Overhead, the aurora borealis blazed forth in ribbons of vivid color in honor of the Solstice.

But when dawn was near, Mar a' Ghealach summoned Rainey to her throne. She leaned forward to whisper in her ear, and Rainey nodded her understanding.

"We will keep a watch over you all," Mar á Ghealach promised.

Rainey smiled. "And you will always be welcome in our home."

Mar a' Ghealach nodded her thanks.

The fairies lit their way home to the edge of the forest. Mar a' Ghealach led them to the garden gate personally. And as the procession retreated into the woods, Matt wrapped his arm around Rainey's shoulders and pulled her nearer.

"What was that all about, what Mar a' Ghealach whispered in your ear, *mo chridhe*?" he asked.

Rainey went up on her tiptoes and kissed him on the cheek. "Mar a' Ghealach said your daughter is growing impatient to join our new family. She has a legend of her own, apparently."

"Then, by all means, we mustn't keep her waitin', Harvard. It seems we're to be quite the legendary family." He kissed her thoroughly.

Emma sighed as she watched Rainey and Matt kiss. "Och, and they're quite the pair, aren't they, Malcolm?" she said wistfully. She swung Sasha's hand back and forth, half in a romantic dream. To Emma's shock, Malcolm threw his arms around her and kissed her squarely on the mouth.

"Mr. MacPherson, no in front of the wee bairn!" Emma cried. But she had to turn her face away to hide her blushing smile. She ran her lucky arrowhead back and forth on its chain flirtatiously.

"Aye, well," Malcolm said as he shuffled his feet. "I'm askin' ye the best I know how not to go back to the Colonies just yet, Emma Ferguson. Yer place is here in the Highlands with the fairies and this wee family." He pulled his trousers a bit higher in a show of courage. "And I want ye here with me permanent, lass, if ye'll give an old digger a go."

Emma looked down at Sasha. "What do ye think

Angus would say, lassie? He's quite a jealous rogue, ye ken?"

Malcolm bristled and started to roll up his sleeves. "And who's this Angus when he's at home, if I may be so bold as to ask? I'll fight the heathen for yer hand, if needs be."

Emma and Sasha laughed until their sides ached at the notion of Malcolm rolling around on the ground, tussling furiously with a little Scottie dog. Malcolm could only scratch his head in confusion, until Emma took pity of him. She took his hand.

"Aye, Malcolm, I'll give it a go with ye." Malcolm whooped with joy. "Stop it, man, ye'll scare the fish away. But mind ye," Emma warned, "I'm a woman of the world. I have my own way of doin' things, and I'll no be ordered about."

Malcolm folded his arms across his chest and considered this for a moment. "Would it be too much of a bother to cook for a man, now and then?" he asked at last.

"It wouldna bother me a bit," she said with a smile.

"Then the two of us will do just fine." He kissed her hand, and she straightened his crown of ferns for him.

Rainey brushed Sasha's cheek with her fingertips, and Sasha touched the locket at her mother's throat reverently. "We're free of them all, now, Sash. All the MacDonnaughs and Evanstons and Malinskys of the world can't touch us anymore. You can talk circles around them in two languages. We're just ordinary people with ordinary problems now, of no interest to anyone but ourselves. How wonderful that sounds!"

Matt lifted Sasha into his arms. "Aye, just ordinary folk who converse with the fairies on a regular basis and turn into ancient royalty once a year." Sasha smiled. "It appears that I have some work to do here, lassie. My father had hopes of keepin' the Highlands free of oil rigs and strip-minin'. Because of his love for me, he had to put his good work aside. And I think perhaps it's a callin' of mine to pursue those noble causes in his name. Do you think you could live here in the Highlands, Sasha?" he asked kindly. "You wouldn't miss California too much?"

Sasha tucked a stray lock of his hair behind his ear. She looked at the gray outline of the Macinnes home and the misty loch beyond in the rising pastel light of dawn. "Mama and I belong here with you, Matt," she replied. "I've been saying it for as long as I can remember. I'm just glad somebody finally listened."

A powerful storm . . .
A dangerous journey . . .
A timeless story.

If you enjoyed
The Starry Child,
you won't want to miss the
spellbinding sequel! Join Rainey,
Matt, and Sasha—who's now
all grown up—as they
set out on another
thrilling adventure!

Coming soon to your
favorite bookstore.

SUSAN KING

☐ *LAIRD OF THE WIND*   0-451-40768-7/$5.99

In medieval Scotland, the warrior known as Border Hawk seizes the castle belonging to the father of the beautiful Isabel Scott, famous throughout the Lowlands for her gift of prophecy. During the battle, Isabel is injured while fighting alongside her men, and placed under Border Hawk's protection. As the border wars rage on, the warrior and prophetess engage in a more intimate conflict, discovering their love for the Scottish borderlands is surpassed only by their love for each other.

Also available:
☐ THE ANGEL KNIGHT   0-451-40662-1/$5.50
☐ THE BLACK THORNE'S ROSE   0-451-40544-7/$4.99
☐ LADY MIRACLE   0-451-40766-0/$5.99
☐ THE RAVEN'S MOON   0-451-18868-3/$5.99
☐ THE RAVEN'S WISH   0-451-40545-5/$4.99
Prices slightly higher in Canada

Payable in U.S. funds only. No cash/COD accepted. Postage & handling: U.S./CAN. $2.75 for one book, $1.00 for each additional, not to exceed $6.75; Int'l $5.00 for one book, $1.00 each additional. We accept Visa, Amex, MC ($10.00 min.), checks ($15.00 fee for returned checks) and money orders. Call 800-788-6262 or 201-933-9292, fax 201-896-8569; refer to ad #TOPHR1

Penguin Putnam Inc.
P.O. Box 12289, Dept. B
Newark, NJ 07101-5289
Please allow 4-6 weeks for delivery.
Foreign and Canadian delivery 6-8 weeks.

Bill my: ☐ Visa ☐ MasterCard ☐ Amex _____ (expires)
Card#_____
Signature_____

Bill to:
Name_____
Address_____ City_____
State/ZIP_____
Daytime Phone#_____

Ship to:
Name_____ Book Total $_____
Address_____ Applicable Sales Tax $_____
City_____ Postage & Handling $_____
State/ZIP_____ Total Amount Due $_____

This offer subject to change without notice.

ONYX

CYNTHIA VICTOR

"Cynthia Victor tells a riveting story!"—Julie Garwood

"Victor evokes [her characters] with skill, a clear ear for their language and a feel for family interaction. Readers...will enjoy this tale."—*Publishers Weekly*

THE SECRET

When an advertising executive becomes a bestselling author of spy novels under a pseudonym, he disappears with a large amount of cash, abandoning his family to write the Great American Novel. Left with three children to support, the wife assumes the identity of the spy novelist, becoming an even greater success than her husband! Embarrassed by this turn of events, the husband plots revenge against his wife, but she's no longer the meek woman he married...
__0-451-18604-4/$6.99

__ONLY YOU	0-451-40606-0/$5.99
__RELATIVE SINS	0-451-17601-4/$5.99
__WHAT MATTERS MOST	0-451-18603-6/$6.99

Prices slightly higher in Canada

Payable in U.S. funds only. No cash/COD accepted. Postage & handling: U.S./CAN. $2.75 for one book, $1.00 for each additional, not to exceed $6.75; Int'l $5.00 for one book, $1.00 each additional. We accept Visa, Amex, MC ($10.00 min.), checks ($15.00 fee for returned checks) and money orders. Call 800-788-6262 or 201-933-9292, fax 201-896-8569; refer to ad # OFIC1

Penguin Putnam Inc.	Bill my: ☐Visa ☐MasterCard ☐Amex_____(expires)
P.O. Box 12289, Dept. B	Card#_____
Newark, NJ 07101-5289	Signature_____
Please allow 4-6 weeks for delivery.	
Foreign and Canadian delivery 6-8 weeks.	

Bill to:

Name_____

Address_____ City_____

State/ZIP_____

Daytime Phone #_____

Ship to:

Name_____ Book Total $_____

Address_____ Applicable Sales Tax $_____

City_____ Postage & Handling $_____

State/ZIP_____ Total Amount Due $_____

This offer subject to change without notice.

SORRELL AMES

LISTENING
IN

A young couple, with two small children, buy a house
across the street from a large Victorian home owned by a
prominent physician and his wife. But when the couple's
baby monitor picks up conversations in their neighbors'
home, the mother learns more than just idle gossip! The
doctor is involved in illegal medical practices resulting in
the deaths of women and babies she finds she must place
her own life at risk in order to stop him....

__0-451-19233-8/$5.99

Prices slightly higher in Canada

Payable in U.S. funds only. No cash/COD accepted. Postage & handling: U.S./CAN. $2.75 for
one book, $1.00 for each additional, not to exceed $6.75; Int'l $5.00 for one book, $1.00 each
additional. We accept Visa, Amex, MC ($10.00 min.), checks ($15.00 fee for returned checks)
and money orders. Call 800-788-6262 or 201-933-9292, fax 201-896-8569; refer to ad #OFIC3

Penguin Putnam Inc.   Bill my: ☐ Visa ☐ MasterCard ☐ Amex _____ (expires)
P.O. Box 12289, Dept. B   Card#_____
Newark, NJ 07101-5289   Signature_____
Please allow 4-6 weeks for delivery.
Foreign and Canadian delivery 6-8 weeks.

Bill to:
Name_____
Address_____City_____
State/ZIP_____
Daytime Phone #_____

Ship to:
Name_____ Book Total $_____
Address_____ Applicable Sales Tax $_____
City_____ Postage & Handling $_____
State/ZIP_____ Total Amount Due $_____

This offer subject to change without notice.